Melcorka of Alba

Melcorka of Alba

The Swordswoman Book IV

Malcolm Archibald

For Cathy

'I am Melcorka the Swordswoman and who dares meddle with me'

Chapter One

The war drums sounded, louder and ever louder, sending bright parrots squawking for shelter, echoing through the humidity of the forest and vibrating in the sultry air.

'They won't be long now.' Melcorka touched the hilt of Defender, her sword, allowing the surge of power to thrill through her body.

'They'll hunt us down and kill us all!' The Taino woman clung to Melcorka's arm. 'Then they'll eat us.'

'No, they won't, Hadali.' Melcorka shook her head. 'Did you order the precautions that I advised?'

Hadali nodded. 'Yes, Melcorka.'

'You dug the ditch around two-thirds of the village?'

'Yes, Melcorka.'

'You readied the palisade?'

'Yes, Melcorka.'

'You sent the oldsters and children to the safest part of the village?'

'Yes, Melcorka.'

'Then all should be well,' Melcorka said. 'I have trained the men and women how to use spears.' She touched the hilt of Defender again. 'The Kalingo are not used to meeting resistance, are they?'

Hadali shook her head. 'The Taino are not a fighting people. We don't resist.'

Melcorka smiled. 'Between us, we will teach the Kalingo not to return to this island.'

'We are not a fighting people,' Hadali repeated.

'I am a fighting woman,' Melcorka said.

'And your man?' Hadali indicated the tall, long-faced man who leaned against the bole of a turpentine tree, thrusting his staff into the sand, listening to everything and saying nothing. 'He does not appear to be a warrior.'

'That is Bradan the Wanderer,' Melcorka said. 'He is a man of peace.'

Hadali eyed Bradan. 'Why are you wandering, man-of-few-words?'

'To seek knowledge,' Bradan said.

'Which knowledge do you seek?' Hadali stood beside him. 'There is much.'

'I seek the knowledge that belongs to me,' Bradan said. 'I saw it once, briefly, and have travelled the world ever since, hoping to recover what I only glimpsed.'

Hadali touched Bradan's arm. 'And Melcorka? Does she also seek your knowledge?'

'Melcorka is her own woman.' Bradan looked up. 'You will soon see what she does best.'

'It is strange for a man who walks in peace to accompany a woman who carries a long sword.' Hadali's gaze did not stray from Bradan's face.

'It is what it is,' Bradan said. 'Melcorka and I have travelled a long road together.'

'Is there an end to the road?' Hadali asked.

'Every road has an end. It could be on this island, at the point of a Kalingo spear, it could be at the bottom of the sea, or it could be in front of a peat fire flame in Alba.' Bradan gave a small smile. 'We will know when we get there.' He looked up. 'It sounds as if your friends are getting restless.'

'The Kalingo are nobody's friends,' Hadali said.

The drums continued, joined now by long blasts on war-trumpets and a rhythmic chant that raised the small hairs on the back of Bradan's neck. A pandemonium of parrots exploded from the trees, while the insects seemed subdued by the threat of the impending horror.

'Here they come,' Melcorka said. 'Keep out of the way until I say otherwise, Bradan. You are no warrior.'

'I know that well, Melcorka.' Bradan tapped his staff on the sandy ground. 'Keep safe.'

Melcorka's eyes were bright. She laughed. 'I was made to fight.'

'Sometimes I think you enjoy it too much,' Bradan said.

There was a clearing between the village and the sea, two hundred paces of animal-cropped grassland which the Kalingo had to cross. Taking a deep breath, Bradan looked around the settlement. He could sense the fear. It was in the sweat of the Tainos, it was in the air they expelled from panting lungs, it was in the shallow breathing and the sharp, nervous gestures of the near-naked men and women. Bradan nodded. He understood the Tainos. They were good people, and Melcorka was right to fight for them.

Standing along the line of the beach, next to the lean pirauas that had carried them to this island, were the Kalingos. They were a seething mass of warriors, preparing themselves for an attack as the thunder of their drums increased, raising the tension.

Amidst them stood a lone woman, staring at Melcorka across the bare ground.

'There are more than warriors among the Kalingos today,' Hadali said. 'Be very careful, Melcorka. There is evil here of a kind you may not have met before.'

They came at a run, hundreds of bare-chested Kalingos with clubs and spears, yelling as they attacked the seemingly defenceless villagers. Some wore a circlet of feathers around their heads, others sported face tattoos. A few stopped partway across the cleared ground to fire arrows into the air, with the shafts plunging down inside the village. Every warrior was painted with bright colours or hideous designs and they raised a war cry to terrify the people they had come to massacre.

'Steady now,' Bradan called, as some of the Tainos shuddered and turned to run. 'Trust in your defences. Trust in Melcorka.'

The Tainos looked at him and then at Melcorka, two strangers from across the sea, two aliens in this island of sunshine and colour.

Hadali stepped beside Bradan. 'If we run, they will hunt us down. I know it is not our way to fight. I know it is wrong to praise violence, but I want to see our babies grow into adults and our oldsters die peacefully in their own homes. I do not wish to see our children skewered above a Kalingo cooking fire, or smell the scent of roasting Taino on the wind.'

The Tainos shuddered, some muttered; only one man turned to flee. Bradan watched him run and said nothing. He understood.

'Now!' Melcorka yelled. 'Barriers!'

The Taino women dashed forward, fifteen paces beyond the edge of the village, to raise the barriers Melcorka had ordered them to create. Made of woven boughs within a wooden framework, they would not stop a serious assault but could slow down any attacker.

'Back!' Melcorka ordered, and the Taino women scurried back, their job done.

The Kalingos only hesitated for a moment, long enough for Melcorka to shout: 'Spears: ready: throw!' At her word, the men of the village stepped forward and threw the spears that Melcorka had them make. Not expecting to meet any resistance, the Kalingos stared as a hundred slim spears rose in the air, hovered at the apex of their flight, and then plummeted downward.

'Bradan!' Melcorka shouted. 'Take charge here.'

'Now you will see Melcorka.' Bradan pushed himself away from his tree. 'Spears ready!'

Melcorka strode forward with her right hand on the hilt of the sword that protruded from behind her left shoulder.

Five or six of the Kalingos were down, transfixed by the defenders' spears. The others gathered their resolve before this unexpected resistance. Two men stepped in front of the mass, one with his face heavily tattooed, the other with a circlet of red parrot feathers around his head and a massive wooden club in his hand. The woman remained in the centre of the warriors, watching.

'Spears... throw!' Bradan shouted. He saw some of the Tainos hesitate. 'Don't worry about Melcorka,' he said. 'You won't hit her.' Leading by example, he lifted a spear from one of the stacks that Melcorka had ordered them to prepare. Twelve feet long, it was lighter than those used in Alba, while the head was of chipped stone rather than steel. Hefting it over his right shoulder, Bradan balanced, poised and threw. He watched the spear rise up until it was only a speck in the sky before it wavered and sliced downward. The air whistled through the holes Melcorka had ordered to be bored in the shaft, making an unearthly noise that unnerved some of the Kalingos, as was intended.

'Here they come!' somebody shouted, as the two Kalingo leaders waved their warriors forward.

The defenders hesitated, with some of them turning to flee. They all knew what to expect if the Kalingos overran their village: slaughter, murder and a cannibal feast. The Tainos had always lived in fear of the Kalingos, whose pirogue fleets ravaged thousands of square miles of this sea and the myriad islands it contained. Only Melcorka's influence had persuaded the Tainos to stand and fight. Only Melcorka's sword could maintain their morale.

Faced with the reality of hundreds of screaming Kalingo warriors, the Tainos' courage rapidly evaporated.

'Don't run!' Bradan shouted. 'Fight!' He could understand the defenders' fear. He also knew that if they ran, the Kalingos would be encouraged and would chase them, whatever Melcorka did. 'Lift your spears!'

A few of the men closest to him did as he ordered. Most did not. Some were crying in terror. Others accepted what they saw as their inevitable fate.

Bradan spoke to those Tainos who remained. 'Well done! Now poise, aim and throw! Follow my movements.'

The two leaders had rallied the Kalingos after their moment of hesitation. Unable to understand the Kalingo language, Bradan did not know what the leaders had said but he did know that it had worked, as the Kalingos surged forward again. The closer they came, the more ferocious the Kalingos looked, hundreds of painted warriors who had only ever known victory and savagery.

'Throw!' Bradan put all his strength into hurling his spear. He saw the missile land somewhere within the Kalingo ranks, to thrum in the sandy ground. The Kalingo leader with the red parrot feathers faced him directly, lifted his great carved club and shouted something.

'He says that he is going to eat you while you are still alive,' one of the Tainos said, dropping his spear.

Bradan felt a prickle of fear. He had faced Norsemen, Caterans and the warriors of Cahokia, yet these Kalingos were different again. They hunted humans for food, which was more chilling even than the ferocity of the Norse or the human sacrifices of Cahokia.

And then Melcorka acted.

Unsheathing Defender, she stood directly in front of the Kalingo warriors. Her voice sounded clear above the clamour. 'I am Melcorka of Alba, and who dares meddle with me?'

The front rank of the Kalingos hesitated before this tall, raven-headed woman with the shining sword, who openly challenged them.

Melcorka ran into the mass of the Kalingos, swinging Defender in a figure-of-eight against which it was nearly impossible to defend. The nearest Kalingos turned to face her. Defender sliced through the club of her first adversary and continued onward to hack off the man's head. Melcorka strode on, swinging.

'Come on, then!' Melcorka felt the power surge through her from Defender, the sword that stored all the skills of its previous owners. To Melcorka, the

Kalingos seemed to move in slow motion, enabling her to block their blows and retaliate with ease. She stepped forward, lopping off arms, legs and heads, moving through a curtain of blood that covered her and the ground over which she travelled. Although the Kalingos were fierce warriors, they had never before encountered such resistance. While some lunged forward to meet the challenge, most hesitated; only a few turned to flee.

'You see?' Bradan shouted. 'Would you leave a woman to fight alone? Throw another volley of spears!'

The bolder of the Tainos were lifting spears and looking toward the Kalingos.

'Throw!' Bradan launched another spear. 'Come on! Help Melcorka!'

Some of the defenders followed Bradan's example. Most could not gather the courage to fight. Bradan shouted again, trying to encourage them as he saw that more of the Kalingos were turning from their assault on the village to face Melcorka. Now twenty, thirty, forty men were massing around the swordswoman, hefting their great wooden clubs or the long stabbing spears.

'Will you let Melcorka do your fighting for you?' Bradan lifted a spear as sudden worry flooded him. 'Come on! Support her! Come on, you men of the Taino! Help Melcorka defend your village!'

Striving to repress his fear, Bradan leapt over the flimsy barrier and ran toward the Kalingos. He hoped that his example would inspire some of the Tainos to follow him, for any one of the Kalingo warriors could kill him in seconds. If the Tainos did not come, well, he had no desire to be stuck so far from home if Melcorka was killed.

That prospect chilled him.

'Come on!' Bradan yelled.

For a moment or two, the Kalingos stared at him. Perhaps they thought he was one of the inhabitants of the village, until they realised he was clothed and knew he was a stranger. An arrow thrummed past him, missing him by a handspan. Another thudded into the ground at his feet.

'Melcorka!' Bradan yelled. 'I'm coming!'

What a place to die, thousands of miles from home on an island whose name I do not even know.

Bradan saw a mass of Kalingo warriors close around Melcorka, clubs rising and falling as they tried to penetrate her defences. Dodging a third arrow more by instinct than by skill, Bradan lunged at the flank of the Kalingos, thrusting his spear beneath the shoulder-blade of a brawny, tattooed warrior. The man stiffened at the unexpected agony, and half turned toward Bradan, who twisted the point to enlarge the wound and tried to withdraw.

The suction of the human body held the spear point fast. Cursing, Bradan wiggled the shaft as his screaming victim struggled to escape, and cursed again as he saw a yelling Kalingo running towards him with his war-club held high.

Bradan grunted. 'That serves me right for acting the part of a warrior. I never was any good at fighting.'

'You never said a truer word.' Melcorka stepped over the body of a man she had just gutted, thrust Defender through the chest of the charging Kalingo, ducked and hacked the legs off another warrior. 'What are you doing in this slaughterhouse, Bradan? I told you not to get involved.'

'I came to help you.' Bradan at last succeeded in freeing his spear.

'That was very kind of you.' Melcorka fended off the attacks of the screaming Kalingos that surrounded them. 'Foolish, but kind. Did you think I had forgotten how to fight?'

'I thought you were on your own against a multitude.' Bradan ducked as an arrow whizzed overhead.

'I was never alone,' Melcorka said.

Bradan winced as another Kalingo charged forward, swinging his great club. 'Who is with you?'

'Why, you are, Bradan. I see you as plainly as I see these savages.' Melcorka parried the swing of the Kalingo's club and hacked off the man's arm. Blood spouted scarlet. 'And you've brought some help.'

'Which help?' Bradan asked, and smiled as the Taino defenders finally struggled over their barrier to run at the Kalingos. 'Well, they took their time.'

'They followed the example of the bravest man I have ever known.' Melcorka began to walk toward the now withdrawing Kalingo ranks.

'Alba!' Increasing her speed to a charge, Melcorka yelled her war cry. 'Alba!' Seeing this blood-spattered woman with the blood-dripping sword running at them from one flank, and the totally unexpected sight of resistance from the Taino defenders on the other, the Kalingos broke. One minute, they were a horde of fierce warriors hoping to kill and eat all they came across, the next, they were a panicking mob of frightened men, all eager to escape.

Only a single Kalingo stood her ground. The lone woman faced the attackers, a female rock in an ebbing tide of Kalingo males. She pointed two fingers at Melcorka.

'Run, you fool!' Melcorka yelled. 'All your friends have gone.'

The woman remained standing. Melcorka slowed down, curious to see why her adversary did not run.

The woman stared directly at Melcorka. Tall and dark, the woman wore a loose cloak that failed to conceal her magnificent physique, while a single white stone gleamed in the golden band that encircled her forehead.

'Who are you?' The woman's voice was clear and calm.

'I am Melcorka nic Bearnas of the Cenel Bearnas,' Melcorka answered at once. 'Some call me Melcorka of Alba. Others know me as the Swordswoman. Who are you?'

'I am a kanaima,' the woman said.

'Why do you not run?' Melcorka was genuinely curious. 'You can see that your warriors are defeated, you can see that your spears and war-clubs are no match for my sword. Your battle is lost, Kanaima. Turn and run. You will not have this village with its peaceful people.'

Kanaima stretched out her arms, pointing the forefingers of both hands at Melcorka. 'You are wrong, Melcorka of Alba. Our battle is only beginning.'

Melcorka hefted Defender. 'I do not like to kill without reason, Kanaima. Go now. Do not give me a cause to end your life.'

In return, Kanaima took a single step forward. 'I curse you. I curse you in your body and in your mind. I curse you in your possessions and your strength. I curse you in your travels and your weather. I curse you until the balance of the world is restored...' She got no further, as Melcorka neatly cut off her head.

'I warned you,' Melcorka said, as Kanaima's head rolled seven times on the grass and came to a stop with the eyes still open, still dark and still staring at Melcorka. 'You could have escaped, Kanaima.'

The laughter inside Melcorka's head mocked her, and for an instant, she thought she felt something long and rubbery slithering around her shoulders. She shook off the feeling. *Imagination.*

'Let the survivors go,' Bradan called to the now courageous Tainos. 'You've won. There's no need for any more killing.'

I was going to grant them quarter, Melcorka said to herself. *Not now. There will be no more mercy.*

'Follow them!' Melcorka countermanded Bradan's words. 'Teach them not to come here! Make them so afraid of you that they never come back.' Chasing after the fleeing warriors, Melcorka swung Defender right and left, cutting off legs and arms, slashing deep, bleeding wounds in backs and shoulders, slicing off heads and hands without opposition. What had been a retreat turned into a rout as the Kalingos fled from Defender's blade.

'Face me or flee from me, I still bring death!' Melcorka shouted.

The Kalingos ran to the beach, dropping their weapons in their panic. Some of the Taino villagers followed, thrusting with their spears, killing or wounding a man here and there, shouting to encourage themselves and muster the courage to continue. Other Tainos retched at the sight of so much carnage, gagged at the stench of raw blood and closed their eyes as they saw once-bold Kalingo warriors writhing and screaming on the ground.

The Kalingo pirauas were pulled up beyond the high-tide mark on the beach, rank upon rank of long, lean piratical craft. The raiders ran to them, pushing the fragile boats into the pounding surf without looking back as Melcorka and the villagers harassed them, killing and maiming.

'Come back!' Melcorka yelled, as the surviving Kalingos paddled desperately away. 'I want to kill more of you.' Charging into the water, she slashed at a piraua, slicing through the hull so it split and the occupants tumbled out, to swim frantically to their colleagues for help. Melcorka watched as Kalingo warriors fought each other with the broad-bladed paddles, refusing to allow others on board their piraua as fear overcame friendship.

'Enough.' Bradan took hold of Melcorka's arm. 'You've killed enough.' He pulled her back as she swung at a final target. 'You don't kill for killing's sake.'

'Let go!' Melcorka pushed him away and dashed deeper into the sea for a final attack on a piraua.

'Melcorka!' Bradan followed, hauling her back, until she lifted Defender to threaten him.

'Melcorka!' Bradan had never seen such madness in her eyes. 'Enough! This is not like you!'

Melcorka nodded. 'Yes, enough.' She was panting, her face and body painted red with the blood of the men she had killed. 'They've learned.' Melcorka took a deep breath. 'I don't think they'll return to this island.'

'I think you are right.' Bradan looked around. Bodies, dead and dying, bobbed on the surface of the sea and the surf, once pristine yellow but now stained crimson with blood, carried yet more corpses onto the beach. Land crabs were already scuttling down from the trees to feast on the bodies.

'This is a beautiful place.' Bradan deliberately looked away from the beach, past the village to the verdant slopes that rose to a range of jungle-clad hills, gilded silver-grey with mist. 'Why does mankind spoil perfection with violence and killing?'

'Because human nature demands it.' Hadali had waded out to join them. Years had added lines of wisdom to her face and sadness to her eyes. 'Long ago, our people decided not to follow the path of violence, even though we knew our decision meant that the Kalingos would hunt us as prey.'

Like the rest of her people, Hadali was naked save for a twist of cloth around her loins. Melcorka tried to guess her age; anything from thirty-five to sixty, although the profound wisdom in her eyes argued for another couple of decades at least.

Hadali put a small hand on Melcorka's shoulder. 'You have done what you think is right, Melcorka of the Cenel Bearnas, but you cannot stay here any longer.'

Bradan sighed. 'I am called the Wanderer,' he said. 'I follow the road seeking knowledge and here, I have found wisdom and the most peaceful people I have ever seen.' He gestured to the Tainos who thronged the beach, shocked at the carnage.

'You defended us,' Hadali laid a small hand on Bradan's arm, 'and you saved our lives. If you had not been here, the Kalingos would have killed us all and eaten our flesh.'

'That is correct.' Bradan ducked under the surface of the sea to wash off the blood that covered him.

Hadali shook her head. 'Despite your help, in killing as you did, you broke our code and you must leave. Your presence as killers would pollute our village.'

Melcorka copied Bradan in washing off the blood. 'We saved all your lives,' she reminded Hadali.

'Sometimes, lives are not the most important things. Beliefs, morality and the human soul matter more. By encouraging our young men and woman to kill, you have damaged those parts of them that are vital to our culture.' Hadali sighed. 'These of my people who fought will have to endure weeks or months of purifying, before they can rejoin the community.'

'I see.' Bradan took hold of Melcorka's arm before she began to argue. 'It is never our intention to make a custom or to break a custom, so we will do as you wish.'

'We have a prophesy,' Hadali said, 'that sometime in the future, men with clothes will come to our lands and they will kill us all. We know that will happen and we accept that is our fate. Until then, we will live the way we have always lived, in peace and generosity.'

'It is a good way to live.' Melcorka cleaned the blade of Defender as she walked back to the beach. 'One day, humankind will learn to live in peace.' She indicated the carnage between the beach and the village. 'One day, good will vanquish evil. One day, there will be no need for people like me.'

Hadali followed, with a frown furrowing her brow. 'That day is far in the future, Swordswoman. Tell me about the Kalingo woman that did not run. What did she say to you?'

Melcorka checked Defender and returned the sword to her scabbard. 'She told me her name was Kanaima, and she tried to curse me.' Melcorka shrugged. 'I killed her before she finished the curse.'

Hadali's frown deepened. She sighed and shook her head. 'No, Melcorka, you did not kill her. You cannot kill a kanaima.' She stepped back. 'Kanaima was not her name. A kanaima is an evil spirit that enters people and makes them do terrible things, or turns them into beasts.'

'Oh?' Melcorka glanced over at the casualties. The woman she knew as Kanaima lay as she had fallen, with her head detached from her body. 'Well, she's dead now. Defender is not an ordinary sword.'

'I hope you are right,' Hadali said.

'You are good people,' Melcorka said. 'I am sorry if we have caused you pain.'

'You meant well,' Hadali woman said. 'We will repair the harm you have done.' She smiled again. 'We will provide provisions for your great piraua and pray for you.'

'Thank you,' Bradan said.

Hadali placed her hand on Bradan's shoulder. 'You are seeking, Bradan, but you do not know what you seek.' Her face contained a wealth of wisdom. 'You seek more than knowledge.'

'That may be so,' Bradan said.

Hadali's expression altered to sympathy. 'Then let me tell you what you seek.'

'If you would.'

'You are seeking a truth you will never fully find and a peace you cannot obtain.' Hadali's eyes were compassionate. 'Not until you have fulfilled your destiny.'

'I did not know I had a destiny,' Bradan said.

Hadali touched his forehead with a cool finger. 'We all have a destiny,' she said. 'It is knowing what we seek that guides us toward what we should ultimately become.'

'I see.' The explanation meant nothing to Bradan. 'Can you tell what we should ultimately become?' He included Melcorka in his gesture.

Hadali put both hands on Bradan's shoulders. 'You cannot be greater than your destiny, Bradan the Seeker. What is the greatest thing you desire?'

Bradan returned to his earlier statement. 'I thought that my greatest desire was knowledge.'

Hadali smiled. 'There is much knowledge in the world, Bradan. You are seeking to fill a bottomless pit. You will never satisfy that desire. What else is important to you?'

Bradan met Hadali's dark eyes. 'To share the knowledge I gain.'

'That is a good desire.' Hadali placed both hands on Bradan's head, frowning.

'What's the matter?' Melcorka had been an interested spectator.

Hadali moved her hands slightly. 'There is trouble and great danger ahead of you both.'

Melcorka smiled. 'We always have trouble and great danger ahead of us,' she said. 'We have trouble and great danger behind us as well. As long as I have this,' she tapped the hilt of Defender, 'we can handle whatever fate throws at us.'

Hadali touched Melcorka on the shoulder. 'You are a brave woman, Melcorka. You only need to learn humility to mature beyond your over-confidence.' She looked directly into Melcorka's eyes. 'You have strength beyond your sword, Melcorka. If you find that, you will become a full woman. If you depend only on Defender, you will stagnate into a sword-for-hire.'

'I am no mercenary swordswoman,' Melcorka said.

'You are capable of becoming much more,' Hadali agreed. 'Or much less.'

'You spoke of destiny,' Bradan said. 'What is the destiny of Melcorka?'

Hadali stepped back a pace. 'Although fate will guide Melcorka, she is a woman who will create her own destiny. Her life is in her hands, not in the blade of her sword.' When Hadali touched Melcorka's head, her expression altered.

'What is it?' Bradan asked, suddenly alarmed. 'What did you see? What can you see?'

Hadali stepped back. 'I saw you lying on your back, Melcorka of Alba, with your sword beside you. I saw a tall man standing over you, smiling. I saw blood.'

Melcorka nodded. 'Such is the way of the warrior.' She patted the hilt of Defender. 'Until that happens, we will stay together.'

'One day, Melcorka the Swordswoman,' Hadali said, 'you will meet a warrior who will defeat you, despite the skills inherent in your sword. One day, you will meet a warrior whose sword is superior to your own.'

'May that day be far off,' Melcorka said. 'You have given me a lot to think about, Hadali.'

Hadali's smile was enigmatic. 'Then think, Melcorka the Swordswoman.' A shadow crossed her face. 'Take care, Melcorka and Bradan. You have faced the Kalingo and lived; not many do that in these seas. Melcorka, you have also met a kanaima face-to-face.'

'I cut off its head,' Melcorka said.

'I know,' Hadali spoke softly. 'It will not forget. Be careful that you do not meet it again.'

Chapter Two

The islands lay weeks behind them, long sunk beneath the horizon so they were little more than a memory of lush trees, peaceful people and exotic fruit. All around was the sea, languid and flat. High above, the sun hammered down on *Catriona*, the single-masted vessel that had carried them from Alba across the Western Ocean and down the great rivers of the New World.

'There is not a whisper of wind.' Melcorka lay at the tiller, fanning her face with a broad-brimmed hat. 'No birds, not even an insect. It is as if God has forgotten to put life into this part of His world.' Standing up, she shouted and the sound of her voice was lost in the vast abyss that surrounded them. 'Nothing!'

'It's hot.' Bradan pulled on the oars, looked up at the sail that hung limp and useless, and pulled again.

'It is.' Leaving the tiller, Melcorka slumped onto her rowing bench and pulled at her oar. 'Are we making any progress?'

'It's hard to tell in this ocean.' Bradan swept the perspiration from his forehead. 'How long is it since we last saw land? Three weeks? Four?'

'Three weeks,' Melcorka said. 'Three weeks and three days. It's at times like this that I could long for a good, old-fashioned Alban gale, with bitter, cold rain and a wind that bends the mast.'

Bradan grunted. 'I'll remind you of that when the weather breaks.' He gave a sour grin and pulled again. *Catriona* slid another few feet through the water, without changing anything. The blue sea merged with the blue sky somewhere on the indeterminate blue horizon.

'How is the drinking water?' Bradan asked.

Melcorka lifted one of their water containers and looked inside. 'Turning green and slimy,' she said. 'I think there are things living in there.'

'Fresh meat,' Bradan said, pulling at the oars again. 'Check the fishing lines, Mel.'

'Nothing,' Melcorka said. 'Even the fish have deserted us.' Her laugh had an edge that Bradan did not like. 'I'll be killing and eating you, soon!'

'That's not funny, Mel.' Bradan rested on his oars. 'You've not been the same since that battle with the Kalingos. Maybe there was something in the kanaima's curse.'

'I killed the kanaima,' Melcorka reminded him. 'I cut off her head.' She made a slicing motion with her right hand. 'Chop! Like that.'

'That's not like you, either, Mel, exulting in killing.' Bradan began to row again. 'I'll be glad to get you to land and back to normal.'

Returning to the tiller, Melcorka suddenly stood up. 'What's that ahead?' She pointed with her chin. 'The sea's changing colour. It's a browny-yellow.'

'I've never seen a sea like that before.' Bradan stared over his shoulder, resting on his oars. 'A yellow sea! Well, Mel, we travel to see new things.'

'It's not the sea that's yellow,' Melcorka said. 'There is vegetation on the surface.'

'The sea is growing plants?' Bradan shook his head. 'Truly, this world is full of marvels, unless it is only seaweed, of course.'

'I'd rather there was a breath of wind than a sea of weed.' Melcorka slumped back at the oars and pulled hard. 'Our lack of progress is terribly frustrating.'

'This is a big ocean,' Bradan said. 'We might be rowing for weeks and travel hundreds of miles and still be only a fraction of the way across.' He pointed to the sun. 'At least we are heading north and east, though. We are heading home.'

'Very slowly,' Melcorka said. 'I would give my arm for a slant of air, something to fill the sail and send us faster over the sea.'

Bradan grunted. 'The old sailor men have a method of calling the wind.'

'What was that, Bradan? What magic trick do they perform?' Melcorka grinned across to him. 'Do they sacrifice one of the crew to the sea-gods? Perhaps a long-faced, staff-carrying man?'

'Nothing as dramatic,' Bradan said. 'They stick a knife into the mast and whistle.'

'Oh?' Melcorka looked a little disappointed. 'Well then, if a knife and a whistle can call the wind, we shall try Defender.'

'No.' Bradan shook his head. 'If a knife can whistle up the wind, imagine what Defender could summon!'

Despite their apparent lack of progress, *Catriona* had inched closer to the browny-yellow sea. As Melcorka had said, it was a plant, but unlike any they had seen before.

'That stuff is moving toward us,' Melcorka said.

'Plants can't move.' Bradan pulled at the oars again. 'Unless the wind shifts them, and we have no wind.'

'This plant does not know it cannot move,' Melcorka said. 'It's reaching out for *Catriona*.'

Melcorka was correct. Even as Bradan watched, the vegetation was easing toward *Catriona*, with one tendril creeping up the prow and crawling along the short foredeck.

'I've never seen anything like that before,' Bradan said.

'Nor have I.' Stepping over Bradan, Melcorka unsheathed the dirk from underneath her arm and sliced at the stem of the plant. 'It's tough,' she called. 'Look at that!' The plant had begun to crawl up her arm. 'It's also fast!' She cut harder, lifted a length of the growth and threw it over the side.

'It's at the stern, too.' Bradan hit out with an oar. 'It's grabbing at my oars.'

'It's everywhere,' Melcorka said. 'It's all around us.'

'Time to get out of this patch of sea.' Bradan pulled hard at the oars, only to swear as the weed wrapped itself around the blades. 'Get away!' He hauled one oar free, just as more tendrils of the brown-yellow plant crawled on board.

'Enough of this!' Melcorka replaced her dirk, drew Defender and sliced at the ever-increasing number of plants that climbed onto *Catriona*. As fast as she hacked, more of the browny-yellow growth arrived.

'Bradan!' Melcorka threw him her dirk. 'Cut us free!'

Even with two of them hacking as fast as they could, the plants continued to advance, crawling up the hull and sending long, yellow-brown tendrils towards Bradan and Melcorka.

'What were you saying about Defender calling up the wind?' Melcorka asked. 'It seems like a good idea.'

Bradan sawed through a plant that began to explore his ankle. 'Be careful, Mel!' He held up a hand as Melcorka rammed Defender into *Catriona*'s single pine mast. 'A weapon like that might summon more than we can handle!'

'Nonsense!' Melcorka said. 'We can't handle these plants. Anyway, it's only superstition and the more wind we have, the better! Give me my dirk!' She chopped at a tendril that was curling around the mast. 'It's not working. Is there anything else I have to do?'

'Whistle!' Bradan said, as the air remained still and the growth spread across *Catriona.* 'Whistle as though your soul depended on it.'

'Whistle?' Melcorka sliced through a plant that was coiling up her leg. 'I can't whistle.'

'Try!' Bradan tried to rip at a stem that curled around the tiller. 'These things are worse than the Kalinga.'

For a second, Melcorka looked over the side of *Catriona* into the yellow-brown mass that seethed across the sea around them. A ship-length to starboard, she saw the vegetation form the likeness of a human face, and the poisonous eyes of Kanaima were watching her.

'You're dead!' Melcorka said, so quietly that Bradan could not hear. Pursing her lips, she whistled as loudly as she could.

Bradan cringed. 'You may be the greatest warrior in the world, Mel, but you cannot hold a tune in your head, can you? That's a terrible noise you are making.'

'Then join me, Bradan! Make sweet music to call the wind.' Melcorka looked again, but Kanaima's face was gone. All she could see was plant-life covering the ocean and gradually smothering *Catriona.*

Bradan increased the volume of his whistling. He doubted it would help, but anything was better than not trying at all. The yellow-tinged sea stretched forever in all directions except upward, where the brassy sun powered down on them. Unless they found land soon, the plants would overcome them, or they would die of thirst in this pulsating yellow-brown expanse. Pushing out his lips, Bradan blew tunelessly.

'That's worse than me,' Melcorka said. 'It's like an old crow rasping on a rusty farm gate.'

Stung by her words, Bradan moistened his lips with a mouthful of their precious water and tried again.

'That's better.' Melcorka continued to hack at the invading plants. 'Now you are whistling like a king. You could charm the birds from the trees if there were any birds around here, or any trees...'

No sooner had Melcorka spoken than the sea altered. A deep swell began to move the plants, so they rose and fell like yellow waves.

'Something's happening.' Bradan wrestled an oar free of the crawling plants. 'It's working!'

The swell rose, carrying *Catriona* up and down as if she were a cork. One minute she was deep in the trough between two mountains of vegetation, the next, she was poised up high, revealing a limitless vista of unbroken yellow-brown. Above, the sky darkened, with thick clouds rolling in from the north and west, some black, others purple-tinged and full-bellied, pregnant with menace.

'What's happening, Bradan?' Melcorka asked.

'We whistled for the wind,' Bradan said, 'and your Defender summoned us up something a bit stronger. Look at the plants!'

Already, the rising swell showed patches of clear water through the vegetation. A spatter of spray rattled against *Catriona's* hull.

'I've never seen anything like this before.' Bradan watched with interest. 'It's a new experience.'

'It's a new experience I can do without. What is that?' Melcorka pointed astern, where a patch of clear sea brightened to flaming orange. She could only stare as the water erupted behind them, thrusting upward in a fiery red mass, edged with orange and purple. 'In the name of God!'

The sea surged skyward in a wave ten, fifteen, twenty, fifty times higher than *Catriona's* mast and still rising.

'Hold on!' Bradan yelled. 'Mel! Find something to hold on to!'

The sea continued to rise, higher and higher until it blocked the sky astern, augmented by a smoky dark cloud and the reek of sulphur.

'It's Hell!' Melcorka shouted. 'The gates of Hell have opened up behind us!'

'Row!' Thumping onto a rowing bench, Bradan grabbed a pair of oars. 'Row, Melcorka! Row as if your soul depends on it.' Leaning forward, he dipped the blades in the seething water and pulled back, with Melcorka doing the same, until they realised that *Catriona* was already rushing forward at a far higher speed than anything they could manage. The smell of sulphur was overpowering, as fish, living and dead, rained down on them, together with water that was so hot it burned their skin. Glowing embers joined the fish, some hissing as they landed in the sea, others hitting the hull or sliding down the much-patched linen sail.

'Get the sail in!' Bradan yelled. 'These burning rocks will set it on fire!' Shipping his oars, he began to furl the fabric, with Melcorka joining him, swearing as the hot rocks hurtled down and fish flapped and writhed in the seething water that lapped at their shins and knees. They bundled the sail on deck, where it smouldered and charred under the onslaught of hot rocks.

'Hurry!' Bradan slapped at the flames until a wave crashed against the hull and sent a bathful of hot water to douse the fire.

'What's happening?' Melcorka yelled, above the roar of water and wind. Her hair beat a mad frenzy against her head, one second covering her face, the next, streaming down her back. 'Is it the devil coming for us?' She glanced toward Defender, thrumming in the vibrating mast. 'I'll fight it, if it is!'

'No!' Bradan shouted. 'It's a volcano! I've heard about them before. It's a mountain exploding and spewing out its flaming insides.'

'We're at sea!' Melcorka nearly screamed. 'There are no mountains here!'

'It must be a mountain under the sea!' Bradan roared.

'I've never heard of that before.' Melcorka tried to control her flying hair.

'Sit down, grab hold of something and pray,' Bradan said. 'There's nothing else we can do.' Balancing in the madly rocking boat, he inched to the stern and clutched at the tiller.

'It's all right, Bradan,' Melcorka said. 'Don't forget that a master-builder created *Catriona*. No sea can sink her.'

'No sea can sink her –' Bradan glanced at the nightmarish mountains of water behind him, shuddered and quickly turned his attention forward, 'but the sea might still capsize her, or toss us out.' He had to bellow to be heard above the roaring of wind and water. 'I'll keep her head straight.'

All around them, the sea was a maelstrom, with waves rising and falling. Debris from the volcano continued to hammer down, lashing the surface of the water like a thousand flails.

As *Catriona* rushed on, Bradan fought the tiller that bucked and reared in his hands, trying to guide the ship through the nightmare of rising and falling water. Twice, he saw colossal sea monsters of a type he had never met before, and each time they vanished again, as some hidden current dragged them away. Melcorka laughed, crawled to the bow and stood there like a splendid figurehead, her head thrown back and her legs braced to challenge this new experience.

'That's my Mel,' Bradan whispered. 'Whatever comes at us, we'll get through it.' His arms ached with the strain of steering *Catriona,* yet knew he had to hold on. If he relaxed, a wave could smash at them from starboard or larboard, capsizing them in half a second. Bradan knew that Finlay MacCodrum, *Catriona*'s builder, had been part selkie, a creature of the sea. Finlay had designed *Catriona* to be unsinkable, but had he taken account of underwater volcanoes?

Had Finlay even known about such things?

Bradan held on, keeping *Catriona*'s stern to the sea, guiding her despite the constant ache of his arms. He lost track of time, he lost track of distance or location. Keeping afloat mattered, keeping alive mattered. Nothing else. Ignoring the pain, ignoring the fatigue, Bradan remained at his post as the sea hissed and spumed and roared around them.

'I'll take over! Have a break!' Melcorka crawled to Bradan's side, her voice sounding dim through the thick cloud of his exhaustion.

'Thank you.' Bradan relinquished the tiller and massaged his arms. 'How long has it been since the eruption?'

'Melcorka shrugged. 'I don't know. Hours, maybe days.' She glanced at Defender, still firm in the mast. 'You were right, Brad. It was our fault. We caused the volcano to erupt by sticking the sword in the mast. If a sailor's knife and a whistle can call up the wind, how much more could a magic sword such as Defender do?'

'It was nothing to do with Defender.' Bradan was not sure if he was correct. He no longer cared. The volcano and subsequent massive waves had pushed them clear of the terrible yellow seaweed and got them moving again, after weeks of floating on a pond-calm sea. Bradan knew they were heading in the wrong direction to go home, but he was the Wanderer; any new nation or unknown people would broaden his knowledge.

'You're trying to make me feel better.' Melcorka brought him back to the present. 'I still don't know the full power of my sword. Retake the tiller.' Stepping forward, she wrestled Defender free from the mast. Almost immediately, the sea began to moderate, the wind eased, and within an hour *Catriona* was sailing at a sedate pace over a sea that was no different from any other, except for the hundreds of dead fish floating on top.

'At least we won't go hungry for a while.' Bradan leaned over the bulwark to scoop up the nearest fish.

Melcorka began to clean Defender's blade. 'I wonder where we are? I think we have travelled many miles.'

'At the speed we were going, hundreds of miles,' Bradan agreed. 'I've never been in a ship that moved so quickly for so long.'

Melcorka slid Defender into her scabbard. 'I wonder what strange lands we will come to next, what adventures we will have and what peoples we will see?'

Bradan smiled. 'I hope there are no adventures, Mel. I want to find myself in a peaceful place, with intelligent people to increase my knowledge. I will settle for somewhere such as Athens, or Rome, or Baghdad.' He yawned. 'But the first thing I want to do is sleep. I feel as if we've been awake for days.'

'We have,' Melcorka said.

Bradan checked the sea. 'It's clear here. We can let *Catriona* drift for a while and catch up on some sleep.' He grinned. 'Let's hope there are no more aggressive plants.'

Melcorka smiled. She did not mention seeing the face of Kanaima among the vegetation. Sometimes, it was better not to share all her knowledge, for Bradan the Wanderer was also Bradan the Worrier. She crawled into the shelter of the small cabin under the foredeck and closed her eyes.

The face of Kanaima returned, ethereal within her head. 'Begone! You are dead!' Melcorka brushed it away.

'Did you say something, Mel?'

'I was dreaming,' Melcorka said. 'Go back to sleep.' She listened until Bradan's breathing became soft and regular, put her arm around him and closed her eyes again.

I am not dead, Melcorka. No mortal blade can kill me.

Chapter Three

'I see a sail, Bradan.' Melcorka perched cross-legged in the bows, staring out to sea as the waves broke silver and blue under the prow.

'Good, we need some navigational advice. How long is it since the storm died down?' Bradan sat at the tiller with the wind pushing them northeast by north and the occasional squall filling their water casks.

'I don't know.' Melcorka stood up. 'It's been weeks and weeks with nothing to see except the sea. That's no longer true, Bradan. There's maybe more than one ship.'

'Where?' Bradan scanned the horizon.

'On the starboard bow,' Melcorka said and swarmed up the mast for a better look. Sitting on the cross-trees, she shouted down. 'I see three sails in close company.'

'I'll steer towards them,' Bradan said.

'They might be unfriendly,' Melcorka warned.

'It's been months since we last spoke to anybody. Have you not had enough of my company yet?'

'More than enough,' Melcorka said. 'These ships are sailing towards us.'

The sails burst over the horizon, one, two, three, close together and moving fast.

'It's only a single ship,' Bradan said. 'It is a single ship with three masts.'

'It must be huge,' Melcorka marvelled. 'We'll soon see if they are friendly or not.'

The ship was long, stable in the water and larger than any they had seen before. Three tall masts were resplendent with square sails, while a bowsprit thrust from the bow, also holding a sail. The master must have placed a lookout on one of the masts for he altered direction toward the diminutive *Catriona*.

'They've seen us.' Bradan steered for the strange ship.

The three-master surged toward them and, with an impressive display of skill, her crew furled all her sails simultaneously. She eased beside *Catriona*, rising and falling on the long, still unbroken swell. Sun glinting from the water around her only enhanced the hush and swish of the waves.

'Well met, stranger!' Bradan shouted across the cable's length between them.

A score of dark brown faces stared at them as a man stood in the stern and called to them in a language they did not understand.

Bradan tried again, in Gaelic, Pictish and Cymric, to meet only smiles and shaking heads. The mariners on the stranger ship also attempted different languages, which had everybody smiling and laughing together.

'At least they're friendly,' Melcorka said.

'I'll try Norse,' Bradan said, 'and then maybe Latin.'

'I didn't know you spoke Latin,' Melcorka said. 'You are full of surprises, Bradan.'

The master of the foreign vessel was broad and smiling under a large turban. He responded to the Latin with a great, booming laugh and words that Bradan understood, despite the strong accent.

'They want to know who we are and where we are from,' Bradan said.

'Then tell them.' Melcorka sat with her back to the mast, studying the strange ship with its large crew of bare-chested, sinewy men. She listened to Bradan speaking, decided that she was not needed and closed her eyes. She opened them briefly when the strange vessel sent over a small open boat with a bird in a cage and closed them again when it was apparent there was no threat to *Catriona*. As she could not communicate with them, there was nothing else she could do.

'They're from a place called the Chola Empire,' Bradan said at length.

'I've never heard of it,' Melcorka said.

'They've never heard of Alba, either,' Bradan grinned. 'This is a completely different world.'

'Is this Chola Empire worth visiting?' Melcorka asked.

'It sounds like it. The shipmaster thinks it's paradise on earth, with hospitals for sick animals as well as sick humans and resting places for travellers.'

'Take us there, then,' Melcorka said. 'We need a friendly place and some time on land after so long at sea.'

'If we head north, and a little east, most of the coastline belongs to the Chola Empire,' Bradan said. 'The shipmaster has given us a navigation bird. He says that when we see seabirds or smell the coast, we should release the bird and it will guide us to land.'

Melcorka looked at the bird, unhappily hunched within its cage. 'The poor little creature will be pleased when we set it free.' Putting her finger through the bars, Melcorka stroked the bird's breast. 'She's a lovely little thing.'

'I don't like to see birds and animals caged,' Bradan said. 'I think we should free her now.'

Melcorka nodded. 'Do it. We can find land ourselves.' She watched as Bradan opened the cage door. The bird hopped out and immediately flew away. 'Safe journey, little bird. Did the shipmaster say anything else?'

'The captain also said to watch out for the pirates of Thiruzha.'

Melcorka laughed and touched the hilt of Defender. 'We have faced Caterans and Norsemen, Kalingo warriors and the armies of Cahokia. We can face pirates as well.'

'You are not invulnerable, Melcorka,' Bradan warned.

'Nor are they.' Melcorka dismissed Bradan's words. 'What else did your Chola friends say?'

'You're not normally so contemptuous of a possible enemy.' Bradan narrowed his eyes. 'You've not been quite yourself since you fought the Kalingo.'

'I'm fine.' Melcorka brushed aside Bradan's worries.

Bradan grunted. 'I'm not so sure. I'm keeping an eye on you, Melcorka nic Bearnas.'

Melcorka arched her back and thrust out her breasts. 'Oh, please do, Bradan no-last-name.'

'That's not like you either, Mel.'

'But you're glad I have this new side.' Melcorka laughed. 'It's all right, Brad, I'm still me. I've not changed. Now, tell me more about these ferocious Thiruzha pirates.'

Bradan altered the angle of the sail and looked around the horizon. 'The captain advised us to watch out for a man named Bhim – he is the worst of them. The shipmaster said if you meet Bhim or a woman named Dhraji, turn and flee.'

'We shall avoid him, then.' Melcorka spoke lightly.

They watched as the Chola ship hoisted its sails and bore away to the East, leaving a spreading white wake behind. Two men waved from the stern.

'I wonder where she is bound and what strange lands await her?' Bradan said. 'Perhaps we should have gone with her.'

'They have their journey,' Melcorka said, 'and we have ours. Let's find this Chola Empire and see if it is as friendly as the seamen said.' She grinned. 'The empires we have found in the past were not always worth finding.'

'As long as there are no warlike falcons there,' Bradan said. 'I do not wish to meet any more falcon warriors.'

'Do you wish to meet a many-legged monster?' Melcorka asked, suddenly serious.

'I never wish to meet a many-legged monster,' Bradan said.

'Don't look behind you, then.' Melcorka drew Defender.

Melcorka had never seen anything even remotely resembling the thing that was rising from the sea. Three enormously long tentacles stretched as high as *Catriona*'s mast, writhing as they sought their prey. On the underside of each arm was a row of circular suckers, equipped with what looked like sharp teeth.

'It's a sea monster, Bradan!' Melcorka shouted. 'Get forward and keep out of my way.'

'I can't leave the tiller!' Bradan shouted.

Grabbing hold of his arm, Melcorka ripped Bradan from his seat and shoved him forward, just as one of the probing tentacles swept across the stern of *Catriona*. 'Move!'

A fourth wriggling tentacle joined the first three, and then a fifth.

'What in the name of God is that?' As always, Melcorka felt the thrill as the power of Defender surged through her, with the skill of the sword's makers augmented by the fighting ability, cunning and strength of all her previous users. 'Come on, you creature from Hades! Melcorka of Alba is here! Melcorka the Swordswoman is waiting for you!'

Three arms settled on the stern of *Catriona*, dragging the ship deeper into the water as the teeth within the suckers scraped at the timber.

Melcorka swung Defender at the closest arm, feeling the bite as the blade sliced into the rubbery thing that writhed and pulled at the bulwark. She swore as Defender stuck fast.

'You're tough.' Melcorka gave grudging praise. 'What in God's name are you?' Wrestling Defender free, she hacked a second and a third time before the arm parted, leaving a four-foot-long length writhing along the deck.

'Mel!' Bradan's voice was hoarse. 'Behind you!' Rushing forward, he crashed down his rowan-wood staff on one of the arms that snaked around the back of Melcorka. The stick bounced from the tentacle without having any effect, but Bradan's shout alerted Melcorka just as the tip of the tentacle curled around her ankle.

The power of the tentacle shocked Melcorka as it lifted her leg. She yelled, turned and sliced downward, chopping the end off the tentacle, which parted, to wriggle on the deck like a living thing.

'There are more of them!' Bradan said, as two more of the long, red arms slithered from the sea, and then a massive head thrust up at the bow, with shield-wide eyes staring at them, on either side of a great, beak-like mouth that snapped in fury.

'What an ugly brute you are!' Melcorka jerked back as the beak reached for her, and more of the creature's arms appeared. One coiled around the mast and another grabbed Bradan around the thigh.

The rings of teeth tore into Bradan's leg. 'Mel!' Bradan beat uselessly at the tentacle with his staff, swearing as the thing tightened its grip, tearing into his flesh.

Melcorka had troubles of her own, as one tentacle wrapped around her waist and another grabbed her right arm, trying to prise her grip free from Defender. Shocked at the monster's power, Melcorka gasped as she fought back, using all the strength she could glean from her sword.

The monster hauled itself further on board, its many arms tangling around the ship, wrapping around the mast and spars as its great, ugly beak snapped close to Melcorka's face. She could see her reflection in the black mirrors of the creature's eyes.

'Mel!' Bradan shouted desperately, as the arms dragged him toward the beak.

Melcorka twisted Defender to the right, stabbing at the tentacle that held her arm. The point of the blade sunk into the rubbery substance and stuck there. Melcorka worked it right and left, enlarging the wound until the tentacle parted.

Gasping with relief, Melcorka yanked her arm free and, without hesitation, sliced right and left, using all her strength now that she knew how tough this monster's arms were. Grunting with satisfaction as first one and then another of the tentacles parted, Melcorka felt the sting where the creature's toothed suckers had wrapped around her waist.

'Get back to Hades!' she yelled, only to swear as she saw the creature dragging Bradan toward its terrible beak. One tentacle was around his thigh, another on his left arm while he swung his staff in futile attempts to break the creature's grip.

'Bradan!' Jumping over the wriggling tentacles and rowing benches, Melcorka lifted Defender high. 'I'm coming, Bradan.'

Fighting desperately against the strength of the creature, Bradan knew he was doomed. The monster's two glaring eyes surveyed him, its beak was open, ready to snap off his arms or head and all he had was his staff. He saw two more tentacles wrap around Melcorka and draw her back.

'Melcorka! Look out!'

Bradan did not mind dying; everybody had to die at some time. However, he did not want to die and be eaten by some multi-armed monster from beneath the sea. Lifting his staff, he thrust it with all his force into the creature's left eye. The beast did not flinch as the end of the staff bounced off the eyeball. The beast prepared to bite, and Bradan saw that the inside of its beak was lined with a double row of inward-pointing teeth. Once that thing closed on him, he would never escape.

Then Melcorka was at Bradan's side, slicing at the tentacles with Defender, before hacking uselessly at the creature's right eye with the point of the blade. The creature's remaining arms curled up and it withdrew from *Catriona* with a massive splash, sending water cascading into the wildly tossing ship.

'It's gone! Thank the gods!' Bradan gasped.

'What was it?' Melcorka held Defender ready in case the creature returned.

'Some monster from the furthest deeps of the sea,' Bradan said. 'I'll wager that the volcano spewed it up.'

'The volcano was weeks ago and hundreds of miles away!' Melcorka paced the length of the ship, sword held ready. 'I've never seen anything so ugly in my life, or fought anything so strong.' She shook her head. 'I stuck Defender into its eye as hard as I could, and it just bounced off. Defender bounced off!' Melcorka lowered her voice and stared at the still-disturbed water. 'That's never happened before.'

'Be thankful the creature has gone,' Bradan said. 'You chased it off and saved my life.' He touched Melcorka's arm. 'Thank you. Now, look at yourself. That thing has opened cuts all over your arms and legs.'

'You're the same.' Melcorka pointed to the blood that seeped down Bradan's legs. 'We'll have to patch up the wounds before they fester.'

'Do you think it will return?' Bradan lifted one of the tentacles. 'Yeuch, this thing is disgusting! Look at these teeth!' Shuddering, he threw it over the side. 'Come on, Mel, let's get the ship cleaned up.'

'I hope it comes back because I want to kill it.' Melcorka wiped thick, clear liquid from Defender. 'Look at this, Bradan. It doesn't even bleed. I've never seen a creature that doesn't bleed.'

'Let's hope we never see it again.' Bradan felt himself shaking with delayed reaction. 'I don't like monsters of any sort.'

With the deck cleansed of the tentacles and scrubbed with sea water, Melcorka and Bradan tended to each other's wounds.

'Seawater to clean them and cloth to stop the bleeding,' Melcorka said and gave a high-pitched laugh that had Bradan looking sideways at her.

'Are you all right, Mel?'

'I want to kill that monster. I like to kill things.' Melcorka laughed again.

'No, Mel. No, you don't.' Bradan took hold of her arms. 'You don't like to kill things. This is not like you, Mel.'

Melcorka pushed him away. 'Where are we?' She had not paid much attention to her surroundings since the volcano erupted, being content to sit in the bows and stare at the sea, or take her turn on a rowing bench. Now, she looked around, seeing choppy blue seas, diamond-sparkled by the sun, with a distant bank of white cloud.

'We're not where we want to be, anyway.' Bradan stepped to the tiller. 'That volcano pushed us far to the south and east, and we've been heading roughly north and east ever since.' He looked upward. 'We're in the torrid zone still, a long way from Alba, that's for certain.'

'I can get used to the heat.' Melcorka stretched out in the bows and looked sideways at Bradan. 'It's fun lying about doing nothing.'

'You've always hated doing nothing,' Bradan said. 'You like to be active.'

'Not any more,' Melcorka said. 'I feel like being lazy now and letting the world drift along.' She pointed to the horizon. 'That mist is getting closer.'

White and clinging, the mist circled *Catriona*. Within an hour, it had slithered over the ship, breaking into long tendrils that flew from *Catriona*'s mast like ripped flags.

'The mist has hidden the sun. I can't see through this muck.' Melcorka flapped a hand in a vain effort to clear away the mist. 'Tell it to go away, Bradan. I have no idea what's out there.'

'It could be anything – more sea monsters, more volcanoes, more savage Kalingo, or even the friendly traders of the Chola Empire.' Bradan half furled the sail. 'We'll move slowly in case there is land nearby, or some other danger.'

Melcorka stretched again, sighed and took control of the tiller. 'Get on the oars, Bradan, and I'll manage the sail and the steering.'

A seabird called, the sound echoing eerily through the fog, while the occasional wave lapped over the low gunwale. Melcorka watched Bradan's long, lean body as he sat on the rowing bench and took the oars. Years of rowing and travelling had created a man of firm muscles without an ounce of spare fat. Although Melcorka had been his companion for some years, she did not know how old he was. He seemed ageless, as if he had always been the same and always would be. She mused over him, smiling as she hummed a small song her mother had sung to her as a child.

'Over there! To the left!' Melcorka pointed with her chin. 'I'm sure I saw land.'

Bradan squinted narrow-eyed into the mist. 'I can't see anything. What was it like?'

'White,' Melcorka said. 'Pure white, like snow. Maybe we're back in Greenland with the Norse and the Skraelings and the Ice King.'

'It's too warm for Greenland,' Bradan said.

'Look!' Melcorka pointed again. 'I'm sure that I can see white land.'

Bradan twisted to see over his shoulder. 'I've heard that the south coast of Britain has white cliffs, but we're not sufficiently far north. We are thousands of miles from Britain.'

Melcorka shrugged. 'Well, I don't know.'

'Something's happening, Mel,' Bradan said. 'Look.'

The mist lifted, leaving *Catriona* bobbing on an azure sea that sparkled under the caress of the sun. A mile to starboard, something white gleamed on an otherwise unbroken, hazed horizon.

'I've never seen a pure white island before.' Bradan lifted his staff and tapped it on the deck. 'It's another new thing.'

'You like new things, Bradan,' Melcorka said. 'You want to land there, don't you?' She altered the angle of the tiller, steering toward the island even as she spoke.

Bradan nodded. 'The Chola Empire can wait. It will still be there tomorrow. We may never sail this way again, and a pure white island is intriguing.'

Riding light, *Catriona* eased across the waves. Melcorka shook out the single square sail, and they closed with the island.

'It's not all white,' Bradan said, as they came within half a mile of it. 'There is a copse of trees back there.'

'It's sand,' Melcorka said. 'It's pure white sand.'

'I had hoped for something more unusual.' Bradan voiced his disappointment. 'Take the sail in, Mel, we're about to land.'

Catriona hissed onto a gently shelving beach where the sea kissed soft white sand. 'I've never seen sand this colour.' Bradan jumped onto the beach and looked around. 'It's warm and pristine. There's not a shell, not a stone, no tide-wrack, not a footprint. There are no birds and no insects. This is the strangest island I have ever seen.'

'Help me haul *Catriona* further up,' Melcorka said, and they pulled the boat a few yards away from the lapping waves. 'You're right, Bradan. There's no high-tide mark, no fringe of seaweed, no line of coconuts or other refuse of the sea. There's not even a breeze to skiff the surface of the sand.'

'We're being watched,' Bradan said. 'I can feel it.'

Melcorka glanced at him. 'Hostile-watched, or curious-watched?'

'I can't tell yet.' Bradan thrust his staff into the sand. It sunk deep. He thrust further until the body of the staff disappeared. 'There's no bottom here. The sand goes on forever. Don't look at the trees, Mel. I think there's somebody there.'

Melcorka turned her back to the trees and stared along the length of the beach. 'There's nothing here except the trees,' she said. 'No buildings, no rocks, no water, no hills. This is a desert island indeed.'

'I don't think the watcher is unfriendly,' Bradan said. 'I can't feel anything unfriendly.'

Melcorka smiled and tapped the hilt of her sword. 'I have a cure for hostility.'

'There is no need for that.' Bradan shook his head. 'Even since you fought the Kalingo, you have been too keen to use Defender.'

'I am the Swordswoman,' Melcorka said.

'You are more than that,' Bradan reminded her. 'You wait here, and I'll walk up to the trees. If I need you…'

'If you need me, I'll be at your side,' Melcorka said. 'I am not letting you walk up to any foreign man alone. If need be, I have this.' She tapped Defender again.

'Try not to kill anybody, Mel.' Bradan lengthened his stride and headed for the trees. A breeze eased up, keeping conditions pleasant without lifting even the surface of the sand. They walked on, feet sinking deeply, yet after a few moments of steady walking, the copse seemed no closer. Bradan turned around. *Catriona* lay where they had left her, smaller with distance.

'A man is sitting amidst the trees,' Melcorka said. 'I can see him as plainly as I see you.'

'I see him.' Bradan tapped his staff on the sand. 'He's watching us.' He raised his staff. 'Halloa there!' His voice faded in the vast spaces around them. The man did not respond.

'I'll try,' Melcorka said. Cupping her hands around her mouth, she shouted, 'Can you hear us? If you hear us, raise a hand!'

'They don't speak Gaelic around here, remember,' Bradan said. 'I'll try Latin.' He shouted again, with the words sounding harsh and guttural to Melcorka's ear. The man remained sitting.

'How old would you say he was?' Bradan asked.

'About thirty,' Melcorka guessed.

Bradan nodded. 'He's all alone, I think.' He looked around. The whiteness stretched from the soft surf of the shore to the still-distant trees, and all around the island. There was only sand, a circuit to adorn the nodding palms.

'Something's wrong here,' Melcorka said. 'There are no houses, no other people, no ships except *Catriona*, and no bird or insect life. Who is that man and how did he get here? How does he survive?' She lengthened her stride. 'Come on, Bradan, we have a mystery to solve.'

They broke into a trot, and then a full run until their legs ached and their lungs burned, without closing the distance to the lone man at the copse of static palms.

'Stop,' Bradan gasped, clutching at Melcorka's arm. 'We're getting nowhere here.'

'You're right,' Melcorka said. They stood side by side, breathing in agonised gasps. 'Look around us, Bradan.'

The sea lapped against the beach a few yards behind them, where *Catriona* lay with her mast slanting sideways and her prow facing the still-distant palms. 'We've moved backwards since I last looked,' Bradan said.

'So I see,' Melcorka said. 'We're no closer to the copse than we were when we started.'

'This island is not normal,' Bradan said. 'It is either enchanted or accursed and either way, it is best if we were not here.' He gestured to the man sitting under his palm trees. 'Whatever that is, wizard, warlock, magi or druid, it has powers that we cannot match.'

'We'll get back to sea then.' Melcorka jerked her head toward *Catriona*. 'This is an adventure that I have no wish to repeat.'

Catriona seemed eager to leave. She slid easily down the sand into the water as Bradan and Melcorka pushed her. They jumped in together, with Melcorka taking the tiller as Bradan hoisted the sail.

'At least you have got some energy back,' Bradan said.

'The wind is from the south-west.' Melcorka did not respond to his words. 'Angle the sail to catch it.'

'Look,' Bradan pointed ahead. 'The island has moved.'

A hundred yards in front of them, the white sands of the island stretched out on either side. Astern of *Catriona* was only sea.

'This is uncanny.' Bradan rubbed his thumb across St Columba's cross that was carved into the tip of his staff.

'That man is still there.' Melcorka altered the angle of the tiller. 'Time we were not.'

The copse of trees seemed only a few hundred paces away, with the man stationary at the edge. There was no trace of their footprints on the beach.

'Hoist all sail,' Melcorka said. 'If we can't get away, we'll fight. Ram the island.'

'We can't sink an island,' Bradan said.

'Get on the oars and pull with all your strength,' Melcorka's eyes narrowed. 'We can't walk to that man, so let's try to sail to him. If he's there at all.'

'If he's there at all?' Bradan repeated.

'We have seen armies before, where none existed.' Melcorka joined Bradan at the oars, sending *Catriona* surging forward. 'That man could be an illusion, a trick of the mind, a conjurer's image and so could the island.'

'As you wish.' Securing the sail in place, Bradan hauled as hard as he was able, grunting with effort. *Catriona* thrust into the sea, her sharp prow raising a bow-wave, and then she rammed hard onto the sand.

Melcorka gasped as the impact threw her backwards. Bradan tumbled on top of her and the oars were thrown into utter confusion.

'That feels solid enough.' Melcorka dragged herself up, feeling for broken bones.

'The island is unaltered.' Bradan pointed to the copse of trees, where the man sat, unmoving, watching them.

'What do you want?' Melcorka shouted. 'What do you want of us?'

'We come in peace,' Bradan roared. 'We only want to talk to you.'

The man still did not move as, once again, Melcorka and Bradan strode forward, with their feet sinking into the white sand and the copse remaining the same distance from them.

'Look behind you,' Bradan said. 'We're making an impression.'

Their footsteps were distinct in the sand, stretching backwards, but every time they stepped forward, the imprint nearest to *Catriona* faded and vanished.

'This man is a magician,' Melcorka said. 'And the only cure for a magician is this!' She unsheathed Defender with a slither of steel on leather. As always, she felt the thrill as the power and skill of all the previous holders of the sword coursed from the hilt through her hands and arms and into her body. 'Now, let us see how good he is.'

'He has not attacked us,' Bradan said.

'Just as well for him.' Melcorka lifted Defender above her head. 'You there! Magician! We came in peace, and you have played with us. Greet us fairly, or by my sword, I will part your head from your body.'

For the first time, the man showed some emotion. He smiled, sitting cross-legged amidst the palm trees, naked except for a minuscule loincloth.

Bradan looked around. They were now only five yards from the man, yet he had not moved since Melcorka drew Defender. 'How did we get here?'

'Magic.' Melcorka tightened her grip on Defender. 'Look behind us.'

Twin sets of footprints extended from *Catriona* to the copse, unbroken save where falling fine sand was blurring the edges of each print. The air was still, without a hint of a breeze.

'Who are you?' Bradan asked.

The man spoke without moving. 'Who I am does not matter. Who are you, man-with-a-staff, and why do you come to my home?'

Bradan gave a little bow. 'Well met, man of this island. I am Bradan the Wanderer from Alba. I seek knowledge of places and people unknown to me. My companion is Melcorka nic Bearnas, also from Alba. Nic means *daughter of*, so she is Melcorka, the daughter of Bearnas.'

'Well met, Bradan the Wanderer from Alba.' The man did not move. 'Knowledge is a powerful tool and one that can be used to help or to injure.'

'That is so, man-with-no-name,' Bradan agreed.

'I do not like talking to a man with no name,' Melcorka said. 'Who are you?'

The man remained still. 'More importantly, my Lady of the Sword, is who you are.'

'I am Melcorka nic Bearnas, of the Cenel Bearnas from Alba.' Melcorka said. 'Bradan has already told you that.'

'Bradan told me your name,' the man corrected gently. 'He did not tell me who you are.'

Melcorka took a deep breath. She did not like people interrogating her, or playing word games. 'People call me Melcorka the Swordswoman.' Melcorka lifted Defender higher. She thought she saw something else beside the man, somebody indefinable, a shimmering black-and-white light between the boles of the trees.

'Melcorka the Swordswoman.' The man nodded. His eyes were older than his body, deep and wise and serene. 'You are a woman who lives by violence and delights to kill.'

'I have no delight in violence, nameless man. I only kill when it is necessary.'

'Meet yourself,' the man with no name said. 'You are coming to see me, as you did and as you are.'

'Turn around,' Bradan murmured. He placed a hand on Melcorka's arm. 'Hold your temper in check, Mel.'

Melcorka did as Bradan asked and gasped in shock. An image of her was striding up the beach, legs thrusting vigorously, face set in determination and with one hand hovering above the hilt of her sword. 'I have a cure for hostility,' she said, tapping the sword hilt. 'I have a cure for hostility.' The image of Melcorka repeated its words and actions. 'I have a cure for hostility. I have a cure for hostility.'

'You are a woman who lives by violence and delights to kill,' the man repeated.

'I was provoked,' Melcorka said.

'You may have felt provoked,' the man with no name said and waved the image away. 'You may be taking offence where none is intended.' When he lifted his hand, the image of Melcorka returned.

'As well for him.' The image of Melcorka lifted Defender above her head. 'You there! Magician! We came in peace, and you have played with us. Greet us fairly or, by my sword, I will part your head from your body.'

The man with no name dropped his hand again, and the image disappeared. 'Would you be so bold without your sword, I wonder? Nobody caused you offence. I merely wanted to see you before you came close.'

'You did not reply to us.' Melcorka found she was defending her stance.

'You chose to come to my home,' the man with no name replied. 'You landed on my island and approached my house uninvited and unannounced.' The expression on his face did not alter. 'You depended on the skill that lies within your sword to look after you if you were unwelcome.'

'How do you know about the skill that lies within my sword?' Melcorka asked.

The man reached forward and put his forefinger on the hilt of Defender. 'Derwen made this sword,' he said. 'It came from long ago, long back, and Derwen made it for Caractacus, who was betrayed by a woman. It was the blade of Calgacus, the swordsman. It was the sword of Arthur, who faced the Saxon and now it is the sword of Melcorka.'

'Who are you?' Melcorka asked. The nameless man had repeated, nearly word for word, what Ceridwen had told her when first she gained Defender.

The man continued. 'It was a sword well made in Derwen's forge. It was made with rich red ore, with Derwen tramping on bellows of ox-hide to blow the charcoal hot as hell ever is. The ore sank down, down through the charcoal to the lowest depth of the furnace, to form a shapeless mass the weight of a well-grown child.'

Melcorka listened, remembering the day when she had chosen Defender, or the sword had picked her.

The man with no name continued. 'It was normal for the apprentices to take the metal to the anvil, but Derwen carried the metal for this one himself, and chose the best of the best to reheat and form into a bar. He had the bar blessed by the Druids of his time, and by the holy man who came from the East, a young fugitive from Judea who fled the wrath of the Romans. Derwen cut his choice of steel into short lengths, laid them end on end in water blessed by the holy one and the chief Druid of Caractacus, and drew them long and long, before welding them together with the skill that only Derwen had. These operations working together equalised the temper of the steel, making it hard throughout, and sufficiently pliable to bend in half and spring together. Derwen tested and retested the blade, then hardened and sharpened it with his own touch and his own magic. In the end, in the final forging, Derwen sprinkled his own white powder of the dust of diamonds and rubies into the red-hot steel, to keep it free of rust and protect the edge.'

'You know it,' Melcorka said.

'The sword told me most of it,' the man with no name said. 'And some came from within you.'

The shimmering beside the man was more definite now, a black-and-white mass that settled on the sand. Melcorka frowned, trying to clear the confusion from her mind. She should know what that shimmer was; she had seen it before, more than once. She delved into her memories and found only a labyrinth of uneasiness.

'That sword is worthy of heroes.' The man interrupted her thoughts.

'It is,' Melcorka said.

'Now you must prove yourself worthy to bear it.' The strange man lifted his hand again, and a circular hole appeared in the sand at his side. As Melcorka and Bradan looked, the hole deepened until they saw water at the bottom. 'Defender will rest here for eternity,' the man said. 'Or until a hero comes along who deserves her.'

Melcorka shook her head. 'No man and no woman can take Defender from me.'

'Perhaps not.' The man fixed his eyes on Melcorka. 'Throw her into that hole.'

'I will not.' Yet even as Melcorka spoke, she unbuckled Defender and held the sword, together with her scabbard and belt, high in the air above the hole.

'Melcorka!' Some unseen source held Bradan back, foiling his attempt to grab at the sword. He struggled desperately, fighting to move. He could only watch as Melcorka tossed Defender into the air. The sword poised there for a second, with the sun catching the bronze bands that encircled the embossed leather of the scabbard, and then it fell into the hole beside the man with no name. Bradan saw Defender plunge down and down and down until it slid silently and without a splash into the dark water.

The black-and-white shimmer reappeared between Bradan and Melcorka. Formless and shapeless, it wavered, as if uncertain which of them it wished to touch, and then vanished into nothingness.

'Melcorka,' Bradan said again. He could do nothing, as the man with no name, together with the copse of palm trees, dissolved before him. One second, Bradan was watching Defender sink into the water and the next, he was lying on the deck of *Catriona* with his back pressed onto the wood and the mast slowly spiralling beneath the vacuum of the sky.

'What happened?' Melcorka was at the tiller, staring around her.

'You threw away Defender,' Bradan said. 'You threw Defender into the hole that the magician created.' He looked around. They were a couple of miles off an unknown green coast with a distinctive, double-peaked hill directly to starboard.

'I know.' Melcorka gave a strangely vacant smile. 'Can we get it back now, please?'

'We have more immediate problems,' Bradan said. 'Look there.'

A mile to port, a dozen two-masted vessels with sails set were spread out in line, abreast. They were closing fast, with the distinctive beat of drums urging them on.

Chapter Four

Melcorka looked dazed. 'My sword,' she said. 'I've lost Defender.' She felt at her shoulder. 'I threw it away.'

'You did,' Bradan agreed.

'I must get her back.' Melcorka stared over the side of *Catriona*, desperate to find the white island with its mysterious occupant.

'We have other things to worry about,' Bradan said. 'Get on the tiller, Mel, and I'll hoist the sails. These vessels may not be friendly. They may be the Thiruzha pirates that Chola shipmaster warned us of.'

The fleet was spread out, with the vessels extending from the coast to the horizon. Drumbeats throbbed across the intervening water, ominous, dangerous, as the drummers marked the time for the oarsmen who propelled the vessels toward *Catriona* with frightening speed.

'That looks and sounds bad,' Bradan said. 'No peaceful merchantmen would use a formation like that, or have drums to keep them at the same pace.'

'We'd best sail away then.' Melcorka's eyes cleared for a moment. 'We can come back later and get Defender.'

'They're travelling faster than we are,' Bradan said, 'but I'm damned if I'll sit tamely by and allow them to catch us. Come on, Mel!'

'My sword!' Melcorka looked dazed again. 'I can't leave Defender!'

'We'll come back for Defender.' Bradan shoved her hard onto a rowing bench. 'Come on, Mel, row like the demons of hell are after us, and they might well be. Run, and live to fight another day!'

By now, the dreadful booming of the drums was echoing around *Catriona* as the strange fleet closed. Bradan could make out men on the cross-trees of the masts, with others standing in the bow of each approaching ship, watching them. The sun glittered on metal, either sword-blades or the points of spears, he could not be sure.

'Row!' Bradan checked the sail. It was drawing as full as it could, gliding *Catriona* over the long rollers. He hauled on the slim oars and watched as Melcorka pulled feebly. 'Come on, Mel, at least try!'

'Defender,' Melcorka said. 'I want my sword back.'

The first arrow fell well short; the second was twenty yards to port, landed on a shallow trajectory and skiffed across the surface of the water. The third arrow whizzed past, to fall in the water with barely a splash. A fourth followed, and then a fifth, missing the hull of *Catriona* by only a handspan.

'I don't think they're friendly,' Bradan said.

Melcorka smiled at him, wordless.

Facing astern, Bradan could see the strange fleet clearly. Each vessel was five times the length of *Catriona;* ocean-going craft with two masts and a score or more of warriors to augment the oarsmen. A forest of spears protruded from behind the wooden bulwarks and rows of round, white objects bounced along the hull. Only when the vessels closed to thirty yards or so did Bradan make out what the white objects were.

'Row, Mel,' he whispered urgently. 'Can you see what they have along the hull?'

'My sword.' Melcorka shook her head, still dazed. 'I've lost Defender.'

'They're skulls – human skulls!' Bradan hauled at the oars again, trying to increase the speed of *Catriona* although he already knew it was hopeless. 'Mel! Try, please try!'

As Bradan spoke, each ship of the unknown fleet hoisted long, swallow-tail flags from their mizzen mast and stern. Each flag showed the head of a snarling yellow animal against a blue background.

When Melcorka said, 'That's quite pretty,' Bradan knew that her mind had snapped. A grown-up child had taken the place of his Melcorka.

'Stay with me, Mel, and we'll try to get you back.' Bradan stopped rowing. He might need his energy for whatever ordeal lay ahead.

The strange fleet surrounded them and closed the net, with brown-skinned, bare-chested men standing in each ship, pointing arrows or spears at Melcorka and Bradan. When a tall man shouted an order, two arrows sliced through the air, to thrum into the rowing bench at Bradan's side.

'That's it now,' Bradan said. 'We can fight and die, or just surrender, and I don't fancy being the prisoner of this lot.' Lifting his staff, Bradan stood over Melcorka. 'Come and take us then, if you can!' He feinted right and left as a horde of men swept over the side of the boat. 'Get off my ship!' Something hit him on the side of the head, and he slumped down. Something else hit him, and he lost consciousness.

'I've lost my sword.' Melcorka smiled up at the man who crashed the butt of a spear on her head.

* * *

Bradan woke with his head pounding and his wrists and ankles tightly tied. He opened his eyes, smelled smoke and heard cries, screams and rough laughter.

'Mel?' Bradan looked around. Melcorka lay beside him, tied up as he was and unconscious, while strange, brown-faced men crowded *Catriona*. Struggling to sit up, Bradan peered over the gunwale. *Catriona* was in the middle of the pirate fleet, a few yards off a shore of yellow sand and tall palm trees. More pirate ships were hauled up on a steeply shelving beach. Flames and smoke rose from a sizeable village of thatched-roofed houses, where armed men chased terrified people, dragged women away and plunged spears and swords into any men who tried to fight back.

Bradan groaned as memories of Norse raids and Hebridean Caterans flooded into his mind. History was repeating itself, except now Melcorka did not have her sword, they had no allies, and they were thousands of miles from home. Screwing up his eyes against the pain in his head and the pounding sun above, Bradan watched, with his heart sinking within him.

What manner of trouble have we landed in this time?

The pirates were not indiscriminate. They only killed the old and weak, the very young or those who showed resistance. The rest, they herded up and shoved towards the fleet.

'What's happening?' Melcorka opened her eyes and smiled. 'Have we found Defender yet?'

'It's a slave raid,' Bradan told her. 'This is a slavers' fleet.'

'Oh.' Melcorka shook her head as if to clear it. 'Are we collecting slaves?'

'No, Melcorka,' Bradan said. 'We are the slaves.'

'Oh.' Melcorka shook her head again. 'If I had Defender, I would not be a slave.'

'I know,' Bradan said softly. 'I know that, Mel.'

Bradan watched as the slavers drove their captives onto the ships, tied them hand and foot and left them lying on the deck. The slavers were laughing, enjoying their work as they decapitated the dead and lifted the still-dripping heads. Some of the men dragged away the more comely of the women, while others laughed and jeered at the screams of the victims.

The sun slid behind a range of hills to the west, colouring the sky ochre and purple in a beauty that seemed obscene beside such a scene of horror. The pirates bundled the slaves onto the boats and followed, blood-smeared, smoke-stained and laughing. Only then did Bradan realise that the oarsmen had not left their places. They were chained to the oars.

'Galley-slaves,' Bradan said, feeling sick. He had heard that the life of a galley-slave was short and brutal. He had no desire for a period of intense toil under the lash of some sadistic overseer, to die at the oar and be pitched overboard as food for the sharks. If he died, what would happen to Melcorka? Ordinarily, Bradan would have no fear for Melcorka's ability to cope with whatever the world threw at her, but now that something had broken in her mind, she was vulnerable to any man, or woman.

I will survive, Mel, Bradan promised. *I will survive whatever these pirate slavers do to me and do my best to get you back to yourself. Somehow.*

Melcorka lay on her side, smiling and singing a small, childish song. Bradan wanted to hold her close, to protect her from all the evil in the world. He also wanted to weep. *No*, he told himself. *I cannot do that. I must keep strong for Melcorka's sake.*

Night fell with the usual swiftness of tropical latitudes, and a sky of brilliant stars gleamed above the fleet. The pirate ships left the village and sailed north, with the drums still beating and the oarsmen giving a hoarse gasp with each haul on the oars. Bradan lay awake, listening to Melcorka's steady breathing as she slept and desperately trying to wrestle free from his bonds.

A guard stood over him, bent down and tested the rope around his wrists and ankles, grunted and stepped to Melcorka. He looked at Melcorka's body and slid a hand over her left breast.

'If you touch her, I swear by every God you know that I will kill you,' Bradan said.

Not understanding, the guard barely spared Bradan a glance. He moved his hand to Melcorka's right breast until Bradan wriggled closer and kicked out with his bound feet. He caught the man at the back of the knees and knocked him to the deck. The guard bounced back in a second, drew a wavy-bladed knife and stepped toward Bradan, until another slaver intervened, laughed and pushed him away. Uncaring, the oarsmen rowed on through the night.

* * *

They were approaching land again. Bradan had been watching the increasing number of birds around the fleet and could smell vegetation and a faint hint of spices. Wriggling backwards and propping himself against the mast, Bradan looked over *Catriona*'s bow, to see the distant serration of mountains. As the steady beat of drums encouraged the fleet forward, the land became more visible and the details more apparent. The fleet was approaching what looked like a large harbour, part-shielded by a long, rocky island. Flags and banners showed that snarling yellow beast, prominent on its blue background, a warning to all to keep clear.

The slavers were talking as they approached the sheltered harbour. A stocky, broad-shouldered man sat at *Catriona*'s tiller, giving sharp orders that saw a man furl her sail as the ship kept formation with the rest of the fleet. Whatever these pirates were, Bradan thought, they were good seamen. They had mastered *Catriona*'s unfamiliar sails and oars within minutes.

'Where are we?' Bradan asked.

Nobody replied.

He tried again in Latin, with the same result. *Catriona* pushed on until they were level with the island. Only then did Bradan see that it was fortified, with stone walls rising from the rock and faces peering from the embrasures. Spear points glittered in the sun and archers waved as the ships sailed in, one by one and line astern. Four large machines stood on platforms a few paces behind the walls; Bradan recognised three of them as catapults that would hurl huge boulders at any threatening ships, and the fourth was a winch with a heavy chain. The slavers had their base well-defended then, for he presumed the chain was a boom to stretch across one of the entrances of the harbour, denying entry to any enemy.

They eased past the island, with the crew cheering as the garrison of the fort welcomed them. On an order from one of the ships ahead, each vessel broke out their flags, the now-familiar snarling yellow beast on a blue background.

The man at *Catriona*'s tiller drank from a human skull, belched, shouted something and drank again.

'We have come into the hands of barbarians,' Bradan muttered. 'Oh, Melcorka, I wish you were yourself again.'

Beyond the island, the harbour broadened out into a large bay with a horseshoe-shaped beach beneath a walled city. The same snarling yellow beast flag flew from the battlements and bastions of the walls, from a massive red-walled fortress that dominated the town and from the ornate tower of what appeared to be a palace. Bradan stared at the scale and size of the city, for it was more extensive and more complex than anything he had seen before. Multiple towers and round turrets nailed the tall wall to the ground, offering a formidable barrier to any attacker.

'Where is this place?' he asked. 'Is this Thiruzha? Or are we in the Chola Empire?'

'Hello, Bradan,' Melcorka said. 'Where are we?'

'I don't know yet.' Bradan tried to wriggle back to back to loosen Melcorka's bonds. A guard grabbed his hair and hauled him away, kicking him with a hard foot.

'Where are we?' Bradan asked.

Nobody replied. The pirates were too busy cheering and yelling in response to the crowds that flooded from the city.

'This is the pirates' lair.' Bradan answered Melcorka's question. 'The den of the yellow beast. It is either Thiruzha, or the Chola Empire that the shipmaster told me about? If it's Chola, it is nothing like he described it.'

The instant that *Catriona* eased onto the beach, the crew sliced open the bonds around the prisoners' ankles and shoved them ashore. 'Keep close to me,' Bradan said, as Melcorka stared at him in evident incomprehension. Pulling her towards him, Bradan gasped as one of the guards swung a long spear against his leg. He contemplated fighting back and realised it would be pointless.

Pushed, jostled, kicked and shoved, Bradan joined the long line of prisoners. The guards – lithe, brown-skinned men in loin-cloths who carried spears, curved swords and round shields – forced them towards the walled town. Despite his situation, Bradan noted his surroundings. The walls were tall and dark, with ornate, pointed battlements and round stone towers set every two hundred paces. Spear-toting warriors in turbans or steel helmets stared down at them from the battlements, talking and laughing.

'We're on display,' Bradan said. 'Keep your back straight and hold your head high, Melcorka. Remember who you are.'

'Who am I?' Melcorka gaped at her surroundings.

'You are Melcorka of Alba,' Bradan said softly. 'Don't ever forget that. Whatever happens, you are Melcorka of Alba, Melcorka the Swordswoman.'

'I haven't got a sword,' Melcorka said.

'I know,' Bradan said, with his heart breaking for her.

The pirates forced the prisoners through the high gateway and into the city, with narrow streets of flat-roofed houses and more noise, colour and confusion than Bradan had ever seen in his life. Animals mingled amongst the crowd, with cattle roaming free and a score of great beasts with long necks and humped backs that Bradan had never seen before.

'Truly there are wonders in this world,' Bradan said. 'I wish we were free to enjoy them.'

Melcorka smiled, her green eyes wide and vacant.

Even the recently captured slaves stared as Bradan and Melcorka shuffled along, with their fair skin immediately marking them as aliens in this world of dark-skinned people. One or two reached out to touch Melcorka, until Bradan snarled at them and pushed them away, much to the amusement of the guards. The pirates herded their long column of prisoners into a vast square, where tall trees afforded shade for hundreds of spectators. In the centre of the square, a group of men in gold-and-white robes stood on a wooden platform, watching over the arrival of the slaves, pointing out individuals and making comments to one another. One golden-caped man remained slightly apart from the others, distinguished by an ornate head-dress and the long stick he flexed.

'Slave market!' Bradan edged as close to Melcorka as he could. 'We're going to be sold! Keep close to me, for God's own sake.' He had a sudden moment of panic that they would be separated. In her present mental state, Melcorka was as vulnerable as any child.

Melcorka looked around her, with her eyes wide. 'This place is pretty,' she said.

'What's happened to you?' Bradan asked. 'Mel! Come back to me.'

'Hello, Bradan.' Melcorka gave a wide grin. 'This is a nice place.' She nodded to the huge, highly ornate palace that took up one complete side of the square. 'I'd like to go in there.'

Bradan looked up at the plumply prosperous people who were enjoying the show from the upper windows of the palace. 'I don't think we'll get much choice of where we're sent, Mel.'

Even with so many prisoners, there was still space in the square. Spearmen and swordsmen lined the outside, facing the prisoners and talking to each other. One of the caped men on the wooden platform blew on a long brass horn, whose blare echoed from the surrounding buildings and gradually silenced the guards. Numbed and afraid, the prisoners huddled together, looking at the men in the long gold-and-white capes.

'Now we'll see,' Bradan said. 'Stay with me, Mel.'

With the square approximately quiet, a group of spearmen hurried into the crowd and grabbed half a dozen of the prisoners. Bradan noticed that all the surrounding buildings had windows facing into the square, and each window had at least one spectator leaning out.

When the guards shoved the batch of prisoners onto the raised platform, the man with the head-dress leapt up, lifted the arms of the nearest prisoner, prodded his muscles with his stick and began a long monologue.

'He's the auctioneer giving the selling points,' Bradan said to Melcorka. 'These people at the windows might be the prospective buyers.'

When one of the spectators at the windows opposite the palace shouted something, the auctioneer pushed the first batch of slaves off the block.

'That's them bought,' Bradan said. 'Mel, come to the back of the crowd. Hopefully, most buyers will get bored and leave so we might get released.' That hope vanished when somebody in the palace gestured to the men on the platform and pointed directly at Bradan and Melcorka.

Bradan felt nausea rise within him. 'Stay close, Mel. I think we are wanted.'

When the auctioneer pointed to Bradan, a group of guards detached from the main body and pushed through the crowd.

'They're coming for us, Mel,' Bradan said. 'Stick by me, and we might get bought by the same person. If we stay together, we can escape together.'

Melcorka gave a smile of pure idiocy.

'Snap out of it, Mel. You must get back to yourself again.'

A body of spearmen grabbed hold of Bradan and Melcorka and shoved them to the platform.

'Don't you hurt that woman,' Bradan snarled, as the smallest of the guards jabbed his spear into Melcorka's leg. The man did not reply.

Close to, the auctioneer with the head-dress was older than Bradan had expected, with soft brown eyes that disguised the callousness of his occupation. He touched Bradan's arm and spoke, evidently asking a question.

'I don't understand,' Bradan said, in Gaelic and then in Latin.

The auctioneer took a step back and replied, also in Latin. 'You are from the far west.'

'The very far west.' Bradan struggled to find the words. 'We could not be any further west.'

'You will fetch a reasonable price.' The man stroked a finger down Melcorka's face, examining the tattoo on her cheek. 'What does this symbol mean? Is it your god?'

Bradan thought quickly. 'It is a charm. If anybody hurts her, a bolt will come from the sky and kill them.'

'I'll keep that quiet then,' the auctioneer said. 'There's no sense in putting a prospective buyer off, is there? We already have one very important party interested in you two.' He laughed. 'Now, strip naked so the buyers can see how white your skins are. That should put the price up. Novelty items are always good for business.' He poked at Melcorka with his stick. 'Do you hear me? I said take your clothes off!'

'Leave her!' Bradan tried to push the auctioneer away. 'She doesn't understand!'

'You tell her then,' the auctioneer ordered, as two of the guards stepped closer, spears ready.

For one desperate moment, Bradan contemplated grabbing Melcorka, forcing her off the platform and running, but there was nowhere to go. They were in the centre of a square surrounded by hundreds of spearmen, with crowds of people watching. If they somehow succeeded in getting out of the square, they would still be within a strange city, where their pale skin and unusual clothing would immediately identify them as strangers. If Melcorka had Defender, even if Melcorka was herself, Bradan might have chanced it. As things were, he knew they would not get ten paces.

'There's no help for it, Mel. Do what I do.'

Smiling, Melcorka watched as Bradan took off his clothes. Aware of the hundreds of eyes watching him, he stood erect on the block and helped Melcorka strip. 'Keep your head up,' Bradan said and repeated, 'if we stay together we'll have a better chance of escape.' He did not know if Melcorka understood him.

'All these people!' Melcorka dropped the last of her clothes and smiled at the crowds. 'They're all looking at us.'

'That's right.' Bradan felt sick. He wanted to hold Melcorka close, keep her safe from the troubles of the world. 'They are admiring your beauty.'

'They're at the windows, too.' Melcorka began to wave to the gaping faces. 'Who are they?'

'I'm not sure,' Bradan said. 'I'm really not sure.'

'Who are we?' Melcorka gave a little giggle. 'What's your name?'

'I am Bradan the Wanderer,' Bradan said, 'and you are Melcorka nic Bearnas, of the Cenel Bearnas from Alba.'

'Oh.' Melcorka looked at him. 'That's a very long name.'

'Yes.' Bradan rubbed her arm, fighting his emotion. 'Most people just call you Melcorka.'

'Keep quiet, you two,' the auctioneer snapped. He lowered his voice. 'Is your woman simple?'

'No,' Bradan said. 'She's just not very well just now.'

'Good. If your woman lacked anything up here,' the auctioneer tapped his forehead, 'nobody would want her for a slave. We'd have to kill her, which would be a shame.' He ran his hand up Melcorka's leg from ankle to thigh. 'She could be a nice-looking woman.'

Ignoring the spears of the guards, Bradan shoved the auctioneer's hand away. 'I know she is nice-looking. If you kill her, the gods would be angry. Remember her tattoo.' Bradan grunted as the small guard jabbed at Melcorka with his spear again. 'That's enough of that, you! I'll see you later, son. I'll remember your face.'

'Don't damage my goods!' The auctioneer pushed the guard away with his stick. Men and women were shouting as the auctioneer lifted Bradan's arm and demonstrated his strength. Months of rowing *Catriona* had given Bradan muscles of whipcord, while his previous life of walking day after day had strengthened his legs.

Men – and and now women, too – leaned out of the windows or stood on top of the flat roofs of the houses, shouting and waving their arms. One woman shoved forward from the crowd and gestured to the auctioneer.

At the auctioneer's word, the prospective buyer stepped up to the platform and examined Bradan with great interest, speaking to the auctioneer in low tones. She ran her hands across Bradan's chest, smiling as the crowd roared their approval.

'You are attracting interest,' the auctioneer said. 'You're a curiosity. Nobody has seen a man of your paleness before. You and the woman – what's her name?'

'Melcorka.'

'You and the woman Melcorka will fetch a fine price, either together or singly.' The auctioneer ran a practised eye over Melcorka again. 'I would buy her myself if I had the money, just to show her off.'

Bradan could see the avarice in the auctioneer's eyes as he responded to the shouts and waves from the windows.

'You're fetching a rare price,' the auctioneer said. 'Oh, Shiva save us all.' He salaamed, suddenly obsequious as a man in ornate clothes climbed onto the platform. The yellow beast's head that roared from his flowing top was the mirror of the flag the pirate ships had worn. A file of female warriors followed, each woman with a pointed steel helmet on her head and a small, round shield on her left arm.

The auctioneer stopped the auction at once. 'That's it,' he said to Bradan. 'You have new owners. You're sold.'

'Who to?' Bradan looked around the crowd. The faces were wide-eyed, curious and without even a trace of sympathy for the plight of the slaves.

'You'll soon see. Get your clothes on and go with these soldiers.' He lowered his voice. 'And for the sake of Shiva, do as you're told.'

The squad of warriors formed around Bradan and Melcorka and marched them from the platform, with thousands of eyes following these exotic strangers. The warriors hurried to the palace and filed through a broad, pointed doorway. Two spearmen stood on guard at the door, faces immobile.

'Where are we going?' Melcorka asked.

'I don't know, Mel,' Bradan said. 'But I know that on the first opportunity, we're going to escape.'

'Are they taking us to my sword?' Melcorka gave an unnervingly high-pitched giggle.

'No,' Bradan said. 'They're not taking us to your sword.'

The warriors hustled them through a walled garden, where fountains splashed amidst close-cropped lawns and trees hung heavy with fruit. The atmosphere was of decadence and luxury, as brightly coloured birds hopped and chirped on the trees and a bevy of servants waited for orders. Two more female warriors stood in a corner, hands on the hilts of long, curved swords.

In the centre of the garden was an open, circular building with a pointed roof and walls of delicately carved stonework. Within this arbour, a man and a woman sat on cushioned swings. Both wore identical blue robes, with the man wearing a yellow turban set with a large pearl and the woman wearing an ornate headdress of smaller pearls.

The warriors stepped back, fingering their swords.

For a long moment, the man and woman within the arbour stared at Melcorka and Bradan, with their swings swishing slowly back and forth. The woman spoke first.

'I understand you speak Latin.' Her voice was clear and low as her dark eyes swept over them from head to foot and back.

'I do,' Bradan said.

'How strange to find education in a man who travels in rags.' The woman left her swing and stepped forward to run her finger down Bradan's face. 'You are very pale, and your skin is rough, like leather.'

'It is the colour of all the people where we come from,' Bradan said. 'And I have been outdoors in all sorts of weather.'

'I've never seen anybody your colour before.' The woman turned her face sideways. 'Are you pale all the way?' She arched her eyebrows and ran her gaze down Bradan's lean body. 'I could not see properly when you were on the slave block.'

'Yes,' Bradan said. 'I am pale all the way.'

'We shall see. Do you have names where you come from? I am Dhraji.' The woman opened up Bradan's travel-stained and much-patched leine and examined his chest. 'Dhraji means whirlwind.' She looked up and smiled. 'So I am a whirlwind. What are you?'

'I am Bradan the Wanderer,' Bradan said.

'A wandering man. How strange. Were you a warrior before you became my slave?' Sunlight caught the pearls on Dhraji's headdress, reflecting in a hundred different colours. The man remained on his swing, watching dispassionately.

'I was never a warrior,' Bradan said. *And I won't be a slave for long,* he thought, as Dhraji pulled open his leine and examined him minutely, making small noises that might have been approval or disapproval.

'You are not built any differently to the men here,' Dhraji said. 'You have the same appendages, yet you are taller and paler.' Raising her voice, Dhraji snapped an order. Two muscular servants immediately ran from the corner of the garden. 'Don't get alarmed, slave Bradan. These men are going to wash the slave-stink from your body and make you presentable.'

'Presentable for what?' Bradan asked.

'For me, of course,' Dhraji said. 'You are my slave, while this woman,' she jerked a thumb at Melcorka, 'belongs to Bhim, if he ever gets off his lazy, fat backside to even look at her.'

Bhim and Dhraji, the two people the Chola shipmaster warned us to avoid. We have fallen among thieves indeed. Pretend ignorance.

'Her name is Melcorka.' Bradan spoke rapidly, trying to protect Melcorka before Bhim got his hands on her. 'She is not herself at present.'

'Oh?' Dhraji looked supremely disinterested as she snapped instructions to the two servants.

'Just be careful, Mel!' Bradan shouted to Melcorka, as the servants led him away. He looked over his shoulder to see Bhim lift his considerable bulk from the swing and saunter across to Melcorka. 'Don't you hurt her, Bhim!'

The servants hurried Bradan out of the garden and into an airy chamber with a stone floor and two large urns of clear water. All the time, the men were talking, with Bradan unable to understand a word. They removed his leine and while one held him, the other emptied one of the urns over him. Unsmiling, they scrubbed him from head to feet with handfuls of dry white sand that made his skin tingle.

'Careful down there,' he snarled, as the men began to work on his groin.

'Oh, let them carry on.' Bradan had not known that Dhraji was present until she spoke. 'If they damage you, I will have them kissing an elephant's foot.'

What in the name of God does that mean?

The two servants salaamed, pressing their hands together as they backed away from Dhraji. When Dhraji snapped something, the servants returned to work, now using an oily substance to wash Bradan's hair and down the length of his body.

'Stand still.' Dhraji watched, smiling. 'They know what they are doing. You people from the west have never experienced soap before. We have much to teach you.'

'Is Melcorka all right?' Bradan asked.

'That woman is no longer your concern,' Dhraji said. 'From this day onward, you will think only of me.' Although she was smiling, something in Dhraji's tone warned Bradan that she was a very dangerous woman. *Stay alive,* he told himself. *I am no good to Melcorka if I am dead!*

'It is hard not to think of you.' Bradan forced a smile.

'Do you find me attractive?' Dhraji emphasised the swing of her hips as she stalked around Bradan.

'You are a wonderful-looking woman.' Bradan spoke only the truth, for, with her long black hair, small, smiling face and shapely figure, Dhraji could be the epitome of all that a man could lust for in a woman.

'Then why do you not look at me, Bradan the Wanderer? I order you to.'

'I did not think it was fitting.' Bradan allowed his gaze to roam the length of her, from foot to head, before resting on her face.

'I desire you to look at me always.' Again, there was steel behind the silk in Dhraji's tones.

'In that case, I shall comply with pleasure.' Bradan smiled.

The two washers finished, salaamed and withdrew, walking backwards. 'Oh, that is much better now.' Dhraji slid her hand across Bradan's body, lingering where she pleased. 'You have underlying strength, Bradan the Wanderer. We will soon see if you also have the stamina to match.'

'How is Melcorka?' Bradan could not resist asking the question, despite the angry shadow that crossed Dhraji's face.

'The tattooed woman is with my husband,' Dhraji said softly. 'And I advise you not to interrupt me again, slave Bradan. I am not a woman it is wise to cross. I own you now, body and soul, and you are mine to do with as I please.' She took hold of him. 'I can make your life full of pleasure,' she squeezed gently, 'or full of more pain than you can imagine.' Dhraji increased the pressure of her fingers, watching his reaction. 'You see?'

Bradan fought to retain his composure. 'I see,' he said.

'You will not speak of that other woman again. You will not think of that other woman again. Your world now revolves around me.' Dhraji smiled.

'Come now, slave Bradan, there are thousands of men who would desire nothing more.'

Stay alive! If you are dead, you can't help Melcorka.

'I can understand that.' Bradan enhanced his words by allowing his gaze to roam from Dhraji's face down the length of her body. 'I know a man who these thousands would envy.'

Releasing him, Dhraji stepped back, still smiling. 'When my cleaning-and-dressing slaves have finished with you, then I shall test you out, Bradan the Wanderer. Tomorrow, I have a treat for you.'

'Your Majesty.' Bradan thought that a show of humility might best suit his cause. He bent in a salaam such as the cleaning-slaves had used. *Pretend ignorance.* 'May I ask where we are? Is this the Empire of Chola? Are you the Empress of Chola?'

Dhraji's laugh sounded genuine. 'Chola? Oh, that is good, Bradan, that is priceless. No, Bradan, this is not Chola. Every slave we captured on that raid is from Chola, and when the Raja returns with his army, he will bring back even more.' Dhraji's face altered. 'When I have Arul Mozhi Chola here as my slave, I will not have him bathed and treat him tenderly.' She pushed her hands together, intertwining her fingers as if wringing the neck of a chicken. 'He calls himself Raja Raja Cholan, the King of Kings, as if he had a divine right over all his neighbours. Well, by Skanda and Yama, Arul Mozhi Chola, the Emperor of Chola, is not raja over me!'

'I apologise.' Bradan salaamed. 'I did not know. I hope you forgive me, Mistress.' He wondered what else he could say to flatter this volatile woman.

Dhraji smiled. 'You know now, Bradan.' She patted his chest, her eyes busy. 'We are in the city of Kollchi, in the land of Thiruzha.'

'I do not know these places,' Bradan said. 'Are we in the Indies? A storm blew us off course.'

'You are in the south of Bharata Khanda.' Dhraji's hand drifted across Bradan again. 'You may know that better as Hindustan, or even India. Now, get along with the bathing-slaves. I'll send for you later.'

'Yes, my Lady Dhraji.' Bradan bowed and salaamed again.

'You learn quickly for a pale foreigner,' Dhraji said. 'I can see I'm going to have fun with you. I hope you learn other things as quickly.'

'For you, my Lady,' Bradan said, 'I will do my very best.' *And when you are asleep,* he thought, *I will find Melcorka and we'll get out of this poisonous paradise.*

Standing in another courtyard within the palace, with a pool of limpid water in front of him and brightly coloured birds calling all around, Bradan stared at his reflection. Scrubbed, with his hair neatly trimmed, sweet scent splashed onto him and dressed in silken blue robes and open-toed sandals, he no longer looked like the wandering man he was.

So here we are, Bradan said, *slaves of a demented pirate in southern Bharata Khanda, somewhere east of the Central Sea and west of the New World. Melcorka has lost her sword, and her mind, and I am dressed like a God-knows-what, await-ing the call to service some powerful, crazed woman who hates the Chola Empire, whatever that may be. I can't think of a way out yet, but I will not give up hope. With Melcorka not herself, everything depends on me. Sorry, Mel, I will do what I have to do until I see an opening. I know you would understand.*

The reflection stared back, a long-faced, weather-battered man with haunted eyes. The bright, unfamiliar clothes only enhanced Bradan's sense of unreality.

The guard wore a red turban on his head and a long, slightly curved sword at his belt. He summoned Bradan with a grunt and beckoned for him to follow, with his very unmilitary soft slippers making no sound.

The palace was more luxurious than anywhere Bradan had visited before, with deep Persian and Afghan carpets on the floor and intricately carved stat-ues of unfamiliar gods standing in prominent places. Colourful tapestries dec-orated the walls, while armed sentries stood at every one of the arched doors in the never-ending corridors.

'Lovely place you have here,' Bradan said.

The guard grunted and shoved Bradan up a flight of marble steps that stretched to a large teak doorway, where two stern-faced female warriors stood on guard.

On the guard's knock, the door opened silently, and Bradan walked in.

'Welcome, Bradan the Wanderer.' Dhraji sat cross-legged on what was un-doubtedly the most enormous bed that Bradan had ever seen in his life. Wear-ing a pair of loose, transparent trousers and a loose, equally transparent jacket, she smiled at him across the width of a green-patterned carpet. A double string of pearls around her neck had joined the pearl headdress.

Bradan salaamed. 'Thank you, Dhraji, Queen of Thiruzha.'

'You are a quick learner, as I suspected, although here, the queen is known as a rani.' Dhraji patted the bed at her side. 'Come and talk to me, Bradan. Tell me about this Alba of yours, and tell me why you wander.'

Bradan salaamed again. Unwilling to give too much information to this dangerous woman, he tried to turn the conversation. 'I'd prefer to talk about you, my Lady.'

'Oh?' Dhraji stretched herself on the bed. 'Tell me why, Bradan.' She twirled the string of pearls around her throat, placed them between her lips and slowly drew them through from one side of her mouth to the other.

Bradan thought of Melcorka, with her new, vacant smile and dazed eyes. 'There are many reasons, my Lady.' He closed the door with his foot and drew the bolt to ensure nobody would disturb them.

'Should I be afraid, all alone with a foreign slave?' Dhraji spoke through the pearls in her mouth.

Bradan guessed that Dhraji had a weapon hidden somewhere on her side of the bed and, even if he did manage to overpower or kill her, he was stuck in the middle of a palace with scores of guards. More importantly, he did not know where Melcorka was. 'You should never be afraid of me, my Lady. I am a wanderer, not a warrior.'

Dhraji gave a throaty chuckle. 'I am not afraid, Bradan. Now, tell me about me.' She lay back, still playing with her pearls. 'Tell me everything you think. Afterwards, I will have another use for you.'

Chapter Five

'You are about to witness history.' When Dhraji put her hand on Bradan's arm, the sun glinted from the single pearl ring on her third finger. 'Today, Bose Raja returns from his raid into the Chola Empire. My clever husband Bhim has created a triumphal arch to welcome him back.'

'Who is Bose Raja?' Bradan asked. By now, he knew that a raja was the equivalent of a king. He was gradually picking up the native language so he could understand snatches of conversation.

They sat in another airy room with ornate pointed windows that looked over the city. Directly below the window, people and animals filled the square where the slave market had been held. Further out, a panorama of roofs and temples stretched around them, with the occasional garden and open space. Birds fluttered outside the window, their calls clear above the jabber from the streets below. In the far corner of the room, the leopard lay quietly, head resting on its paws and its yellow eyes occasionally opening to watch what was happening.

'Bose is our raja and Bhim's father.'

Bradan nodded. 'I thought you were already the rani, your highness. I had not realised your father-in-law was the raja.' He remembered the warning the Chola shipmaster had given him.

Dhraji gave her throaty laugh. 'I am only the rani apparent, Bradan the Wanderer.'

'I am honoured to be your slave, Dhraji Rani.' Bradan salaamed again. Dhraji enjoyed men bowing and scraping to her. 'I am happy that Bhim allows you such freedom.'

Although Dhraji's smile remained in place, her eyes altered from laughter to something much darker. 'Bhim could not stop me from doing anything I want.'

So you are the power here. Bradan salaamed again. 'I could not imagine why anybody would ever wish to deny you anything, Your Majesty. Your people are indeed fortunate in having such a ruler. I have never before met a woman quite like you.' *Well, the last part was genuine.*

'Be careful now, Bradan.' Dhraji's expression altered again. 'Although Bhim does not rule me, he is my husband. I do not need another.'

'One at a time is sufficient for anybody.' Bradan leaned forward, hoping to make Dhraji think he had genuine feelings for her.

Dhraji took Bradan's hand and placed it on her upper thigh. 'One husband and a few lustful lovers would be my best choice – the husband for heirs and the lovers for pleasure.'

'A good husband could provide both.' Bradan looked directly downward, where a group of guards drove a long file of chained slaves across the square. Although his position was precarious, his day-to-day life was more comfortable than these poor devils.

Dhraji raised her eyebrows again in that engaging manner. 'Don't presume, Bradan. One night or one week does not make a man a good husband, however skilled he may be at the two-backed beast.'

'Indeed, my Lady Dhraji,' Bradan said. 'Devotion and loyalty make a man a good husband.'

Dhraji laughed, looked away, glanced back at Bradan, shook her head and looked away again. 'You intrigue me, Bradan.' Standing up, she walked to the window with her transparent clothing hiding nothing of her shape. 'You call yourself a wanderer, you are our slave, yet here you are acting the courtier with me. We separated you from your woman, and you adapted as my lover without hesitation.' Dhraji turned to face him, perching on the window ledge with her legs crossed. 'I have had many lovers, Bradan. Most don't last more than a few days.'

Bradan did not want to ask what happened to the men Dhraji rejected. He remained silent. For one moment, he contemplated rushing forward and pushing her out of the window to her death. *That would be suicide; that would not help Melcorka.*

Dhraji placed both hands on the window ledge. 'I would like you to last a while, perhaps two weeks, three, maybe even longer.' She swung her legs from side to side. 'Do you like me, Bradan?'

'You don't have to ask,' Bradan said.

'I do have to ask.' Dhraji slid off her perch. 'You should hate me for what I have done to you and Melcorka.'

Bradan held her eyes as he smiled. 'There are compensations.' He tried to sound casual. 'Is Melcorka still alive?'

Standing at the window so that the light silhouetted her, Dhraji shrugged. 'I believe she is. I will ask my question a second time; I do not ask things thrice. Do you like me, Bradan?'

'More than like,' Bradan said.

'I wonder.' Dhraji remained where she was, with Bradan unable to see her face against the bright sky, or discern her expression. 'I wonder if you do, or if you are lying to me.'

'I could prove it if you like,' Bradan said brightly. 'I can think of a way.'

'No.' Dhraji stepped away and walked around the room, so Bradan had to turn to look at her. 'That is lust. Men can lust after anything that even hints of a female.' She stopped and put both hands on Bradan's shoulders. 'You should hate me, Bradan and you probably do hate me.' Her laugh broke the mood. 'Even if you do, there is nothing you can alter. Come with me, Bradan. I want you. No! Wait!' Dhraji changed her mind and held up a hand. 'Look down below.'

A column of Thiruzha warriors marched across the square, faces to the front and each carrying a long spear, a circular shield and a slightly curved sword.

'We don't have much time.' Dhraji was smiling again. 'What do you think of my soldiers, Bradan? How do they compare to your warriors from the West?'

'Your fighting men seem very skilled,' Bradan said. 'However, I have not seen them fight real soldiers so I cannot compare them with the men from Alba.'

Dhraji's smile broadened. 'Our men are as good as any warrior the Chola Empire can produce, and the Chola soldiers are the best in the world.'

'Are they that good?'

'The Chola Empire is expanding and will continue to expand.' Dhraji led him out of the room and into her bedchamber, with the leopard following, its paws noiseless on the thick carpet. 'It controls the southern half of the

Bharata Khandan peninsula and half the island of Ceylon, while Chola fleets are continually probing south into the ocean and east toward China.'

Bradan did not admit that he had never heard of the Chola Empire until the last few days. He watched as Dhraji poured them both a drink of some clear liquid. She handed a silver cup to him and drank from a golden goblet, set around with pearls.

'Drink, Bradan. It will increase your lust. We don't have much time for dalliance.'

'I don't need this when I am with you,' Bradan said.

Dhraji smiled to him across the rim. 'How much can I trust you, I wonder?' She shifted slightly, deliberately allowing her legs to rub against his. 'How much, Bradan?'

'As much as you wish,' Bradan said.

Dhraji sipped again, rubbing her foot the length of Bradan's leg. 'I wonder.'

'You have no need to fear me.' Bradan spoke only the truth.

As she put down her goblet, Dhraji altered her smile to something far more serious. 'I do not understand you, Bradan. You are unlike any man I have ever met before.'

Bradan said nothing.

'You are not a warrior, you are not a priest. You are not a farmer, or a landowner, or a dancer, or a bard. What are you, Bradan?'

'I am a wanderer,' Bradan said. 'I seek knowledge.'

'Why?'

'To find out why we are here.' Bradan said. 'I seek knowledge to find out why people exist in this world and to see strange things and different cultures.'

Dhraji seemed amused. 'Have you found out yet, why we are here?'

'No, my Lady.'

'Then I shall tell you.' Dhraji scratched the head of the leopard, which lay purring at her feet. 'People are here for my pleasure and entertainment.' She flicked her head forward, so stray strands of hair shaded her eyes. 'What do you think of that, Bradan?'

'As long as you are happy, my Lady, I have no objections.'

'Do you plan to kill me while I sleep?' Dhraji pushed the leopard away.

'I have no plans to kill you or anybody else.'

Dhraji shook her head slowly. 'I believe you, Bradan. Except for priests, I have never met a man who was less violent than you. I have no reason to be afraid at all.' She looked up sharply as somebody knocked at the door. 'Who is there?'

The female guard was tall and capable-looking. Her eyes flicked to Bradan and away again. 'The border patrol reports a body of Chola cavalry outside Rajgana pass.'

'What sort of cavalry? Who are they?' It was the first time Bradan had seen Dhraji even slightly agitated.

'Seventeenth Troop,' the guard said. 'They've moved closer to the pass since our raid.'

'Who leads them?' Dhraji seemed to have forgotten that Bradan was present.

'We don't know his name,' the guard said. 'He was a young officer with no reputation.'

Dhraji visibly relaxed. 'All right. Who brought the news?'

'The captain of the roving patrol, Highness.'

'Wait here. I will speak to this captain.' Dhraji hurried from the chamber, still holding the goblet in her hand. The leopard followed, its tail swishing slowly from side to side.

The guard took up position inside the bedroom, her face impassive.

'Try this, soldier.' Bradan handed over his cup. The guard looked surprised and took a single sip.

'That's a powerful potion.' The guard was about twenty, with a determined face and the large brown eyes that seemed common in Thiruzha. 'You can trust Dhraji to have the best.'

'Royalty always keeps the best for themselves.' Bradan took a sip and handed the rest over to the guard, who drank greedily.

'Laced with opium, I'd guess,' the guard said. 'How long will you last before Dhraji tires of you?'

'As long as I can,' Bradan said. 'Have you seen anything of the woman I came with?'

'I heard about her. She was as pale as you, was she not?'

'That's her.' Bradan tried to hide his fear. 'Is she still alive?'

The guard nodded. 'I think so. I've not heard of any executions since you came. You've been keeping the Dhraji busy, so I'm told.' She smiled. 'Lucky man, as long as it lasts. She's some woman.'

'She is. Where would Bhim hold the pale woman?' Bradan wondered if he should try flattery with this woman, and decided it was best not to.

'Bhim would hold her in his room if he wanted her body. In the dungeons if not. Dhraji allows Bhim to do as he wishes with his slaves.'

'Dhraji's not scared of him then. Is she ever afraid of anybody?' Bradan asked.

The guard considered. 'You saw her jump just now when I mentioned a Chola patrol. Dhraji is afraid of only one man. The best warrior there has ever been.'

'Why is that and who is this man?'

'I don't know.' The guard shrugged. 'There is a story that only one man can kill Dhraji. He is said to be a mighty warrior, as I said – the best there has ever been. That's why she examines all the prisoners and singles out any she suspects may be that warrior. If she finds him, she will have him kiss the feet of an elephant, or try his hand at flying.'

Bradan nodded. He had no idea what kissing the elephant's feet or flying meant, but suspected both would be unpleasant. The guard's revelation explained why Dhraji had been questioning him about the warriors of Alba and had been relieved to discover that he was peaceful. His lack of fighting prowess had probably kept him alive.

Dhraji returned before Bradan could ask any more questions. 'Get out,' she ordered the guard, drained the goblet she carried and pointed to the bed. 'And you get on there, slave Bradan.'

The leopard lay across the doorway, rested its head on its paws and watched.

Chapter Six

The crowds packing the streets created a riot of colour and noise. Women and children in bright, flowing clothes carried garlands of flowers, while companies of warriors gathered near the gate. The sun glittered on steel and brass and on the animals of every description that mingled with the people, bellowing or lowing as women threw flowers over their necks.

'What's that?' Bradan could not control his words as he saw the great, grey monster that lumbered toward them, driven by a man sitting on its neck.

Dhraji took hold of his arm. 'Have you never seen an elephant before?'

'Never,' Bradan said. 'Does it bite?' The huge beast was many times larger and heavier than a horse and had huge, flapping ears and great curving tusks, together with a long trunk that swayed in front of it. A silk-covered box sat on its back, as colourful as anything in the city of Kollchi, with gold tassels bouncing around the back of the elephant.

'That one does not,' Dhraji said. 'We use elephants for warfare as well and they very effective. That one is for our personal use.' She smiled, evidently amused at Bradan's ignorance. 'Come with me, slave Bradan.'

Bradan kept back as the elephant slowly got down to its knees.

'Come on, Bradan. This compartment is called a howdah.' Dhraji dragged him to the elephant and into the silk-lined howdah on its back. There were cushioned seats inside, with a couple of bows, two quivers of arrows and a long whip. Sitting facing forward, Dhraji motioned that Bradan should sit opposite her. 'You'll enjoy the ride.' Her mouth opened slightly, with her tongue flicking out. 'I know that you enjoy riding and other experiences.'

'Yes, my Lady.' Bradan sat down. Behind him, a near-naked man straddled the elephant's neck, driving the elephant with a spiked pole.

'That man is a mahout,' Dhraji explained. 'If he guides the elephant well, he is rewarded. If he does not...' She shrugged. 'Their deaths can be entertaining.'

'I see, your Majesty.' Sometimes, Bradan found it hard to imagine that this charming, sensual woman was probably a cold-blooded killer. Dressed in wide blue silk trousers and a top of blue decorated with rows of small pearls, Dhraji looked as beautiful as Bradan had ever seen her. Only the shadow of cruelty in her eyes and the sensuous curl to her lips reminded him of the reality beneath.

Two more elephants marched with them toward the eastern gate. Bhim rode on the beast immediately behind them, with Melcorka sharing his howdah, smiling at the crowds as if they had gathered specifically to see her pass. Bhim was dressed in magnificent robes, his portly form dignified as he sat straight-backed, raising his arm to acknowledge the cheers of the crowd. Wearing transparent clothes that hid nothing, Melcorka half stood, to the delight of the crowd.

Thank God that you're still alive, Mel. Bradan wished desperately to reach over and touch Melcorka, but he fought the temptation, aware that Dhraji was watching and probably testing him.

'You're looking even more attractive than usual today, my Lady.' Bradan hid his emotional agony behind flattery.

'Do you find me more alluring than that stringy woman?' Dhraji nodded to Melcorka.

'I see her there.' Bradan glanced at Melcorka and returned his attention to Dhraji. 'I'm glad she is still alive.' He paused for effect. 'But I'm happy to be sharing your howdah and not hers.'

Dhraji gave a light laugh and snapped an order to the lithe mahout. Their elephant halted at once. Melcorka barely looked at Bradan as her elephant lumbered past and then Dhraji ordered the mahout to follow it out of the great, pointed gate.

'See what we have prepared for Bose Raja.' Dhraji pointed with an elegant hand.

Bradan could hardly have missed the tremendous triumphal arch that stood a hundred paces outside the eastern gate. Twice as tall as an elephant, the arch was made of intricately carved stone, so that the elephant-headed god Ganesha and the monkey-headed god Hanuman combined in a multi-armed goddess that jolted Bradan with unpleasant comparisons with sea monsters.

'That's Kali.' Dhraji responded to Bradan's unspoken question. 'She is one of our goddesses. Do you like your archway?'

'It's very impressive.' Bradan looked up as a fast column of dust indicated that a horseman was approaching at a gallop. 'Somebody's coming.'

It was significant that the rider approached Dhraji rather than Bhim. Dhraji nodded toward her husband and the horseman reined up beside Bhim's elephant. 'Bose Raja is coming!' he shouted.

'That's not hard to see.' Bradan pointed to the haze of dust that nearly blocked their view of the distant Ghat Mountains. The air was sultry here, with insects clouding around and the smell of vegetation mingling with the various stenches from the city.

The music drifted across a few minutes later as the dust cloud came steadily closer, with the howdahs of a score of elephants looming above the dust like ships floating on a dun-coloured sea. Outriders charged forward, to wheel in front of the triumphal arch, raise their swords, yell in salute and gallop past in a flurry of flapping cloaks, glittering steel and thundering hooves.

'Here they come!' Dhraji sounded quite excited as she gripped Bradan's arm and leaned forward. 'Watch closely now, Bradan. You are about to see history being made.'

As they neared the arch, horsemen broke from the approaching army and formed two lines on the outside, a standing guard of honour for Bose Raja on his elephant. On a word from the cavalry captain, each horseman drew his sword and raised it high, creating a corridor of glittering steel. The raja raised his flag, the same snarling yellow beast on a blue background that had graced his fleet. The silk flowed and fluttered as the elephant walked sedately forward. With the cover of the howdah removed, Bose Raja stood up so that his people could see him. Tall and broad, with a luxurious, down-curving moustache decorating the stern face of a warrior, Bose Raja raised both hands in the air as he approached the great arch.

'Bose Raja is returning from an expedition to the Chola borderlands,' Dhraji explained. 'He has a hundred camel-loads of treasure to add to our vaults, and three hundred more slaves for labouring and domestic duties.'

'No wonder the crowd is happy,' Bradan said.

The crowd was cheering, the warriors raising swords, shields and spears in salute as the raja's mahout guided his elephant under the magnificent stone arch. For a moment, the shadow of the arch concealed Bose Raja.

'Now,' Dhraji said softly and lifted her left hand. Bradan heard the rumble before he saw the movement, and then the entire left side of the arch collapsed. Scores of tons of stone fell, knocking the elephant down, instantly killing the mahout and tossing Bose Raja onto the ground. The raja struggled to his feet, shouting something and staring at Bhim and Dhraji. Above him, the remaining side of the arch tottered but held.

'Now,' Dhraji repeated softly and lifted her right hand. The remainder of the arch shook, shuddered and crumbled. A block of carved stone fell directly on top of Bose Raja, crushing him, so only his head protruded. A smear of blood spread from underneath the stone.

Bradan saw a quick smile cross Dhraji's face before she masked her emotions with a look of horror.

A shuddering gasp arose from the crowd as men and women clustered around to try and save the raja. Bradan made to jump from the howdah, only for Dhraji to grip his arm. 'Stay there, Slave Bradan,' she said quietly. 'This situation does not concern you.'

'He might still be alive,' Bradan said, more in hope than expectation.

'He is dead.' Dhraji regained her smile. 'He is dead and now Bhim and I are Raja and Rani in truth.' She patted Bradan's thigh. 'I told you that you would witness history today, Bradan.'

'You mean...?' Bradan gestured to the mass of masonry that lay in a tumbled heap on top of the late Raja. 'You knew this was going to happen?' He remembered Dhraji's small gestures before the masonry collapsed.

Dhraji intended this; I am not sure how she did it. That woman is not merely evil, she has some sort of power. She is even more dangerous than I had thought.

'Of course.' Dhraji looked surprised that Bradan should have to ask. 'I wanted to be Rani, and Bose Raja was in my way. What better time to get rid of him than when he is at the height of his prestige, all proud and gallant and brave – and with his defences down!' She laughed again. 'And with such a public death, nobody can blame Bhim for Bose's death. It was obviously a tragic accident. Now I will execute a few builders for their shoddy workmanship, purge the palace of any of Bose's most loyal supporters and rule through Bhim.'

'I see.' Bradan hid his disgust. 'I underestimated you, my Rani. You are indeed the cleverest of queens.' He bowed and salaamed. 'It is a privilege to serve and learn from you.'

Dhraji smiled. 'Now we must all appear sorrowful and mourn the death of our great leader, who was so foolish as to trust his heir apparent.' She leaned toward Bradan and rubbed her hand up his thigh. 'You will need your stamina tonight, Bradan.'

'I look forward to it, My Lady.' Bradan was very aware of Melcorka riding close by on Bhim's elephant as it walked past. With Dhraji holding his gaze, he could not look round.

* * *

Bhim declared ten days of national mourning to honour the death of his father. During that time, the people of Thiruzha had to wear only sombre clothes and no jewellery or finery. They had to drink only water and eat the simplest of fare, walk with their heads bowed and keep their children under the strictest control.

'We'll place Bose Raja's body on a raised platform in the centre of the square,' Dhraji said, as she inspected the crushed remains of her father-in-law. 'I rather like him like that.' She smiled at Bradan. 'He's even easier to control now.'

'Did you control him, my Lady?'

'He did as I wished,' Dhraji said. She snapped her fingers to the captain of the palace guard. 'Have Bose Raja's body put on public display in the square,' she ordered. 'I want every man, woman and child to pass him and leave a token of their respect.'

'It shall be as you wish, Rani.' The captain salaamed.

'Those that do not leave a token shall be enslaved,' Dhraji said.

'It shall be as you wish, Rani.' the guard salaamed again.

'Those who do not attend shall be put to death.'

'It shall be as you wish, Rani.'

'Come with me, Bradan.' Although Dhraji spoke with a gentle smile, there was no doubting her authority. As usual, the leopard followed. 'You shall see what happens to men whose shoddy workmanship killed a king.' When she laughed lightly, the leopard lifted its head and licked her hand.

The crowds gathered in the great square again, some laughing, some sober-faced and most in a holiday mood. Bradan sat opposite Dhraji in the howdah, with the sun pouring its heat down and the leopard's head resting on Dhraji's feet. Dhraji and Bhim had provided entertainment before the main event, with a hundred sinuous dancers writhing through the approving crowd. A line of guards kept the more enthusiastic men back with ungentle blows from the butts of spears and the flats of swords.

'Do you like my dancers?' Dhraji asked.

'They are excellent.' Bradan was not sure what answer Dhraji expected. The dancers were the best he had ever seen, shapely, skilled and with every movement calculated to arouse the senses of the audience.

'Do they stimulate you?' Dhraji raised her eyebrows in that suggestive look that Bradan had come to recognise.

'When I have you beside me, I need no other stimulation,' Bradan said.

'Remind me later,' Dhraji said, 'and I will dance for you.' She jiggled her breasts, smiled and placed one finger to her lips. 'Now, watch the justice of the Raja and Rani.'

The crowd hooted and cheered as ten scared men were led into the square, which now looked even larger with the slave platform removed. Weighed down with chains, the men stood still, looking around at the mob, while men and women at the windows waved and shouted to each other. Some women carried children, which they balanced on the sills of the windows so they could obtain a better view of the proceedings. Peddlers weaved through the crowds, selling carved wooden figures of elephants.

'Who are these men in chains?' Bradan already guessed the answer.

'These are the master builders,' Dhraji said. 'These are the men who created the triumphal arch that so tragically collapsed and killed the last raja. It is fitting that they should be punished.'

Knowing he could not help the condemned men, Bradan nodded. 'I see.'

'I know that you agree with me,' Dhraji said. 'Justice must be seen to be done. The death of a raja must be marked.'

'As your majesty pleases.' Bradan salaamed.

'They are slaves, of course,' Dhraji said. 'They were captured during one of the late raja's raids on the Chola Empire, so no doubt they deliberately built a flawed structure to avenge themselves on their captor.'

'That must be what happened.' Bradan wondered if Dhraji was warning him of the possible price of treason.

The ten builders huddled together in the centre of the square, as if the proximity of other condemned men gave them security. Even from his elevated position in the howdah, Bradan could smell their fear. Their eyes were wide and one was openly weeping, while another fell to his knees, hands raised in supplication, to the amusement of the crowd.

'Wait!' Dhraji rose in the howdah and shouted in a high, clear voice. 'Release these men from their chains.' She sat down again. 'One must appear merciful, Bradan. It also gives the prisoners false hope and lengthens the time of the execution.'

'How are they to be killed?' Bradan looked in vain for a gallows or a headsman with an axe.

'Watch and learn. You may enjoy it as much as I do.' Dhraji was smiling as Bhim shouted an order and an elephant ambled into the square.

At the sight of the great grey beast, the condemned men set up a wail of terror and tried to run into the crowd, only for the guards to push and prod them back. The air of anticipation increased. Dhraji leaned back in her chair with a small smile in her face, one hand fondling the ear of the leopard. Bradan studied the crowd, who watched with slack jaws and mounting excitement as the elephant thudded into the square, with the mahout guiding it with a pointed, iron-shod stick.

'I could have put in more elephants,' Dhraji's voice was taut, 'but using only one makes the execution last longer. Now, watch. Watch and learn.' She leaned forward, smiling as the condemned prisoners tried to run away and the mahout guided the elephant toward them. The mahout selected his first victim, who gave a high-pitched scream and tried again to escape into the crowd. Grinning guards caught him and threw him back. The crowd roared and one woman at a window held her child close, pointing to the execution and whispering in his ear.

Bradan saw Dhraji's smile broaden as the victim stumbled and fell face-down on the ground. The mahout stopped the elephant in front of the unfortunate builder and had it raise its right foot. The man's constant screaming was the only sound in the square except for the panting breath of the audience. Dhraji leaned forward, one hand reaching for Bradan.

'Good, good,' she said, as the elephant slowly lowered its foot. The man crawled away, so the elephant missed his head and instead crushed his left leg. The victim twisted and screamed, long and shrill.

Dhraji's eyes were bright. She leaned forward, her tongue licking her lips and her hand busy on the leopard's ear. Bradan knew that he had been forgotten; the Rani's entire attention was on the deliberate murder being enacted in front of her.

The elephant lifted the builder with its trunk, swung him, a bleeding, squealing mess, around its head and threw him into the crowd. Drops of blood sprayed the audience, with one landing on Dhraji's arm. She licked it off, still smiling and, for the first time, looked at Bradan. Her eyes glowed with pleasure, and a smear of the victim's blood was on her lips. Her tongue darted out, removed the blood and explored her lips for more.

With the first victim a bloody smear on the ground, the other condemned men ran in panic as the mahout guided the elephant toward them, choosing his next target.

Bradan looked away. He had seen too much bloodshed and suffering in his life to find any interest in more. Instead, he watched the crowd as they roared and cheered and laughed at the antics of the condemned men, and he watched Dhraji as she leaned forward with intense eyes and darting tongue. He had never despised her more, yet knew that her lust would be at its height later. For the first time, he contemplated escaping on his own.

No. I will not leave Melcorka in the hands of this woman... if she is a woman and not some terrible creature from another world.

By the time all ten builders were dead, the square was a mass of blood and brains, crushed bones and slithering entrails. The crowd was in a state of high excitement, with hysterical laughter and cheering, although Bradan was pleased to see that some were looking sick and a few had slid away from the horrific scenes.

There is hope, he thought. *Even though these people are inured to horror, a spark of decency remains. That can be built on.*

'Take us back to the palace.' Dhraji's voice was husky as she addressed the mahout. 'And quickly.'

'Come, Bradan.' Dhraji took hold of his arm the second they left the howdah. 'I won't be dancing for you just yet. Executions always arouse me.'

The leopard followed, padding in Dhraji's wake with its head held low and its eyes smouldering yellow.

* * *

They sat in the corner of Dhraji's chamber playing chess, as the setting sun coloured the sky a brilliant orange-red and silhouetted the serrated peaks of the Ghats. Small birds darted beyond the window and occasionally invaded the room.

'Do you have this game in your Alba, Bradan?' Dhraji asked.

'We do,' Bradan said. 'We have slightly different pieces there.' He lifted a small ivory chariot. 'In Alba, we have a rook rather than a chariot, and we have a bishop where you have an elephant.'

Dhraji smiled. 'This game was invented in Northern Bharata Khanda.' She lifted the king. 'Here, we call this piece the raja. Where you have the queen, we have the mantra, or minister, a politician. The queen, the mantra, is the most powerful piece while the king, the raja, is merely the symbol of authority.'

'That seems to be the case here, too,' Bradan agreed.

Dhraji laughed openly. 'It may be the case in your Alba as well. What you call chess, we call chaturanga, which means four divisions – cavalry, elephantry, infantry and chariotry.'

'I see.' Bradan surveyed the board.

'I rather like you.' Dhraji surveyed him once more. 'You have intelligence and stamina.'

'It's all that walking and rowing.' Bradan moved an elephant on the board. It would take him a while to get used to the different pieces.

Dhraji continued her lecture. 'Chess spread to Persia and when the armies of Islam invaded Persia, they adopted the game and carried it with them.' She moved her mantra. 'When I take over the Chola Empire, I may march my army north and destroy the Islamics.'

'Yes, my Lady.' Bradan perused the board, wondering if he should allow Dhraji to defeat him, or if she wanted a real challenge.

'I wonder how loyal you are?' Dhraji shot him a sideways look. 'I wonder how far I can trust you?'

'You have always treated me well,' Bradan said. 'You have no reason to distrust me.'

'We'll see,' Dhraji said.

'How large is your realm?' Bradan asked.

'It is not large yet, only a couple of hundred miles north to south,' Dhraji said, 'and from the coast, we extend as far as the Ghats.' She nodded to the now-darkening mountain range.

'And how large is the Chola Empire?'

'Much larger,' Dhraji admitted. 'It is hundreds of miles north to south and it stretches right across to the East coast and even to the island of Ceylon.' She smiled. 'But it is old and creaking. We are young and vibrant. We will raid and weaken the Cholas until their Empire collapses and then,' she clapped her hands, smiling, 'we will move in and take over.'

'And then,' Bradan said, 'you will be Rani of the New Chola Empire, with all their lands and all their power.'

'It will be Bhim's land, not mine. I am only a poor woman. What do I know about affairs of state?'

'Everything there is to know, I wager,' Bradan said, 'and maybe more than has ever been written.'

'You have a silver tongue, Bradan the Wanderer,' Dhraji said, 'but it is not that part of you I wish to exercise.' She stood up. 'Leave this foolish game.'

The sun had long gone as Bradan lay awake in the great bed, with the distant noises of the city faint beyond the palace walls and the fluttering of moths and steady breathing of the leopard only a distraction. Bradan sighed, wondering if he could ever escape this silken prison, and wondered, as he did a hundred times a day, if Melcorka was still safe. Every time he asked a guard about Melcorka, they refused to answer his question, leaving him frustrated and worried. He had lost count of time since he first entered the palace. It was weeks, he knew; three weeks perhaps, or maybe four.

He sighed again. If he could find Melcorka, he would try to escape with her and make their way to the Chola Empire, which might afford them sanctuary; or the Chola soldiers may kill them out of hand as spies of the Raja of Thiruzha.

The haze drifted through the window and hovered beside the bed. Bradan half sat up; he had last seen that indefinable black-and-white mass when Melcorka had thrown away Defender. What was it? Brushing away a whining insect, he peered into the darkness. He heard the leopard give a low growl as if in warning, and the black-and-white mass moved toward it, settling on the leopard's head. The leopard sank down, instantly asleep.

'What are you?' Bradan whispered. 'Are you friendly? Or are you not friendly?'

The mass moved toward him. Bradan reached out, but his hand penetrated the mass, vanishing into the interior. When he withdrew his hand, the mass disappeared. Bradan heard a new sound. Something was scratching. It was not the scratching of a rat or a mouse, or even the leopard; nor was it the slight sound of an insect. Bradan lay unmoving on the bed, aware that something was wrong; something had changed.

Asleep beside Bradan, Dhraji stirred, shifted, snored slightly and relaxed into slumber. She lay naked and serene, with her hair a black fan on the pillow and her eyelids flickering with dreams. Even in sleep, her mouth seemed to be smiling, as if at some secret joke, or with smug pleasure at the path her life had taken.

The sound came again, this time more like a scraping than a scratching. Bradan lay still, his eyes hooded as he examined the room. Faint moonlight ghosted through the pointed windows, casting a gloss over the luxurious furnishings. Bradan sensed movement in the far corner, where Dhraji's full-length mirror stood. He shifted slightly, hoping his movement seemed natural. The leopard remained still, unmoving. What had that black-and-white mass done to it?

There was definite movement there, a darker shadow among the shadows, a blurred shape against the window. Bradan distinctly heard the slither of feet on the ground. For a moment, he wondered if he should lie still; if the intruder was an assassin, then Dhraji thoroughly deserved death. He considered quickly; if he remained still and did nothing, and the assassin, if it was an assassin, killed the Rani, what was the possibility of survival?

Not high.

Remember what had happened to the completely innocent arch builders.

Think of Melcorka. Stay alive, whatever it takes.

'That's far enough!' Bradan rose from the bed, wishing desperately that he had a weapon. Even his old rowan-wood staff would do. As it was, he had only his hands, feet and voice.

The shadow solidified and rose, and Bradan leapt on top of it, roaring.

'Dhraji! Take care!'

Bradan did not think. He knew he was no fighting man and any half-decent warrior could dispose of him with ease. He also knew he had the advantage of surprise and that Dhraji had guards within call. So he yelled as he lashed out with his balled fists and kicked out with feet toughened by years of constant walking. His fist made surprisingly solid contact, but the intruder fought back, with one hand around Bradan's throat and the other holding a wavy-bladed knife.

'Dhraji! Get out of here!'

Dhraji was also shouting, sitting up in bed as Bradan wrestled with the intruder. The door crashed open, and three of Dhraji's guards burst in. The first held a lantern aloft and the other two carried short, curved swords. Bradan just had time to see that the man he wrestled was small, lithe and dressed in black, before the guards reached them.

'Kill him!' Dhraji screamed. 'Not the pale man! The other.'

Without hesitation, the guards hauled Bradan away and chopped the intruder to pieces, hacking and slicing at his body as it lay supine on the floor.

Kneeling naked on the bed, Dhraji watched. 'Good,' she said, nodding. 'Good. You may leave now.'

'Shall we take away the body, your Majesty?' The guard with the lantern asked.

'No, leave him there.' Dhraji said. 'Go now.'

The guards departed without another word, leaving Bradan shaking beside the window and the late intruder lying in a dozen pieces amidst a spreading pool of blood.

'Good.' Dhraji dipped her finger in the blood and licked it clean, smiling. 'I wondered how you would react.'

'You wondered?' Bradan asked.

'I hired this man.' Dhraji was evidently pleased with her own cleverness. 'I wanted to see if you would defend me.'

About to say, 'I could have been killed,' Bradan changed it to, 'You might have been killed, your Majesty.'

'Can you see a weapon?' Dhraji dipped her finger in the blood again, smiling.

'Yes.' Bradan lifted the wavy-bladed knife the intruder had carried.

'Oh.' Dhraji shook her head. 'He really was going to try and kill me. How foolishly brave of him. If I had known that, I would have fed him to my pet.' She kicked the leopard. 'He should have been my first line of defence. It was lucky for the murderer that you are brave and loyal.'

'You know I care you for you, Majesty,' Bradan said.

'I do now,' Dhraji said. She produced a curved knife from beneath the pillows. 'That fool was paid to shake me awake. If he had done so, I would have killed him. He knew that. I wanted to test your loyalty. I wanted to see if you would help him, or help me.'

'Did I pass?' Bradan asked.

'You know you did.' With the dead man's blood dribbling down her chin, Dhraji held out her hand. 'Come back to bed, Bradan.'

* * *

'Do you like them?' Dhraji held up a string of finger-nail-sized pearls before draping them around her throat. 'I know other women prefer emeralds and rubies and diamonds, but I like pearls.'

'So I see.' Bradan sat beside the window as Dhraji paraded her pearls against her naked tawny skin, admiring herself in her mirror. 'How many do you have?'

'Hundreds and hundreds,' Dhraji said. 'I send out my ships to capture the pearl divers of Ceylon, and use the divers to scour the ocean bed for them.'

'How many do you want?'

'All of them,' Dhraji said. 'I want all the world's pearls.' She lifted one of the strings from around her neck and held the pearls up to the light. 'They are beautiful, are they not?'

'They are,' Bradan agreed. 'That will be a lot of pearls.'

'All mine.' Dhraji selected a long string and draped them around her hips, so they bounced and danced as she swayed around the room. 'I once said that I would dance for you,' she said. 'Do you like this?'

Despite himself, Bradan felt his heart beat faster as he watched.

I am betraying Melcorka. I should not watch this woman.

'I like this,' Bradan said.

Dhraji wriggled closer, with the pearls catching the light and her eyes dark and inviting.

I have to do this. If I do not, Dhraji would kill me without a qualm and then what would happen to Mel?

'Come closer.' Bradan smiled. 'Much closer.'

'Are you not scared of me, Slave Bradan?'

'Yes,' Bradan admitted freely.

'That is as it should be.' Dhraji smiled as she further emphasised the sway of her hips. She danced closer, brushing against him. 'Soon, you will forget Melcorka, Bradan, as she has forgotten about you.'

And then her revenge will be one step closer to completion.

Bradan did not know from where the words came until he saw the black-and-white haze hovering just within the window.

Revenge for what? Bradan stretched out a hand to touch Dhraji as she bent toward him. 'Fear can be an enhancement in certain situations, my Lady.' *And I will never forget Melcorka. I will get her back to herself and then we shall see how dangerous you are, my vicious little beauty.*

'Enjoy me, Bradan,' Dhraji said as she straddled him, 'for there is red war ahead. The Chola Empire will seek to retaliate for our raids.' Her smile broadened. 'There is blood and gore and death on the horizon.' It was evident that Dhraji enjoyed the prospect.

Chapter Seven

'To invade the land of Thiruzha, Rajaraja of the Chola Empire had a choice. He could send a fleet up the coast and attack our city of Kollchi, where we all stand now, or he could send an army through the passes of the Ghats.' Bhim spoke impressively slowly. 'Instead, Rajaraja has done both. He has attacked Kollchi and sent an army to the Ghats.'

'So here we are.' Dhraji and Bhim stood in the Council Chamber, with the war leaders and shipmasters gathered around them and two of Dhraji's guards standing sentinel at the door. Bradan stood with his back to the wall, awaiting Dhraji's orders, listening to everything and trying to keep as low a profile as possible. The Thiruzha warriors looked a handy bunch, some with scarred faces as souvenirs of previous battles, and all with long, slightly curved swords at their belts. Bradan was happy to note that Dhraji's leopard was not with her.

Bhim spread a large map of Thiruzha over a low table. 'Come closer,' he ordered. 'My spies have informed me that the Chola Raja, or Rajaraja as I shall call him, has gathered a strong flotilla and will send it up the coast to Kollchi, here.' Bhim jabbed his sword into the map and the watchers all nodded, as if they needed reminding where their own city was.

Bhim looked around at his mariners and warriors. 'At their present speed, the Chola fleet will arrive in three days.'

The nautical men of the audience grunted and looked at each other, evidently worried about the lack of time they had to prepare to meet the threat. Bhim raised a podgy hand to regain everybody's attention.

'In the meantime, Rajaraja has also gathered an army to force through the Rajgana Pass in the Ghats.' Bhim drifted his sword across the map to a dark pass marked in the east. 'Here.' He stabbed down. 'We estimate that the Chola army will take two weeks to reach Rajgana.'

Dhraji, resplendent in tight blue trousers and a transparent top, with three rows of pearls around her neck supplementing her pearl head-dress, clapped her hands and spoke for the first time. 'So, gentlemen, Rajaraja's fleet will come here in a few days. We will defeat them and then we must gather our army and force-march to fend off the Chola army at the pass.'

The lords, chiefs and seamen nodded. One middle-aged man raised his voice. 'We are not sufficiently strong to defeat the Chola fleet, your Highness. We have only three days, barely enough time to load up the ships with all we can carry and run.'

'Who said that?' Dhraji asked, smiling. 'Who gave that opinion?'

Everybody shuffled away from one man, who stood erect beside the map. 'We can raid and burn, Rani,' he said. 'We cannot fight against the entire Chola Empire. I am only thinking of the good of your people, Your Highness.'

'Tell me what you advise, Chera.' Dhraji stepped beside the man and rubbed her hand over his arm. 'My, you are strong, aren't you?'

'We could load up everything and sail further up the coast before the Chola fleet arrives,' Chera said.

'We could do that.' Dhraji pressed her near-naked body against him, lowering her voice to a whisper as she smoothed her hand over Chera's chest and stomach. 'Do you think that is best?'

'Yes, Rani.' Chera was looking nervous. 'I don't want to think of you in danger.'

'That is good of you,' Dhraji said. 'Is your brother not also a ship's captain?'

'Yes.' Chera's finger shook as he pointed to a tall, clean-shaven man with a sizeable green-and-red turban.

'Good. Do you agree with your brother, Dee?' Dhraji asked.

Dee looked from his brother to Dhraji and back, evidently reluctant to make a decision. 'No, Rani,' he said at last.

'Do you think Chera is a coward?' Dhraji asked smoothly. 'He is strong and muscular, and he looks brave. Is he brave?'

Dee closed his eyes as sweat broke out on his forehead. His voice dropped to a whisper. 'Yes, Rani. He is brave.'

Bradan breathed as softly as he could in a room that had gone very quiet. He could hear voices rising from the city below and even the rustle of a bird's wings as it flew past the window.

'Your brother says you are brave,' Dhraji said to Chera. 'Are you brave?'

'Brave enough.' Chera evidently knew there was no escape.

'Prove it to us.' Dhraji's smile did not falter.

'What? How can I prove my bravery?'

'Jump out of the window.' Still Dhraji's smile did not falter.

The room was five storeys above the square. Chera stepped back, with Dhraji still smiling. 'Jump out of the window,' she ordered, 'or I will have four elephants pull you apart an inch a day in the square.'

'No!' Chera looked at his colleagues for support. When they stepped further back, he pulled out his sword and rushed at Dhraji. 'You evil whore!'

Nobody moved. The seamen and warriors seemed frozen in horror as sunlight glinted on Chera's curved blade. Even the guards appeared paralysed. Dhraji continued to smile. It was instinct that forced Bradan to thrust his foot forward. Chera tripped and staggered, which gave Dhraji's guards sufficient time to rush from their position against the wall and remove Chera's sword. They held him securely on the ground, awaiting Dhraji's orders.

Dhraji had not moved. 'Strip him,' she said pleasantly, 'and hang him by his left ankle outside the window. He can sun-dry there for a day or two until I decide how to execute him.' She looked at Bradan and nodded, once. 'That one was not a test,' she said and watched as her guards suspended Chera from the window, as she had ordered. None of the men lifted a finger to help.

'Now, here is what we will do,' Bhim continued, as if a naked man was not slowly swinging outside the building. 'Our ships will meet Rajaraja's fleet in the open sea. We will harass them and attack the stragglers and the loolas, their scout ships.' Bhim looked around to ensure that everybody was paying attention.

'We will strike, kill, withdraw and strike again. We will not oppose the Chola fleet in an open battle. Our job is to thin their numbers and unsettle them.'

The shipmasters nodded. They were raiders and slavers; they understood tip-and-run fighting.

'When we get within half a day's sail of Kollchi, we will break off and sail home.' Bhim's grin restored some spirit to his audience. 'We have some surprises for Rajaraja's men here, and I'll need your nautical fighters to man the walls. We will put out the boom and hold them in our harbour, with fire and steel.'

Bradan nodded. It was an excellent strategy. He began to have a little respect for Bhim.

'We will defeat them. No fleet can breach our defences, island and city,' Bhim said. 'What is more troubling is the Chola army. Our border fort at Rajgana is only lightly held, so we need to send reinforcements to the pass.'

'We have a week to defeat the Chola fleet,' Dhraji said. 'Don't let me down.' She pulled Dee close to her and patted his cheek. 'Can I trust you, Dee? Can I trust you, knowing what I have done to your brave brother?'

'You can trust me.' Dee did not look as Chera struggled desperately outside. With all his weight suspended on one ankle, the strain would already be becoming intolerable.

'Good.' Dhraji kissed his forehead. 'If you stay loyal, I will make it easy for your brother. If you let me down, then you will join him. I rather like the idea of having two brothers decorating my house.'

Ignoring Dhraji's words, Bhim lifted his voice. 'Thank you all, gentlemen. You may go and prepare for war.'

The ship captains and war lords filed out, leaving Bradan alone with Dhraji and Bhim.

'You did well, Bradan.' Dhraji eyed him. 'That is twice you have intervened to save me. You deserve a reward. What shall I give you? A slave girl, perhaps? Or some golden trinkets? What do you desire most?'

'Your Majesty,' Bradan salaamed to Dhraji, 'I crave a favour from Bhim'

'You are my wife's slave.' Bhim's eyes were as smoky as Dhraji's leopard's. 'Your favour is remaining alive.'

'He has proved his loyalty twice now,' Dhraji said. 'The first time, he thought to protect me from a night assassin and he saved me again today. Let him speak. He is an intriguing slave.'

'Thank you, My Lady.' Bradan salaamed to Dhraji and then to Bhim. 'You may not recall, Bhim Raj, that when I was captured, there was a woman with me.'

You may not like me mentioning Melcorka again, Dhraji, but I must find out.
When Bhim nodded, folds of fat flapped around his chin. 'I remember.'

'Is she still alive?'

Bhim nodded. 'The pale woman is still alive.'

Bradan felt Dhraji's eyes on him and wondered if the Rani was jealous, or if she was now so secure with her power and undoubted charisma that such emotions were beyond her. *I must take the chance.* 'She was unwell when we were captured. I would crave permission to see her again.'

Dhraji tilted her head to one side. 'Were you as loyal to this woman as you are to me?'

'I was, and I am,' Bradan said. 'My loyalty does not falter or die, your Majesty.'

'How strange.' Dhraji touched Bradan's arm. 'It is curious that you should remain loyal to somebody else, even after meeting me... even when you know how much I value total submission.'

That was undoubtedly a threat. 'You are easily the most enchanting woman I have ever met.' Bradan chose his words carefully.

'So why keep your loyalty to another?' Dhraji seemed genuinely confused.

'My loyalty is steadfast,' Bradan tried to explain. 'It is a custom, a tradition, where I come from. It cannot be bought or sold or transferred. Once I fix my loyalty on somebody, it remains there.'

'I have never heard of that before,' Dhraji said. 'It is a strange concept.'

'You may visit this pale woman.' Bhim dismissed Bradan with a flick of his hand. 'One of my guards will take you.'

'Thank you, Your Highness.' Although Bradan salaamed to Bhim, he intended the words for both. He had no doubt that Dhraji would exact a price for his request.

* * *

Bradan gagged at the stench. They were far underground in a place of stone chambers and iron chains, where rats and mice scurried over their feet, and sinister jailers loomed from the shadows. Hidden under the arches were dozens of dungeons, some packed with suffering humanity, men, women and children crammed together, others with a solitary inhabitant, heavily chained to the wall.

'Why is Melcorka held down here?' Bradan asked. 'She is no harm to anybody.'

'I would have killed her.' The head jailer was a stocky, lugubrious man with arms as thick as most men's thighs and a cynical twist to his mouth. 'If Lord

Bhim had not wanted her alive, I'd have tied her big toe to her thumb and thrown her in the river. Lord Bhim says she may recover from whatever ails her, and if so, her pale skin could amuse him.'

In the chamber furthest from the entrance, amidst piles of filth and a thousand scrabbling insects, Melcorka was chained to the wall. She lay there unmoving, as Bradan entered.

'Mel!' Bradan knelt at her side. 'It's me!'

Melcorka looked up, her eyes still vague and a stupid smile on her face. 'Hello.' Her hair was knotted and filthy and her face bloated with insect bites.

'It's me,' Bradan repeated. 'Do you recognise me?'

'Hello,' Melcorka repeated. 'Do you like my house? They feed me nearly every day.'

Oh, dear God in his Heaven. 'What's happened to you, Mel?' Despite the filth that covered Melcorka, Bradan held her close. 'Mel, where are you?'

'Who's Mel?' Melcorka lay back again, still smiling through the dirt. Her breath was foul, her teeth yellowed and her eyes bloodshot, yet it was her blank mind that hurt Bradan the most. *I'll get you out, Mel; I swear I'll get you out of this hellish place.*

'Is she always like this?' Bradan asked the jailer, who shrugged.

'Every time I've seen her.'

'I want her moved to better accommodation,' Bradan said. 'I want a clean dungeon at least, with fresh straw and daily food and fresh water.' Bradan knew the jailer would have no power to release Melcorka. 'Can you do that?'

'I could, but why should I?' The jailer sized Bradan up with a single look and shrugged. 'You have no authority over me. You're a slave, while she's just a foreign prisoner. Either she'll die soon, or my Lord Bhim will order her executed.'

'Will Lord Bhim order her to kiss the elephant's foot?' Bradan asked.

'No!' The jailer shook his head as if that idea was amusing. 'She's not important enough for a public execution.' He indicated the heavy club at his belt. 'I'll come in and finish her off.'

Bradan shuddered. The thought of his Melcorka, scourge of the Norse, Melcorka of the Cenel Bearnas, Melcorka the Swordswoman, being bludgeoned to death by a fat jailer in a filthy dungeon was more than he could bear. If Melcorka had to die, it should be in battle, fighting against great odds like the hero she was.

'I want her moved,' Bradan repeated.

The jailer laughed. 'Who are you to want anything? You are a slave, a nothing, and a foreign slave, a less than nothing.' He waddled up to Bradan. 'Do you think your position as Lady Dhraji's current lover impresses me? I've seen them come, boy and I've seen them go – handsome young gallants who danced on Dhraji's bed and thought they were oh-so-important. Don't you ever think of your predecessors?'

Bradan kept a rein on his temper as the jailer continued.

'Some are dead. They either took the long step from the battlements to the ground below –' The jailer extended his arms and yelled, like a man falling to his death, 'or they kissed the elephant's foot. Some were less lucky. I have two here still. Come with me.'

Bradan followed the jailer to a dungeon next to Melcorka's, where a naked man lay curled up on the bare stone floor. As the jailer opened the door, the prisoner howled like a dog and backed to the furthest corner, holding his hands up in supplication.

'You see what I mean?' Then jailer poked the prisoner with his feet. Bradan saw in horror that the prisoner had been mutilated, with his eyes put out and his nose and ears sliced off.

'This fellow was Dhraji's previous lover.' The jailer held his torch up. 'Her Ladyship blinded him in person, and had great pleasure in emasculating him as well.' The jailer laughed. 'I have orders to beat him every third or fourth day. Her Majesty occasionally visits, to enjoy his suffering.'

Bradan stepped back from the dungeon, feeling sick. He had to escape from here and bring Melcorka with him, although he could not think of a way out. 'If you hurt Melcorka,' he said. 'I will kill you. I will hunt you down and kill you.'

The jailer shrugged. 'Aye, maybe,' he said. 'It's much more likely that I'll have you down here in a few weeks, or even a few days.' He turned away without showing any visible concern. 'Well, Bradan the pale man, you've seen the mad foreign woman. Now, get out of my domain.'

Bradan raised his voice. 'Don't give up, Melcorka. I'll be back for you.'

Lying on her filthy straw, Melcorka smiled. There was no expression in her eyes.

* * *

It was good to be back at sea, with the wind fresh on his face and the movement of the ship lively under his feet. Bradan looked around at the Thiruzha fleet, with each of the fifty two-masted vessels manned by fifty well-armed warriors, while a drummer beat time for the naked slave oarsmen.

'You were a seaman once,' Dhraji had said to him.

'I was,' Bradan agreed.

'You can keep me company then,' Dhraji decided. 'Bhim is in command of matters military on land or sea. I am only here to observe.' Her smile broadened as she patted his thigh. 'You might come in handy if I get bored.'

Bradan forced a smile. 'I look forward to that, your Majesty.'

He had watched with interest as the Thiruzha sea-masters loaded their vessels with spears and arrows, containers of water and baskets of food. Bhim had launched one new ship across a line of tethered slaves, with a crowd cheering as her keel ripped them open and the ship was born in a shower of blood.

'Now she will not be scared of battle,' Dhraji had explained and ordered one of the now-dead slaves to be decapitated, to provide a dripping figurehead for the new ship. She had personally placed the head in position, licking the blood from her fingers.

The Thiruzha fleet rowed from Kollchi harbour in a long line, with the yellow-and-blue flag fluttering at the mast-heads and the drums beating time.

'Do you like the flag?' Dhraji asked. 'It is my leopard, of course.'

'Of course.' Bradan looked around for the animal.

'I don't take him to sea,' Dhraji explained. 'He gets seasick.'

The sharp prow of Dhraji's vessel dipped into the waves, bouncing the row of skulls that decorated her hull and raising a curtain of fine spray that spattered onto the deck. Dhraji laughed, shaking her head. 'Lovely,' she said. 'I love the feel of water on me.'

'I'll bear that in mind, your Majesty,' Bradan murmured. 'It could be useful for variety.'

Dhraji eyed him sideways. 'You are indeed a strange man, Bradan,' she said. 'I may keep you for a long time.'

'I certainly hope so, your Majesty,' Bradan said. 'I have no desire to kiss the foot of an elephant or try to learn how to fly.'

Dhraji's laugh pealed across the ship. 'There are worse ways to die.'

Bradan thought of the mewling thing in the dungeon and said nothing.

There was something exhilarating about being part of such a fleet, witnessing the power and the colour, feeling the excitement as the oars thrust the ship onward and watching the leopard standards flail and crack at the mastheads. Bradan tried to analyse his feelings. Although he could understand the excitement of the warriors, his primary concern was to stay alive and get Melcorka free. After that, he would try and find a cure for whatever malaise affected her. He could not see beyond that point. Only Melcorka mattered. To survive, Bradan knew he needed to keep in Dhraji's good graces. He had no illusions that she genuinely liked him, or would retain his services once she tired of his company. To Dhraji, he was a temporarily entertaining novelty and nothing more. He closed his eyes and immediately saw Melcorka lying in her dungeon.

I'll survive, Melcorka, and I'll get you out, somehow.

While Bradan had been thinking, the fleet had hoisted the sails and was far out to sea. Bhim sent outriders, fast scout ships, to search for the Chola fleet. They sailed ahead, with the drummers pounding out the time and the oarsmen sweating on their benches.

'Send out the outrider scouts,' Bhim ordered through a brass speaking-trumpet and half a dozen smaller, faster craft pushed forward in a flurry of spray and flickering oars. As they sped ahead, Dhraji walked the length of the ship, pointing out any of the slaves she considered was not working hard enough and smiling as a man with a whip laid into them. The sun rose higher and arced to the west, a brassy orb that scorched the ships, bubbled the pitch between the planking and tortured the slaves as they worked unprotected on their benches.

The fleet sailed through the night, south by south-east, relentless, spread into a great line abreast so they would not miss any prey or any sign of the enemy. There was no respite for the slaves. They rowed through the darkness and were still rowing when the sun gleamed faintly orange above the eastern horizon.

'Look!' A lookout pointed to the south. 'A sail. Two sails! One of our outrider scouts is returning!'

The beating of the drum carried far in the hush of the morning. Bradan squinted into the silver dawn as the Thiruzha outrider came closer. It was travelling so fast that Bradan could nearly smell the oarsmen's sweat from a mile away.

'Lord Bhim!' the master of the scout shouted, even before the two ships closed. 'The Chola fleet is just beyond the horizon.'

'How large is it?' Bhim asked.

The answer came at once. 'The Cholas have a hundred and twenty vessels and twenty fast loolas.'

Bradan noticed the arrows that protruded from the hull of the outrider and the blood that dribbled from the scuppers. Men had died to bring that fragment of information, and more would die before this day was done.

'They've moved faster than I expected,' Bhim said. 'Damn their skins. We'll lure their loolas in and dispose of them. Outriders!' The speaking-trumpet magnified his voice, so it carried easily across the Thiruzha fleet. 'Sail out, lure them in!'

Bhim gave a string of orders that saw the fleet alter into a half-moon formation, with the outriders arrowing forward toward the enemy, leopard flags streaming out in their wake.

'Row!' Bhim roared. 'Drummers! Increase the pace!'

Each ship had a broad-shouldered man in the stern, with a massive drum in front of him. At Bhim's orders, the drummer quickened the beat, and the oarsmen kept pace, with brawny men wielding long whips to encourage the exhausted. The twin sails bellied out with the wind, adding to the speed.

'Isn't this invigorating?' Dhraji breathed deeply of the scent of sweat and excitement. 'I love the tension before battle.'

Bradan nodded. He wondered how many of these men and women would still be alive at nightfall; how many would be floating face-up in the sea and how many would be screaming, broken wrecks with arms and legs lopped off.

Dhraji squeezed Bradan's bicep. 'Are you thinking the same as I am, Bradan?'

'I was thinking of you, My Lady,' Bradan lied.

Even approaching battle, Dhraji wore three strings of pearls, with one large pearl in the centre of her ornate head-dress. 'Of course you were.' Dhraji moved her hip against him. 'If you ever stop thinking of me, I must get rid of you, and I'm not at all ready for that yet.'

'I'm glad to hear it, your Majesty, for I am not yet finished with you.' Bradan managed what he hoped was a lecherous leer.

Dhraji slapped him sharply. 'Have patience, Bradan. You are only a slave.'

'Your slave, My Lady.' Bradan bowed and salaamed. He thought of Melcorka in her foul dungeon and bent lower. 'Always your slave.'

'Here they are!' the lookout called from the masthead. 'The outriders are returning, with the Chola loolas in pursuit.'

'How many loolas?' Bhim asked.

'I see fourteen, no, fifteen, Lord Bhim, and maybe more on the flank.' The lookout was counting as he reported, balancing on the masthead as the ship bounced to the rhythm of the waves.

'Stand to your oars!' Bhim roared. 'Archers! Prepare your arrows! Drummer, increase the beat by one-half.'

As the Thiruzha scouts withdrew before the pursuing Chola loolas, the Thiruzha fleet spread even further out, with the flanking vessels increasing their speed faster than the others.

'Can you see what we are doing?' Dhraji asked.

'I see,' Bradan said. 'We are luring the Chola ships into a trap.'

'Exactly so.' Dhraji nodded. 'Now, come with me and watch.' Agile as any monkey, Dhraji climbed to the masthead, balanced easily on the slanting yardarm and smiled as the initial stage of the battle developed. Bradan followed, every bit at home on the ship as Dhraji was. He looked out to sea, enjoying the view of the limitless horizon and wondered if he and Melcorka would ever again find themselves sailing in *Catriona*, free of the land.

We will. I must not think otherwise. We will get away.

When the leading Chola vessels finally realised that the entire Thiruzha fleet was surrounding them, they turned to flee.

'You're too late, by Shiva!' Bhim roared 'We have you! Close the mouth!'

Like the jaws of a leopard, the two wings of the Thiruzhas closed, catching the bulk of the Chola loolas in between. Three of the Chola vessels managed to escape, with Bhim ordering his scouts to hunt them down before they reached the Chola fleet.

'Catch them and sink them!' Bhim shouted. 'Don't return until they are all destroyed. I'll have the head of any shipmaster who fails me!'

The entire flotilla of Thiruzha scouts raced after the three Chola loolas, with the drums hammering like the hooves of a galloping horse and the slave-drivers cracking their whips on naked shoulders and backs.

'Without their loolas, the Chola admiral is blind,' Dhraji said. 'He can only blunder forward, not knowing what we are doing or where we are.' Her smile broadened as she borrowed Bhim's speaking-trumpet. 'No quarter!' she shrieked. 'No quarter!'

The Thiruzha fleet closed the net, with the Chola loolas, fast vessels but much smaller than their adversaries, searching frantically for a gap that did not exist.

Dhraji licked her lips, eyes bright with excitement as the Thiruzha archers poured volley after volley of arrows into the Chola loolas.

'Take that one!' Dhraji pointed to the furthest forward of the Chola loolas, which was trying to break through the Thiruzha line by speed alone. A second Chola loola followed the first, speeding toward a hopeful weakness in Bhim's trap.

Dhraji's ship altered course slightly, with the drummer pounding his drum and the oarsmen hauling as if their lives depended on it – as they probably did, Bradan thought. Dhraji watched with her mouth slightly open and her tongue flicking around her lips.

'Catch them,' Dhraji whispered and then raised her voice. 'Archers! Aim at the oarsmen! Loose!'

A volley of arrows hummed through the air, some to thunk into the hull of the Chola craft, one or two to plop into the sea and a few to transfix the Chola oarsmen.

'Archers, keep firing,' Dhraji ordered as the Chola vessel replied in kind, so arrows flew in both directions. An arrow ripped into the sail a handspan from Dhraji's left foot. She looked down in amazement. 'Somebody's firing at me,' she said and laughed. 'It's that man there!' She nodded to an archer who balanced in the crosstrees of the Chola vessel. 'It's that man in the red-and-yellow turban. What fun!'

Bradan inched closer to Dhraji. 'Stay close to me, your Majesty and I'll protect you.'

'Oh, Bradan, you are the most amusing slave I have ever owned. Let's play a game with this archer.' Dhraji stood and stepped further along the spar, spreading her legs and arms. 'There, you impudent little man. There's a target for you. Let's see if you can hit me, or not.'

Bradan shook his head. 'No, my Lady!' If the Chola archer killed Dhraji, Bradan knew his life would be short and unpleasant, leaving Melcorka very vulnerable. 'You are too valuable. I need you, Lady Dhraji!'

'Oh, Bradan, where did I find you? Are there others like you in Alba?' Despite the arrows that hummed and screamed around her, Dhraji smiled at

Bradan. 'Perhaps I should order a raid on Alba and bring home a hundred men like you!'

Bradan thought of the fierce swordsmen of the Lord of the Isles and the disciplined Pictish spearmen. 'As Your Majesty pleases,' he said.

'You could guide us there.' Dhraji toyed with the idea. 'We'll discuss it later.'

A second archer had joined the first, with both firing at Dhraji as she stood static on the spar. She laughed as the arrows zipped and plunged around her.

'We're going to ram!' Bhim shouted. 'Up oars!' The Thiruzha oarsmen rapidly lifted their oars as the prow of the Thiruzha ship ripped along the side of the loola, snapping and splintering Chola oars. Chola oarsmen tumbled from their benches as both vessels came to a halt. The terrible jerk of contact sent Bradam sprawling. He grabbed the spar, with his feet kicking and scrabbling for purchase on the taut canvas of the sail. As the ships collided, he saw Dhraji overbalance and fall silently into the sea. She hit the water with barely a splash and vanished into the blue.

'Dhraji!' Bradan held on for a moment more and then dived after her. He had no choice: Dhraji was his link to Melcorka.

The water was warm and welcoming as Bradan entered, to surface, spluttering, a few yards away, searching desperately for Dhraji. He could not see her. He could only see a confusion of fighting ships littering the sea, with Dhraji's ship locked with the smaller Chola loola and men striving desperately with sword and spear. A Chola warrior screamed as an arrow sliced into his face, penetrating both cheeks. He plucked at it, and another bolt slammed into his belly, throwing him back onto the deck of the loola.

'Dhraji!' Bradan ignored the carnage and searched desperately for Dhraji. He peered over the tops of the chopped waves for her long, black hair or a glimpse of her pearl headdress. Seeing neither, he took a deep breath and dived back below, searching. He surfaced again, gasping for breath. If Dhraji was dead, what chance had he of rescuing Melcorka? *Virtually none.*

'Dhraji!' He dived under again, with the same result.

Thiruzha warriors were running along the deck of the Chola loola, pushing back the Chola crew by force of numbers. However, the second Chola loola was approaching. Her master had the choice of running for safety through the minuscule gap, or steering to help her colleague. He chose the more gallant latter course. Bradan could see men massing in her bows, with the sun glinting on spear points and steel helmets – and then the impossible happened.

The sea rose up beside the Chola ship, erupting like a miniature volcano. Bradan stared for a second and then swam away, hoping for safety as a multi-armed monster emerged from the depths. The creature wrapped its long tentacles around the loola's masts and dragged sideways, toppling the vessel into the water. Some of the loola crew tried to hack at the arms with their swords; others thrust spears at the enormous eyes, but most jumped into the sea. More tentacles appeared, grabbing at the men in the water, tearing off their heads and arms, lifting them out of the sea and dashing them against the hull of the loola, or throwing them bodily skyward.

'Oh, dear God,' Bradan said, as the monster hauled at the Chola ship until it capsized and lay bottom-up on the waves. The creature pulled itself onto the hull and crouched there, with its shield-sized eyes glaring at the battle and its parrot-beak snapping at the Chola warriors who struggled to escape. Blood smeared the sea.

Melcorka, hold on! Bradan pleaded. *How can I get you back? I know where your body lies, but where is your mind?*

Bradan knew his world had ended. With Melcorka an empty shell of herself, and Dhraji drowned, or killed by this monster, he was stuck in this terrible land of slavery and cruelty. His wandering had brought them both to this end. The monster glared directly at him before sliding back under the waves.

Bradan shook his head. *I will not give up. There is always hope. Somehow, I must get Melcorka free. Somehow, I will get us back to Alba.*

'What are you doing in the water?'

The voice was familiar, and Bradan looked up. Lost in his thoughts, he had not seen the monster disappear, and now he floated a few yards from Dhraji's ship. The Thiruzha leopard banner hung from the stern of the captured Chola loola and those few of her crew who survived sat in a frightened clump amidships, with their grinning captors tormenting them with jabbing spears and barbed insults. Dhraji leaned over the stern. 'Did you fall into the sea?'

'No.' The shipmaster was drinking from a gold-embossed skull. He was a stocky, muscular man with a twisted turban on his head and a short sword at his belt. 'He roared your name and jumped in to try and save you.'

Dhraji's laugh tinkled across the water. 'What a loyal little slave you are.' She threw a rope. 'I will reward you later. Up you come, slave.'

'I was worried about you.' Bradan hauled himself on deck, shaking from reaction. 'Did you see that thing in the water? Did you see that monster with the many arms?'

'No.' Dhraji shook her head. 'What was it?'

'A monster,' Bradan said. 'It was a gigantic beast with ten long arms, that dragged a Chola ship under the water and killed the crew.'

Dhraji shook her head again. 'I was trying too hard not to drown,' she said. 'There are lots of terrible things in the sea.' She pointed overboard, where a school of sharks were busy with the dead and dying from the battle. 'I rather like sharks,' she said absently.

Bradan shook his head. 'This thing was worse than any shark.'

'Oh?' Dhraji shrugged. 'Well, whatever it was, it's gone now. Let's see what Bhim's next plan is. He's calling all the ships together.'

The Thiruzha ships gathered, some looking battered, with rents in their sails and arrows protruding from their hulls. One had lost her mizzen mast; another was smeared with blood, with the crew throwing their dead overboard.

'We have disposed of their loolas,' Bhim shouted through his speaking-trumpet. 'Now, you outriders, here's your chance to show what you can do. Hit and run, sail to arrow-length, fire a few volleys and turn away. Lure some of their main fleet. We will wait beyond the horizon and destroy any Chola vessel foolish enough to follow you.'

The scout captains and crews cheered and left at once, with their oars flailing the sea to white foam and the yellow leopard ensign streaming behind them.

'Ten slaves to the fastest man!' Bhim shouted after them, and their speed increased even more.

Dhraji quickly lost interest in watching the scouts race away. 'Bring me the prisoners,' she ordered and crowed in delight when she noticed the archer with the red-and-yellow turban, bleeding from a wound in his right arm.

'Tie him to the mainmast,' she ordered, 'and bring me a bow and arrows. That man tried to kill me!'

Bradan did not watch as Dhraji used the archer for target practice, firing ar-row after arrow and puncturing her victim in his legs and trunk a dozen times, smiling as he writhed and groaned without the mercy of death. Eventually, growing tired of her game, Dhraji ordered all the prisoners thrown overboard and watched their struggles with interest. The sharks were busy that day.

'Men are such frail things,' Dhraji said to Bradan. 'I don't know why they are so brave, knowing that they have only a short spell in this world.'

'We all must die sometime.' Bradan felt sickened by her cruelty.

'Not I,' Dhraji said. 'I will live forever. Death fascinates me, and the manner of death can be so amusing.'

Bradan could not think of anything to say to that.

'Go away now.' Dhraji pushed Bradan astern. 'Go away, I said! My sharks are more entertaining than you.'

Bradan moved at once. If Dhraji decided he was no longer wanted, his life would be short. It was far better to get out of her way. He moved as far aft as he could.

'Did you see the sea monster?' Bradan asked the helmsman, who shook his head, wordless.

'Did anybody see the sea monster?' Bradan raised his voice. 'The many-armed thing that sunk the Chola loola?'

Nobody spoke, although there were a few shaken heads and down-turned faces.

'What do you think happened to the other loola? Do you think it just sunk by chance?'

Again, there was no response. Bradan began to realise that something was seriously wrong. *Is it because I am a slave? No. There is something else. What is it?* They were scared, Bradan realised. They were scared to admit that they had seen the monster. *Why?*

'Best keep quiet.' The helmsman spoke from the corner of his mouth. 'If you value your life, for the sake of Shiva, say nothing and see nothing.'

Bradan glanced at him, realised that Dhraji was watching, her eyes hooded, and shrugged. 'Maybe I imagined things.'

'That would be it,' the helmsman said at once. 'It's the strain of the battle.'

Bradan felt the atmosphere in the boat lift with his words and wondered again what was wrong. In the meantime, there was a battle to win. The Chola fleet was still full of fight.

Chapter Eight

The Thiruzha fleet had survived their fighting retreat back to Kollchi. They had lost seven ships to the Cholas and every vessel now carried the scars of battle. Sails were torn, oars broken, arrows stood out from each hull like the spines of hedgehogs and the decks were strewn with dead or dying men. In return, they had accounted for nine Chola ships as well as the loolas and had killed an unknown number of Chola warriors.

'You fought well,' Bhim shouted through his speaking-trumpet. 'Now it is time to stand behind our defences and watch the Cholas' attack splinter against the stone walls. Withdraw to the harbour!'

Like the excellent commander he was, Bhim waited until the last of his fleet had entered the harbour before he followed with his flagship. Once again, Bradan could only admire the Raja's tactics as his fleet slid past the defending island into the magnificent harbour of Kollchi and onto the horseshoe-shaped beach. The warriors filed out, to enter the Seagate of the city and take their places with the other defenders.

'Now we will see how skilled the Chola warriors are,' Dhraji said. 'Now we will see the breaking of bones and the ripping of intestines, the crushing of skulls and the spilling of blood.' Her eyes were bright with anticipation. 'Come with me, Bradan.' She led the way to the tower that topped the gatehouse, giving them a view over the harbour and the fortified island that was their outer defences.

'What is the island called?' Bradan asked.

'Kalipuram.' Dhraji seemed to have rekindled her liking for Bradan as she took hold of his arm. 'It will give the Cholas some surprises.' Her laugh contained genuine humour.

The Chola fleet, no doubt eager for revenge after their losses on the voyage north, formed two lines so they could pass on either side of the Island of Kalipuram. The island's defenders greeted them with volleys of archery that forced the Cholas further away from the fort and perilously close to the rocks on either entrance of the bay. The Chola archers fired back, standing on deck in positions that made them even more vulnerable to the defenders' arrows. Bradan saw Chola warriors drop under the arrow hail, and then the smoke started.

'Fire-arrows,' Dhraji said, with satisfaction. 'I told you Kalipuram held some surprises.'

Bradan could only watch as the archers in the fort fired volleys of fire-arrows that arched through the air to land on and around the Chola ships. The sails of one ship immediately caught fire, to flare up, dropping burning shreds onto the deck. When the crew fought the flames with buckets of water, they exposed themselves to the archery from the fort, with more men falling as the fire spread.

Dhraji watched, smiling, with her hands gripping the parapet.

The burning vessel veered to port, upsetting the tight Chola formation and forcing all the ships astern to steer to starboard. With the burning vessel now closer to the fort, the defenders' archers concentrated on this easy target. The sheer volume of missiles in the air and the smoky trails of the fire-arrows combined to darken the sky.

'I've never seen anything like this before,' Bradan said.

'My warriors know how to fight.' Dhraji's eyes seemed to glow.

The captain of the burning vessel tried to steer her away from the fort, with the result that the oars on the port side clacked and crashed against the rocks, making her course even more erratic.

Bhim had anticipated the Chola ships trying to avoid Kalipuram and had stationed a company of mixed archers and spearmen among the rocks. They opened up on the vulnerable burning ship, so in minutes, it was a charnel house of screaming men. At the blare of a horn, Thiruzha warriors emerged from their positions, thrusting their long spears into the survivors who staggered ashore, pleading for mercy that the Thiruzhas would never grant.

Another Chola ship was on fire now, with men leaping into the water rather than face the flames. As the island's defenders used them as targets, one of the Chola vessels eased out of line to pick up survivors.

'The day goes well,' Dhraji was still smiling, 'and the Cholas have not met our main defences yet.'

As Dhraji spoke, Kalipuram's catapults opened up, launching their rocks against the Chola fleet. The first salvo failed to hit anything, but the immense splashes must have caused consternation among the battered seamen. The second salvo was more effective, crashing onto one of the Chola ships. Bradan saw the rock hurtle down amidships, heard the resulting chorus of screams and yells and saw splinters of wood rise high in the air. The ship immediately began to sink, with the Kalipuram archers ignoring it to concentrate on the more dangerous vessels.

'This is a slaughter,' Dhraji said. 'I thought the Cholans were skilled warriors. They have no imagination at all.'

As if they had heard her speak, the Cholans changed tactics. Four of their ships landed on Kalipuram Island and the crews poured out with spears and swords, to try an immediate assault on the fort.

The defenders responded at once, sending a third of their archers to the threatened wall. That movement weakened the defences of the other walls, so the remainder of the Chola fleet was under less threat as it tried to squeeze past the island.

'Now!' The speaking-trumpet altered Bhim's voice to a metallic rasp.

There was a scurry of activity on the walls of the fort and Bradan saw the water between the first and second half of the Chola fleet rise. 'That's the boom,' he said, as the huge chain rose from the bed of the sea to block the passage of the Chola ships.

'Their fleet is split,' Dhraji said. 'The ships behind the boom can either run or remain, for the Kalipuram garrison to destroy at will.'

The remainder of the Chola fleet formed up, out of arrow range, in front of Kollchi. They were battered and bloodied, but they had passed the outer defences and now hoisted giant flags in defiance. The red tiger of Chola sprung from a yellow background.

'Now watch,' Dhraji said quietly, licking her lips.

The single word, 'Fire!' sounded as Bhim gave the order and a score of catapults loosed from the walls of Kollchi. Heavy rocks soared high in the air, hovered for a few seconds and then plunged down with ever-increasing speed. The water splashes were huge, higher than the Chola masts and before the water fountains subsided, the next volley of rocks was on its way.

'Now the Chola admiral has a difficult choice,' Dhraji said. 'He can try to scale the walls of Kollchi, try to capture Kalipuram to rescue his doomed ships, remain anchored and lose his ships, or run with his tail between his legs.' Her smile broadened. 'He had better choose quickly. Things are about to get worse for him.'

The catapults fired again, with large bundles of oil-fuelled flaming rags rising up and falling among the Chola ships. Only one landed on target, and the Chola seamen ran to douse the flames as a new sound echoed around the harbour.

It was like nothing Bradan had heard before; an echoing crash, as if a hundred archers had fired at once, followed by a heavy scream as a massive bolt shot from the city walls. Bradan watched its progress as it soared across the harbour, to pass between two of the anchored ships and smash against the rocks near the harbour entrance.

'Missed,' Dhraji said. 'That should cost somebody his skin.'

'What was that?' Bradan asked.

'That was our new weapon.' Dhraji said. 'It is a bow that fires an arrow as long as two men and as broad as a man's thigh. Bhim has three more of these weapons under construction.'

Bradan could sense the thrill of horror that passed through the Chola fleet. Rather than the aggressors, they were floating targets for the fire-catapults and the giant arrows of the Thiruzha defenders.

'Things are going well,' Dhraji said. 'I wonder what the admiral of the Chola fleet plans to do now?'

'He'll have to try and take the city,' Bradan said. 'If he sits there, your defences will shoot his ships to pieces.'

'Good, good.' Dhraji clapped her hands together. 'Oh, I do hope so. I don't want him to run away until we have given him a proper drubbing. I want to weaken Chola so much that they never try again and we can rule the seas from here to the Andaman Islands and over to Java.'

Bradan had never heard of these places. 'You will have to take me there sometime.'

Dhraji laughed, pressing against him. 'Are you not tired of me yet, Bradan, the slave?'

'I will never tire of you, my Queen.' Bradan thought of Melcorka suffering in her dungeon and swallowed his pride. He allowed his left hand to touch Dhraji's arm. 'You are unlike any woman I have ever met before.'

Dhraji laughed again. 'Oh, my sycophantic little foreign slave! When I conquer the Cholas, I will undoubtedly take a fleet to your Alba and find out if all the men of Alba are like you. How would that be, Bradan? You can be my guide.'

Bradan thought of the mists and coolness of Alba again... the feel of winter sleet against his skin, the sweet scent of a peat-fire flame, the sound of harpers drifting across a western loch and the sight of the sun rising above the grey granite peaks of Drum Alba. 'My people would make you most welcome.'

With sword and steel and fire and blood, they would.

The warriors of Donald of the Isles, the Picts of Fidach and the stubborn spearmen of the Lowlands would not bow before any piratical potentate. Bradan stilled the sudden surge of passion within him. He started as something flew past – something black-and-white. He did not know what it was. It had not been a bird; it was shapeless, formless and sad. That thing was back, that vague mist that had appeared on the island where Melcorka had thrown away her sword. *What was it?* Somehow, Bradan knew it was not unfriendly. That black-and-white mist had put the leopard to sleep.

'What is in your mind, my slave?' Dhraji had caught his mood.

The black-and-white image had gone. 'I was wondering how you would like Alba,' Bradan said. 'It is cooler than here, with winters of snow and sleet and winds that can blow the roofs off houses.'

'I've never seen snow,' Dhraji said.

'It's cold and white,' Bradan began, just as the catapults fired again. Bhim had loaded half with rocks and half with something else; things that writhed and screamed as they soared through the air, to plummet on and around the Chola ships.

'Oh, look!' Dhraji laughed out loud. 'Bhim is letting his prisoners go!'

It was true. Bhim had loaded the Chola prisoners onto the catapults and fired them against the Chola fleet. That action seemed to sting the Chola admiral into action, for his ships suddenly surged forward towards the beach.

'They're going to attack!' Dhraji shouted. 'Now we'll see how good they really are!'

Bradan could only watch as the Chola ships raced for the walls of Kollchi. The Thiruzha catapults fired again, hurling rocks and fireballs through the now-darkening sky, with one Chola ship set ablaze and another broken in half. The artillery only stopped when the Chola fleet was under the arc of their rocks and closing on the walls.

Most of the population of Kollchi seemed to be waiting to repel the attack, women as well as men, with archers firing non-stop and the rest throwing spears, stones and anything else they could find. Bradan saw a group of women emptying a cauldron of boiling oil onto the Chola warriors and another group throw pots and burning cloth on them.

That black-and-white mist was back, hovering a few feet from him, fluttering like a bird above the parapet. *What are you?*

The Cholas thrust ladders against the wall and clambered up, with Thiruzha archers picking them off in dozens while spearmen and swordsmen waited on the top. One brave Chola warrior reached the battlements, felling three of the defenders, before a female thrust a spear into his belly and slowly pushed him backwards. Other women joined in, until the man was balanced on the parapet, roaring defiance and spurting blood.

'Oh, there's a brave man,' Dhraji said. 'He would make an excellent slave if he could be tamed.' She smiled and licked her lips. 'What fun the taming would be!'

An archer fired at the Chola warrior, and then another. Under the impact of two arrows, he toppled slowly backwards, still slashing with his sword. His ladder followed a few seconds later.

Despite all the effort and bravery, the Chola attack ebbed back, with the defenders standing on top of the battlements to fire arrows and hurl missiles at the retreating warriors.

'Now!' Bhim rasped through his speaking-trumpet. Horns immediately blared out across Kollchi, their sound filling the air until the city gates crashed open. A squadron of horsemen poured from each gate, to harry the disorganised Chola warriors. The angle of the walls impaired Bradan's vision so he could not see details of the battle, only the Chola's surge back to the ships. He heard a rising cry of triumph from the ranks of the Thiruzhas and the defending archers fired non-stop. Chola warriors were falling fast, with a few dozen raising their hands in surrender as the Thiruzha horsemen slashed and stabbed and whooped in delight.

One by one, and then in a great clump, the Chola ships put back out to sea, with the Thiruzha horsemen riding into the shallows to hack and slash at them. Only a few desperate Chola warriors turned to fight. When the Cholas' spears struck down some of the horsemen, Bhim ordered his horns to sound again, recalling the cavalry.

Once again, the catapults and that massive bow fired on the Chola ships, turning their retreat into a panicked rout, which the defenders of Kollchi intensified as they surged from the gates. Attacked on all sides, the discipline of the Chola fleet completely broke.

The horns sounded again, three sharp blasts followed by one long one, and the Thiruzha seamen poured out of the city, passing the panting cavalrymen as they re-launched their ships.

'With the boom up, the Chola ships only have one channel to squeeze through,' Dhraji said. 'There won't be many going home. We'll harass them until dark, catch the stragglers and create so much panic that the Cholas will never return to this coast again.'

'There is still the Chola army advancing on the eastern frontier,' Bradan reminded her.

'I anticipated that it would take a week to defeat the Chola fleet.' Dhraji sounded smug. 'It has taken only two days.' Her smile wrapped around Bradan like the tentacles of the monster from the sea. 'We have time for other things, Bradan.'

* * *

When Bradan woke in the morning, Dhraji was gone. For the first time since his enslavement, he lay alone in the vast bed. Shadows striped the room as the moon glowed above the Ghats.

'Where's Her Majesty?' Bradan asked the guard who still lolled outside the room.

'She has gone on her own business.' Used to Bradan, the guard was offhand. She barely spared him a glance.

'Will she be back soon?'

'I do not inquire into the Rani's business.' The guard was older than most, perhaps thirty, Bradan estimated, with tiny crows' feet around her eyes and a small scar disfiguring her mouth.

'You've been in the palace for some time, haven't you?' Bradan asked.

'Yes.' The guard was not inclined to talk. Her scar writhed around her lips with every short phrase.

'You are fortunate, working for the Rani.' If the guard reported the conversation to the Rani, she might as well have something ingratiating to say.

'We all are, even you, her slave.' The guard regarded Bradan much as she would look at something unpleasant in which she had trodden. 'You've already lasted longer than most.' Her smile taunted him. 'I hope you don't expect to live much longer.'

'I'll live until it's my time to die,' Bradan said. 'Does the Rani often go wandering in the night? I can't remember her ever doing it before.'

'When she wishes to.' The guard scanned Bradan up and down and gave a scornful smile. 'She leaves her chamber when she tires of her current slave.'

'I'll go and look for her,' Bradan said. 'I don't like the thought of her wandering around alone in the dark.'

'You're a naïve sort of fool, aren't you?' The guard stepped aside. 'My job is to keep people from attacking the Rani, not to prevent lunatic slaves from getting killed.'

When he stepped away from Dhraji's chamber, Bradan felt as if shackles had been removed from his limbs. He took a deep breath and hurried down the carpeted corridor, found a flight of stairs and moved downwards as fast as he could. *Melcorka – I'm coming to see you.* Trying to remember the route from his previous visit, Bradan took a few wrong turnings, ended up in the kitchen where cooks were toiling in unbelievable heat and continued downward.

That black-and-white haze was back, forming in front of him as if trying to pass on a message.

'What are you?' Bradan asked. 'I know you're not unfriendly. Who are you? Are you trying to help?'

For a moment, the haze nearly formed into something tangible. Bradan saw a flash of orange amidst the black-and-white, before the shape faded away and he stood in a bleak chamber of bare stone walls.

'Hey! You!' Bradan accosted a passing servant. 'I have a message from the Rani. Which way are the dungeons?'

The servant goggled at Bradan. 'You're Dhraji's foreign slave. You shouldn't be here.' He started in sudden alarm and salaamed. 'Is the Rani with you?'

'I know what I am and no, she's not,' Bradan said. 'Which way are the dungeons?'

The servant indicated a plain wooden doorway. 'Through there and follow the steps.' Bradan could feel the servant watching as he opened the door. 'Get used to the dungeons,' the servant called out. 'The Rani's last two bed-slaves are still there, waiting for you!'

The atmosphere chilled immediately Bradan began the descent. Small torches spread faint light, sufficient to see the stairs and no more. Bradan followed the stairs, walking slowly and carefully on steps that were slippery with slime. He came to an arched wooden door, turned an iron handle and pushed; the door led to yet more stairs, descending down and down into a dark mist. Lifting the nearest torch, Bradan coughed and stepped on, cautiously, slowly, hearing his sandals rustling on damp straw.

'Who in Shiva's name are you?' The voice boomed from the surrounding dark as a bulky figure emerged from a semi-hidden door.

'Bradan the Wanderer.' Bradan lifted the torch so the jailer could see his face. 'Come to see the foreign woman.'

'Are you still alive?' The jailer sounded genuinely surprised. 'You've lasted a long time. I thought the Rani would have made you kiss the elephant's feet days ago.'

'I'm still alive,' Bradan said. 'Take me to the foreign woman.'

'You're too late,' the jailer said.

'Too late? What do you mean, too late?'

'She's dead.' The jailer spoke without emotion.

Chapter Nine

'Dead? Bradan stared at the jailer in disbelief. 'When? How?' He grabbed the wall for support as all the strength drained from his legs. *Melcorka can't be dead. She's too vital, too alive.*

The jailer grinned. 'In about two minutes' time. Do you want to watch?'

'You said she is dead,' Bradan said.

'In all but name.' The jailer nodded. 'Bhim sent the order just a few moments ago. "Kill the useless," Bhim said, "to make room for officer prisoners of war from the Chola Empire."'

Bradan tried a deep breath but the foul air caught in his throat, so he gagged and nearly threw up. He thought quickly. 'You just want the space, then?'

The jailer shrugged. 'Yes.'

'I'll take her away,' Bradan said. 'Give her to me.'

'The Raja gave an order. If I let her go, I'll be given to the elephants, or be food for the leopard, or go swimming with...'

'Go swimming with what?' Bradan asked. 'With that great monster that everybody denies seeing?'

The jailer looked away. 'I'm going to kill the foreign woman.'

Bradan pressed again. 'What is that great monster?'

'Don't be naïve. Now, get out of my way and let me do my job.' The jailer stepped back through the door and returned holding a heavy club. The length of a man's arm, it was studded with iron knobs and must have weighed fourteen pounds.

'Make it quick,' Bradan said. 'Please.'

The jailer sighed. 'I'll make it quick.' He hefted the club. 'I'll use this heavy one.'

'I want to make sure it is quick,' Bradan said.

'You can watch.' The jailer was magnanimous. 'Your own death won't be so quick when Dhraji gets rid of you. It never has been for her ex-lovers.' Unlocking the door to Melcorka's dungeon, he pushed in, with Bradan at his back.

Melcorka lay as Bradan had last seen her, filthy, stinking and vacant-eyed, chained to the far wall. She looked up when the jailer and Bradan entered.

'Hello, Mel.' Bradan spoke in the Tamil language so that the jailer could understand him. 'I've come to say goodbye.'

'One minute only.' The jailer lifted his club. 'I haven't got all day to waste on one blasted prisoner.'

Kneeling at Melcorka's side, Bradan held up the torch. Melcorka smiled up at him. Nobody's killing my Mel. For an instant, Bradan saw the shimmering black-and-white presence again, fluttering between Melcorka and the jailer, and then he thrust his torch hard into the jailer's face. 'You're not killing Melcorka!'

Letting out a high-pitched scream, the jailer clutched at his face. As the club fell to the floor, Bradan grabbed it, smashing it as hard as he could on the jailer's head. He hit again and again until the jailer lay prone with his skull smashed and his blood soaking into the filthy straw. Mice ran toward the body, fearless in this abode of suffering.

Melcorka watched with a look of wonderment in her eyes. 'Why did you do that?'

'Come on, Mel, I'm getting you out of here.' Circumstances had taken control. Bradan had not intended to kill the jailer and rescue Melcorka. He had intended making sure she was safe and later persuading Dhraji to release her.

'Where are we going?' Melcorka asked.

'I have no idea.' Bradan knew he had probably only extended Melcorka's life for a few moments, or at most a couple of hours, while forfeiting his own, for Dhraji and Bhim would both wish him dead now. Kneeling beside Melcorka, he examined her chains. He had hoped for a simple catch, but they were securely locked. Bradan cursed in frustration when a quick check of the jailer found nothing. *Where would the jailer keep his keys? Presumably in that chamber from where he obtained the club.*

'I'll be back in a minute, Mel,' Bradan promised, adding a foolish, 'don't go away' as he lifted his still-spluttering torch and ran into the dark.

Disorientated in the vast, echoing chambers, Bradan tried a few wrong doors before he saw the black-and-white shimmer hovering outside a familiar entrance and he arrived at the jailer's abode. Luckily, the door was open; he pushed in and stopped. He had expected a bare place of horror. Instead, he entered a room where tapestries decorated the walls, and a statue of Shiva stood on a small altar. A kitten purred on a silken cushion while a brass kettle sat in the corner. More important was the bunch of keys that hung from a hook beside a short whip and a bunch of aromatic flowers.

Grabbing the keys, Bradan ran back outside, with the torchlight pushing back the horrors of the darkness. Melcorka was sitting beside the body of the jailer, with the black-and-white shimmer a few yards away.

'The man's hurt,' Melcorka said. 'He was a nice man. He brought me food.'

'Let's get you out of here.' One by one, Bradan tried the keys until there was a sharp click and the shackles around Melcorka's ankles sprang open.

She giggled and lifted her legs in the air. 'Look!'

Bradan nodded. 'You'll feel strange with that weight off your ankles. It will take time to get used to it again.' He tried the same key with the lock around her wrists, swore softly when it did not fit and tried another, glancing over his shoulder at every sound. *I asked too many people where the dungeons were. Dhraji will have no difficulty tracing me.*

'Got it!' The key clicked in the lock and the manacles around Melcorka's wrists sprang open. 'Can you stand?'

Melcorka rubbed her wrists and ankles. 'Yes.' She swayed on her feet. 'I can't walk,' she said.

'I'll carry you.' After weeks of little food, Melcorka was as light and weak as a child. Bradan slipped her over his shoulder and stepped out of the dungeon. He heard the rattle of chains from the dungeons all around him, swore and placed Melcorka on the ground again. 'Don't run away,' he said. 'I won't be long.' The more prisoners that were loose, the more difficult it would be for Dhraji and Bhim to round them all up.

Lifting the keys, Bradan tried three before he found one to fit the nearest lock. The first prisoner within the dungeon cringed away when his door opened and stared in astonishment as Bradan unlocked his chains. The second man was a slight, dark-skinned youth with huge eyes and a body so thin that Bradan could count each one of his ribs.

'Thank you,' the youth said softly, rubbing at his ankles. Bradan saw the tracks of tears down his filthy face.

'Here,' Bradan threw him the key. 'Free the rest.' Returning to Melcorka, he balanced her over his left shoulder, lifted his now sadly depleted torch and hurried for the entrance.

'Wait!' The slender youth had already freed another man and passed on the key. 'Not that way!'

Bradan hesitated. 'Is there another way?'

'Yes, if you can swim. Can you swim?'

'I can swim.' Bradan glanced at Melcorka. 'Mel can't, in her condition.'

'Then you'll have to leave her,' the youth said.

'Never.' Bradan was aware of that shapeless black-and-white mass hovering at the periphery of his vision. 'I'll carry her, wherever it is.'

'She'll slow us down.' The youth's voice rose, as if in panic.

'Lead on,' Bradan said. 'Melcorka and I stay together.'

Glancing at Melcorka, the youth scurried in the opposite direction to the door. He hesitated at the heavily barred door to a cell that was apart from the others. 'We could free Dhraji,' he said.

Bradan stared at him. 'What do you mean, free her? She's the last person I want down here.'

'Dhraji is in there. We could free her. The woman, the *thing* taking her place, is not the real Dhraji.' The youth was babbling, looking all around in case Thiruzha guards flooded in to arrest him. 'She is a demon, a rakshasa, which has taken Dhraji's place. The real Dhraji is in there,' he indicated the door again. 'The rakshasas can only take somebody's shape and face as long as that person is alive.'

Bradan fought the rush of horror that threatened to overcome him. He had been living with a demon for weeks, a rakshasa, as these people called it. In a flash of insight, Bradan thought of the multi-armed monster that appeared when Dhraji had fallen into the water. Dhraji had vanished, the monster had appeared; the monster vanished and Dhraji reappeared.

Dear God! Was that monster Dhraji's real shape? There was something else: had Dhraji not said she would live forever? I had thought that mere vanity at the time. Now, I am not so sure. There's no time to think of that now. I'll worry about it later.

Stepping forward, Bradan tried the door. While all the other dungeons had only been bolted or had the key in the lock, this dungeon's door was securely locked, with two massive iron bolts across the front and three locks. 'Where is the key?'

The youth shook his head. 'I do not know. I thought the jailer might hold it, but none of these fit.' He held up the bunch that Bradan had handed him.

Bradan shook his head and came to a decision. 'My priority is in getting Melcorka away safely. I don't have the time to wrestle with doors. Take me away.'

'This way.' The youth led Bradan through the dungeons, ducked under a low stone arch and nearly slid down a sloping stone platform to a circular hole. Bradan heard the gurgle and roar of fast-moving water.

'This is where the jailer throws the dead, or those that the rakshasa no longer requires,' the youth said.

'Where does it lead?'

The youth shook his head. 'I don't know. Maybe it leads out to sea. As long as it is away from here, I don't care.' He looked up. 'We might drown.'

'We might,' Bradan agreed.

'I'll go first.' The youth jumped in without another word.

'This might get dangerous, Mel,' Bradan said. 'Take a deep breath.' He demonstrated by opening his mouth wide and drawing in air with as much noise as possible. Melcorka smiled and copied him, giggling like a two-year-old.

'Ready?' Bradan lifted her up, and, unable to stop himself, kissed her on the forehead. 'God go with us, Mel.' As he dropped into the river, he had another glimpse of that black-and-white shimmer.

The water was surprisingly warm. Bradan had no time to think, concentrating on gripping Melcorka tightly as the current whirled him away, plunging downward with the force of a waterfall. Melcorka struggled against him, trying to break free. Bradan held her close, hoping that they would reach air before Melcorka took deep draughts of water and they drowned here in the terrible darkness under Dhraji's dungeons.

Pain mounted in Bradan's chest. Fighting the desire to breathe, he slipped his hand across Melcorka's mouth as she struggled against him, her eyes wide with uncomprehending fear. She kicked and pushed, making small noises of panic, until suddenly, they exploded into fresh air and dawn's dim daylight, with the youth bobbing at their side and a gaggle of washerwomen staring at them. When Bradan slid his hand away from Melcorka's mouth, she dragged in a great mouthful of air, staring at him as if he were torturing her.

'Hurry!' The youth was not even out of breath. 'This way.' He jumped from the river and ran past the women. One woman gestured shyly at the naked youth, covering her mouth with a delicate hand. The others began to chatter, pointing to Bradan.

'They know you're a foreigner,' the youth shouted. 'Hurry! Run! They'll tell the Thiruzha soldiers.'

Glancing over his shoulder, Bradan saw the city walls a good quarter of a mile behind them. He wondered what the monster he knew as Dhraji would think when she found him gone, dismissed the thought and concentrated on following the youth, who seemed to be able to swim and run non-stop without drawing breath. They moved through dense woodland, jinking and dodging between the trunks of trees and leaping over increasingly tangled undergrowth.

'Where are we going?' Melcorka asked.

'I don't know.' Bradan held her as tightly as he could. 'Hold on to me.'

They ran for an hour and stopped beside a small stream. The youth picked some fruits from a tree, passed them to Bradan and smiled. 'What's your name?'

'I am Bradan the Wanderer, from Alba.' Bradan put Melcorka gently onto the ground. 'This is Melcorka of Alba.'

'I am Banduka,' the youth said. 'You are very pale-faced. Is it a disease?'

'In Alba, where we come from, everybody is this colour.'

The youth shook his head, evidently not believing Bradan's story.

'Where are you taking us?' Bradan asked.

'Not far now.' The youth stopped at the sound of a whistle.

'He is taking you nowhere.' A deep voice sounded from behind the trees as a man emerged. He held a bow, with the arrow pointed directly at Bradan's chest. Others followed, dark-skinned, broad-chested men with crude bows in their hands.

'I know you,' the deep-voiced man said. 'You were with the rakshasa called Dhraji.' He pulled back the string of his bow. 'You're going no further.'

'No!' Banduka stepped between Bradan and the arrow. 'He saved my life. He is running from the demon.'

'We should kill him,' the deep-voiced man said.

'No, Kosala! He is a friend!' Banduka said. 'He rescued the woman, killed the jailer and set me free.'

'He might be a Thiruzha spy.' Kosala moved sideways, keeping his arrow pointed towards Bradan.

'We can ask Chaturi,' Banduka said. 'She will know what is best to do.'

Much to Bradan's relief, Kosala finally lowered his arrow. 'We will do that. If she says to let him live, we will let him live. If she says to kill him, we will kill them both.'

'Melcorka is harmless,' Bradan said. 'She is sick in her mind just now. You cannot kill her.'

'Yes, I can.' Kosala looked more than capable of following up his words. 'Stay in front of me, Rakshasa-lover, and if I even suspect you are signalling to anybody else, or leaving a trail for the Thiruzha to follow, I will gut you and leave you to die in slow agony.'

'I will come with you,' Bradan knew he had no choice. Sometimes, he wished that he was a fighting man. It was getting a little tiresome, coping with threats from all these violent people.

Bradan counted twenty people in the group, most looking more like refugees than warriors. Kosala took charge, organising them into a central column with scouts out on the flanks, one man in front and another in the rear.

'I can walk,' Melcorka said.

Kosala placed himself two paces behind Bradan, growling threats every time Bradan slowed to support Melcorka over a rougher-than-normal section of ground. They walked steadily, covering the ground at a trot and barely making a sound as they threaded through the trees. Twice they stopped, while Kosala checked the track behind them as they continued deeper into the forest, gradually moving onto rising ground. Insects plagued them, while birds competed with monkeys to chatter and scream in the trees all around.

Bradan had lost count of the time when they eventually halted. They had travelled through the day and night and well into the next day, so the sun was halfway to its zenith. He was flagging through hunger and thirst, his muscles ached from supporting Melcorka, yet he knew that every step took them further from Kollchi and its memories. As Melcorka fell for the twentieth time and Kosala gave a warning snarl, Bradan lifted her bodily and draped her across his back.

'If she falls again,' Kosala said, 'I will slit her throat.'

'If you even touch her,' Bradan glared at him, 'I will kill you.'

'Up there.' Banduka pushed them apart and pointed to a steep, forest-covered hill.

Bradan nodded. All he could see was a tangle of trees and undergrowth. 'Is there a path?'

'Blindfold him,' Kosala said, and within seconds, somebody had slipped a cloth over Bradan's eyes. 'Now, walk!'

Stumbling in the sudden dark, Bradan felt somebody grab his arm and half pull, half guide him onto what was evidently a narrow and very steep track. He followed, with Melcorka staggering at his side.

'I could kill them now,' Kosala said.

'No. They are friends,' Banduka reminded him.

Bradan swore as he slipped and nearly fell. He struggled up an ever-steepening slope that seemed to last for hours and then eventually, with his heart hammering, his leg muscles on fire and his breath coming in short gasps, his guide stopped him.

'Here we are.' Banduka sounded cheerful.

Bradan blinked in the sudden light as his blindfold was removed.

He stood in the centre of a small village, with the houses built of mud and wood, roofed with palm leaves. A circle of dark-skinned, lithe, wary-looking people stared at him, with the men carrying short bows or swords and the women wearing colourful saris.

'Where am I?' Bradan blinked in the sunlight. A myriad flies buzzed around his head, while monkeys screeched from the bough of a tree.

'In a village.' Kosala fingered his sword. 'Chaturi will examine you.'

'Who is Chaturi?' Bradan looked around.

'I am.' The woman sat cross-legged on a small, three-legged stool in front of one of the huts. 'I hear they call you Bradan the Wanderer and you were the lover of the rakshasa Dhraji.'

'That's correct,' Bradan said.

'And your woman is Melcorka of Alba.'

'That is also correct,' Bradan nodded. 'Melcorka is not well inside her head just now.'

'I will speak to you first,' Chaturi said. 'Leave the woman here.'

'She needs water and food.' Bradan did not leave Melcorka's side. 'And she needs shade from the sun.'

Chaturi gave a small smile. 'Banduka will ensure she is comfortable. I give you my word that nobody will harm her unless I think you are a spy for the rakshasa.'

'Melcorka cannot be a spy.' Bradan jerked a thumb toward her. 'She's not at all well. She hardly knows her own name.'

Chaturi glanced at Melcorka and gestured to the hut behind her. 'Come in, Bradan the Wanderer.'

The interior of the hut was simple, with an earth floor and minimal furniture. Chaturi sat on a stool and handed another to Bradan. 'Sit opposite me. How did you get that scar on your head?'

'That was a war club in another country far away.' Bradan touched the scar as the memories slid back.

Chaturi nodded. 'How did you get to this country?'

'We have a small boat. There was an underwater explosion that caused a storm. The storm drove us off-course. We did not know where we were. We sailed north and ended up here.'

Chaturi asked questions and listened to the answers as Bradan gradually revealed details of the adventures he and Melcorka had endured.

'Tell me about Dhraji,' Chaturi asked. 'Tell me all you know about her.'

'She is the rani of the country, a powerful woman, cruel and cunning and very dangerous.' Bradan became aware that Chaturi's gaze seemed to bore right inside his head. 'Killing intrigues her. She finds it stimulating. Your friend Banduka told me that the Dhraji I knew was a demon, a rakshasa, in disguise.'

'You lasted longer than any of her previous lovers,' Chaturi said. 'People think you are the same as her.'

'I do not understand what you mean,' Bradan said. 'I am no rakshasa, and I do not kill for fun.'

'Look at me.' Chaturi put her finger under Bradan's chin and lifted his face. 'Let me inside your mind.'

About to protest, Bradan realised he was already too late. He could feel Chaturi's presence within his mind, probing his thoughts, exploring his memories of Dhraji, testing his motives and actions. He felt the sweat breaking out on his forehead as Chaturi investigated his most intimate memories. The sudden jerk as she left surprised him.

'You are very loyal to her,' Chaturi said.

'I was trying to keep alive, and keep Melcorka alive.' Bradan defended his actions. 'If I had allowed anybody to kill Dhraji, my life and Melcorka's would have been very short.'

'You misunderstand me.' Chaturi gave a small smile. 'I did not mean you were loyal to the false Dhraji. I meant you are very loyal to Melcorka.'

'We've been together for a long time,' Bradan said.

'It is more than that.' Chaturi's smile broadened. 'Come with me.'

The entire population of the village was waiting outside, with the men fingering their weapons and the women looking anxious.

'This man is no spy,' Chaturi said quietly. 'We can trust him.'

'Thank you.' Bradan breathed out slowly. He saw something like regret cross Kosala's face.

Chaturi nodded to Melcorka. 'Bring in the woman.'

'I'd like to be present while you examine her,' Bradan said.

'I know you would.' Chaturi smiled with her eyes. 'You may stay beside her, Bradan.'

'Where are we going?' Melcorka asked, as Bradan helped her to her feet.

'This lady is going to talk to you,' Bradan said. 'Just do as she tells you, Mel, and everything will be fine.' That black-and-white mass was back, drifting beside them as Chaturi led them back into her hut.

'Hello, Melcorka,' Chaturi said quietly, as she placed Melcorka opposite her. Bradan sat cross-legged in the corner, watching intently.

'Hello.' Melcorka smiled at Chaturi. 'Where am I?'

'You are somewhere safe.' Leaning forward, Chaturi touched Melcorka's forearm. 'You tell me where you are.'

Melcorka retained her smile and the dazed look in her eyes. The black-and-white cloud formed beside her. 'I am here,' she said.

'Do you know where *here is?*' Chaturi asked.

'Somewhere safe,' Melcorka said.

'I want you to help me,' Chaturi said. 'Could you do that?'

Melcorka nodded, as eager as a child. 'Yes, I can do that.'

'Thank you.' Taking hold of both Melcorka's hands, Chaturi stared into her eyes. 'I want you to let me inside your head. Is that all right?'

'That's all right,' Melcorka said.

'Look at me, please,' Chaturi said. 'Look into my eyes and don't look away.'

Bradan desperately wanted to help. He ached to get Melcorka back to herself again. He watched as Chaturi focussed on Melcorka while that black-and-white miasma drifted around them both. Chaturi's face altered as she concentrated, and there was a definite wince as she connected with Melcorka.

Oh please, dear God, help Melcorka. Whatever it takes, help Melcorka. Take my life and my mind if it restores Mel to herself.

The black-and-white miasma moved toward Bradan and returned to Melcorka, as Chaturi's face altered.

Bradan was not aware of the passage of time. He only knew that Chaturi was probing within Melcorka's mind. He saw the pupils of Chaturi's eyes dilate until there was no white left, and then shrink back to normal. The miasma remained, formless, hovering beside Melcorka. A bird called outside, the notes strangely elongated, as if time had slowed down.

Bradan again felt the jerk as Chaturi emerged from Melcorka's mind. Chaturi slumped, with perspiration sliding down her face and her eyes wild and unfocused.

After a few moments, Chaturi asked, 'Who did this to her?'

'Who did what?' Bradan already knew the answer. *The kanaima's curse.*

Chaturi touched Melcorka's head. 'Somebody has cursed this woman. Who put a curse on her?'

'There was a kanaima on the other side of the world,' Bradan said. 'Melcorka was herself before then, and has not been right ever since.'

'I've never heard of a kanaima,' Chaturi said. 'If you can find him, he might lift the curse.'

'She is dead,' Bradan said. 'Melcorka cut off her head before she could finish the curse.'

'That is a pity.' Chaturi sighed. 'Dead people cannot remove their curses.' She thought for a few moments, with her hand remaining on Melcorka's head. 'I saw blankness inside here, yet Melcorka is still there. She is inside, striving to get out, desperate to escape the prison of her mind, fighting to remove the swamp of unease and doubt and negativity of the curse.' Chaturi looked into Bradan's eyes. 'A curse of this strength would have killed most people. Melcorka is a very strong woman to survive.'

Bradan felt a surge of relief. 'Is there hope for her?'

'With this woman,' Chaturi nearly smiled, 'there will always be hope. Your Melcorka will not give up until she is dead, and I doubt she will give up even then.' She looked directly at Bradan. 'What did this kanaima say? What were the exact words of the curse?'

Bradan thought back to the battle on the island. 'She said: "I curse you. I curse you in your body and in your mind. I curse you in your possessions and your strength. I curse you in your travels and your weather. I curse you until the balance of the world is restored." She was going to say more but Melcorka cut off her head.'

'A pity your friend had not been a little faster. I suspect this kanaima was a black witch, which are evil things whatever name they go under. They can communicate with demons and do nothing but harm.' Chaturi sighed. 'But at least we know what we have to do to restore Melcorka to herself again.'

'What is that?'

'Why, what did the curse say? The kanaima cursed Melcorka in her body – well, you can see how weak she is – and the kanaima cursed her in her mind, which has evidently been altered. Melcorka now has the mind of a child. The kanaima cursed her in her possessions, now she has lost her sword, and the Thiruzhas have taken your ship.'

'That is all accurate,' Bradan said.

'The kanaima cursed her strength, and by the look of Melcorka she can barely stand upright. It cursed her travels; soon afterward, a storm drove you well off-course.' Chaturi sighed. 'Whatever that kanaima was, it had power; it was in touch with the demons of the underworld.' Chaturi lowered her voice. 'It may even have been a demon itself.'

Bradan nodded. 'How can I lift the curse?'

Chaturi sighed. 'It won't be easy. The kanaima said your friend was cursed until the balance of the world is restored. Are you sure that is what it said?'

'As far as I can remember,' Bradan said.

'All right then. If the balance is restored, then Melcorka will recover.'

Bradan held Melcorka as she swayed to one side. 'Is the world unbalanced? And if so, how can we restore it?'

Chaturi looked grave. 'Have you heard of the nine Siddhars?'

'I have not,' Bradan said. 'Educate me.'

'We do not have time to learn all about our religion,' Chaturi said. 'Perhaps I can tell you later, if you wish to learn.'

'I always wish to learn,' Bradan said.

Chaturi nodded. 'In that case, you are already a practitioner. Now, listen and I will say this simply. A Siddhar is a spiritual seeker who has attained his goal. There are Siddhars who practise Sadhana, a form of spiritual meditation to seek liberation on a higher plane than this earth.' Chaturi struggled to explain. 'In your western culture, the equivalent would be mystics or monks who seek solitude in desert places.'

Bradan nodded. 'We have men in Alba who live solitary lives on remote islands.'

'You understand the concept, then.' Chaturi said. 'Good. We have nine Siddhars who have reached the required highest level. These Siddhars control time and space by using yoga and meditation.'

'That's impressive.' Bradan held Melcorka as she slumped to the ground. He placed her in a more comfortable position. 'Please continue.'

'Siddhars are a bit like your Christian saints, but with the addition of being alchemists and doctors.' Chaturi smiled. 'Does that make sense to you?'

'It does,' Bradan said.

'Good. When all nine Siddhars are together in their mystic mountain...'

Bradan held up a hand. 'I'm lost now,' he said. 'Where is this mystic mountain, please?'

'It is called Sathuragiri, and it's in the Ghats,' Chaturi said. 'You know the Ghats?'

'I've seen them in the distance,' Bradan said. 'They run parallel to the western coast of Bharata Khanda, some miles inland.'

'That's right,' Chaturi approved. 'When all nine Siddhars are together on Sathuragiri, the world has balance. Good and evil counterbalance each other, men and women live their lives, and things are as they should be.'

Bradan glanced at Melcorka; he was not sure if she was listening. 'I see. Am I right in understanding that the world is not balanced at present?'

Chaturi indicated Melcorka. 'If the world were in balance, the curse would have had little or no effect on your friend there. The power of Melcorka's sword would have protected her.'

Bradan nodded. 'So why is the world not in balance?'

'The nine Siddhars are not on Sathuragiri.' Chaturi said. 'There are only seven on the mystic mountain. Until all nine are there, the power of evil will gradually take control, rakshasas will enter our world and eventually, we will live solely in evil and violence when people will either suffer or enjoy the suffering of others.'

Bradan stiffened. 'I have heard Kosala mentioning the rakshasas.'

'Kosala is a pragmatic warrior, not a man of deep thought, yet he understands the principle of good and evil. He recognises a demon for what it is.'

Bradan felt a cold shiver run from the base of his spine to the nape of his neck. 'These rakshasas, are they ugly creatures with many arms and a beak of a mouth?'

'That is one shape they can take.' Chaturi was not smiling. 'You already know the answer. I have been inside your head, remember?'

'I remember,' Bradan said.

'You saw it attack the Chola ship.' Chaturi spoke quietly. 'Did the Thiruzha remark on it?'

'No.' Bradan shook his head. 'They were too scared even to mention it. The sight of the monster... the demon... must have been too much for them.'

'They were too scared,' Chaturi agreed, 'and they were right to be afraid, for the demon lived among them. You knew it as Dhraji. That thing is a rakshasa, one of the more malignant demons.' She touched his arm. 'You already knew this.'

Bradan closed his eyes. 'Yes, I lived with a rakshasa.'

Chaturi nodded slowly. 'You lived with and loved with a rakshasa in human form and your friend there, Melcorka the Swordswoman, fought it when it took its demonic form.'

Bradan took a deep breath. 'How can we get the nine Siddhars back onto Sathuragiri?'

'Seven are already there,' Chaturi reminded him. 'Two are not. We know where the eighth is, but nobody can reach him, and the ninth is missing.'

'Where is the eighth? Nobody can reach him? By the love of God, I will reach him for Melcorka's sake.'

'The rakshasa you knew as Dhraji captured one of the Siddhars. His name is Machaendranathar,' Chaturi said. 'Dhraji suspended him in an iron cage from her border fortress of Rajgana.'

Rajgana! The armies of Chola and Thiruzha are marching to Rajgana. If we are to free this Machaendranathar, we will have to get there before the fighting starts.

'Can't we save him?'

'We hope to,' Chaturi said. 'My Singhalese people, the people who presently live in this village, are not warriors, although they carry swords and spears. Only Kosala is a genuine fighting man. The others are fishermen and divers. Your rakshasa, Dhraji, enslaved us to dive for her pearls.'

'Dhraji loves her pearls,' Bradan agreed.

'Some of the rakshasas do.' Chaturi frowned. 'They are a vain breed. My pearl-divers cannot fight the Thiruzha army. We need soldiers for that – warriors to face warriors.'

'You might have some soon,' Bradan said. 'Dhraji and Bhim spoke of a two-pronged Chola attack on Thiruzha. The Chola navy was defeated, but their army will be attacking Rajgana within the next few days. If they are successful, we can free this Machaendranathar fellow.'

'Rajgana is impregnable,' Chaturi said.

'Nowhere is impregnable,' Bradan said. 'Let's go to Rajgana and see if we can help. Your divers may not be the fiercest warriors in the world, but they seem a handy enough bunch to me, while Kosala would fit into anybody's army.'

Chaturi shook her head. 'If only it were that easy. Have you ever been to the Western Ghats? Have you seen the Rajgana frontier fortress?'

'I have seen fortresses before,' Bradan said. 'They can be assaulted, they can be undermined, or they can be stormed or starved into submission.'

'I admire your optimism.' Chaturi gave a sad smile. 'I hope you feel the same after you have seen Rajgana.'

Rajgana. For some reason, the name chilled Bradan, as if somebody had walked across his grave. 'I will carry Melcorka with us.' He lifted his chin, expecting Chaturi to object. 'I won't leave her alone.'

Instead, Chaturi smiled. 'We'll help.'

'Thank you,' Bradan said. 'Now, I have one more question. I have only seen Dhraji nervous on one occasion, and that was when she heard that a cavalry patrol was nearing the Rajgana Pass. I have been told that she is scared of one man.'

'That is so,' Chaturi said. 'Rakshasas should live forever, yet there is a legend that says that one warrior will kill Dhraji.'

'Who is this warrior?' Bradan asked.

'The legend says that he will be the greatest warrior there has ever been.' Chaturi said. 'That is all that I know.'

Bradan nodded. 'I hope he comes soon. Dhraji is a source of great evil.'

'No.' Chaturi's expression altered. 'The rakshasa we call Dhraji is not a source of great evil. It is the living personification of evil!' When she looked up, Bradan saw the dark shadows of fear in her eyes.

Chapter Ten

With Bradan and a smiling diver carrying the swinging litter that held Melcorka, the Singhalese left their hill-top camp for the Ghats. They travelled warily, alert for Thiruzha warriors as they jogged along a succession of narrow forest tracks, avoiding villages in case spies reported them to Dhraji. Twice, they passed crossroads decorated with the twisted bodies of men and women, executed in various hideous ways.

'Dhraji's work,' Chaturi said. 'These people are better off dead than under her power.'

Ignoring the colourful snakes and hordes of biting and crawling insects, the Singhalese made good progress. After two days, Kosala lifted a hand and signalled them to stop. He pointed ahead, unsmiling but evidently pleased.

'There,' Chaturi said. 'We are on the foothills of the Western Ghats.'

Close to, the mountains were even more impressive. Higher than any hills Bradan knew in Alba, they were also lusher, covered in dense vegetation that would provide a formidable barrier to any army.

'There is only one pass into Thiruzha that is suitable for an army,' Chaturi said. 'Even so, the troops would have to squeeze between two steep peaks, neither of which has ever been climbed, and which are only a stone's throw apart. A fort sits on top of a spur of each mountain, with a slender bridge connecting them. Each fort has a large garrison, and the whole defensive complex has the name Rajgana.'

'So if the Cholas take the forts, this Rajgana, they can enter Thiruzha,' Bradan said.

'Neither of the forts has ever been captured,' Chaturi said. 'You will see why in an hour. An attacker needs to capture both, for any one of them could make passage into Thiruzha impossible.'

They rested in a clearing partway up a steep ridge, with the Ghat range reaching as far as they could see, until it faded into the northern distance. Behind them, the forest tops spread to the distant blue haze of the sea.

'How large is this Bharata Khanda?' Bradan asked.

Chaturi shrugged. 'As far as one can travel and even then you will still not reach the end. To the far north, there is the sacred river Ganges and beyond that is the great Himalaya mountain range, that makes our little Ghats appear like pimples on a teenage girl's bottom.' Chaturi smiled. 'There is a mysterious kingdom in the Himalayas, and the lands of the Chin lie to the east of that. To the northwest are wild, terrible mountains and beyond that are vast steppes that extend to the birth of the wind.'

'Once Melcorka is herself again, we may visit these places.' Bradan said. 'Show me these fortresses of Rajgana.'

'Follow,' Chaturi said and strode on with a speed that belied her years. 'It's not far.' The others trailed in her wake.

Chaturi led them to a steep, wooded slope with extensive views to the east. 'This is as good a place as any. Any further and we might meet Thiruzha patrols.'

'We are sufficiently close,' Bradan said. 'That is indeed an impressive fortress.'

The pass rose steeply from the forested plains on the eastern side of the Ghat Mountains and threaded through a defile so narrow that only a single wagon, two packhorses or four men abreast could advance together. At some time in the distant past, an engineer had carved this path from the living rock. Later, or perhaps at the same time, an architect with a genius for the dramatic had designed the twin forts of Rajgana.

Bradan looked upward, following the sheer cliff on either side of the pass. In places, trees, creepers and other vegetation clung to cracks in the cliff; else-where, the rock seemed smooth as ice. Three hundred feet above the pass, the walls of the fortress looked like a vertical extension of the cliff. They were sheer, tall and impossible to scale, with a series of overhangs provided with a hundred dark holes through which objects could be dropped on anybody negotiating the pass.

An arched bridge connected the two halves of Rajgana Fort. Stone-built and perhaps sufficiently broad to hold two men walking side by side, the bridge was again pierced with holes and arrow slits, so that the defenders could drop unpleasant objects onto any force passing beneath. No army could force the pass without suffering horrendous casualties.

'Whoever controls Rajgana controls the pass,' Chaturi said.

'What is that?' Bradan pointed to an iron cage that slowly swung thirty feet beneath the bridge, at least three hundred feet above the pass. Even from this distance, Bradan could see somebody sitting within the cage.

'That is the prison where Dhraji holds Machaendranathar,' Chaturi said. 'As you see, the Siddhar has no shelter, no floor except iron bars and no way out.'

Bradan whistled. 'I see why nobody can free him.'

'Why is that man in a cage?' Melcorka waved her hand.

'He is a prisoner there,' Bradan told her.

'Why is he a prisoner there?' Melcorka waved again. 'He doesn't like it there. He wants to be free.'

'A bad woman put him there,' Bradan said.

'Can't somebody let him go?' Melcorka frowned. 'He's miserable. I can feel his sadness.'

'We're going to try and let him go,' Bradan said.

'Good.' Melcorka nodded. 'He's a good man.'

'You are right, Melcorka,' Chaturi said. 'He is a very good man.'

Bradan sighed, desperately wishing that Melcorka was herself again. 'How strong is the garrison of the fort?'

Kosala answered. 'We estimate that they have about two hundred and fifty men on each individual fort.' He held up a hand. 'Listen!'

The sound was clear; the regular tramp of marching feet accompanied by the heavier tread of animals. A trumpet blared, followed immediately by the blast of horns and the high squealing of elephants.

'There's an army approaching.' Bradan said. 'From the west. Thiruzhas.'

'Melt into the trees,' Kosala said. 'There are too few of us to face an army, especially with Rajgana so close.' When he fingered the hilt of his sword, Bradan knew the Singhalese warrior longed to throw himself into a fight with the Thiruzhas. Melcorka had that same look whenever she grasped Defender.

The Singhalese took cover in the forest, burrowing behind the trees and bushes until they had virtually vanished. The sound of marching increased;

small pebbles rattled on the ground and alarmed birds exploded from the trees. Monkeys shrieked and gibbered as they gathered in curious clusters in the topmost branches.

'There they are.' Kosala pointed to the west.

Dhraji had come in style. Perched in her howdah, she led an array of twenty war elephants with spikes around their legs, iron on their tusks and archers sitting on their backs. Behind the elephants rode troop after troop of cavalry, followed by five companies of archers and spearmen, fresh from their successful defence of Kollchi.

'That is a formidable force,' Bradan said.

'The Chola army will have to fight hard to force the pass.' Kosala's fist wrapped around the hilt of his sword. 'If only I had more men. With just fifty, I could create a diversion on this side of Rajgana.'

'You and Melcorka will get along famously,' Bradan said. 'Once she is better.'

Kosala looked at Melcorka who lay smiling at the monkeys, grunted and shook his head. 'A simpleton will not be any use in a battle.'

'She's no simpleton.' Bradan looked up at the Siddhar swinging in his cage and wondered how he could possibly get him free. As long as the Thiruzha held Rajgana, Machaendranathar was doomed to captivity. Everything depended on the skill of the Chola commander.

Bradan watched as Bhim made his dispositions. He set his spearmen in solid phalanxes along the road and among the woodland on either side, with blocks of archers positioned amongst them. He sent another company of archers to the Chola side of the pass, together with the bulk of his horsemen, presumably so they could skirmish with any Chola army or disrupt their advance.

The marchers' dust settled. The Thiruzha army settled in its positions, with some playing musical instruments, others singing or cooking. Flies clouded around while hunting birds circled above, waiting for the dead they sensed would come.

It was Kosala who first felt the approach of the Chola army. 'Here they come,' he said. 'It's two hours past noon, about four hours to sunset. That leaves time for a short battle.'

'Let's hope for a decisive Chola victory,' Bradan said.

'It's in Shiva's hands,' Chaturi said.

From the Singhalese position halfway up the hillside, Bradan could see both sides of the pass and the rolling cloud of dust that marked the advance of the Chola army. Bhim was equally alert and sent two squadrons of cavalry forward, the men yelling shrilly and waving swords and lances in their excitement.

'Shiva, grant success to the Chola,' Chaturi prayed.

'They're coming fast.' Kosala gripped his sword. A few moments later, they heard the cries and screams above the hammer of marching feet.

'They've made contact.' Bradan held Melcorka's hand.

'Now we wait and hope,' Chaturi said. 'If the Chola win, then we can rescue Machaendranathar and begin to restore some balance. If Bhim's Thiruzha win, then may Shiva and all the gods help us.'

'The Chola have halted,' Bradan said, as the trembling stopped and the dust created by thousands of marching feet settled down. As the air cleared, Bradan could see what was happening on the further side of the pass.

The Thiruzha cavalry returned, some wounded, and with a dozen empty saddles. They were laughing as if satisfied with a good job done.

'Oh, dear Lord.' Bradan gripped Melcorka's hand tighter.

The Chola had halted five hundred yards short of Rajgana. For every man that Bhim had, the Chola Empire had ten, with fifty war elephants standing in line amidst regiments of cavalry and infantry. The reflection of the sun on spear-points and swords, helmets and shields dazzled the watchers.

'What force can stand against so many?' Bradan asked. 'It makes the armies of Alba and the Norse seem puny in comparison.'

'Our hope is constant in Chola,' Chaturi said.

A horn blared out, and then another and another, echoing back and forth from the surrounding hills. War drums began their insistent rap-a-tap-tap, driving men to battle as flags fluttered and snapped above the dust and the helmets of thousands of warriors. In response, the defenders of Rajgana hoisted the yellow leopard of Thiruzha.

'The Cholas are advancing,' Bradan said.

'And Bhim's men are retreating.' Chaturi did not sound elated as the Thiruzha forward force withdrew through the narrows beside the fort.

The Chola general sent in his elephants first, massive battering rams to try and force the pass. They moved ponderously, great grey monsters with spiked trunks and steel-reinforced tusks, offensive weapons whose feet clumped down slowly, steadily, inexorably toward the western side of the pass. At first, nothing happened, and then the defenders of Rajgana began to fire. A torrent of arrows poured down from both forts, so the elephants soon resembled grey hedgehogs with the number of arrows that were embedded in their thick hides.

'It's not stopping them,' Kosala said. 'They're still coming on!'

The archers altered their targets, aiming at the howdahs from which the Chola warriors were firing back. Now the arrows whistled down on them, wiping out the archers and the mahouts on all three of the leading elephants in minutes. With the mahouts dead, there was nobody to guide the animals; they veered from side to side, slowing the advance.

Bhim shouted an order, the horns blared, and a company of infantry rushed out from the western side of the pass, thrusting long spears at the elephants. Trumpeting in pain and fear, the beasts reared up, with Thiruzha spear-points penetrating their mouths and the tender underside of their trunks.

'Bhim knows his stuff,' Bradan said.

The Chola commander proved he also had some military skill when he ordered his archers to scatter Bhim's spearmen, then sent his cavalry to destroy the fugitives. The Chola cavalry covered the withdrawal of their elephants as the remaining Thiruzha spearmen scurried back to their own side of the pass. Following his small advantage, the Chola commander ordered his spearmen to advance, with shields over their heads as protection against the arrows.

'They look like human tortoises.' Kosala was watching the battle closely.

'It's like a game of chess,' Bradan said, 'with human lives as pawns.' For one betraying moment, he was with Dhraji, smiling over the chess pieces as she displayed her splendid body. *Why do I still think of that creature?*

Bradan did not see from where the rock came. He only saw it land in the middle of the human tortoise. Another rock followed, and then another, scattering the men under the shields. Presented with this easy target, the Rajgana archers fired again, joined by others in hidden locations on the flanks of the hill.

'The Thiruzha have catapults, too,' Bradan said, as he saw the scores of Chola casualties left by the abortive attack.

Now they had started, the Rajgana defenders followed up with volleys of rocks that clattered and crashed onto the Chola army, forcing them to retreat out of range and leaving an elephant wounded and squealing on the road.

'First day to the Thiruzha,' Kosala said. 'Time is drawing on. The Chola won't wish to fight in the night.'

However, Kosala underestimated the determination of the Chola commander, who tried another advance under cover of darkness. Bradan heard hoarse shouts first and then the screams and yells of the wounded. The defenders dropped kegs of burning oil from the battlements onto the pass, where some exploded into pools of flame and others rolled and bounced toward the advancing Chola army. As the flames flickered upward, Bhim sent his cavalry forward to harass the Cholas, chopping at the infantry and clashing with the Chola horsemen.

'The Thiruzha are too outnumbered to chance losing men in pointless skirmishes like that,' Kosala said.

After a few moments, a horn sounded three urgent blasts, and the Thiruzha cavalry broke off the action and hurried back to the western side of the pass, with two squadrons of the Chola horse in hot pursuit.

'They're running!' Kosala said. 'The Thiruzha are on the run!'

'It's a trap,' Bradan told him. 'Bhim used similar tactics with his fleet.'

The Thiruzha cavalry streamed through the pass as if in panic, the sound of their hooves echoing from the high walls as they passed underneath the stone bridge. When the Chola horsemen followed, laughing as they thought they had broken the Thiruzha attack, Bhim sprang his ambush. As one phalanx of spearmen ran from the side of the fort to block the pass behind the Chola horsemen, two other companies formed in the Cholas' path, forcing them to rein-up or face hundreds of eighteen-foot-long spears.

The Chola horses screamed, pawing the air as the riders hauled on the reins, unsure which threat to face. Other riders were too slow and ran onto the spears, and then Bhim ordered his archers to fire. Flight after flight of arrows hissed into the trapped Chola cavalrymen, killing, maiming, and adding to their confusion. Within ten minutes, there was not a single Chola horseman left mounted. The ground was a mess of dead and wounded men and horses, lit by the oil barrels' flickering flames.

'Look!' Chaturi pointed. 'There's the rakshasa now.'

Bradan heard the Singhalese shuffling further away, as if fearing Dhraji could see them through the dark at half a mile's distance.

Despite himself, Bradan watched Dhraji as she walked among the dead and wounded, dipping her finger in the blood. In the oil-barrel's dying light, Dhraji looked even more sinister.

'She's a monster,' Chaturi said.

'She gets inside your head.' Bradan noted the well-remembered curve of breast and flank, hip and thigh. *Oh, dear God, why am I thinking like this?* He could not look away until the black-and-white miasma drifted across his line of sight.

What is that thing?

Bradan realised that Kosala had unsheathed his sword and had crept beside him. 'It's all right, Kosala, I have no intention of letting Dhraji know we are here.'

Perhaps it was a coincidence that just then, Dhraji, still licking the blood from her fingers, turned to face their direction. For one moment, the flickering firelight reflected from her face, and Bradan could swear he recognised the lust in her eyes. Even at that distance, he felt the menace that emanated from her.

'She is the most evil woman I have ever met.'

'She is the personification of evil,' Chaturi agreed. 'No mortal blade can kill her, no arrow can pierce her skin, no spear, axe or mace can hurt her. Only something immortal can destroy her, and until the balance of the world is restored, no force for good can come to our aid.'

Bradan looked up to where Machaendranathar hung in his iron cage hundreds of feet above the pass. Unless the Chola army succeeded in forcing a passage, there seemed no hope of rescuing the Siddhar. Melcorka would remain physically weak, with the mind of a child and no memory of the woman she once had been.

'May my God and your Shiva aid the Chola army,' Bradan said.

'The Cholas are attacking again,' Kosala had replaced his sword in its scabbard. 'All of them.'

Aware of this new threat, the garrison of Rajgana suspended oil lanterns from the walls, making the pass nearly as clear as daylight. No longer playing Bhim's game, the Chola general had sent forward his entire army. They advanced at speed, with the remaining cavalry in front and the elephants and infantry in the rear. Massed archers fired volley after volley ahead of the cavalry to clear a path.

'They mean business this time,' Chaturi said. 'The Chola general doesn't seem to be worried about taking casualties as long as he forces the pass.'

Bradan agreed, as he watched the Chola army advance straight into the Thiruzha barrage. Arrows, spears and rocks poured down, felling men by the score. Still they pressed on, stepping over the bodies of the dead, leaving the wounded to lie.

'They might make it...' Bradan heard the hope in his voice.

'Let it please Shiva that they do,' Chaturi prayed. 'And may Shiva protect the Siddhar from a stray arrow.'

'What's that?' Kosala lifted a hand. 'I heard something.'

The sound started as a faint rumble and increased to a growling that echoed from the rocky slopes. Bradan looked up as a slot opened in the solid cliff underneath the fortress. Scores of Thiruzha soldiers slowly rolled a fifteen-foot-high iron fence across the pass.

'It's on wheels.' Bradan could hardly believe what he saw. 'It's a barrier on iron wheels.'

'Nothing will get past that.' Kosala sounded sick. 'I've never seen anything like that before.'

'Neither have I,' Bradan said.

Ignoring casualties, the leading squadrons of Chola horse pressed on, to erupt on the Thiruzha side of the pass a few seconds before the barrier closed. Wheeling, one squadron attacked the Thiruzha soldiers who pushed the mobile fence.

'There are not enough of them,' Kosala said. 'They are doomed.'

A sudden hot wind sent the oil lanterns dancing along Rajgana's walls and bounced surreal shadows on the ground. As the wind strengthened, it blew out most of the lights, plunging the pass into darkness. The battle halted except for arrows flying in both directions. The Thiruzha horn sounded again, long and low, and one by one, the lanterns were replaced. As the light strengthened again around Rajgana, details of the battle became apparent.

The detachment of Chola cavalry that had passed the gate milled in confusion as they realised that they were trapped between the iron fence and the entire Thiruzha army. With the light restored, the Thiruzha arrow hail increased, humming and whistling toward the couple of hundred Chola horsemen. A Chola captain trumpeter blew a series of short blasts and the cavalry formed into an arrowhead and charged toward the Thiruzha army. Sitting on his elephant, Bhim ordered his spearmen into a solid, spiked hedge.

Rather than a battle, it was a massacre as the cavalry ran into the spears, with the Thiruzha archers sending a non-stop stream of arrows toward the rear of the Chola force. It was over in five bloody minutes, leaving the ground littered with Chola dead.

All the time, the defenders of Rajgana Fort had been busily firing at the Chola host, with catapults, rocks, spears and arrows whistling down on the confused and largely impotent force that had seemed so formidable only the previous day. Some Chola warriors had advanced as far as the iron barrier, only to die in frustrated fury as the defenders fired arrows and dropped rocks on top of them. A few ragged survivors limped back.

The Thiruzha horn sounded again, five short blasts and a long drone. The defenders dragged back the metal gate and the Thiruzha army surged through, cavalry in front, followed by the elephants and the infantry.

'I've never seen a battle on this scale,' Kosala said.

Bradan said nothing as the Thiruzha cavalry charged straight into the disorganised Chola and sent them reeling back.

'We've lost the battle.' Kosala shook his head. 'Oh, Shiva! I wish I could help.'

'One sword would not make much difference in a battle of thousands,' Chaturi said.

Bradan thought of Melcorka and said nothing.

The horn sounded again, five long blasts, and the tail end of the Thiruzha army filed under the stone bridge and through the pass to the east. Last of all was the war elephant of Dhraji, deliberately stepping on the Chola wounded.

'Look,' Banduka said. 'Rajgana's gates are opening. The garrison is joining the pursuit.'

Bradan had expected the garrison to march down a path from one of the towers. Instead, a door opened beside the metal gate. Hundreds of men filed out, to trot towards the east in pursuit of the retreating mob that had once been the Chola army.

'Dhraji and Bhim must be confident of victory,' Chaturi said. 'They've stripped every last man from Rajgana.'

Every last man! Rajgana is nearly empty. 'They've given us a chance,' Bradan said quickly.

'A chance for what?' Banduka asked.

'Our chance to rescue that poor fellow there.' Bradan gestured upward, to where Machaendranathar swung in his iron cage. Bradan's mood lightened with this first stroke of good fortune for days. 'With most of the garrison gone, I can slip into the fort and get him out. There must be a way into his cage from above; how else will the garrison feed him?'

'You can't go in there,' Banduka said. 'You've just escaped from Dhraji. You can't go back into her den.'

Bradan glanced at Melcorka, lying supine and vacant-eyed on her litter. 'I have to,' he said.

'I know you do.' Chaturi touched his arm.

'I'll come with you,' Banduka said.

'No.' Kosala shook his head. 'I will. The pale foreigner might need a sword to guard his back.' He touched his sword hilt. 'Or he may be planning to betray us, in which case he will need a sword in his back!'

'He is no traitor,' Chaturi said. 'Move fast in case the rakshasa's men come back, and keep out of trouble.'

'Come on then, Kosala.' Bradan hesitated, looking at Melcorka.

'I'll look after her,' Chaturi said. 'Whatever happens to you.'

'Thank you, Chaturi.'

Glad to be doing something positive, Bradan negotiated the wooded slope with Kosala at his back and the night already beginning to fade. A slanting overhang half-hid the door in the rock, which the garrison had left unlocked.

'That was fortuitous,' Bradan said.

'Or one of Bhim's traps,' Kosala drew his sword. 'I'll go first, Bradan, in case there is a sentry.'

The door opened onto a flight of stairs that spiralled up inside the rock wall of the cliff. Without lighting to show the way, Kosala moved up slowly, testing each step, keeping his sword ready as Bradan followed, biting back his impatience. Within a few minutes, Bradan felt dizzy with the constant spiralling.

'Wait.' Kosala put out a hand.

Footsteps echoed from above. Bradan felt his heart racing. His mouth dried.

A Thiruzha warrior ran down toward them, buckling on a sword belt and trying to adjust the round shield he carried on his back. He stopped when he realised that Kosala blocked his passage.

'Who are you?'

In reply, Kosala slid his sword in the man's belly and sliced upwards. The man died without a sound, falling onto the steps.

'That's one less.' Kosala cleaned his sword on the dead man's turban.

They moved on, silent in the dark, upwards and ever upwards. Twice, they stopped when they heard movement above, and each time Bradan held his breath. He was a man of the open spaces, not a thief to work in such confinement. Then he thought of Melcorka, lying with a vacant smile on her face and the mind of a child. *I must press on. I must do my best.*

After an eternity of climbing, the stairs ended at a heavy wooden door, studded with iron. Kosala placed a hand on Bradan's shoulder to stop him, pushed the door gently and eased in.

'Who's that?' Bradan heard the question, followed by a strangled gasp.

'Only one guard,' Kosala reported, wiping the blood from his sword.

'I'm glad you're here,' Bradan said.

'Follow me.'

They entered what was evidently a guard room, an austere stone chamber with nearly empty weapons-racks on the wall. Lifting a long, slightly curved knife, Bradan thrust it through his waistband. He did not wish to use it but knew that if he needed a weapon, he would need it desperately. Again, he steeled himself with the image of Melcorka lying helpless as a baby.

Kosala opened the door in the opposite wall, and they stepped into another long room. Faint light seeped through eastward-facing arrow slits, revealing that dawn was already greying the eastern sky. Within half an hour, full daylight would make their position in the fort even more precarious.

'Hurry,' Kosala said.

They hurried, with Kosala disposing of another Thiruzha soldier on the way.

'Bhim has emptied the fortress of everybody except the sick and the menials,' Kosala said. 'None of the men we've met have been top quality warriors. Bhim must be supremely confident of victory.'

Bradan peered out of an arrow-slit as the rapidly rising sun glossed the sky brilliant red. 'I think he is right to be confident. I can't see a single living Chola soldier.'

Dead bodies covered the pass to the east. Men and horses lay singly or in small mounds, with grey heaps showing where the Chola elephants had also died. There was no sign of either army.

'We have to find that bridge,' Bradan said. 'We must release Machaendranathar.'

'Hey!' The voice was strong and authoritarian. 'Who are you? Why are you not fighting the Chola?'

The man was tall, broad and carried a long, wavy-bladed sword in a manner that suggested he knew how to use it.

Thinking quickly, Bradan faked a cough, hoping to be taken for a sick man.

'That won't fool me,' the tall man said. 'You were talking normally a minute ago, the two of you. Come here!'

'No,' Kosala said. 'You come here.'

'What?' The tall man stared at him from under a pointed steel helmet. 'Do you know who I am?'

'No,' Kosala said. 'But I know *what* you are. You're a fat, bullying pig. You're a ranting coward that sends others out to fight, while you strut around waggling your fat arse and trying to look important, you useless lump of stinking lard.'

The man strode forward. 'I'll have you flogged!' he roared. 'By Shiva, I'll have you thrown over the cliff, flayed alive and hanged by the heels.'

'Well, which will it be? Make your mind up before you give birth, you waddling barrel of fat.' Kosala leaned against the wall. 'Which death is it to be?'

'Give me your name!' The broad man increased his speed.

'I am Kosala.'

'I am Bradan from Alba.' Bradan slipped a foot between the angry man's heels, making him stagger.

Kosala stepped aside, grabbed the man's head and cracked it hard against the wall. 'These Thiruzha are so overconfident, they are easy to fool.'

Bradan nodded. 'Dhraji was the same,' he said. 'She believed all my flattery. Vanity seems to be their downfall.'

'Now...' Kosala relieved the guard of his sword, 'let's find out where the bridge is.' He pricked the man on the side of the neck. 'A minute ago you threatened me. Now, I am the man with the power. Tell me how to cross to the fort on the other side of the pass or I will cut you up very slowly.' He twisted the blade until it was just under the surface of the skin and slid it downward, avoiding any vital spots. 'This could take all day.'

'Why do you want to go there?' Sweat slithered down the guard's face.

'Dhraji ordered us to,' Bradan said.

'You don't know Dhraji,' the guard blustered.

'I do indeed,' Bradan said. 'From the top of her head to that interesting little mark she has on her left buttock. You must know the one? It's shaped like a fish.'

'Of course I know it. You go through that way.' The guard's eyes swivelled left. 'And it's the second door.'

'Thank you,' Kosala said.

'Why did you not just ask?' Blood flowed from the guard's neck.

'This way is more interesting,' Kosala said and thrust in his blade. The guard died with hardly a sound. 'Bradan, does Dhraji really have a mark like a fish on her arse?'

'No.' Bradan shook his head. 'I was playing on the vanity of these people, as we said.'

'It worked,' Kosala said. 'Through here.' He searched the guard and swore softly. 'I hoped he might have the key to Machaendranathar's cage with him.'

The passageway led to yet more stairs, narrow, with arrow-slits providing the only illumination. As the large man had said, the second door opened onto the bridge.

Built of stone and with a vaulted roof, the bridge crossed the path in a high arch, with light shafting through from a score of arrow-slits. Cavities in the wall held spears, bows and quivers of arrows, while there were three iron ring bolts in the floor, one a few paces from each end and a much larger one in the centre.

'Machaendranathar must be beneath here.' Kosala hurried to the central ring-bolt. 'There is a single slab here, but it's heavy, Bradan. I need your help!'

Even working together, they could hardly budge the central slab. They turned the ring bolt and heaved, with the slab moving about a finger's width from the floor and slamming back down as their strength failed.

'There must be a knack to this,' Kosala said. 'I'm as strong as any man, and you're no weakling.'

'We'll have to lift it and wedge it open with something,' Bradan looked around the covered bridge. 'We'll have to hurry. Bhim's army could return at any time.'

'We'll try this!' Grabbing a spear, Kosala hurried back to the slab. 'Now, on the count of three. One, two, three!' Again they managed to lift the slab a crack before Kosala thrust the spear butt into the small opening. 'Now rest and gather your strength.'

Bradan nodded and relaxed his grip. Immediately he did, the slab slammed back into place, snapping the spear-butt as if it had been a twig. 'That didn't work. There must be another way.'

'Two spears?' Kosala asked. 'No...'

'The other slabs are smaller,' Bradan said. 'If we can lift one of them, we might use it as a wedge.'

It took them only a minute to lift the much smaller slab nearest the north-ernmost tower and carry it back.

'Lift!' Kosala said, and for the third time they hauled the central slab up. 'I'll hold it.' Kosala's muscles trembled with the strain. 'Hurry!'

Bradan scraped the smaller slab into place. 'There!'

Kosala relaxed. They looked at each other, sweat dripping from their faces.

'If we twist the smaller slab onto its side,' Bradan suggested, 'it will force the larger one higher, and then we can maybe push it all the way up.'

Twisting the smaller slab was easier than expected, and gradually they cre-ated a sufficiently wide gap for them to grab the central slab and scrape it free. The gaping hole revealed the dizzying drop beneath.

'Maybe you're not a spy for Dhraji!' Kosala was gasping with effort.

They looked down on the iron cage that swung slowly back and forth. 'How do we get down there?' Bradan asked.

The cage was a good thirty feet below them, suspended by a single chain attached to the underside of the bridge by an arm-thick staple. As it rubbed against the staple, the chain creaked ominously, with fragments of rust falling every few seconds. Sitting cross-legged inside the cage, Machaendranathar looked up, his eyes quiet above a long beard. 'You don't get down,' he said. 'The other guards lower food and water by a rope. There is no other way.'

'How did you get in?' Bradan asked.

'They put me in when the cage was on the bridge,' Machaendranathar said. 'Twenty men and the rakshasa that pretends to be Dhraji lowered me down.' He sounded as calm as if he were sitting under a tree in the centre of a village.

'We're going to try and rescue you,' Kosala said.

'I know.' Machaendranathar did not move.

'Do they ever let you out?' Kosala asked.

'No. This is where I am.' Machaendranathar continued to sit cross-legged on the bars that made up the floor of his cage.

'Hello, man in the cage!'

129

Even Machaendranathar seemed surprised as the female voice interrupted them.

'Who said that?' Kosala spun around with his sword ready. There was nobody else on the bridge.

'I said that.' Melcorka climbed on top of the cage and sat there, smiling, as it swayed hundreds of feet above the ground.

'Mel! How did you get here?' Bradan stared at her.

'I climbed.' Melcorka sounded surprised at the question. 'How else could I get up? I can't fly like the birds. I climbed up the cliff and hand-walked along the underside of the bridge.'

Bradan looked down the vertical cliff with its meagre patches of vegetation and stretches of ice-smooth rock. He remembered that Melcorka had grown up on a small Hebridean island where much of the diet comprised birds' eggs retrieved from the cliffs. 'You have to be careful, Mel!' Bradan tried to still the hammering of his heart.

'It's fun,' Melcorka said and proved it by pushing with her feet, so the cage swung harder. 'Do you want out, man?'

'I do,' Machaendranathar said. 'And so do you, I believe. You want to be released from the cage that is trapping your mind.' He looked at Bradan. 'I see you know this young woman.'

'That is Melcorka from Alba.' Bradan made quick introductions. 'A witch or a demon cursed her to lose her strength and her mind.'

'I thought as much.' Machaendranathar remained calm.

'Where is the door to your cage?' Melcorka asked.

'There is no door,' Machaendranathar said. 'The whole bottom swings open. One day they will open it and allow me to drop.'

'If I open it, you will be free,' Melcorka said.

'If you open it, young woman, I will fall to the ground.'

'Not if I catch you,' Melcorka said.

'You haven't the strength,' Machaendranathar said.

'Bradan has.' Melcorka looked upward. 'Bradan carried me for miles.'

Bradan glanced at the fearful drop to the ground and looked away quickly. 'I can't come down there. I am dizzy even looking down.'

'Yes you can, silly.' Melcorka hung over the edge, balancing with one hand. 'See? It's safe unless you let go.'

'It has to be you, Bradan,' Kosala said. 'I am not built for climbing, and the woman doesn't have the strength. Hurry, before the garrison return.'

If he did not free Machaendranathar, Bradan reasoned, the nine Siddhars would never be together and the world could not be balanced, which meant that Melcorka would be cursed forever. He had to try.

Oh, dear God, give me strength.

Taking a deep breath, Bradan gathered his nerve and swung over the gap. Taking hold of the chain, he lowered himself cautiously down, one link at a time. The wind grabbed at him, pushing him this way and that until his feet made contact with the iron bars of the cage roof and he slowly released his breath. He felt sick. *Don't look down. Don't let go. Think of Melcorka.*

'I told you it was easy.' Melcorka leaned back, still holding on with one hand. Grinning, she changed hands. 'Now, you have to come down here so that when I open the bottom, the man doesn't fall out.'

Bradan nodded, breathing hard. 'You may be cursed, Mel, but you've kept some of your brains and all of your nerve.'

Machaendranathar grunted. 'A demon's curse should have reduced her to a baby, or worse. Something inside that woman is fighting back. She is right. You will have to help me.'

Oh Lord, give me strength and balance, Bradan prayed, as he inched to the end of the cage and slid his feet over the side. Melcorka grinned at him, flicked back her dark hair and rattled the cage.

'Come on, Bradan! It's easy!'

'I'm coming.' Bradan manoeuvred himself beside Melcorka, clinging to the lowest horizontal strut of the cage with his feet, while clinging to the vertical bars with both hands. He felt the drop sucking at him, inviting him to release his hold and fall down and down forever.

''You'll have to release one hand to help me,' Machaendranathar said.

This is worse than fighting the Kalingo.

'I can do that.' Bradan forced a death's-head grin as the immense drop beneath him appalled and fascinated him in turn. Gripping tightly with his right hand, he forced his left to open. 'All right, what's next?'

Grinning, Melcorka slipped free the simple bolt that secured the bottom of the cage and laughed when it crashed open. The sound echoed from the cliff walls, bouncing back and forth before it slowly decreased. The cage swung back and forth, forcing Bradan to cling on with both hands once more.

'Shiva! The garrison can't miss that racket,' Kosala said. 'Hurry, Bradan!'

Clinging to the sidebars of his cage, Machaendranathar moved toward Bradan. 'I may be an aesthete,' the Siddhar said, 'but I place too much value on this life to throw it away.' He extended a slender hand, which Bradan gripped.

'Out you come, man.' Melcorka ignored the terrifying abyss. 'Then we'll climb up the chain or down the cliff.'

Machaendranathar's hand tightened on Bradan's as he manoeuvred himself from the cage and slowly began to climb up the bars to the roof. Refusing to look down, Bradan licked dry lips and pushed from below until they reached the top of the cage. Large pieces of rust flaked from the chain, which creaked alarmingly under the increased weight.

Kosala's voice was strained. 'Hurry! I can hear people moving!' Drawing his sword, he glanced right and left along the interior of the bridge.

Melcorka swarmed up to the bridge without hesitation. 'Come on! It's easy.' She poked her head through the gap, grinning.

Pushing Machaendranathar in front, Bradan hauled himself up the rusty chain, swearing in a constant monotone that helped relieve his feelings, while not aiding his climbing ability in the slightest.

'Come on! Come on!' Kosala urged, leaning forward with his hand extended. 'Somebody's coming. Shiva! It's an archer! Shiva help us!'

The first arrow whined past Bradan's ears, clattered against the chain and ricocheted away. The second pinged between two links and stuck there, with the feathers of the flight vibrating. Blaspheming, Bradan shoved Machaendranathar up the final few inches, where Kosala hauled him up bodily as a third arrow bounced from the ceiling of the bridge.

'Come on, Bradan! Run!' Kosala unceremoniously pushed Machaendranathar in front as he raced along the bridge. Bradan pulled himself out of the hole, gasping for breath. The archer had dropped an arrow but half a dozen men were running toward him, swords raised and yelling loudly.

'Run! Run!' Melcorka had caught Kosala's agitation.

Lifting a spear from a rack on the wall, Bradan threw it toward the advancing Thiruzhas, turned and fled along the bridge. He heard the twang of a bow and ducked as an arrow hissed well past him.

'We're lucky that these are the Thiruzhas' worst warriors,' Kosala gasped. 'If the best ones had not pursued the Cholas, they'd have killed us long ago.'

With his legs still shaking, Bradan could only nod as they plunged through the door. He looked for a bolt to lock it, swore when he saw none and ran again, to see Kosala propelling Machaendranathar through a wooden door while Melcorka laughed.

'Men chasing us,' she said.

'Come on, Mel!' Scooping Melcorka up, Bradan nearly threw her in front of him. 'Run! They're bad men, Mel, run!'

'Bad men,' Melcorka repeated. 'They're bad men!'

Going down the stairs was even worse than coming up, with Machaendranathar stiff and slow after his months in the cage and Melcorka looking over her shoulder every few seconds. Bradan heard the door at the top of the stairs crash open, followed by the raised voices of their pursuers. A spear clattered down the steps. Picking it up, Bradan wedged it in a crack on the stonework with the tip pointing upward. With luck, that may slow his pursuers down a fraction. With great luck, one of the pursuers might run into it.

'Come on, Bradan!' Kosala roared.

'Bad men!' Melcorka reminded him.

An arrow whistled down, and another, but the nature of the circular staircase made such weapons virtually useless. The Thiruzha pursuers had to catch them. Bradan heard the unmistakable sound of a man falling and nearly smiled.

'Keep going,' Kosala ordered. 'It's not far now.'

Voices echoed behind them, hollow in the staircase. They ran, sliding on the worn steps, gasping for breath, swearing, keeping together. Melcorka began to giggle hysterically until Bradan reminded her that there were bad men behind them.

'Don't waste breath,' Kosala said. 'Run!'

After an interminable downstairs run, they barged open the final door and emerged into the pass, to be greeted by a volley of arrows from the fort and the bridge high above.

Kosala jumped back into the shelter of the overhang. 'Shiva! We're trapped!'

'We can't stay here.' Bradan held Melcorka close to him. 'They're close behind us. We must run.' Lifting a shield from one of the many dead Chola warriors that littered the pass, he passed it to Melcorka. 'Everybody, grab a shield.'

They did so, nervously, shaking with reaction, cursing as arrows hissed and bounced around them. Bradan took a deep breath. 'Hold the shield above your head, Mel, and when I say so, run. Run as if the devil himself was after you, and don't stop until you reach that tree there.' He indicated a taller than usual palm that marked the edge of the pass. 'Don't run straight, jink from side to side. Don't stop for anybody or anything. Do you understand?'

Melcorka nodded. 'Run and jink and don't stop.'

'On the count of three, we run out,' Bradan said. 'Don't keep together. A group is an easier target than an individual. Are you ready?'

Only after they nodded, one by one, did Bradan slowly count: 'One, two, three!'

They exploded from the overhang. Bradan had expected the arrows. He had forgotten about the other missiles and swore as a large rock smashed down a few yards from him, disintegrating in a mass of splinters. Something sliced into his thigh and he gasped, hopped and continued, fighting the pain.

'Run, Melcorka! For God's own sake, run!'

He heard Melcorka giggle, saw Kosala help Machaendranathar over a rough stretch of ground, and then he was at the trees with his left leg throbbing and the breath rasping in his throat. Melcorka was right beside him, holding her shield with both hands.

Chaturi was there to greet him. 'Hurry,' she said. 'The demon's army is returning!'

Chapter Eleven

'I can't run another step,' Bradan gasped.

'You'll have to,' Chaturi said. 'Now that we've freed Machaendranathar, the rakshasa Dhraji will never rest until she kills or captures him and us. We have to flee quickly.'

Two Singhalese produced a litter, placed Machaendranathar on it and trotted away in that ground-covering pace that made light of obstacles and distance. Banduka gave Bradan a wide grin and joined the others.

'We did well.' Kosala checked the edge of his sword. 'I wondered about you, Bradan.' He nodded. 'Maybe I was wrong.'

'Are you coming?' Bradan asked.

'I'll go last.'

'As you wish.' Bradan said and moved on. Melcorka ran at his side for the first few hundred yards before she staggered. Bradan caught her, wincing in pain.

'You're bleeding.' Chaturi glanced at Bradan's leg.

'It's nothing,' Bradan said.

'Perhaps. Don't let it slow you down.' Chaturi shouted for two of her men, who bundled Melcorka onto another makeshift litter and trotted on.

They pushed on along a winding forest track, with birds squawking around them and insects clouding at their faces. Monkeys watched curiously and once, a small herd of deer bounded in front of the column.

'Watch out for snakes,' Chaturi said. 'There are a lot around here.'

'Dhraji can call them up.' Machaendranathar spoke quietly from his litter. 'Where are you headed?'

'Anywhere,' Chaturi said. 'We're headed anywhere away from the Thiruzha.'

'Permit me to guide you,' Machaendranathar said. 'Open your minds. All of you – open your minds.'

'How do I do that?' Bradan asked, and felt the jolt as Machaendranathar entered his head. Unsure what to expect, he saw a map of the country spread out before him, with a clearly marked paththat led through the maze of forests to a narrow pass over the Ghats. The Chola Empire waited in the east.

'Follow the path,' Machaendranathar ordered. 'Don't think – let your mind guide you.'

The forest paths straightened as Bradan followed his feet, with the Singhalese moving without a sound. When Melcorka slipped clear of her litter and walked beside him, it seemed natural to hold her hand, although whether it was as a child or a woman, Bradan did not know. Nor did he know how long that journey lasted. It seemed natural to walk and keep walking as if in a dream, with one footstep following the next and the trees a blur around him and Melcorka at his side. Time did not matter; weariness was accepted; the pain in his thigh was as much a part of his life as the clouding of insects and the green-hazed light though which they passed.

The forest path rose beneath them as they weaved through the foothills of the Ghats, but this time, the pass was too narrow and steep for any army, and there was no fort to avoid. Birds of prey screamed and circled overhead and twice, Bradan saw that shapeless black-and-white mass hovering between him and Melcorka before dissolving into nothingness.

The pass rose higher until it seemed they could touch the sky, levelled out and descended in a dizzying zig-zag towards a vast forested plain, smeared with the smoke from a hundred village fires.

Welcome to the Chola Empire. The words came to Bradan's mind. With his invisible guide in control of his feet, he had no need to worry about direction or time. Step, step, and keep walking until they saw the mystical mountain.

Sathuragiri. Again, the word formed itself as everybody stopped to stare ahead. The mystical mountain rose four-square from a bed of mist, with waterfalls and clear streams easing down its flanks. Sathuragiri: the name eased itself across Bradan's mind, like balm soothing his worries. When he pulled Melcorka closer, she came willingly.

'We can rest here, safe from Dhraji,' Machaendranathar said.

An aura of peace descended on Bradan as Machaendranathar led them to a small temple set beside a bubbling spring. Birds called all around, and monkeys chattered and played without any fear, watching these newcomers through inquisitive eyes.

'We will eat.' Machaendranathar clapped his hands.

Bradan did not see where the food appeared from. He only knew it was delicious and that he was hungry. He ate with relish, wondering at this new sensation of total tranquillity.

'This place is holy,' Bradan said.

'It has been holy in the past, it will be holy again in the future,' Machaendranathar said. 'At present, it is incomplete. The rakshasas have damaged us.'

'It is a place of great wisdom and knowledge.' Bradan crouched to touch the ground. 'I have been searching for knowledge all my life, wandering the byways and highways to glean scraps of information here and there. Once, when I was at the temple of Callanish in Alba, I imagined that I grasped everything, as the knowledge of the Druids and the wisdom of the Greeks combined within me, but alas, it was fleeting and temporary.' He smiled. 'My mind could not hold on to so much learning.'

Machaendranathar's smile was as much sympathetic as understanding. 'Wisdom is like that,' he said. 'It cannot be retained without great effort, a build-up of knowledge and experience that takes years to obtain. One must meditate and add layer upon thin layer, learn about oneself through inward contemplation, as well as finding knowledge by observing people and events.'

'It is hard to maintain such concentration,' Bradan said. 'Our old Druids spent many years amassing knowledge before they could be priests and alas, they did not write their knowledge done. Much of it, most of it, is gone now. We only have fragments of what they knew. As I said, I glimpsed it once, and the power was too much.'

'You are young,' Machaendranathar said. 'It takes a lifetime to gain wisdom, as your Druids knew. Their loss is the world's loss.'

Other men appeared, to sit in a circle beside Bradan and Machaendranathar. Bradan did not know them; nor did he not recognise where he was. The newcomers had the same intense eyes as Machaendranathar, where profound wisdom merged with worldly compassion.

'Carry on.' The circle of men spoke in unison, although not one of them opened his mouth.

'Are you the Siddhars?' Bradan knew he had no need to ask the question. They answered without speaking, probing him for his knowledge and sharing such of theirs as could benefit him.

'In Alba, we have Celtic Christian priests,' Bradan said. 'They meditate to become closer to God. We can find them on desolate islands... barren, bleak, wave-lashed places where no man or woman could live without intense spirituality and a disregard for bodily comforts.'

Bradan knew that the Siddhars understood. The Celtic priests and the Siddhars were engaged on a similar spiritual journey, each embarking on a search for truth and enlightenment in the way their particular culture and religion guided them.

'The truth is within you.' The words eased into his mind. 'Only you can find the mental peace you seek and the enlightenment you crave. You wander physically while your mind is restless, jumping from experience to experience and event to event. You will find what you seek, Bradan the Wanderer, but what you seek may not be what you think you seek.'

There was a light around the Siddhars, soft yet bright, an aura of peace and acceptance that Bradan had met only once before, that day at Callanish.

'What do I seek?' Bradan asked.

'You seek that which you need most.' The answer was cryptic, as all these answers seemed to be.

'Where will I find it?'

'Where it already is.' The answer was frustrating.

'When will I find it?'

'When you are ready to accept it.'

'How can I help Melcorka?' That was a question Bradan knew he should have asked first.

'By following your guide.'

'Who is my guide?' Bradan asked, as the black-and-white mass appeared before him, although not quite as shapeless as before.

'You know the answer.'

The peace remained as Machaendranathar knelt beside Melcorka.

Bradan looked around. They were still on the slopes of the holy mountain, with the sun beating on them and a circle of white cloud shifting around the forests. Machaendranathar's voice sounded again. 'Now I can see to this unfortunate young lady.'

'Can you cure her?' Bradan's repressed anxiety surfaced with a rush. 'Can you remove the curse?'

'Allow me to speak to Melcorka,' Machaendranathar said. 'She and I have much to discuss.' He placed his hand on Melcorka's forehead, chanting softly. 'You have a troubled mind, Melcorka.'

Melcorka looked up at him with that simple smile that cut Bradan so deeply. Bradan stepped closer. 'She was cursed.'

'I remember,' Machaendranathar said. He signalled to the seven other Siddhars who gathered around. 'A witch or a demon cursed this young woman, yet she still had sufficient goodness and strength to climb up and rescue me.'

The Siddhars spoke without words, their wisdom encircling Machaendranathar and Melcorka. Although he knew his words were not needed, Bradan broke in. For weeks, he had tried to control his anxiety about Melcorka. Now that the immediate danger was past, he allowed his fear to surface. He felt himself tremble as he spoke.

'Melcorka is like that. She will risk her life a hundred times to help people who need her. If you ever had the opportunity to see her when she is well...'

'I would like that opportunity,' Machaendranathar said. 'Sadly, I may never get it, and nor might anybody else.'

'Why is that?' Bradan asked.

'You know that we have a Siddhar missing, so the world is out of balance,' Machaendranathar said.

'Chaturi informed me of that.' Bradan put a hand on Melcorka.

'Unless all nine Siddhars are together on this sacred mountain,' Machaendranathar continued, 'the world will continue out of balance, allowing the demons to enter. Already one rakshasa, the creature you knew as Dhraji, has entered this world. There may be others.' The Siddhar sighed. 'You know what Dhraji is like, with her taste for blood and death.'

'I know what she is like,' Bradan said.

'There are hundreds, maybe thousands more, waiting for the imbalance to increase. Unless all nine Siddhars are back on the mountain, praying and meditating, the balance will never return, and the rakshasas will infest and invade this world. There will be endless wars and suffering. Blood and pain will rule supreme.'

'How can we get all nine of you back together?' Bradan saw the shimmering black-and-white mass slide toward him. He knew it was carrying a message.

He knew it was striving to tell him something. He wished he knew what it was. He watched as the mist slid around Melcorka and merged with her.

'We have one Siddhar missing,' Machaendranathar said. 'Matsyendranath, the Lord of the Fishes.'

'Matsyendranath is not missing,' Melcorka said, with a smile. 'He's on an island.'

Bradan sat up with a jerk. 'Mel, you don't know that for sure.'

'Yes, I do,' Melcorka said. 'Matsyendranath is the man who made me put my sword down a pool so I would come back to him.'

'Open your mind to me,' Machaendranathar said. 'I want to see your history.'

'You won't,' Melcorka said. 'You can't see my history. The kanaima blocked it.'

'Mel,' Bradan said and stopped. This young-minded Melcorka would not know about the kanaima. The original Melcorka, his Swordswoman, was missing. So who could supply this information? It came from Melcorka's mouth, so the only source could be that black-and-white mist that had entered her.

'Do you know of this island?' Machaendranathar asked Bradan.

'I was there when Melcorka lost her sword,' Bradan answered carefully. 'I do not know if the man who took it was a Siddhar or not.'

'Describe him,' Machaendranathar said. 'Give me as many details as you can.'

Bradan recounted their experiences on the white island as Machaendranathar listened, his eyes gentle yet piercing. 'Your friend was correct; that is Matsyendranath,' he said. 'Could you find this island again?'

Bradan shook his head. 'It moved,' he said. 'It moved when we tried to sail away.'

Machaendranathar smiled. 'The island did not move. It was never there except inside your mind. Could you find the patch of sea where you *think* you landed on the island?'

'Oh, yes. I took sea-marks – that is, I took note of the salient points on the nearest coastline – and if I see it again, I can sail to the same angles.'

'That will do,' Machaendranathar said. 'Take me there.'

'I no longer have a boat,' Bradan said. 'The Thiruzha took it.'

Chaturi had been listening closely to their conversation. 'We can get you a boat,' she said.

Chapter Twelve

Bradan rechecked the sea marks. They were a couple of miles off the green coast, with a distinctive double-peaked hill directly to starboard. He checked the angle between the boat and the double-peaked hill. 'Here we are,' he said. 'This is the exact spot where we found the white island.'

The sea stretched all around, unbroken to west, north and south and level as far as the coastline to the east. There was no island. A flight of birds passed so close overhead that Bradan heard the whirr of their wings and saw the glint of their eyes.

Chaturi looked disappointed. 'Are you sure, Bradan? All the sea looks the same. It might have been a different mountain that you saw. The Ghats are only a little to the north. Could it not have been one of them? Or a hill inland?'

'It was here,' Bradan said. 'That double-peaked hill is quite distinct.'

'There is no island in this patch of sea,' Banduka said. 'I know this coast. Dhraji makes us dive for pearls here.'

'Maybe it sank,' Kosala said. 'Maybe it's one of the sinking kinds of islands. Did you see a sunken island when you were underwater, Banduka?'

'No.' Banduka took the question seriously. 'No, I did not.'

'You have to call for it,' Melcorka said. 'If you call, it will come.' Raising her voice, she shouted out as the others watched her.

'Look!' Bradan pointed to a gleam of white that had appeared on the surface of the water. 'That's what we saw.'

'Is that an island?' Kosala was sceptical. 'It doesn't look like an island.'

'Steer towards it, anyway,' Chaturi ordered.

The Singhalese boat was more cumbersome than *Catriona*. Bradan steered as Kosala and Banduka worked the sails. The white smear got no closer.

'It's in your mind,' Machaendranathar told them. 'It's there if you wish it to be there.'

Melcorka stood up. 'I remember,' she said, as the boat slid up the white sand that only a moment before had not been there.

Bradan saw the man sitting beneath the palm trees watching them, as if it had only been a few minutes since they last saw him.

'Hallo!' Bradan shouted. 'Are you Matsyendranath? Are you the Lord of the Fishes?'

The man remained still, with the palms rustling above him and the sea hushing along a beach that seemed to have no end.

'This is very familiar.' Bradan began to walk toward the sitting man, with the others following a few paces behind. The man remained static; the distance neither diminished nor increased.

'Look. There are two men now,' Melcorka said. 'Machaendranathar has got there.'

What had Machaendranathar said about the island? It's there if you wish it to be there. 'Think yourself there,' Bradan said. 'Come on, Mel, we've done this before.' Taking Melcorka's hand, he stepped onward, while trying to envisage himself standing within the copse of trees.

'You're back again.' The sitting man had not moved. He was only an arm-span away.

'We are,' Bradan agreed. 'Are you Matsyendranath?'

'I am,' the sitting man said.

'You are wanted in Sathuragiri,' Bradan said.

'I know.' Matsyendranath did not move.

'Have you always known?' Bradan asked.

'I have always known,' Matsyendranath said.

'Why do you stay here?' Bradan asked.

'A rakshasa has trapped me,' Matsyendranath said.

'There was no need to stay trapped,' Bradan said. 'Melcorka and I had a boat. We would willingly have taken you away last time we were here.'

'My body was not the problem,' Matsyendranath said. 'A rakshasa had trapped my mind.'

'Can we free your mind?'

Matsyendranath pointed to Machaendranathar. 'That man has freed me by his presence. I needed him here. That's why we sent for you.'

'Nobody sent for us,' Bradan said.

'Why do you think you are here?' There was humour in Matsyendranath's eyes. 'The nine Siddhars have to be together on the Sacred Mountain to restore the balance of the world.'

'So I have been told,' Bradan said.

'Seven are on Sathuragiri, one was locked in an iron cage, and I was trapped here. I cannot be freed without Machaendranathar's help, so I had to get him here.'

'Was there nobody else that could help?' Bradan thought of the horrors of the past few weeks. Had this Siddhar been manipulating them all the time?

'There was nobody else with your unique gifts,' Matsyendranath said. 'Nobody except Melcorka could climb to rescue Machaendranathar.'

'Melcorka is not herself,' Bradan said.

'Melcorka had you to look after her,' Matsyendranath said. 'A kanaima has cursed her, but her essential goodness is intact. I knew you would bring her to Machaendranathar and I knew she would rescue him.'

'How could you know that?' Bradan asked, just as the black-and-white miasma formed beside Melcorka. 'What is that?'

'You already know,' Matsyendranath said.

'Last time we were here, you took Melcorka's sword,' Bradan was not prepared to play word games with Matsyendranath.

'We've no time to look for swords.' Chaturi interrupted the conversation. 'We have to get all nine Siddhars back to Sathuragiri, before the rift opens wider and more rakshasas pour into our world.'

Bradan felt his stubborn streak coming to the fore. Ignoring Chaturi, he addressed Matsyendranath directly. 'When we were here last, you said that Melcorka was not fit to use her sword. You were right. She is not fit because a kanaima cursed her. I will help you get back to your famous mystical hill, but not until you help my Melcorka get her sword back.' He felt the atmosphere alter around him and stepped closer to Melcorka, ready to defend her if need be. He heard the slither of steel as Kosala unsheathed his blade.

'Melcorka is safe.' Matsyendranath had read Bradan's fears. 'There is no violence on this island. Put your sword away, Kosala. It is not needed here.'

Bradan faced the Singhalese warrior, knowing he was outmatched if it came to a fight. Kosala slipped his sword back into his scabbard, although his gaze never strayed from Bradan's face.

Matsyendranath lifted his hand, and the dark pool was back. 'How much do you want your sword back, Melcorka? How much have you learned, Bradan?'

'Melcorka's not well,' Bradan said. 'She's not going down there.' *Was this a test?* If so, he would not back away. Feeling no embarrassment at all, Bradan stripped off his clothes, took three deep breaths and prepared to dive into the water.

'No, Bradan!' Banduka smiled as he stepped forward. 'I'm a pearl diver. I am better in the water than you, and you saved me from the dungeon.' He dived in without another word, leaving hardly a ripple on the surface.

Bradan watched air bubbles rise to the surface of the pool.

'We don't have time to search for a sword,' Chaturi said. 'I can feel the rakshasas massing.'

'Go then,' Bradan told her. 'Go without us. Leave Melcorka and me here.'

'No.' Machaendranathar placed a hand on Chaturi's arm. 'Melcorka needs her sword.'

'There are other swords in the world,' Chaturi said. 'You, Kosala, give your sword to Melcorka, although I don't know what she will do with it in her state.'

'Melcorka needs her own sword. It is special.' Bradan held Kosala's arm and nodded to the pool. 'I hope that young lad is all right. He's been down there for a long time.'

'Get everybody else back to the boat,' Chaturi said. 'Kosala, you escort the Siddhars in case the Thiruzha come here. 'Bradan, you can do what you like. We have what we came for. I'm not wasting any more time.'

At that second, Banduka surfaced in an eruption of water. He leaned against the edge of the pool, gasping for breath as water streamed from his hair onto the sand. 'Nothing,' he said. 'I could not reach the bottom. I went down as far as I could.' Banduka took a great, heaving gasp of air. 'I've never been so deep before. There were no fish even. There was nothing, only water, a void of dark water.'

Bradan felt nausea rising within him. Melcorka without Defender was only another woman. Oh, she would be as brave and strong and stubborn as ever, but... There were no buts. Bradan looked down at Melcorka as she sat propped up against one of the palm trees, smiling. He suddenly did not care if she was

Melcorka the Swordswoman, or plain Melcorka from the islands. He did not care if the Singhalese remained or left. *I want Melcorka back, not her blasted sword.*

'You tried, Banduka. Thank you. We will not forget how you tried. Now, you had better get back to the boat.'

'Are you not coming, Bradan?'

'We are staying.' Melcorka answered for them both. 'We are staying until I get my sword back.'

Melcorka spoke with such simple conviction that Bradan could not resist smiling. He sat at her side.

'Anyway,' Melcorka said, 'the rest haven't reached the boat yet. The man told me to think my sword back.'

'Which man?' Bradan asked. He rose to return to the pool, determined to dive in and try again, for Melcorka's sake.

'The man inside my head,' Melcorka explained, with infinite patience.

Bradan saw the black-and-white mass shimmer in front of him. 'What are you?'

There was no reply. The pool was shrinking even as Bradan watched it. The black-and-white mist had settled beside them, sitting an arm-span above the sand. Bradan looked into the miasma. It seemed to extend forever, as if he could step inside and lose himself in the mist, yet at the same time, he could see through to the other side. The dark pool continued to diminish, closing over Defender.

The black-and-white mist remained.

'What are you?' Bradan asked again. 'Why are you here?'

There was no reply.

Bradan saw somebody emerge from the pool – or was it some*thing*? The shape was indefinable, vague, ethereal. He shook his head as the thing gradually took shape. Defender sat on a bed of sand, as clean and pristine as if she had never been under hundreds of feet of water. The leather-and-brass scabbard was gleaming as if Melcorka had oiled it only ten minutes before.

Bradan looked at Defender for a moment as the memories flooded back. The sword was long and ancient, with the sparkle of jewels in the blade, the upturning quillons of the Highlands and the long, sharkskin-bound grip. Defender was as familiar as his own face. He remembered Melcorka wielding that sword against the Norse and against the terrifying Shining One. She had carried it throughout the New World and against the Kalingo. Now Melcorka smiled as if she had recovered a lost toy.

'There's my sword.' Melcorka lifted it. 'Now we can leave, Bradan. Come on, the rest are waiting for us.' She strapped it across her back as naturally as if it were part of her.

'Melcorka has learned,' Machaendranathar approved, from within Bradan's mind. 'Battles are won with the will and the mind as much as with muscle and steel.'

Despite the time they had been gone, the Singhalese had made no progress across the sand. Bradan and Melcorka joined them within half a dozen steps.

'Where have you been?' Chaturi looked puzzled. 'We've been walking for hours.'

'The island does that,' Bradan said. 'It warps and distorts time and distance. We'll be on the boat soon.'

'Here we are already,' Kosala said. 'I swear we covered that last mile in only a few steps.'

The boat lay as they had left her, hauled up above the rippling sea with her mast at an angle and the tide no different to when they had left it, half a day or five minutes before.

'Hurry!' Chaturi urged them on. 'We must get the Siddhars back to Sathura-giri before the rift widens further.'

'The Siddhars are moving as fast as they can,' Machaendranathar said. 'We know the dangers better than you do!'

The second they stepped into the boat, the seascape altered. For one moment, Bradan had a vision of a vast continent that stretched as far as he could see to the south and east, and then, without a sound, there was only the sea, blue and warm and shifting.

'Hoist the sail,' Chaturi spoke quickly. 'Get to the oars. Hurry, before the Thiruzhas are out searching.'

'I think they already are.' Banduka pointed to the north, where the sails of a small flotilla punctured the horizon.

Chapter Thirteen

'Hurry!' Bradan had never seen Chaturi more agitated. She pushed the crew into their places. 'How far is the land?'

'It's only about two miles away,' Bradan said. 'We should reach it long before these vessels reach us. With luck, they might not even see us.' He gave quick instructions. 'Don't hoist the sail as it will make us more visible. Row, fast and hard.'

Taking the steering oar, Bradan pointed the bow toward the double-peaked hill. 'Pray to Shiva, people, and I will pray to my own God.'

'I think we're too late,' Banduka said. 'They're altering course.'

The shape of the Thiruzha sails had altered, as the vessels moved toward the Singhalese boat.

'They're much larger than us,' Bradan said. 'They are two-masted Thiruzha scout ships. They'll carry thirty men and twenty oars each, with two or three times our speed.' A shift of wind brought the thunder of drums to them.

Bradan glanced at Melcorka. 'I won't let them take you. Forget what I said and hoist the sail. Move!'

The sail bellied for a moment, pushing them forward, then sagged as the wind died. The boat's speed dropped.

'Everybody row,' Bradan ordered. 'Everybody, find what you can and row as if your lives depended on it. You too, Melcorka!'

'More than our lives depend on this,' Chaturi said. 'The balance of the world depends on us.'

The Singhalese fishing boat was broad-beamed and bulky, built for carrying a cargo of fish, not for racing predators across the sea. The Thiruzha scouts outmatched them, approaching at an angle, trying to cut off the Singhalese boat before it reached the land. Bradan glanced at the scouts and then at the line of palm trees that marked the land. They might make it. They might not.

'Row!' Bradan ordered. 'Row!' He again heard the beat of the drum as the Thiruzha shipmasters urged their slaves to greater effort. The bow-wave from each Thiruzha vessel was tall and silver-white, with spume and spindrift rising in a manner Bradan would have found beautiful if the situation had been different. As it was, he saw only the menace. Now, the Thiruzha vessels were so close that he could make out the features of the men on board. He saw the glint of sunlight on spears and helmets and heard the hoarse cries of the warriors.

The first arrow whizzed out a moment later, to fall a cable's-length short in the smooth swells of the sea.

'They're firing at us,' Banduka said.

'They are,' Bradan agreed. He glanced ahead. They were less than a quarter of a mile from land, with everybody straining to row, but the Thiruzha scouts were nearly within hailing distance and arrows were landing all around.

'One last effort!' Bradan urged. He saw Kosala eyeing a bow and shook his head. 'No, Kosala. I know you want to fight back, but it's more important you use your muscles to move us forward.'

Chaturi nodded agreement, ducking when an arrow thudded into the planking at her side. 'Row!'

They hit the beach with a crunch of timber on yellow sand and tumbled out before the next wave broke. The beach was long and smooth, backed by a line of rustling palms, with a group of shacks from which bewildered villagers stared at them. A woman in a long pink sari waved, while two plump-bellied children laughed to see these curious strangers on their beach.

'Run!' Bradan shouted. 'Run for your lives! The pirates are coming!'

'No,' Chaturi said. 'Don't warn them. They might distract the Thiruzha, which will give us space and time.'

Bradan shook his head. 'I'm not sacrificing these innocent people just to save our lives.'

'We're not sacrificing these people to save our lives,' Chaturi said. 'We're sacrificing them to save the lives and souls of thousands, perhaps millions of people for all eternity.'

'Sometimes,' Machaendranathar said, 'the few have to be sacrificed to save the many.'

'Not this time,' Bradan said. 'There will be no sacrifices.' He raised his voice, 'Run you, people! The pirates are coming!'

With his warning given, Bradan grabbed Melcorka's hand and pulled her up the beach toward the palm trees.

'It's nice here,' Melcorka protested. 'I want to stay.'

'Not this time, Mel,' Bradan said. 'Run!'

Inland of the palm-thatched village, a network of paths ran in every direction. For a second, Bradan hesitated until Machaendranathar's voice spoke inside his head.

'Follow the map,' Machaendranathar said. *'Follow your instincts.'*

Glancing over his shoulder, Bradan heard shouts, rough laughter and frantic screams. Chaturi had been right; the Thiruzha had stopped to ransack the village. He swore, hating himself for knowing that the suffering of the villagers increased his and Melcorka's chances of survival.

'Horses!' he shouted. 'Is there anywhere around here we can get horses?'

'No,' Chaturi said. 'These are poor people. Only the rich have horses.'

'Just like back home,' Bradan said. 'We'll have to keep moving then. Come on, Mel. We have a choice. We can head directly for Sathuragiri, which may be quicker but which the Thiruzhas will expect, or we can head north and then west. It will take us longer, but could throw the Thiruzhas off the scent.'

'They are busy ravaging that fishing village,' Chaturi said. 'We'll make as much distance now as we can.'

'Follow the map.' Machaendranathar's voice sounded again. *'Follow your instincts.'*

Again, the route was clear. Bradan allowed his feet to take their own course, slipping from one track to another as he came to crossroads and junctions. He was hardly aware of the people around him, except that Melcorka was dragging; she could not go much further. The old Melcorka could have run forever, but this one was thin and weak.

Keep going, Bradan told himself. *Keep going*. He walked in a daze of exhaustion, carrying Melcorka on his back and limping along forest tracks as the wound in his leg throbbed and opened. Ignoring the insects that feasted on his blood, Bradan concentrated on carrying Melcorka. The world shrank to tiredness, sweat and pain as the wound in his thigh drained his strength.

Walk, keep walking. Move. Ignore the pain. Ignore the rasp of tortured breathing. Ignore the blood flowing down my thigh. Walk. Carry Melcorka. Ignore the screaming agony of my back and arms. Keep walking. Just one more step. And another. And another. Walk. Don't give up. How long, oh, God, how much longer?

'There's Sathuragiri!' Chaturi pointed ahead. The square-sided mountain thrust skyward, ringed by a halo of white cloud. 'We're nearly there.'

Bradan nodded, too spent to waste breath on speech. He looked behind him, where the Thiruzha warriors were spread out in two lines, the sturdy, brown-skinned men jogging tirelessly over the undulations.

'Come on,' Chaturi said. 'Hurry up.'

'We are hurrying,' Machaendranathar said.

Bradan had no idea how old the Siddhars were. One minute they appeared as vital and healthy as teenagers and the next, they had the wisdom of centuries in their eyes. Either way, they kept moving, sometimes labouring, other times trotting. The sight of Sathuragiri invigorated them, increasing their speed.

'The Thiruzhas have also seen the mountain,' Kosala said. 'They're breaking into a canter.'

'One last effort,' Chaturi said. 'Come on, gentlemen. One last effort to reach Sathuragiri and then we can start to set things right.'

Machaendranathar was suddenly exhausted, drawing in each breach with a painful gasp and staggering on his legs. He nodded and continued, with Chaturi supporting him as best she could.

'How far to go?' Banduka asked. 'How far?'

'Only one mile,' Chaturi said. 'Only one more mile and we're there.'

'I can't make another mile,' Machaendranathar gasped. 'I have to stop.'

'We can't stop,' Chaturi encouraged. 'If we stop, the consequences are unthinkable.'

'If we don't stop, you'll be carrying a dead Siddhar to Sathuragiri, and that won't help anybody.' Machaendranathar halted, whooping in great breaths.

'Is there anywhere nearby where we can stand and fight?' Bradan fought the agony of his weary body. 'Is there a natural fortification of some sort?' He looked ahead, where Sathuragiri seemed a distant dream, a mountain of unattainable promise. Behind them, the Thiruzha warriors had closed the distance to a quarter of a mile. They were moving fast; Bradan estimated they would catch up within five minutes.

'There!' Kosala pointed to a river that lay between them and Sathuragiri. 'We have to cross a ford here. There's deep water on one side and rapids on the other, so the Thiruzha cannot outflank us. It's not great, but it's better than nothing.' He glanced at Bradan. What's in your mind, Bradan?'

'I will stand and fight them off. Chaturi takes the Siddhars to the mountain.'

'You'll die,' Kosala said.

'We all have to die.' Bradan gestured to Melcorka. 'Could you look after Mel for me? If Chaturi is correct, she'll be herself again when all nine Siddhars are together.'

'I'd rather stay and fight,' Kosala said. 'You can't face them all yourself.'

Chaturi and Banduka pushed the two Siddhars through the ford, with the water splashing on either side. Upstream, sad trees dipped in dark water and a white bird hunted for fish beneath a precipitous cliff. Downstream, the river descended in a series of roaring rapids, with white water foaming over ragged rocks. 'Come on, you three.'

'I'm staying.' Bradan took Banduka's sword. He tested it, swinging right and left. It was small and light compared to the longswords of Alba, but well-balanced. 'You get the Siddhars to safety. Take Kosala and Mel with you.'

Chaturi nodded, immediately understanding. 'May Shiva go with you, Bradan.' She turned and pushed on, with the two Siddhars limping in front of her. Birds called in the air, their sounds harsh.

'So here we are.' Bradan took a deep breath and stepped to the middle of the ford. The water came up to his thighs, slowing his movement but cleaning and soothing his wound. Upstream, the white bird continued to fish, standing on a water-smoothed boulder. *So here I die, Bradan the Wanderer, acting as a warrior to save Melcorka.* He gave a sour grin. *I wish I could die back in Alba. I don't want to leave my ghost here, thousands of miles from home.* Finding a rock at the side of the ford, Bradan sat down, with the sun warming his head and the water cooling his legs.

Thiruzha voices sounded, loud and querulous. A handful of warriors arrived above the ford. One tested the depth with his spear, found no bottom and hunted up and down the bank for a crossing place. Another swam noisily to the other side, realised there was a steep cliff and returned, to the hoots and jeers of his colleagues.

'Take your time,' Bradan said. 'The longer you take, the more time the Siddhars have to get to their mountain and the more chance of Melcorka becoming herself again.'

The Thiruzhas clustered at the riverbank, some looking downstream and others poking at the ford. One man pointed to Bradan, who sat on his rock, waiting.

'Here they come.' Bradan stood up, sword in hand. 'May God and all his saints look after you, Melcorka. I have done the best I can.'

The Thiruzha mustered on the far bank. Two men stepped into the water, checking the depth. Bradan lifted a rock from the bed of the river, tested it for weight and threw it. The leading Thiruzha jerked aside; the rock flew wide, to land with a splash a yard away. The white bird looked up, spread its wings and returned to its fishing.

A Thiruzha threw a spear that thrummed into the riverbed, and then two men rushed toward Bradan.

'Here we go,' Bradan said. He threw another rock, felt momentary satisfaction when it cracked against the face of the leading warrior, and prepared to defend himself when the second Thiruzha pushed forward. He was shorter than Bradan, with the water reaching his upper thighs.

'Stand aside, Bradan.' It was Kosala's voice. 'You're no warrior.'

Blocking the Thiruzha's lunge with ease, Kosala thrust his blade upward into the man's groin, ripping into his belly. The man screamed shrilly and toppled into the rapids, which swept him away. The second Thiruzha warrior, bleeding where Bradan's stone had caught him, hesitated and withdrew.

Bradan stopped Kosala from charging forward. 'No, Kosala. We are here to delay them, not to make our names as heroes.'

'You are right, Bradan,' Kosala agreed. 'You have some wisdom for a foreigner.'

Such was the nature of the ford that the Thiruzha could only advance on a narrow front. The next man moved more warily, throwing a spear to unsettle Kosala before splashing forward with a swinging sword. Kosala parried the blow and tried the groin stroke again, only for the Thiruzha to block in turn and thrust for Kosala's throat.

'You are a warrior,' Kosala said, as he ducked the thrust and hacked downward, taking the Thiruzha in the thigh. The Thiruzha gasped and retaliated with a wicked thrust to the stomach that forced Kosala to sidestep. The Thiruzha's blade nicked Kosala's ribs; he winced, and for a moment tottered on the edge of the rapids. Seeing his advantage, the Thiruzha thrust at Kosala's throat. Kosala blocked, turned the Thiruzha's blade and pushed him. When the Thiruzha slipped, Kosala stabbed him in the throat before shoving him into the seething white water below the ford.

'They're getting better.' Kosala was gasping with effort. He had to shout above the roar of the rapids.

'You're wounded.' Bradan pointed to Kosala's blood coiling in the river. 'Let me take over for a while.'

'No time.' Kosala readied himself for another fight as two Thiruzha warriors advanced at once.

Lifting the spear the Thiruzha had thrown, Bradan leant his staff against a rock and stepped behind Kosala. 'Here they come again.'

As the Thiruzhas charged forward, their colleagues on the bank unleashed a volley of spears. Bradan parried one with a desperate swing that jarred his arms and then both Thiruzhas were pressing on Kosala.

The Thiruzhas attacked at once, forcing Kosala to withdraw step by step. 'I can't hold them!' he panted.

Another group of Thiruzhas advanced into the ford, shouting as they thrust past their colleagues with long spears and shorter swords.

Swearing, Bradan pushed with his spear, felt a quick surge of satisfaction as he pricked a Thiruzha chest, then gasped as a spear-point scraped along his left arm. Kosala withdrew another step, forcing Bradan to edge further toward the bank. Once they were there, the Thiruzhas would flood past them, and the fight would be over.

Hold them! Gain time for the Siddhars. Gain time for Melcorka.

Kosala grunted as he stabbed his immediate opponent in the throat, and then took another backward step as a fresh Thiruzha warrior opposed him.

'There are too many,' Kosala said. He slipped on a round stone, nearly fell and winced when a Thiruzha slashed his face with the point of a sword. Kosala withdrew another step, forcing Bradan to do the same.

'You fight well, Kosala!' Bradan felt the ground solid behind him. One more step and he would be on the bank of the river. 'Do you want to break off and escape, Kosala? I'll hold them as long as I can.'

'No!' Bleeding from his face and his side, Kosala shook his head. 'We fight for as long as we can.' He gave a lopsided grin. 'We will be remembered as heroes, Bradan. This fight at the ford will be told and retold in stories, legends and lies.'

'Mostly lies.' Bradan forced a smile.

The Thiruzhas withdrew a few paces, regrouped and came again, yelling their war cries as they powered forward, knowing that Kosala was weakening and victory was virtually assured.

Kosala took a deep breath. 'It's nearly time, brother,' he said. 'We will die together.'

'Not yet, I think.' The voice came from behind them.

Bradan turned around. 'Melcorka! What are you doing here? Get back where it's safe!'

Melcorka stood at the edge of the pass. She was so thin that her clothes hung from her gaunt frame. Her grin made her face appear like a skull. 'You two have had your fun. It's my turn now.' The hilt of Defender thrust from behind her left shoulder.

'Mel? Mel, are you back? Are you yourself again?'

Kosala spoke before Melcorka could reply. 'This is no place for you, woman. This is a warrior's work. Go back to Chaturi and stay safe.'

Sliding past Kosala and Bradan, Melcorka strode into the ford, smiling. 'I am Melcorka nic Bearnas of the Cenel Bearnas.' Standing with the water surging up to her thighs, Melcorka raised her voice to a shout that sounded even above the roar of the waterfall.

'I am Melcorka of Alba! I am Melcorka the Swordswoman and who dares meddle with me!'

Chapter Fourteen

'Something has happened,' Kosala said. 'The air is different.' He looked toward Sathuragiri. 'Bradan! Look at the sacred mountain!'

Torn between watching Melcorka and following the direction of Kosala's gaze, Bradan spared only a second to glance at Sathuragiri. The cloud around the base had dissipated, and a golden glow diffused from the square slopes. It did not last long, perhaps three seconds, yet there was sufficient time for Bradan to see ten huge figures standing in a circle. For one instant, he experienced that same sensation of peace that he had found on his previous visit to Sathuragiri.

Bradan saw nine of the figures merge into the mountain, while the tenth rose into the air, to soar toward him in the form of the black-and-white miasma. As it moved, it changed shape into a bird that fluttered around Melcorka, piped through its orange beak and landed on a rock.

It was an oystercatcher, the black-and-white bird of the shores of Alba; Melcorka's totem bird and the physical manifestation of Bearnas, Melcorka's dead mother.

Bearnas, Bradan said. That mist was Bearnas. The Norse had killed Bearnas years before and ever since then, she had appeared to help Melcorka in times of her most desperate need. *All this time, Bearnas has been watching over her daughter.*

When the first of the Thiruzha saw that only a woman opposed him, he splashed carelessly forward. Melcorka barely shifted her stance as she unsheathed Defender and sliced off his head in the same movement. The second Thiruzha's hesitation cost him both legs. He fell, screaming, into the rapids.

Balancing Defender on her right shoulder, Melcorka surged forward, silent save for the splash of her legs through the water.

One Thiruzha threw a spear at her; Melcorka sliced it in half. Another crouched behind a rock to thrust his spear at her. Melcorka chopped the shaft in two and cut off the warrior's right arm, leaving him shocked and bleeding to death.

While the braver of the Thiruzhas bunched together to attack, the majority realised that they were facing something beyond their experience. They began to edge away. Melcorka heightened their fear by sweeping Defender waist high, cutting a man in half, recovering her blade and killing a second. After that display, none of the Thiruzhas chose to oppose her. They fled, with Melcorka chasing them, fleet as a deer and dangerous as any leopard that haunted the forests.

Bradan sat on a rock, breathing hard. He closed his eyes. The nine Siddhars were back where they belonged. That meant that the world must have been restored to balance and, more importantly for him, Melcorka was undoubtedly back to normal. Now he had to feed her up, get her back to full strength, and regain *Catriona*. He had had enough of this place with its rakshasas and slavers and Siddhars, however intelligent and knowledgeable the latter might be.

'Who is that woman?' Kosala had bound up the wound in his side and was pressing leaves on the gash in his face.

'That is Melcorka,' Bradan said.

Kosala shook his head. 'No. I've seen Melcorka these past few days. She is an imbecile, a woman without a brain. That must be her double.'

'You are wrong.' Bradan shook his head. 'A demon cursed Melcorka and reduced her to the shell you saw. The Siddhars must have managed to lift the curse. The world is back in balance again.'

Kosala hefted his sword. 'I will help your Melcorka.' His grin reopened his facial wound so that blood dribbled down his chin. 'She is a woman I could learn to like.'

'She's mine,' Bradan said.

Kosala spun his sword around his hand, threw it in the air and caught it again. 'A woman like that would prefer a warrior to a man who only wants to wander.'

'Go and help her if you wish,' Bradan said. 'You still cannot have her.' He swayed, as the mental trauma and physical exhaustion of the past weeks caught up with him once more. The rocks seemed to rise up toward him as he slumped down. The sound of the rapids and the calls of birds were the only things he heard.

* * *

Bradan woke to find the nine Siddhars surrounding him, serene and unsmiling. The atmosphere of tranquillity was so overwhelming that he had no desire to be anywhere else. He smiled up to them.

'He needs information,' one of the Siddhars said.

'He is not yet ready,' said another.

Bradan wished to remain in this place of peace and wisdom forever. There was no lust here, no desire for power or conquest, no overriding ambition for material gain, no hidden motivation to dominate or control. There was only acceptance, wisdom and a connection with Creation that Bradan did not fully understand.

'Bradan.' The Siddhars spoke as one unit. 'With our reunion, the world is more whole, yet there is more danger.'

'There is always danger,' Bradan said.

'We cannot tell him all...' The voices shifted within Bradan's mind. He tried to listen, to pick out the words and phrases that could help him, yet he knew that if he opened his mind to everything that was there, madness would consume him. His brain could not yet digest this vast volume of knowledge, although he knew that each encounter and experience helped it to expand.

One voice stood out amongst the rest. 'Tell him what he needs to know. Tell him what he needs to know, or the rakshasas will be victorious despite all we can do.'

'The war between Good and Evil is fought on two levels.' The words were clear in Bradan's mind. 'It is fought on the spiritual level and the physical level.'

'I understand that,' Bradan said.

'You and Melcorka are the two levels,' the voices said, 'although the links are shared and the elements mixed.'

'I do not understand.' Bradan tried to grasp the concept. He could see the truths floating around his head, yet, when he reached for them, the words and the wisdom slipped from his grasp, leaving him only a residue, a rump of knowledge where he needed the entirety.

'You both have a measure of the spiritual.' The voice was patient. 'And you both have a measure of the physical.'

Bradan heard another voice speak. 'These two do not have enough of either to defeat the rakshasa. They need help.'

'Time is short,' a third voice said. 'The rakshasas are at the gate. We must close the great gate before it is too late.'

Bradan felt the new urgency around him. The Siddhars were worried about something. 'Tell me!' Bradan said. 'Tell me what we must do!'

The words came in a babbling rush, as if the Siddhars were too busy to explain correctly.

'Use the steel from the west bathed in the water from the north to defeat the evil from the south when the sun sets in the east.'

'What? What does that mean? The sun never sets in the east. The sun can never set in the east! Tell me!'

Bradan sat up with a jerk. He was on the slope of a hill with the sun hot on his face and birds chattering around him. Monkeys were playing in the copse of trees nearby. Chaturi sat at his left side, with Melcorka on his right. Nearby, Kosala lounged, sharpening his sword and singing a soft song.

'Where am I?' Bradan asked.

'You are safe.' Chaturi pushed him back down. 'You are safe, and Melcorka is safe. The world is in balance.'

'No,' Bradan said. 'There is still work to be done. We have to use the steel from the west bathed in the water from the north to defeat the evil from the south when the sun sets in the east.'

'Oh? What does that mean?' Melcorka was chewing on a piece of fruit, with juice dribbling down her chin. Although she had washed and her hair shone like varnished ebony, her face was gaunt, there were dark shadows around her eyes, and her frame was skeletal thin.

'I hoped it might mean something to Chaturi.' Bradan faced Melcorka. 'Are you back, Mel?'

'I am back.' Melcorka finished her fruit and started on another. She glanced down at herself. 'I am a walking skeleton, with so little strength that I can hardly walk, let alone lift Defender, but I am back.'

'The way you have eaten since the Siddhas balanced the world,' Chaturi said, 'it won't be long until you are as fat as a pig.'

Bradan struggled to sit up. His gaze did not stray from Melcorka's face. 'I was a little concerned.'

Chaturi gave a barking laugh. 'He worried about you constantly, Melcorka. He bullied and harassed us into taking care of you every waking minute and dreamed about you when he was asleep.'

Bradan filled the awkward silence with an attempt at humour. 'I needed her sword.'

'Now, about this woman you were seeing when I was gone...' Melcorka inched closer, still chewing. 'Tell me about her.'

'I had little choice in the matter,' Bradan said. 'And she was a rakshasa, not a woman.'

'So you say,' Melcorka said. 'I will speak to her later, rakshasa, woman or whatever she pretends to be.' She touched his arm. 'Chaturi told me what you have done.' She said no more. Both knew that there was no need for either of them to say more. Words did not matter.

'How did it feel, Mel? When you were gone?'

Melcorka considered. 'I am not sure,' she said. 'At first, in the immediate aftermath of the curse, it didn't feel like anything. I knew I was not quite myself, yet without anything definite. I felt very aggressive, as if I wished to fight everybody and everything. After that, I seemed to float away. I could see you and hear you. I knew what you were saying and doing, without being able to respond. I knew what I wanted to say.' She shrugged. 'I just could not say the words.'

'You should have wasted away and died weeks ago,' Chaturi said. 'That sort of curse kills slowly and terribly. After this length of time, even the Siddhars should not have been able to get you back. You are a strong woman.'

Kosala stepped up. 'She is a warrior. I have never seen any woman fight as she did. I would be proud to have a woman like you, Melcorka.'

'Thank you, Kosala,' Melcorka touched his arm. 'Coming from a noted champion such as you, these words mean a lot.'

Bradan sat further up. 'I thought I might never get you back.'

'If it had been anybody else except you, Brad, I might have stayed in that place forever, not quite alive and not quite dead. I won't forget what you did.'

'So you forgive me the other woman, then?'

Melcorka laughed. 'I did not say that. I have to think what to do to you.' She touched the hilt of Defender. 'I have business to finish with this Dhraji, rakshasa, demon, witch or rani. I have red words to say to her with a tongue of steel. Now,' Melcorka looked up, 'I need more food.'

They ate beside a copse of trees on the side of the sacred mountain, with the air warm and the high green slopes of the Ghats spreading before them. 'I'm glad you've found your appetite,' Bradan said, grinning as he watched Melcorka eat everything that was put before her.

'Are you going to finish that?' She pointed to a slice of fish that Bradan had been saving for last. 'No? Then it must be for me.' Smiling, she lifted it. 'I need to keep my strength up.'

'As Chaturi said, you'll soon be as fat as a pig,' Bradan told her. 'It's good to have you back, Mel.'

'You'll soon have all of me back.' Melcorka slapped her stomach and grinned. 'Not a human twig!'

'If you two love-birds can stop cooing,' Chaturi said, 'we can talk about something more serious than the shape of Melcorka's belly.'

'Maybe more serious,' Bradan said, 'but not as interesting.'

'We were a fraction too late,' Chaturi said. 'We succeeded in getting the nine Siddhars together, but not before at least one more rakshasa entered our world.'

Melcorka sighed. 'Your delay was my fault. If you had not tried to help me, you might have been faster with the Siddhars.' She glanced at Bradan. 'If Bradan agrees, we will stay in this Bharata Khanda and help remove these rakshasas.'

Chaturi shook her head. 'You cannot, Melcorka. Although you are a skilled warrior with a fine sword, you cannot kill them. No mortal blade can kill a rakshasa.'

Melcorka tapped the hilt of Defender. 'My sword was not made by mortal hands. The People of Peace made Defender. She is a thousand years old and absorbs all the skill and cunning of each warrior who wields her. Calgagus, Arthur, Bridei Mac Bili and Angus MacFergus are only some of the warriors who have held her.'

'I do not know these names,' Chaturi said.

'There is no reason why you should,' Melcorka replied. 'They come from Alba, my country, many thousands of miles to the north and west of here. Calgagus fought the Romans; Arthur fought the invading Angles and Saxons; Bridei led the Picts to a famous victory over invading Angles at Dunnichen; Angus MacFergus was a great Pictish leader.' Melcorka smoothed her hand over Defender's hilt, enjoying the sensation of power. 'I am not immortal. I am only the latest in a sequence of warriors chosen to carry this sword. I can be killed in battle, or I will die of disease or old age, and then Defender will pass to somebody else and somebody after that, until the days of swordplay are over.'

'May I touch your sword?' Chaturi asked.

Melcorka passed Defender over.

'I can feel nothing.' Chaturi sounded sceptical. Brushing against Melcorka, Kosala also reached forward and put a hand on the hilt of Defender.

Kosala looked disappointed. 'I also feel nothing.'

'If Defender chose you, then you would feel a thrill of power that heightens your senses, increases your vision and hearing, and quickens your reflexes, so you move and think faster.' Melcorka was smiling as she spoke. 'With Defender, I am a good warrior. Without her, I am not. I'm really a bit clumsy,' she said, 'and I do love to eat sweet things. I might even put on too much weight!' When she slapped her bony right hip, even Chaturi joined in her laughter.

'Did you choose the sword's name?'

'I chose her name. Every owner of this sword, if indeed we own her and she does not own us, chooses whatever name they think best. For instance, Arthur broke his first sword, Caliburn, in a fight. Only then did this sword think him suitable to be chosen. Some versions of the old tale call her Caledfwlch, others say she is Excalibur or Cut-steel. Some say that Arthur drew her from a stone, others say a lady rose from a lake to hand her over.'

'Which is true?' Chaturi seemed interested.

'Maybe one of the legends is true, perhaps neither. I do not know.' Melcorka accepted Defender back and slid her into the scabbard. 'I had to climb a sea-stack to gain her, and she came with certain rules. I cannot use Defender for an evil purpose, or wield her in revenge.' Melcorka patted the hilt. 'She is a force for good, if killing can ever be good.'

'Killing rakshasas must be good.' Chaturi steered the conversation back to the main subject.

'I have things to straighten out with Dhraji,' Melcorka reminded her, 'so I have to be careful that I fight her for the correct reason and not for revenge.'

'A human female is only its shape in this realm,' Chaturi said. 'A rakshasa can assume any form it wishes, on land and at sea.'

'I am not concerned about her other shapes,' Melcorka said. 'I am more concerned with the female form it used with Bradan.'

Chaturi frowned. 'I see. What do you intend doing now?'

'I will escort you and your people back to the coast near to Ceylon,' Melcorka said, 'and then I will attend to Dhraji and her pirates of Thiruzha.'

'You did not understand me, Melcorka,' Chaturi said. 'Dhraji is only one of the demons. There are others. They could turn up anywhere, in human form or otherwise.'

'Well,' Melcorka shrugged, 'if they come, they come. I'm sure that Defender will take care of herself.'

'I hope you are right, Melcorka,' Chaturi said, but Melcorka saw the shadow of doubt that crossed her face.

Chapter Fifteen

The Singhalese filed into their boats, with a warm wind from the north ready to ease them toward their island of Ceylon.

'You will be safe now,' Melcorka said. 'You are nearly home. Just keep clear of Thiruzha raiding parties in future.' She raised her voice and stamped her feet on the ground. 'Come, Bradan, we have work to do.'

'Are you sure you must leave us?' Chaturi asked. 'You are welcome to stay with us as long as you like.'

'Thank you, Chaturi.' Bradan salaamed. 'I am not yet ready to settle down, and Melcorka has a mission to fulfil.'

'In times of war, the enemies of our enemies are our friends,' Melcorka said. 'We are going into the Chola Empire.'

'They are a great people,' Chaturi said. 'They might welcome you, or they might kill you.'

Melcorka nodded. 'That is true of any empire.'

'Are you sure you wish to visit the Cholas alone?' Kosala half-drew his sword. 'Another warrior might be useful, Melcorka.'

'Your people will need your sword if the Thiruzha come again.' Melcorka touched Kosala's arm. 'I thank you for your offer and your companionship. I have decided to get rid of this Dhraji creature. I might be victorious and I might not. She, or *it,* has a large and well-led army and Raja Bhim is undoubtedly a good tactician. Bradan has informed me of his skills.' Melcorka chewed on a hunk of pork as she spoke. 'Dhraji and Bhim have already defeated the Cholas in at least two encounters. I aim to ensure that the Cholas are successful next time.'

'One sword, even a magic sword, will not make much difference.' Chaturi said. 'Stay with us and welcome.'

'Perhaps Defender will kill a rakshasa, perhaps she will not,' Melcorka said. 'I can only try. I chose the warrior's path that may end in glory, or a sordid death in a ditch. Either one or the other may be my destiny.'

'And Bradan?' Chaturi answered her question before anybody else could speak. 'Bradan's destiny is to wander until he finds his truth, whatever that may be.' She smiled, with wisdom in her eyes. 'Perhaps he has already found it.'

Bradan looked confused. 'I am sure I would know if I did.'

'Perhaps your destiny, wandering man, is to be with Melcorka.' Chaturi handed over a small bag. 'There is sufficient gold in there to buy horses for your journey. It is a long distance to Thanjavur.'

'Thank you.' Bradan salaamed again, much to Kosala's amusement. He glanced at Melcorka. 'Perhaps that crazy woman is my destiny. I do not know.'

Melcorka gave a little bow. 'We will bid you farewell here, Chaturi.'

'May Shiva go with you,' Chaturi said, 'and whatever god you worship.'

'And may Shiva be with you,' Melcorka replied and turned away. She heard movement behind her and knew that Kosala was watching. She wondered if he would settle in Ceylon or follow the warrior's path. Well, he was a grown man and had to make a choice. His destiny lay at the end of a road, as did hers.

* * *

'Whoever runs this Empire knows what he is doing.' Bradan tapped his staff on the flank of his horse. It was not the rowan staff that he had carried halfway across the world, but it was serviceable enough to support his weight.

'It's like Fidach,' Melcorka said, 'but on a much larger scale.'

Each road was marked out and well maintained, with smooth surfaces, marking-stones giving directions, and rest-houses for weary travellers. The villages were neat and orderly, governed by the headman and a local council. Farmers diligently worked the fields, and the animals looked sleek and healthy.

'A lot of nations could learn from this Chola,' Melcorka said.

Bradan fondled his horse's ears. 'We've ridden for three days across the Empire without seeing a single soldier or warrior. Nobody has threatened us or demanded tax or bribes to cross their land. This is one of the best-run countries we have ever visited, Mel.' He looked around at the fields and villages between the swathes of forest. 'They do like their temples to Shiva, though.'

'Their architecture puts anything we have to shame.' Melcorka nodded ahead. 'Here's another temple coming up now.'

As she always did, Melcorka stopped to admire the sheer scale of the temple, with its myriad carvings of unfamiliar gods. 'Any nation that has the skill to build a temple like this is far in advance of Alba.'

They saw their first soldiers the next day, a small troop of horsemen who trotted up to them as they passed between two copses of trees.

'Good day, travellers.' The captain saluted them with a smile on his face. 'Are you journeying far?'

'Good day, Captain,' Melcorka replied. 'We are riding to your capital city of Thanjavur to seek an audience with Rajaraja, the Emperor.'

The captain surveyed them, curious more than unfriendly. 'You are strangers in these parts,' he said, 'yet you speak our language.'

'We have been in the area for a few months,' Melcorka said, 'long enough to learn the languages and something of the culture.' Her smile was not forced. 'We don't wish to embarrass ourselves in front of the emperor.'

The captain met Melcorka's smile. 'Rajaraja is a tolerant man,' he said. 'He is always willing to meet strangers in his domain as long as they come in peace.' The captain's glance at Defender was significant. 'That is an interesting sword you carry.'

'I will only draw it for the good of Rajaraja,' Melcorka said.

'That will reassure him.' The captain's smile widened into a grin. 'It will save his guards the trouble of killing you.'

'Then we will both be happier,' Melcorka said, 'for I have no desire to be killed.'

'I'm glad we have that settled,' the captain said. 'We happen to be returning to Thanjavur. We'll show you the way.' When he lifted his hand, his men formed around Melcorka and Bradan. On a single word of command, the troop started at a slow walk, increasing the pace to a trot as soon as the captain was sure Melcorka and Bradan could keep up.

The cavalry moved as a single body, in silence except for an occasional word of command. They stopped at a small river to water the horses, shared their rations with Melcorka and Bradan, moved aside for the occasional caravan of merchants and passed through a country of fertile fields and industrious farmers. Two hours before dark, they reached the gates of an impressive city.

'This is Thanjavur.' The captain's voice hinted at his evident pride. 'The capital of the Chola Empire.'

Melcorka nodded her appreciation of the array of temples that peeped over the surrounding walls. The gate to the city was tall and impressive, surmounted by circular turrets and with four stalwart guards who snapped to attention when the captain barked at them. The cavalry clattered into a place where camels swayed along wide streets and men and women haggled with merchants over merchandise from half the known world. In the centre, as expected, an elaborate palace dominated everything. 'You have a fine city here.'

'It suits us.' The captain did not try to hide his pride. 'Come this way.' The sound of the horse's hooves echoed from streets of low, mud-walled and flat-roofed buildings with small windows and round-headed doorways. Men and women in colourful clothing looked up as they passed and hordes of naked children screamed and shouted to them, with a few running to keep pace with the horses.

They passed three ornate temples, decorated with the usual figures of men and women and gods that were still strange to Melcorka, all painted and bright in the late evening sunshine.

'This is a prosperous place,' Bradan remarked, as they passed through a wide market square where people crowded around a hundred stalls and shops. Merchants in long robes were trading and women and men exchanged greetings, money and goods. 'Your Rajaraja appears to be a successful ruler.'

'We have no complaints. I will take you to the palace, but whether Rajaraja will see you, I cannot say.' The captain smiled again. 'I am only a poor soldier. The ways of rajas and maharajas are well beyond my ken.'

'Beyond mine, too,' Melcorka assured him.

The captain laughed. 'Rajaraja does his best. We are having some local difficulty on the western frontier at present, but nothing that can't be resolved.'

'The slavers and pirates of Thiruzha,' Melcorka said.

'That's the ones,' the captain said. 'Here's the royal palace now. I'll leave you at the gate and after that, it's up to you.' He dismounted, shaking the dust of the journey from him. 'May Shiva go with you.'

'Thank you, Captain.' Melcorka looked up at the palace. 'I hope that Shiva also blesses you.'

The gate was open, with an impressively ornate guard stationed on either side of the wide doorway. The palace walls extended around what seemed to be a single, brightly painted building decorated with carved stone figures.

'We seek an audience with the Emperor,' Melcorka said.

The guards spoke in unison. 'The public Durbar chamber is open for two hours every day and two hours every evening. The Emperor will listen to requests and pleas then and will give judgement.' Their mouths shut as one. Both men stared resolutely ahead as if their duty had been done.

'Thank you.' Melcorka gave a little curtsey, then a salaam. 'Could you direct us to the public Durbar chamber, please?'

The guards spoke again. 'The public Durbar chamber is on the left side of the main corridor, three doors along. The guard at the door will care for any weapons. If you do not hand him your weapon, he will have you arrested and tried.'

'Thank you.' Melcorka salaamed again. 'Where can we leave our horses?'

'The stable lads will look after them.' The guards whistled in unison, summoning two eager youths who prepared to lead away the horses. 'Rajaraja will supply free food, water and shelter for the animals of genuine travellers.'

Melcorka fondled her mount for what she imagined would be the last time. 'May we enter?'

Again, the guards spoke as one man. 'You may enter.' They stiffened to attention.

The interior of the palace was even more lavish than Dhraji's in Kollchi, with beautiful carpets on the ground and tapestries enlivening the walls. Ornate carvings filled every possible niche, while incense drifted from an unknown source.

'We have entered paradise.' Bradan tapped his staff on the ground. 'It's a long way from Dunedin.'

'It's a different world,' Melcorka said. 'I don't like the idea of parting with Defender so soon after getting her back.'

'There is no choice,' Bradan said. 'Anyway, if this Rajaraja fellow made a habit of stealing the weapon of every guest in his palace, he would soon have a foul reputation. I imagine Defender will be safe enough.'

'That may be true,' Melcorka said, reluctantly. 'You like this place, don't you?'

'After Kollchi and Thiruzha, anywhere would be welcoming,' Bradan said.

'Oh?' Melcorka widened her eyes. 'I heard that Dhraji made herself very welcoming to you.'

Bradan grunted. 'You heard more than is good for you, Melcorka nic Bearnas.'

The guard at the Durbar room overtopped both Melcorka and Bradan by a head, while his shoulders nearly filled the doorway. 'I will take your weapons,' he said, in a deep but not unfriendly tone.

Bradan handed over his staff. 'When will we get them back?'

'When you leave the royal palace,' the giant growled.

'Will they be safe?' Melcorka unbuckled her sword belt, holding Defender in both hands.

'I will look after them.' The giant's eyes were soft as they regarded Melcorka. 'Only one man has the key to the armoury.'

'Who is that man?' Melcorka already guessed the answer.

'Me!' The giant dived inside his baggy blue clothes and produced an iron chain with a brass key half the length of a man's arm. 'Your sword will be safe with me, Lady.'

'I believe you.' Melcorka handed over Defender, feeling as if she was parting with one of her limbs.

'You may enter.' The giant stepped aside to allow unobstructed passage.

Melcorka did not know what to expect when she entered the public Durbar room. It was more significant than the doorway suggested, with the last of the daylight easing in through three pointed windows. A plethora of carved sculptures provided decoration, with a massive statue of Shiva dominating everything.

A score of people were already seated on the Bokhara carpets that covered the ground, while a group of musicians played soft music in the corner. A graceful young woman danced on a raised platform to entertain the waiting supplicants.

'This is very civilized.' Melcorka remembered the roaring, ranting, drunken mobs that filled the halls of Alban and Norse nobility. 'We have come up in the world, Bradan.'

'I feel as if I am a barbarian in a much more advanced culture.' Bradan watched the dancer, thought of Dhraji and quickly looked away.

'We are barbarians compared to these people.' Melcorka settled down on the carpet. 'We are travelling to gain knowledge and learn about new places.

Well, Bradan, here is an Empire that can teach us much, as long as it does not succumb to Dhraji and the rakshasas.'

Bradan stretched out on the carpet. 'We have seen no sign of any rakshasa since we entered Chola lands. I am beginning to wonder if the Siddhars were correct. They could well have been exaggerating, or perhaps the rakshasas have already returned to their own domain.'

'I hope they have.' Melcorka admired the fluidity and grace of the dancer. 'If so, we can spend a pleasant few weeks in this Empire and then continue our journeying.'

'You are forgetting Dhraji,' Bradan said. 'We still have to deal with Dhraji and Bhim.'

'I'm not forgetting Dhraji,' Melcorka said. 'I have things to settle with that woman. I have a message for her, written in red ink with a very sharp pen.'

Keeping in perfect time to the music, the dancer, her face a mask of concentration, writhed and contorted in a variety of moves that held the attention of every person in the chamber. As Melcorka watched, the dancer left the platform at the head of the room and moved among the waiting supplicants, enticing yet not quite touching any as she danced around them.

'The women here are quite different to any in Alba,' Melcorka said, as the dancer circled Bradan, wiggling her hips and with both arms raised in the air. Dressed in her transparent, shimmering jacket and loose trousers, she was more sensual than anything Melcorka had ever seen before.

The music eased to a halt, and still the dancer paraded herself a handspan from Bradan, with her subtle perfume drifting over him and her gaze fixed on his face.

'She likes you.' Melcorka could not control her unease. She shifted slightly, wishing she had not relinquished Defender so easily.

'She is testing me.' Bradan said. 'And I rather think she is testing you.'

'I have no sword,' Melcorka said, 'but if that woman slithers any closer, she will find out that a woman of Alba does not need a sword to defend her man.'

The dancer altered the angle of her gaze from Bradan to Melcorka, staring directly into Melcorka's eyes as she continued to grind her hips, now a finger's width from Bradan's face.

'He's mine,' Melcorka said softly, in Gaelic and then in Tamil. Her smile would have frightened a stone carving into terrified flight.

The dancer moved to the next group of supplicants, the music began again, and the incident seemed closed. Melcorka fingered her shoulder where Defender should have been, glanced over to Bradan, and pursed her lips. 'There are some things about this Chola Empire that I do not like.'

Bradan smiled. 'You are safe with me, Mel.'

'That is one thing I do not doubt,' Melcorka said. 'I only wonder if you are safe with these voluptuous women.' She put an edge to her voice. 'And I wonder if these women are safe with me.'

'Hush now.' Bradan touched Melcorka's shoulder. 'Something is happening.'

The dancer slipped away. The musicians changed the tune to something much grander, and a man in scarlet clothes stepped gravely into the room and onto the platform in front. Two others followed, each carrying a large chair with a carved back, which they placed facing the supplicants. The music stopped. The man in scarlet ordered everybody to stand as a quiet-footed servant lit a dozen lamps to illuminate the darkening room.

'That must be Rajaraja coming now,' Melcorka murmured. 'All rise for the king of kings.'

Two people walked slowly to the chairs and sat down. One was undoubtedly Rajaraja Cholan. Taller than the majority of his people, he wore the loose clothing that was common in this part of the world, with most of his upper body bare and three strings of pearls around his neck. Rather than a crown, he wore an elaborate head-dress that glittered with jewels, while a long, slightly curved sword hung from a cobalt-blue belt.

'I do like his ear-rings.' Melcorka murmured. 'And his moustache.'

Bradan grunted. The ear-rings nearly descended to Rajaraja's shoulders. 'Look at the rani.'

The woman who sat at his side was graceful and elegant in her near-transparent jacket and trousers. She looked utterly composed, even though she had been dancing only a few moments before.

'That's the dancer,' Melcorka said. 'She must have listened to every word we said. What a clever system of gauging the temper of her people. I will still kill her if she tries to steal you from me, Rani or no Rani.'

Two musicians raised great, curved horns to their lips. The resultant blast of sound silenced everything else in the chamber, then the musicians lowered their horns and a herald stepped forward to proclaim the raja.

'All praise Arulmozhi Thevar, son of Parantaka Sundara Chola, Rajaraja Chola, Emperor of Chola, conqueror of the Pandyas and Cheras, victor over the fleet of Bhaskara Ravi Varman Thiruvadi, conqueror of Gangapadi and Nurambapadi, scourge of the Chalukyas.'

Rajaraja sat upright on his chair, one hand on the hilt of his sword and his gaze roving over the room. It settled on Melcorka and Bradan, hovered for a moment as he scrutinised these foreigners in his empire, and moved on.

The horns blasted again, and the herald continued: 'Also praise the Rani of Chola, Panchavan Madeviyar.'

The rani sat in dignified silence. Melcorka ran her gaze over the toned, supple body and decided that Rajaraja had chosen a very suitable wife. He wondered what she had heard and how much Melcorka had damaged their cause by challenging her.

'Rajaraja will now hear your supplications,' the herald announced and stepped back as one of his underlings chose who should speak first.

Melcorka listened as Rajaraja dealt with the questions, one after another. The raja decided upon complex cases about inheritance and land ownership, legal rights and village disputes, before the herald at last indicated Melcorka.

'These two are foreign travellers,' the herald announced. 'They are known as Bradan the Wanderer and Melcorka nic Bearnas from Alba.' He stumbled over the unfamiliar names. 'They have come to speak to your Majesty.'

Melcorka felt the power of Rajaraja's personality when the ruler's gaze fixed on her. 'What is it you seek, travellers from Alba? Is it a trade concession?'

Melcorka and Bradan stood up together, with Bradan salaaming and Melcorka giving a formal curtsey. 'We have come from a far-off land,' Bradan said. 'And we crave a private audience with the raja on an urgent matter of state security.' Thinking he should be more dramatic, Bradan added, 'There is a serious threat to your Majesty's empire.'

Rajaraja sat up straight in his chair as Panchavan frowned at Bradan. Melcorka felt the atmosphere chill and wished she still had Defender.

'It is unusual for anybody to make such a request,' Rajaraja said slowly, with his gaze roving from Bradan to Melcorka, 'especially somebody from outside our borders.'

'I do assure your Majesty that we come with only the best intentions,' Bradan said. 'I do not wish to say more in front of your subjects.'

Rajaraja conferred with Panchavan for a moment, with both glancing over to Bradan and Melcorka. Eventually, Rajaraja raised a finger and a man equally as large as the guard on the door approached. Apart from Rajaraja, he was the only armed man in that room, so Melcorka guessed he was Rajaraja's personal bodyguard. 'Take the strangers to the private Durbar room,' Rajaraja ordered. 'Search them thoroughly and wait there with them.'

The large man nodded and gestured that Melcorka and Bradan should follow him. 'If you give Rajaraja any trouble,' he said in a deep bass, 'I will tear off your heads.'

'We will not give Rajaraja any trouble,' Bradan promised. 'I'm rather attached to my head.'

The private Durbar room was one level higher than the public Durbar chamber and was more luxuriously appointed with carpets and silken divans, with the expected carved statues and incense wafting from a tall candle. As in the public Durbar room, a statue of Shiva dominated.

'Strip,' the deep-voiced man said. 'Both of you. Down to your skin.'

Melcorka sighed. 'How often have men said that to me?' She looked at Bradan, hoping for a glimmer of humour.

'Best do as he says, Mel.'

The guard ran his gaze up and down both. 'Turn!' he ordered, prodded at both and grunted. He inspected their clothes for hidden weapons and then ordered them to dress again. 'Wait here,' he said, then took up a position between the two windows and stood with his massive arms folded and the sword naked at his waist.

'We'll wait here.' Melcorka sat on one of the divans and watched Bradan pace the room, looking out of the windows as his right hand sought the staff he no longer possessed.

'Settle down, Bradan. You'll wear yourself out.'

'The longer this takes, the more trouble there might be.' Bradan paced back and forward.

'And the more weary you are, the less sense you'll make when you talk to Rajaraja.' Melcorka leaned back on the couch. 'This thing is very comfortable.'

'You have not seen the cruelty of these rakshasas,' Bradan said. 'If Dhraji is an example of them, and there are indeed others, things could get very bloody indeed.'

'All the more reason for you to conserve your energy,' Melcorka said.

Sighing, Bradan perched on the edge of one of the divans, only to bounce up when the door opened and Rajaraja stepped in, flanked by Rani Panchavan on one side and his bodyguard on the other. The herald stepped in front of them, with the horn-blower at his side.

'All praise Arulmozhi Thevar, son of Parantaka Sundara Chola, Rajaraja Chola...'

'Enough of that nonsense,' Rajaraja said. 'Thank you, Herald, but I am sure shouting my praises once a day is sufficient for you.'

Stopped in mid-sentence, the herald looked slightly disappointed.

'These light-skinned people from Alba already know who I am,' Rajaraja said. 'You already told them, remember? I am sure they will remember from a couple of hours ago. You do your job very well.'

The herald now looked confused, unsure whether to feel pleased or insulted.

'Go and have a rest,' Rajaraja said. 'Spare your lungs for tomorrow's public Durbar.'

Salaaming, the herald withdrew, taking the horn-blower with him.

'Now then.' Rajaraja was immediately businesslike. 'What's all this about a threat to my empire?' He listened without interruption as Bradan told his story. 'You say that Dhraji of Thiruzha is a rakshasa?'

'She is,' Bradan said. 'The real Dhraji is held in the dungeons below Kollchi.'

'And Bhim? Is he a Rakshasa as well?'

'I do not know,' Bradan said. 'I have not seen him alter into any other form, so I think he is human.'

Rajaraja grunted, exchanged glances with Rani Panchavan and continued. 'And she and Bhim combined to defeat the forces I sent to reduce Kollchi?'

Bradan nodded. 'Bhim was the strategic brains behind both the Thiruzha victories. Dhraji changed into a monster to help sink your Majesty's vessels.'

'I can do nothing about these possible other rakshasas,' Rajaraja said. 'If they come, then they come. I don't like Dhraji or the threat Thiruzha poses on my western border.'

'We could help, your Majesty,' Melcorka said. 'Bradan knows the layout of Dhraji's lair at Kollchi, plus the defences at Rajgana and I am a bit of a warrior.'

'Indeed?' Rani Panchavan made a rare contribution to the conversation. 'Then I am lucky you did not choose to reveal your skills when I danced to your man.' Her smile broke any tension. 'It is all right, Melcorka nic Bearnas. I have no designs on Bradan, or on anybody else.'

'I am glad to hear that, Your Majesty,' Melcorka said. 'Nor do I have any designs on Rajaraja.' When she met Rani Panchavan's smile with one of her own, both women looked at each other in perfect understanding.

'I'll call together my commanders and devise a plan,' Rajaraja said. 'We are experienced in war. We know how to gain a victory.'

'You are experienced in a war against mortal enemies,' Melcorka said. 'War against the rakshasas is different.'

'War is war,' Rajaraja said. 'One may require different tactics and weapons than the other, but they all require striving against an enemy who is as determined to defeat us as we are to defeat them.'

'Your Majesty is wise,' Bradan said.

'My Majesty does not need to be flattered,' Rajaraja said.

Bradan salaamed, hiding his smile. Rajaraja was not like Dhraji.

'We will call for you if we need you,' Rajaraja said. 'In the meantime, you are free to wander around my city, Bradan and Melcorka.'

'My sword...' Melcorka began.

'You are my guests,' Rajaraja said. 'And as such are under my protection. You will not need a sword in Thanjavur. Besides,' Rajaraja's smile was of sad humour, 'if you had your sword, you might feel tempted to ensure that Panchavan did not dance to Bradan again!'

'As you wish, Your Majesty.' Melcorka marvelled to find a king with a sense of humour.

'If you need anything,' Rajaraja said, 'say my name and it will be provided. View the great temple of Shiva, I have been told that travellers admire it, and watch for Kulothunga, my champion warrior. His skill is known far beyond my boundaries.'

'We will do that, Your Majesty,' Melcorka said.

Chapter Sixteen

'So this is the great temple of Shiva?' Melcorka leaned back to admire the architecture. The building was larger than any religious building they had seen before, a massively elaborate temple with the exterior a montage of sculptures of gods. There was the four-headed god Brahma, Ganesha the elephant god and Hanuman, the long-tailed monkey god. As expected, Shiva dominated all. 'Somebody has gone to great trouble to build this.'

'These Cholas are a very religious people,' Bradan said.

'We think we are civilised,' Melcorka said. 'This surpasses anything we can build, or have ever built.' She stepped back to further admire the building. 'We have a long way to go yet.'

'We'll get there,' Bradan said.

The temple was set within an exterior wall that also enclosed a large garden containing fountains and smaller temples and other buildings. Melcorka looked around her in awe, never having seen anything on this scale before.

'Do you like it?' Although the warrior had an immense spread of shoulders, his height made him appear rangy rather than muscular, and he sported a magnificent moustache that curled across his cheeks nearly to his ears. The long sword that hung from his belt was only a finger's width from the ground.

'It is a most impressive building,' Bradan said.

'What?' The warrior looked confused for a moment and then shook his head. 'Not the temple. A temple is just a temple. One is much like another, bigger or smaller but all full of statues. I meant the sword. You must have come here to inspect Vijayalaya's sword.'

Melcorka did not wish to admit that she had never heard of Vijayalaya, let alone his sword. 'Vijayalaya was a feared warrior, was he not?'

The moustached warrior puffed out his chest and struck a pose that showed his profile. Melcorka guessed that same pose had impressed a string of women. 'Vijayalaya was the founder of the Chola Empire. He was one of the greatest warriors the world had ever known. Vijayalaya was greater than Sekundar, as great as Rajaraja and perhaps as great as me!'

'He must have been a magnificent warrior to be as great as you.' Melcorka hid her smile. 'Everybody knows your name. Why, even in Alba people speak about you.'

'Of course.' The warrior struck another pose that showed the depth of his chest. 'The name of Kulothunga is known from the Andaman Islands to the lands of the Chin and from the Ganges to Persia.'

Melcorka glanced at Bradan, who kept his face straight. 'Were you at the latest battle against Rajgana Fort?'

Kulothunga shrugged. 'That was no battle. That was a skirmish, hardly worthy of my attention.'

'Ah,' Melcorka said. 'If you had been there, would the outcome have been any different?'

'If I had been there,' Kulothunga said, 'we would have won. The King sent one battalion and a few auxiliaries to take the Thiruzha's border fort. Bhim's pirates humiliated them.' He strutted past the fountain, head up and shoulders back. 'I heard that the pirates killed all the survivors and nobody is sure what happened.'

'I saw the battle,' Bradan spoke quietly. 'I saw the Chola attack with great courage and the Thiruzhas fend them off with archers and catapults, fire and elephants.'

Kulothunga preened his moustache. 'You are a foreigner,' he said, with one hand on the hilt of his sword. 'Yet you do not look like a Chinese or an Arab trader. Are you a mercenary who fought for the Thiruzha?'

'I am Bradan the Wanderer. I am not a fighting man at all.'

Kulothunga's interest waned. 'If you are no warrior, you cannot tell me about the battle tactics.'

'I am interested in Vijayalaya's sword,' Melcorka said.

'You are only a woman.' Kulothunga dismissed Melcorka with a shrug. 'Why would you be interested in a sword?'

'I have been called a swordswoman,' Melcorka said.

Kulothunga looked her up and down. 'Yet you carry no weapon.'

'We are guests in the Empire.' Bradan put a hand on Melcorka's arm to hold her back. 'Your king requested that Melcorka should hand in her sword before we met him.'

Kulothunga's eyes flickered from Melcorka's feet to her head. 'You are very skinny for a warrior.'

'Melcorka has not been well,' Bradan defended her.

Reaching forward, Kulothunga felt the muscle in Melcorka's bicep. 'There is no strength in you at all. You would not last five seconds in a fight with me.'

'If I had my sword,' Melcorka exploded, 'I would show you how I fight, you swaggering buffoon!'

Kulothunga laughed. 'You have fire, my pale Lady Foreigner with the decorated face. I like fire in a woman.' He faced Bradan. 'When you have finished with her, I would like to try her out.'

Once again, Bradan prevented Melcorka from launching herself at Kulothunga. 'She is too much of a woman for you. You would not last the pace. Now, my brave warrior, where is this famous sword you speak of?'

For a moment, Melcorka thought that Kulothunga would draw his sword and kill them both. Instead, he laughed again. 'You evidently have not heard that I have as much skill with women as I do in battle. I will forgive you, as you are only foreigners.'

'And I will forgive you,' Melcorka smiled through gritted teeth, 'as you evidently have never met a woman from Alba before.'

Vijayalaya's sword sat in a special case, within a small building in the grounds of the temple. Protected from the elements by glass screens, the sword was long, with a slight curve to lend weight to the business end, and a green grip on the hilt.

'When I am old and done,' Kulothunga said, 'I will seek one last battle and die with my face to a hundred foes. Men will venerate my sword as they do Vijayalaya's. Our swords will be displayed side by side and people will come to talk about my exploits.'

Bradan winked at Melcorka. 'Men already talk of your martial exploits,' he said. 'And women talk in wonder of your prowess in other areas.'

'That is true,' Kulothunga said, without a hint of irony. He puffed out his chest again. 'These markings on your woman's face; what do they mean?'

'Ask her,' Bradan said.

'What do they mean, Lady Swordswoman without a sword?'

Melcorka touched the tattoo on her left cheek. 'They are the symbols of my people,' she said.

'Are they sacred? Are they sacred to your gods?' Kulothunga continued, before Melcorka could reply. 'This temple is sacred but so is the fountain.' He was smiling again, proud to reveal his knowledge. 'Did you know that, foreign woman with the unpronounceable name?'

'I knew the temple was sacred,' Melcorka said. 'I did not know about the fountain.'

'Follow me!' Kulothunga walked to the fountain that tinkled and splashed in the centre of the garden. 'The water in this fountain is from the Ganges,' he said. 'The Ganges is our sacred river, many weeks' march to the north.'Dipping his hand in the water, Kulothunga touched it to his forehead. 'Rajaraja sent an expedition north with barrels and containers and brought back the sacred water.' He spoke with genuine awe in his voice.

For the first time, Melcorka felt some liking for Kulothunga. 'Does the water have special powers? When the holy men in our religion bless water, it has holy powers.'

'The Ganges is always holy,' Kulothunga said. 'Wherever I go, I carry some Ganges water with me.' He showed a small bottle. 'If I fall, then carrying holy water will ensure that I ascend to the next level of creation,' he smiled, 'or at least that I do not descend to a lower level. Could you imagine me as a farmer or a sweeper?' He laughed at the very idea.

'I could not imagine that.' Melcorka kept her voice serious. 'Not a warrior such as you.'

Kulothunga accepted Melcorka's praise as his due. 'Before I die,' he said, 'I wish to lead a Chola expedition to the Ganges. Could you imagine?' He lowered his voice in awe. 'Could you imagine elephants from Chola dipping their trunks in the Sacred River?'

Melcorka nodded. 'If such a thing happens, I know that you will be there.'

Kulothunga touched the hilt of his sword. 'If I were to be even part of such an expedition, I would die happy. I would have achieved deeds that no Chola warrior, not even the great Vijayalaya, has ever achieved in the past.' He puffed out his chest again, stroking his moustache and rattling the earrings that all Chola warriors seemed to affect. 'Do you wish to see me fight?'

'I would like that very much,' Melcorka said.

'Come then.' Kulothunga put his hand on Melcorka's shoulder. 'It is something that all women should see. After only a single demonstration of my skills, you will forget this peace-loving wandering fellow and wish to bed a warrior.'

Melcorka kept her expression solemn. 'In that case, perhaps I had better not come. Bradan and I have been through many adventures together. It would be a shame to turn my back on him now.'

'It is such a shapely back.' Kulothunga ran his gaze over her. 'I am sure he will admire the view as you walk away from him and towards me.'

Melcorka changed the subject. 'Show me your skills.'

Between the temple and the palace stretched a parade ground on which a company of Chola infantry were marching and counter-marching. Kulothunga approached the officer in charge, an impressively authoritarian man with the ubiquitous moustache of the Chola military.

'I wish to demonstrate my fighting skills to these foreigners,' Kulothunga said. 'Give me five of your best fighters.'

'Only five?' The officer did not seem to be joking. 'You are surely feeling weak today, Kulothunga.'

'Give me seven, then.' Kulothunga glanced at Melcorka to make sure she was listening. 'Form the rest of your men into a hollow square so they can all watch, and have the pale foreigners come inside as well.' He laughed, gripping the hilt of his sword.

Wishing she had Defender, Melcorka stepped inside the square, as Kulothunga stood with his head up and one leg forward and bent in a dramatic pose.

The officer selected seven men. They stepped forward willingly.

'Handy-looking bunch,' Bradan said.

Melcorka agreed. The soldiers were well-disciplined and fit, each man equipped with a spear, sword and shield. 'If appearances are anything to go by, these warriors would trouble any army in the world.'

'First two soldiers,' Kulothunga said. Two men stepped forward. The first soldier poised and threw his spear, which Kulothunga sidestepped with ease, and the second advanced at a run, thrusting his spear in front of him. Kulothunga slipped sideways, grabbed the shaft of the spear, pulled it past him and tripped the soldier with one fluid movement. As Melcorka watched, Kulothunga reversed the spear and pressed the point to the soldier's chest.

'That was neatly done,' Bradan said.

Melcorka watched through narrowed eyes. 'There's nothing new there,' she said. 'Children at play do that.'

Kulothunga glanced over to Melcorka to ensure she was still watching. 'Next two!' he shouted, unsheathing his sword.

Two men approached with swords out, and circular shields held on their left arms. Without a word, they broke into a run. Kulothunga adopted a half crouch, holding his much longer sword one-handed. He parried the blow of the man on his right, locked his opponent's blade with his own and turned aside, so his opponent's body shielded him from the second man. Laughing, Kulothunga twisted away from the first man's sword and stabbed across his body to slightly nick the second soldier on the chest.

'You're both dead!' Kulothunga shouted and returned his sword to its scabbard.

'Well done!' Melcorka clapped her hands. 'That was as neat a piece of swordplay as I have seen.'

Kulothunga smiled.

'Three men this time.' Kulothunga unbuckled his sword and spread his arms out. 'No weapons.'

'That's unusual.' Melcorka watched closely as the three soldiers dropped their weapons and advanced. Rather than waiting and counterattacking as he had done on his two previous encounters, Kulothunga ran towards his opponents. He avoided the grappling move of the first and jabbed at the chest of the man with straight fingers, sending him to the ground. When the second grabbed Kulothunga in a headlock, Kulothunga lifted his arms above his head, slid free and again jabbed with his straight fingers. The man gasped and fell, still conscious but apparently paralysed. Seeing his companions disabled, the third man shouted and threw himself on Kulothunga, to be treated in precisely the same manner.

'Now, that was very impressive,' Melcorka allowed. 'I've never seen anything like that before.'

Kulothunga smiled at her, aware of her admiration. 'Do you want me to show you how I did that?'

'I do,' Melcorka said.

'I shall show you in private.' Kulothunga replaced his sword belt and smoothed a finger over his moustache. 'Where there are no witnesses to learn my skills and use them against me.'

'As long as I have Defender.' Melcorka was reluctant to be unprotected and alone with this dangerous man.

'You will not need your sword for a wrestling match,' Kulothunga said, as the officer took his company of soldiers on a complicated manoeuvre that involved both spear and shield exercises.

'I will trust you.' Melcorka decided.

'Come this way.' Kulothunga smoothed his moustache again. 'Your wandering friend may come as well, although my skills will not be any use to a man such as he.'

Kulothunga brought Melcorka to an enclosed space between a copse of trees and a small temple. 'Here,' he said, 'is where I practice my swordplay and my wrestling.'

'I have never done any wrestling,' Melcorka said.

'Never?' Kulothunga smiled. 'Have you never wrestled with your brothers, or that strange fellow over there?' He nodded to Bradan, who sat on the stump of a fallen tree, watching.

'I have no brothers,' Melcorka said.

'I have seven,' Kulothunga said. 'And three sisters.' His smile widened. 'I wrestled with them all. They never bested me. Not once. Come!'

Melcorka advanced cautiously. Within a minute, she was pinned and helpless on the ground. 'We'll try again,' she said, only to experience the same result.

'You are not as good as I am,' Kulothunga shrugged. 'Nobody is.'

'Teach me,' Melcorka ordered and listened intently as Kulothunga explained each move, step by step. After half an hour, Melcorka had the basics of one movement. After an hour, she had the gist of another, which meant that their bouts lasted longer, although invariably with the same result.

'Now show me how you put these soldier lads to sleep.' Melcorka knew she could practice wrestling with Bradan whenever she wished, while her time with Kulothunga would inevitably be limited.

'Stand up,' Kulothunga said. 'Attack me again.'

Melcorka did so, using every trick she had learned that day, and nearly succeeded in putting Kulothunga on the ground before he knocked her down with a bare touch with the tip of his finger. Kulothunga threw himself down, and they lay on the ground, panting. Melcorka grinned across to Kulothunga. 'You are very good at that.'

'It is called Varmam.' Kulothunga ensured that his moustache was as neat as ever. 'It is a fighting method that we Tamils have developed over the centuries.' When he was talking seriously, Kulothunga revealed his intelligence, and Melcorka realised that she liked the man. He smiled, showing perfect white teeth. 'It is also a method of medical treatment, although I create employment for doctors rather than doctoring the sick myself.'

'How does it work?' Melcorka asked.

'I don't know how it works,' Kulothunga admitted, 'but I can tell you what I do know.'

'Please do so,' Melcorka said.

'Varmam are points in the body, here,' Kulothunga pointed to a spot below Melcorka's left breast, 'and here, and here.' He touched her lightly in various places. 'When somebody touches these pressure points, they can either cure or debilitate, depending on the type of pressure used. You know that the body is made of blood and bones and muscle and sinew? Well, there is also an invisible life force that ten vital channels carry through our body. We call these channels Vaayu, with the most important one being praanan. This vital energy is focussed in one hundred and eight special points of the body, known as Varman points. If we strike these points, we can kill the enemy, or else paralyse him, either permanently or temporarily.'

'How does that work?' Melcorka asked.

'I am not clear about that,' Kulothunga admitted. 'Hitting any of the one hundred and eight points seems to stop the vital energy flowing around it, so your enemy will be disabled.'

'How did you learn these things?' Bradan asked.

Kulothunga shrugged. 'Lord Shiva taught his wife, Parvathi about Varman. Parvathi taught their son, Lord Murugan and he taught Siddha Agasthiyar, who wrote it down for the rest of us.'

'Can you show me these pressure points?' Melcorka asked.

'I will show you.'

The following day, they met again as dawn painted the eastern sky ochre-red, with clouds the ominous colour of blood.

'I have brought two swords of equal length,' Kulothunga said. 'These are the swords our soldiers carry.'

'I am better with my own sword,' Melcorka said.

'So am I,' Kulothunga said. 'I will be superior to you with either weapon.'

'Possibly.' Melcorka tried the primary Chola weapon for balance. It was shorter than Defender, with a broad, slightly curved blade.

Kulothunga's stance was less orthodox than Melcorka had expected. He stood with his left foot extended and his sword held above his head, point down.

'I've never seen anybody stand like that before,' Melcorka said and realised that Kulothunga was no longer smiling. 'Are we fighting to the death?'

'We are practising,' Kulothunga said. 'There is little amusing about swordplay that results in the death of your enemy. There is even less amusing about swordplay that results in your own death. Defend yourself!' Kulothunga advanced quickly, watching every move that Melcorka made as he closed the gap between them.

Melcorka stepped forward. Although she lacked the skill that Defender provided, the scores of encounters she had fought with the sword had taught her more than just the rudiments. She parried Kulothunga's advance, twisted under his arm and swung at his ribs. Kulothunga blocked her sword, ran his blade up to her hilt and pushed backwards.

His superior strength and weight told and Melcorka staggered, to find Kulothunga's blade at her throat.

'You're dead,' Kulothunga said. 'Don't look so depressed, Melcorka, I am the best there has ever been.'

'Does the Chola Empire give praise for modesty?' Melcorka was annoyed at the ease with which Kulothunga had bested her.

'If it did, I would win that, too.' Kulothunga threw Melcorka's sword back to her. 'Defend yourself!'

'No!' Melcorka said. 'You defend yourself!' She attacked with speed, feinted to Kulothunga's right, ducked low and slashed at his legs. Kulothunga gasped, jumped to avoid Melcorka's blade, landed to her left and landed a stinging whack across her backside with the flat of his sword. 'There! You nearly got me, woman!'

'Oh!' Melcorka rubbed at herself. 'You pig! Defend yourself!' She attacked again, feinted left, then right and thrust left, nearly catching Kulothunga, but once again the warrior dodged her sword, and again his blade thwacked her.

'Oh!' Melcorka yelped. 'That's enough of that, Kulothunga.'

'Would you prefer that I used the edge of the blade?' Kulothunga asked. He looked around. 'I think that is sufficient for just now. The sun has risen, and people are beginning to gather. 'You have some skill. I have more. We will leave it at that. Besides,' he smiled, 'you may need to nurse your bruises.'

'You are a pig, Kulothunga,' Melcorka said. Despite this man's posturing, she liked him. She met his smile, as he replaced the borrowed sword with his own.

'You will be glad that we are on the same side,' Kulothunga said. 'That way, you will not have to face me in battle. I am the greatest warrior there has ever been.'

'Yes,' Melcorka said. 'I am glad that I won't have to face you in battle.' *But not for the reason you believe. I would not like to kill a man that I am beginning to like.*

Bradan was standing under the trees. He was leaning on a staff, his face impassive and his eyes thoughtful.

Kulothunga claims to be the greatest warrior there has ever been. Dhraji is scared of one man, said to be the greatest warrior there had ever been. Is this the warrior who is destined to kill her?

Bradan was also aware that Kosala was standing at the gate, watching everything that was happening, with his gaze fixed on Melcorka.

I thought you were back in Ceylon, Kosala. What are you doing here?

Chapter Seventeen

Rajaraja held his council of war in the public Durbar room, with his son Rajendra, half a dozen commanders and three admirals present. Torches sent out flickering light and cast shadows over the faces of the gathered men who studied the map of the Chola Empire that was spread over the low, carved table.

'What we did wrong last time,' Rajaraja said, 'was to divide our forces too quickly. We struck too far apart. If we had attacked both places at the same time, we might have been more successful. Nobody, not even a rakshasa, can be in two places at once.'

The generals and admirals nodded. Melcorka thought they looked a professional bunch; warriors experienced in the art of war, men who knew that one setback did not mean the end of a campaign.

'What do you suggest, your Majesty?' one grizzled admiral asked. A white scar ran down his face, removing his left eye, a souvenir of some half-forgotten campaign when the Chola Empire was expanding at the expense of its neighbours.

'I suggest we plan our campaign to strike at Kollchi and Rajgana Fort the same day, so this Dhraji creature cannot face both our forces. Man for man, we are better than they are. There is no doubt about that. We have the skill, the numbers and the knowledge.'

'Skill, knowledge and manpower might not be sufficient. We don't have supernatural powers,' a younger man said, rubbing a hand over his chin. 'We are not immortal, while this thing they call Dhraji is.'

The silence lasted a good minute as the men looked at each other. Fighting against warriors was one thing; combating an immortal rakshasa was something else.

Melcorka looked from man to man. 'May I say something here?'

'Who are you?' The assembly of warriors and admirals stared at her as if they had not previously noticed the strange foreign female in their midst.

'I am Melcorka of Alba. You do not know me, and there is no reason that you should,' Melcorka said. 'This man,' she indicated Bradan 'is Bradan the Wanderer. We both have knowledge and experience that you may find useful.'

'I invited these people to this council-of-war,' Rajaraja said. 'Listen to what they have to say.'

At Rajaraja's words, the assembly settled back and the hostility eased, although Melcorka still felt tension and scepticism.

'If I may speak?' Bradan stood up and salaamed. 'Melcorka was a prisoner of Dhraji. She also fought her before, when Dhraji had assumed her rakshasa form, so she knows what we are facing. I was immured within Dhraji's palace for some weeks, and I witnessed the Chola naval assault on Kollchi harbour and Kalipuram Island. Both Melcorka and I were present at the Empire's abortive assault on Rajgana Fort.'

A general with long, curling moustaches spoke directly to Rajaraja. 'They could be spies.' He shot the Albans a suspicious look. 'If they were as close to the rakshasa as they claim, they could be here to gather information about us.'

'They are not,' Rajaraja said. 'I invited them.' The word of the King of Kings was sufficient to quash any but the most suspicious of doubters.

'In Alba and elsewhere,' Melcorka said, 'I have been reckoned as something of a warrior, a swordswoman. If Rajaraja permits me to regain my sword, I will walk in the forefront of the battle and face Dhraji's forces. No spy would do such a thing.'

'If you are with us,' Rajaraja said, 'you will certainly fight the enemy.'

'Dhraji and Bhim defeated us by sea and land on our last attack,' the one-eyed admiral reminded the assembly. 'Any information about the reasons will be helpful.'

'Let the strangers talk,' Rajaraja said.

Bradan waited until the group settled down. 'Firstly,' he said, 'can we vouch for the loyalty of everybody present?'

The atmosphere altered again as men either looked at each other, or glared at Bradan in indignation. Bradan waited for the murmurs of protest to die down.

'These men have served me in half a dozen campaigns,' Rajaraja said. 'They have proved their loyalty in blood.'

'The rakshasas can take the form of any living thing,' Bradan said. 'I worry that there could be one amongst us.'

'Here is a cure.' Kulothunga stalked in from his position at the door. 'I have some water from the Ganges. Let every man present drink from my flask. No rakshasa can drink water from the blessed Ganges.'

'Do as Kulothunga suggests,' Rajaraja ordered. 'I will drink first.' He watched as the flask was passed from hand to hand, with everyone present taking a swallow. Melcorka and Bradan were last.

'Good,' Rajaraja said. 'Well thought of, Kulothunga. You may continue, Bradan.'

'Very well, Your Majesty,' Bradan said. 'I was on board a Thiruzha boat in the latest battle.' Once again, he waited for the Chola rustle of unease to pass. 'The Thiruzha scouts enticed your loolas out of formation and the Thiruzha war-galleys ambushed them. Once your loolas were gone, your fleet was blind, and the Thiruzha ships stabbed and ran, inflicting casualties and weakening your ships both in numbers and morale.'

The Admirals were listening intently, leaning forward with their eyes fixed on Bradan.

'By the time the Chola fleet came to the harbour, it was rattled and uncertain, with many casualties. The Thiruzhas have a chain boom to guard the northern entrance to the harbour, and catapults and many archers on the island of Kalipuram.'

'We had a sufficiently large fleet to take the island and the town.' Rajaraja did not like to hear of the deficiencies of his armed forces. 'I heard that our admiral was killed early in the battle.'

Bradan nodded. 'I did not know that, Your Majesty. That would explain why the attack was disjointed. Your men fought bravely.'

'I would expect nothing else.'

Bradan continued, explaining about the Thiruzha catapults and the bolt-firing weapon, as well as the fire that had burned so many of the Chola ships.

'Bhim has Kollchi harbour well defended.' Rajaraja gave grudging respect to his enemy. 'We shall have to devise a way of neutralising his weapons.'

He paused, drumming long fingers on the table. 'I also heard some garbled talk about a great sea monster that attacked our ships.' He looked directly at Bradan. 'Was that Dhraji?'

'That was Dhraji,' Bradan confirmed. 'It is one of her forms. Perhaps it is her true form, I am not sure.'

The assembly murmured in disquiet. 'How do we fight a rakshasa?' the one-eyed veteran asked. 'Mortal weapons cannot kill it.'

'You don't fight it,' Melcorka said. 'You let me fight it.' She expected the rising tide of disbelief. 'Before I tell you,' she said, 'please allow Bradan to explain about Rajgana Fort.'

This time, it was the generals who listened with more attention as Bradan spoke of the stone bridge across the narrowest part of the pass, the iron barrier, the catapults and the number of defenders.

Rajendra waited until Bradan had finished speaking. 'Does the garrison illuminate Rajgana at night?'

'There are lanterns on the walls,' Bradan tried to remember. 'The pass itself is not lit.'

Rajendra drummed his fingers on the table. 'And the door beside the metal gate; was it guarded?'

'I believe not, Your Highness. I was not aware it existed until the garrison marched out.'

Rajendra gave a slow smile. 'That is our way in then, at night and quietly. Rajgana is not impregnable.'

'Perhaps so, Rajendra,' Rajaraja said. 'Bhim has ensured that Thiruzha is well defended. We cannot allow him to remain as a threat on our western border. His ships harass our shipping and raid our coastal villages and his armies loot and rob our lands. He must hold hundreds of our people as slaves.'

'Thousands,' Bradan said. 'Those that survive.' He remembered the dungeons under Bhim's palace and the horror of the executions. 'Bhim and Dhraji rule by terror and Dhraji, at least, plans to overthrow Your Majesty and take over your empire.'

Rajaraja grunted. 'Does she indeed? Now, Melcorka, you mentioned that you could fight Dhraji. What makes you think you can face a rakshasa when my experienced generals and warriors cannot? I have men in my army with twice or thrice your experience of warfare.'

'There are reasons.' Melcorka was reluctant to mention the power of Defender. 'I will keep them to myself at present.'

'Why?' Rajaraja gave the direct question.

'It is against Melcorka's religion to answer that question.' Bradan gave an answer he knew the Cholas would understand.

'I see.' Rajaraja raised his hand in acceptance. 'I cannot say how successful you may be until the day I see you face a rakshasa.'

Melcorka remembered her previous failure to kill the multi-armed sea-monster and said nothing.

'When we attacked the Thiruzha pirates, I only sent one flotilla of ships and a couple of regiments, with a few auxiliaries.' Rajaraja said. 'I underestimated Bhim and Dhraji. I will not do that again. This time, we will muster five regiments with cavalry, elephantry, infantry and archers to attack by land and two hundred and fifty ships to attack by sea. We may not be able to kill the rakshasa, but we will destroy her minions.' When Rajaraja looked up, Melcorka could see the personality that had made the Chola Empire such a significant power.

Every bit as tall and broad as the Raja, Rajendra stepped forward. 'If I may, Father, I would wish to command one of the two forces.' He stood at his father's side, his eyes shining with the anticipation of a new campaign.

Rajaraja's smile was full of paternal pride. 'Choose which you will, Rajendra.'

'I would like the land force,' Rajendra said. 'I would wish to take Rajgana and show Bhim that a Chola army can destroy his pet fortress, despite all his tricks and ploys.'

'Then you shall command the army,' Rajaraja said. 'I will take the fleet and between us, we will squeeze these pirates. Select whichever five regiments you desire, Rajendra, and prepare them with food, water and supplies. I will send Kulothunga with you.'

'No, Father.' Rajendra shook his head. 'I wish to win this battle on my own, without a hero to take credit for my victory.'

Rajaraja gave a faint smile. 'You wish to make your name, I see. So be it, Rajendra. Fight well.'

'Fight well, Father.'

Rajaraja rapped his knuckles on the table, calling the meeting to a halt. 'Gentlemen,' Rajaraja nodded to Melcorka, 'and Lady. In our last campaign,

I merely flicked my little finger at Thiruzha. This time, I will use an iron fist. The Chola Empire is going to war. May Shiva be with us all.'

Chapter Eighteen

With further to travel, Rajendra led out his army a full six days in advance of the fleet. Melcorka watched them march past the walls of Thanjavur: the superb cavalry with swords, lances and prancing horses; the elephantry tramping heavily as the mahouts perched behind the huge creatures' ears and the archers and spearmen crammed in the howdahs, waving to the assembled crowds; and company after company of infantry with spears and swords or bows.

The column seemed to go on forever, thousands of soldiers marching to death or glory with the sun glinting on steel, while mothers and sweethearts watched with a mixture of pride and fear and worry.

'It was ever thus,' Bradan said. 'Men marching to war and women wishing that wars were a thing of the past.'

'Some women march to war, too,' Melcorka reminded him.

They stood side by side on the ramparts of Thanjavur as dawn flushed the eastern sky pink and a thousand birds fluttered and flew around them.

'I had thought the army that attacked Rajgana was large,' Bradan said. 'This one is five times larger. Rajaraja is making sure.'

'I hope that Rajendra takes heed of your advice about Rajgana,' Melcorka said.

'So do I,' Bradan nodded. 'I would wish that we were with him.'

'If you were,' the voice came from below, 'I would be at your side.'

'Kosala?' Melcorka watched the Singhalese warrior hurry up the steps to the rampart. 'What are you doing here? I thought you were back in Ceylon!'

'I've been here all the time, in case you have need of my sword, Melcorka.' Kosala salaamed. 'I thought that you were only a foolish woman until I saw you fight.'

'I'm not sure if that is a compliment or an insult.' Melcorka moved slightly as Kosala stepped to her side.

'I would never insult the best warrior I have ever seen, or the most alluring woman.' Kosala salaamed again.

Melcorka glanced at Bradan and raised her eyebrows. 'I am not sure if either label is correct,' she said. 'Recently, both Kulothunga and Dhraji have bested me, and there are many thousands of better-looking women in this Chola Empire. For instance, the Rani Panchavan is a woman who would turn heads in any company. I am but a plain island girl.'

'You are my goddess,' Kosala said. 'I would die for you, Melcorka.'

'I am no goddess,' Melcorka said, 'and I do not wish anybody to die for me.' She touched his shoulder, smiling. 'I do thank you for the sentiment, Kosala. Now, we had better prepare for war. I think that Dhraji and the Thiruzhas will be a tough enemy to defeat.'

'There is a way,' Bradan reminded her. 'Remember the words of the Siddhars. Use the steel from the west bathed in water from the north to defeat the evil from the south when the sun sets in the east.'

'I remember these words,' Melcorka said. 'I do not know what they mean.'

Kosala frowned. 'The sun never sets in the east,' he said.

'If ever it does,' Melcorka said, 'then we shall defeat the rakshasa.' She did not admit how worried she was.

* * *

With their loolas patrolling ahead and all around, the Chola fleet sailed parallel to the coast. The long swells of the ocean caressed the hulls, with the sun turning the white spray into diamond-bright sparks. Melcorka stood near the stern of the royal yacht *Akramandham,* while Rajaraja sat on a raised platform on the quarterdeck, watching everything that was happening.

Touching the hilt of Defender, Melcorka hoped that her arrangements would be successful. Although she usually had confidence in her ability to defeat any enemy, apprehension gnawed at her as the fleet slipped south, rounded the extremity of the sub-continent and then headed north toward the lands of

Thiruzha. Bhim and Dhraji awaited, one an astute military tactician and the other a rakshasa from the underworld.

'Do not worry,' Melcorka.'Kulothunga stood beside Rajaraja. 'I am here. We cannot lose.'

'Thank you, Kulothunga. That is reassuring.' Melcorka did not hide her smile.

The red tiger flag of Chola snapped from the mizzen mast and stern of each vessel, with men posted at the masthead as lookouts, watching for the movement of the loolas and scanning the sea for any sudden Thiruzha incursion.

Melcorka surveyed the fleet. She had learned the name and function of every class of Chola vessel. The loolas were the light vessels used for scouting, or escorting merchant ships to protect them from stray pirate attacks. The vajaras were the next class up; longer, stronger and better armed, these vessels had provided the mainstay of the previous Chola fleet to attack Kollchi. The dharani were even larger; they tended to work in small flotillas. Finally, there were the thirisdais, the battleships. More massive than anything Melcorka had seen before, these vessels carried hundreds of fighting men and alien war-machines of a type that intrigued her.

'What are these weapons?' Melcorka asked.

'Don't you have them in Alba?' Kulothunga asked.

'We have nothing like them,' Melcorka said.

Kulothunga smiled. 'Hopefully, the Thiruzha pirates have not seen them, either. We might give them a very nasty surprise.' His laugh was totally devoid of humour as he scanned the horizon.

'We're nearing Thiruzha waters,' a ship's officer warned. 'Any vessel here could be hostile.'

'Good,' Kulothunga said. 'I hope the Thiruzhas send out their entire fleet, so we can smash them to splinters and send them to the bottom.'

The first loola returned within an hour, her oars churning the sea into a silver-white froth and her master urging more and ever more speed.

'I think your loolas have made contact with the Thiruzha, your Majesty,' Bradan murmured. 'Now, Bhim's scouts will try and lure them into a trap.'

'You said that Bhim used that tactic with my previous fleet,' Rajaraja said.

'That is what happened,' Bradan said.

'Then we will do the same to them.' Rajaraja said. 'Bring the captain of the loola to me.'

The loola captain was a slim, elegant-looking youth with a ready smile and a thin moustache. Rajaraja gave him orders, patted him on the shoulder and sent him away again. The loola hurried to another vessel of the same class, and within a few moments, the instructions had been passed from ship to ship around the fleet.

'Your Majesty,' Melcorka called out. 'May I crave your permission to serve on one of the loolas?'

Rajaraja looked at her. 'I prefer you to remain where I can see you,' he said. 'I do not wholly trust you yet.'

Kulothunga smiled and touched the hilt of his sword. 'If you wish, Your Majesty, I can go with her. I have already bested her in swordplay and wrestling. If I see her doing anything against your Majesty's best interests, I will cut off her arms and feed her to the sharks.'

Rajaraja nodded. 'If anybody can control a female, Kulothunga, you can. You hear that, Melcorka? My best swordsman will be watching every move you make.'

'I heard,' Melcorka said.

Kulothunga touched a hand to the hilt of his sword and frowned at Melcorka. 'Don't forget, woman.'

'I will also keep your man here, Bradan the coward.' Rajaraja smiled. 'If you do not fight your best for me I shall hang him from the yard-arm by his ankles and let the sun roast him to death.'

'There is no need for threats, Your Majesty.' Melcorka said. 'I have rights to wrong with Dhraji and Bhim.'

'So you claim,' Rajaraja said. 'Keep both eyes on her, Kulothunga.'

'I will,' Kulothunga promised. 'Come, Melcorka, and we shall see if you know anything about using that graceless old sword of yours.'

Rajaraja signalled to the closest loola. 'Take these warriors with you,' he ordered, 'and make sure the foreign woman is at the fiercest of the fighting.'

The loola's captain was named Jasweer, a shapely woman with a scar on her chin and chain mail covering her from throat to thighs. For a moment, Jasweer looked disgusted that a foreign woman should burden her vessel, and then she replied, 'Aye, Your Majesty!' She raised her voice to a clear shout. 'You heard Rajaraja! Bring this useless luggage on board and steer for the enemy!'

Melcorka found that the deck of a loola was very different from the quarter-deck of the royal yacht. Men, woman, weapons and equipment took up every square inch of space, and the crew were all vibrant young people, wiry rather than muscular and eager to get to grips with the enemy. Most were sailors, but, in common with every other vessel of the Chola fleet, the loola carried a contingent of marines, who looked capable of taking on anything.

'Come on then, Kulothunga,' Jasweer said, 'and, if you must, bring that ugly foreign woman with you. We can use her for ballast, I suppose.'

The crew and marines laughed. The sailors pulled at the oars in unison as the lookout sat cross-legged at the masthead.

Jasweer nodded to Kulothunga's sword. 'Do you think you'll get close enough to use that?'

'I hope so!' Kulothunga said. 'I want to kill the Thiruzha.'

'We have archers and marines for fighting,' Jasweer said. 'Landsmen are better on land. They can't handle the sea.' The crew laughed again. 'And as for *that*,' Jasweer jerked a thumb toward Melcorka, 'what can I say?'

'You can use her as bait,' one of the forward oarsmen said, as others gave alternative and cruder uses for Melcorka that caused Jasweer to laugh and shake her head.

'You! Ugly foreign woman! You stand over there and keep out of the way.' Jasweer pointed to the mast. 'When the fighting starts, you can either hide or dive overboard, I don't care which, as long as you don't get in the way or put any of my crew in danger.'

The loola raced onward with her prow kicking up spray and the wind whining in the rigging. The smell of sweat filled the air as the crew bent to the oars, hauling like heroes. A breeze kicked spume from the wave-tops, cooling the rowers as Jasweer scampered to the masthead, agile as a teenager despite her chain-mail.

'Enemy ahead!' she shouted. 'Two, three, four Thiruzha scouting craft and they've seen us. Archers, get ready!'

'Are we going to fight them?' Kulothunga drew his sword in readiness.

'Naturally!' Jasweer said. 'Do you think we've come here to salaam politely and worship Shiva?' She raised her voice. 'We're the point of the sword! We're the sharp end of the Navy! We're Rajaraja's finest killers! We're Jasweer's Sharks! Who are we?'

'We're Jasweer's Sharks!' the crew shouted.

Melcorka remembered hearing similar chants when her mother had first taken her to war against the Norse. Some things transcended cultures, races and continents. People were the same, despite outward differences.

'I can't hear you,' Jasweer said. 'Who are we? Tell the Thiruzha!'

'We are Jasweer's Sharks!' The crew called again. 'We are Jasweer's Sharks!'

'Break out our battle flag!' Jasweer ordered and a lithe sailor hoisted a second flag from the stern of the loola. A red shark on a black background, the flag snarled defiance at the leopard of Thiruzha.

The three Thiruzha scout ships spread out and headed toward Jasweer's loola. Melcorka heard the rhythmic beat of the Thiruzha drums, repetitive, unhurried and sinister through the swish of the oars and the lap of the sea.

'Helmsman!' Jasweer shouted from her position at the masthead. 'On my word, break to port.'

'Aye, Captain.' The helmsman was a broad-chested, sturdy man with a small green turban and an expression of utter composure.

The Thiruzha vessels were closing, rowing steadily through the long seas with their flag alternatively fluttering and sagging in the fluky breeze. A trio of seagulls screamed past, wings flapping and beaks open.

'Helmsman...' Jasweer lifted her right hand, 'ready... *ready*... break now!'

The helmsman shifted the tiller and the loola sliced to port as the oarsmen adjusted their rowing accordingly.

'Archers! Man the starboard side!' Jasweer yelled. 'Wait for my command!'

The loola had left two of the Thiruzha scouts astern and concentrated on the vessel on the left. As soon as that ship's captain realised that they would soon be fighting one-to-one without the support of his colleagues, he ordered his archers to fire. The captain's timing was flawed; the archers fired on a rising wave, and their irregular volley rose too high.

'Two points to port!' Jasweer did not flinch as just three arrows hissed past her, two to rip into the sail and the third to thunk harmlessly onto the deck. 'Now, three points to starboard,' Jasweer ordered, as the enemy archers fired again. One of the Chola oarsmen yelled as an arrow lodged in his thigh. 'Take that man away,' Jasweer shouted. 'Replace him with a marine.'

The two vessels closed, with the Thiruzha archers firing continually and their drummer increasing the beat.

'Stand by to ram!' Jasweer shouted, when the loola closed to within fifty feet. 'Helmsman, port your helm. Archers... at the quarterdeck... now!'

The loola veered, so her starboard side was parallel to the Thiruzha scout. Melcorka saw the straining faces of the Thiruzha crew, the row of bobbing skulls along her hull and the pot-bellied drummer hammering at his drum. Chained to their oars, the oarsmen could only stare up in miserable apathy.

The Chola archers pulled back their bow-strings, aimed and fired a perfectly co-ordinated volley that peppered the quarterdeck of the Thiruzha craft. Melcorka saw the Thiruzha commander fall, with two arrows in his chest and another in his neck. One bolt slammed into the left leg of the Thiruzha helmsman, who staggered, but retained his post with bravery that deserved a better cause.

'Hard a-starboard! One last pull! Up oars and ram!' The strengthened prow of the loola crashed into the starboard side of the Thiruzha scout, splintering three of her oars, killing a despairing oarsman and thrusting deep into the hull.

'Marines! Board, fight and listen for my orders! Oarsmen, sit still!' Perched on the masthead, Jasweer yelled commands to her sharks.

'Come on, Melcorka!' Drawing his sword, Kulothunga followed the Chola marines onto the deck of the scout. Melcorka slipped Defender out of her scabbard, relishing the familiar rush of power as she leapt into the midst of the Thiruzhas. The Chola archers continued to fire, concentrating on the Thiruzha officers on the scout's quarterdeck.

The Chola marines had formed a wedge on the Thiruzha scout, cutting down everybody who stood in their path. They worked as a disciplined team, supporting each other in a systematic attack that no lone warrior could break.

'These marines are good,' Melcorka said.

'So am I!' Kulothunga shouted. His smile was even more extensive than normal as he vaulted over a dead Thiruzha oarsman to get in front of the Chola marines. Melcorka followed and stood at his left as the Thiruzha defenders rushed at them, roaring their battle cries.

Two warriors opposed Melcorka, one with a stabbing spear, the other with sword and shield. Melcorka sliced sideways, chopped the spearman's arms off and, in a single fluid motion, parried the swing of the sword and thrust forward, with Defender's longer length giving her an advantage. The Thiruzha swordsman died without a sound, and Melcorka moved on, ignoring the slave oarsmen as she disposed of the desperate Thiruzha warriors.

'I am Melcorka of Alba! Alba! Alba!'

Out of the corner of her eye, Melcorka saw Kulothunga fighting in a controlled fury; killing and wounding without emotion save for his permanent smile. Melcorka nodded; Kulothunga was as good a fighting man as she had ever seen, fast and powerful, without any wasted energy.

'You're good, Kulothunga!' Melcorka shouted.

'I'm better than good.' Kulothunga gutted a warrior with a twist of his sword, sliced a spear in half and drew his blade across the spearman's chest. 'I'm the best. I am Kulothunga, the best the world has ever seen.'

Dodging a wild swipe from a mace, Melcorka decapitated the wielder with a casual back-handed blow. 'I still admire your modesty, Kulothunga!'

'Naturally you do.' Kulothunga ducked under the swing of a curved sword and chopped the man's legs off at the knees. 'You admire everything about me. Every warrior and every woman admires everything about me.'

'Marines!' Jasweer's voice rose clear above the tumult of battle. 'Marines! Return to the ship! Return!'

The Chola marines began a fighting withdrawal, one steady pace at a time, still fighting, still killing. Melcorka and Kulothunga glanced at each other.

'Best be going,' Melcorka said. 'We don't wish to be left behind.'

They withdrew with the marines, stepping on board the loola just as Jasweer gave the order for the oarsmen to 'back water before that vessel takes us down with it!'

Jasweer's loola eased back into the sea, leaving the Thiruzha vessel a wreck, strewn with dead and wounded men. Greasy blood flowed from her deck into the sea, as water poured into her from the hole that Jasweer's loola had made. The scout tilted to the side and began to sink as, unable to escape, the slaves shrieked in despair.

'You fought well, foreign woman,' Kulothunga said. 'Nearly as well as me.'

'You fought well, too, Kulothunga,' Melcorka said. 'For a man.'

They grinned at each other and simultaneously began to clean their swords as the Chola marines ordered their ranks and counted their casualties.

'This is no time for a holiday!' Jasweer roared from the masthead. 'Oarsmen, double your strokes. Marines, ready your swords. Archers, as soon as the Thiruzha scouts come into range, fire at them. Aim for the quarterdeck and the oarsmen. Slow them down!'

A further two Thiruzha scouts had joined the original vessels speeding toward Jasweer's Sharks, evidently intending revenge for the sinking of their sister. Melcorka scanned the seas. Thiruzha and Chola vessels were locked in combat to port, with ships speeding this way and that as Thiruzha scouts and Chola loolas skirmished, closed and parted in a confused melee.

'Survivors in the water!' the lookout shouted.

'Ours or theirs?' Jasweer asked.

'Theirs!' the lookout said.

'Ignore them. Row on!'

The oarsmen bent to their oars, with some of the blades cracking on the heads of the frantic swimmers. When Thiruzha scouts came within range, the Sharks met them with disciplined fire. Arrows hummed through the air, to splash into the water or thrum against the timber of the respective hulls. One Chola oarsman gasped as an arrow landed on the haft of his oar. Another swore as an arrow sprouted in his arm. He stood up, and another arrow smacked into his side.

'Marines! Take that man's place,' Jasweer ordered. 'Archers, keep firing!'

A Chola dharani powered up. Longer, heavier and more powerful than the loola, its archers supported Jasweer's vessel with four times the loola's volume of arrows. Melcorka grunted approval as a Thiruzha scout veered sharply away, with its commander and helmsman lying dead on the quarterdeck.

'Captain Jasweer!' the commander of the dharani shouted. 'Orders from Rajaraja. You have to delve as deep as you can into the Thiruzha fleet and then return.'

Jasweer raised a hand in acknowledgement. 'Did you hear that, my sharp-toothed sharks? We are given the position of honour! We are to lead the attack and lure the Thiruzha pirates back to our heavy units! Jasweer's Sharks!'

'Jasweer's Sharks!' Jasweer's crew roared. 'Lead on, Captain! Jasweer's Sharks!'

'The Thiruzha know I am aboard,' Kulothunga said. 'Rajaraja is sending me to kill the enemy.' He pulled his shoulders even further back. 'He knows that they will be scared of me.'

'That must be it,' Melcorka said. 'Even in Persia and China, they will know of Kulothunga's deeds.'

'I suppose they do,' Kulothunga said.

Jasweer looked down from the masthead. 'There are three Thiruzha scouts ahead and then a formation of their larger vessels. We are going to ignore the scouts and race for the larger ships. We'll fire on the closest, turn and run back to the fleet.' Jasweer paused as her crew contemplated her words. 'We might not all get back safely. We might all get killed. I do not know. All that I know is that we are Jasweer's Sharks and we will leave a name that will astonish the *world*.' She ended on a rising note that had the crew cheering. Even the wounded looked up from their beds of pain, to yell and shout once more.

'Jasweer's Sharks! Jasweer's Sharks!' The crew chanted the slogan as Jasweer guided her loola toward the centre of the Thiruzha fleet. 'Jasweer's Sharks!'

'Break out all the battle-flags!' Jasweer yelled. 'Let there be no mistake! Let the enemy know with whom they are dealing!'

A further two huge flags exploded from the masts. One depicted the royal tiger of Chola. The other showed Jasweer's own red shark.

'Jasweer's Sharks!' the crew yelled again, as the oarsmen hauled, powering the loola through the sea. As one of the Thiruzha scouts came close, the archers fired an accurate volley. Melcorka saw the arrows as a small dark cloud that seemed to hover in the air for a second, and then they sliced down on the enemy's quarterdeck. A chorus of yells and screams followed.

'Good shooting,' Jasweer yelled. 'Now, target the oarsmen!'

The arrows flew again, and two of the scout's oars jerked out of the water, showing that the oarsmen had been hit.

'Keep firing,' Jasweer ordered, as the loola raced on. A few arrows buzzed back in return, and a marine fell without a sound as he was hit in the neck. His blood spouted in gradually receding jerks that stained the deck and drained into the scuppers.

'Clear the decks,' Jasweer shouted. 'Throw that poor fellow overboard!'

A second Thiruzha scout came marginally closer, fired a salvo that fell short and rowed away, followed by derisive jeers from Jasweer's Sharks.

'Give me a bow,' Kulothunga demanded. 'I am a better archer than anybody on this ship.'

'There are plenty of bows under the deck,' a marine officer told him. 'It's about time you and that pale foreign woman made yourselves useful. Standing about waving your sword and weighing down the boat does not help anybody.'

For a moment, Melcorka thought that Kulothunga would kill the marine where he stood. Instead, Kulothunga lifted two bows and handed one to Melcorka.

'A contest, Melcorka,' Kulothunga said. 'I have already bested you with the sword and at wrestling. Let me demonstrate how to fire a bow.'

Melcorka smiled. 'You do like to boast, Kulothunga, yet I heard some girls giggling about what you cannot do.' She allowed the words to sink in before continuing. 'They mentioned something about inadequacy in bed.'

Melcorka waited to see the reaction. Most men she had known would have responded with bluster and an immediate rebuttal. Kulothunga, with his vastly greater ego, had no need for such things.

'Little girls can say such things,' Kulothunga said, 'but only before I have bedded them. Afterwards, their eyes are full of wonder and their bellies full of my seed.' His great laugh boomed across the boat.

'We'll have less hilarity and more work down there,' Jasweer shouted. 'Get to it, you two! If you can't row, then let's see what else you can do.'

The third Thiruzha scout was racing toward them, firing a constant stream of arrows from a platform in the bows.

'There's our target.' Kulothunga strode forward, bent his bow and sent an arrow across the sea in a single movement.

Melcorka watched as the arrow reached the apex of its flight and plunged down, to land on the hull of the Thiruzha craft. 'You missed, Kulothunga. You were nowhere near your target.'

'You try,' Kulothunga said. 'That was only a ranging shot.'

The bow was of an unfamiliar pattern to Melcorka; longer, double-curved and more powerful than those she had used in Alba. Pulling back the string, she aimed and released, for the arrow to fly far over her mark.

'You see?' Kulothunga laughed. 'I am the better shot.'

'We'll try again.' Melcorka did not like to be second best at anything. Fitting another arrow to the bow, she fired quickly, and missed again, while Kulothunga's arrow thudded into the quarter-deck of the Thiruzha craft.

'Archers!' Jasweer yelled. 'Show these two land clowns how it's done. Show them how Jasweer's Sharks fire!'

The archers grinned and loosed, with every single arrow finding the enemy ship. Melcorka watched their technique and copied it as best she could, so her next arrow landed closer to the Thiruzha vessel, and then there were other things to worry about than a contest with Kulothunga.

'We're approaching the main Thiruzha fleet,' Jasweer said. 'I want every available sailor and marine on the port side, and everybody to have a bow. That means you two boasting land-sloggers as well.'

Fifty strong, the Thiruzha fleet carved through the sea, every ship wearing two flags, the yellow-and-blue leopard of Thiruzha and a plain black flag.

'What's that black flag?' Melcorka asked.

'It means no quarter,' Kulothunga said. 'The Thiruzha are not taking prisoners.'

'There is Bhim.' Melcorka touched the hilt of Defender and, in an instant of sudden clarity, she saw Bhim drinking from a gold-and-pearl-mounted skull. Bhim raised the skull and red liquid dribbled down his chin. In that second, Melcorka knew with utter certainty that Bhim was drinking blood; he was not human. The creature who posed as Bhim was a rakshasa. The knowledge sent a cold chill through her. She had been unable to kill one of these demons; how could she destroy two?

'We are facing forces from another place,' Melcorka said, 'a place of shadows and horrors beyond our imagining.'

'Is that so?' Kulothunga caressed his sword. 'Well, I would gamble all the gold in the Empire that my sword and I are the equal of any number of rakshasas.' He raised his voice to a shout that carried across the intervening water to the Thiruzha flagship.

'Did you hear me, Bhim? I am Kulothunga, and I am not afraid of you, whoever or whatever you are. I am not afraid of any man, any woman, any warrior or any demon in this world or the next.'

Bhim altered his stance to stare directly at Kulothunga. For one fraction of a second, Melcorka caught his glance. She shuddered at the force of pure evil in his smoky yellow eyes.

'Be careful, Kulothunga. It is better not to stir these creatures up.' Melcorka put her hand on Kulothunga's arm.

'I will not stir it up,' Kulothunga said. 'I will kill it.' He raised his voice again. 'Do you hear that, Bhim? I am going to fight you, and I am going to kill you.'

In response, Bhim lifted his skull-cup in salute, took a deep draught and turned his head away. He must have given an order, for the Thiruzha flagship pulled out of formation and headed directly for Jasweer's loola.

'We've caught their attention.' Jasweer's voice carried to every quarter of the ship. 'I want everybody with a bow to fire at the Thiruzha flagship. Fire and keep firing as fast as you can. Don't stop until you have no arrows left. Try and kill Bhim. Oarsmen, keep rowing. Helmsman, wait for my orders.

All the rest, I want you to retrieve any enemy arrows that land on our ship and give them to our archers.'

Jasweer guided them to within seventy yards of the Thiruzha ship, with long-range arrows humming from both sides. 'Helmsman! Hard a-port. Archers, move to the stern.'

Melcorka knew that the next few moments would be dangerous as the loola slowed down to turn and presented her vulnerable side to the Thiruzha flagship. Sure enough, the Thiruzha vessel closed the gap, and more of her arrows found a mark, but Jasweer had timed her move perfectly, allowing the loola to escape with only two casualties. One female archer had an arrow through her stomach, and a male oarsman shrieked with an arrow in his groin.

'Attend to these wounded,' Jasweer ordered. 'Oarsmen, keep the pace. Don't increase it.'

'Don't increase it?' Kulothunga grinned. 'I see! Jasweer wishes Bhim to board us so I can kill him man-to-monster. In fact, I will kill them all.' He spared Melcorka a glance. 'You may help if you wish.'

'Thank you.' Melcorka gave an exaggerated salaam. 'However, I believe Jasweer has other ideas. Rajaraja wants Jasweer to lure the Thiruzha into a trap, much as the Thiruzha did to our last fleet.'

Larger and more powerful than the loola, the Thiruzha vessel surged through the waves with the archers firing non-stop. In return, Jasweer jinked from side to side, using her boat's greater agility to dodge the enemy missiles. Other Thiruzha vessels had broken formation and were streaming behind their flagship, so the sea astern of Jasweer's loola was a mass of enemy ships. Scout vessels tried to close with Jasweer, while the heavier vessels powered through the waves in showers of spray and spindrift.

'Look ahead,' Melcorka said.

The Chola fleet was also approaching, mighty thirisdais with the war machines on board, fast vajaras that had already closed with the more impudent of the Thiruzha scouts and the dharanis, the workhorses of the fleet with their crews of seamen and marines.

'The Thiruzha have seen them,' Kulothunga said. 'They're turning away.'

'Too late, I think,' Melcorka said, as the Chola vajaras sliced through the Thiruzha scouts in a welter of broken oars and fragmented men, followed by the indestructible majesty of the massive thirisdais. 'What a sight! Now, that's something I can tell my grandchildren about.'

'Ha! Wait until you see me at the forefront of the battle,' Kulothunga shouted. 'Your grandchildren will listen with open mouths to the tales you tell them.'

'No doubt.' Melcorka heard Bhim roaring to his oarsmen to back water, but the weight of the Thiruzha flagship kept her moving forward.

'Hard to port!' Jasweer shouted. 'Oarsmen, row as if a hundred rakshasas were breathing fire on your collective arse!'

'Our captain has an interesting turn of phrase,' Melcorka said approvingly.

Kulothunga laughed. 'She is right, except it won't be a rakshasa breathing fire.'

Two Thiruzha scouts raced between Bhim's ship and the leading thirisdai, firing arrows uselessly at the massive hull of the Chola vessel. The thirisdai sailed on, brushed the first scout aside without a quiver and capsized the second with her ram.

'Bhim's next,' Melcorka said.

Melcorka was wrong. Although the scout ships had only lasted a couple of moments, Bhim had used the time to alter course and call up two of his larger vessels to challenge the thirisdai. While arrows whistled in both directions, marines clustered around the strange machine on the thirisdai's deck.

'What are they doing?' Melcorka asked.

'Watch and learn, woman of Alba,' Kulothunga said. 'We of Chola have much to teach you.'

The machine was like a giant funnel set on the base of a chariot. Ignoring the arrows that felled some of their number, the marines pushed the device toward the bow of the ship. When the shipmaster snapped an order, two middle-aged men ran forward, with a body of marines protecting them with a barrier of shields.

'These men are engineers,' Kulothunga explained. 'They will operate the machine.'

Guarded by the shield-carriers, the engineers pointed the end of the funnel toward the nearest Thiruzha vessel, and it gushed out a clear liquid.

'What's happening?' Absorbed in the machine, Melcorka barely noticed the arrows that were falling on the deck of the loola. She brushed one casually away with Defender.

As some marines fell under Thiruzha arrows, others took their place to pro-tect the engineers. Within a few moments, the liquid caught fire and a long tongue of flame leapt from the machine toward the enemy ship. Melcorka heard the terrified screams on the unfortunate Thiruzha vessel, with men either fighting the fire or retreating in panic. One seaman, his clothes and hair ablaze, leapt into the sea. Others followed, with prowling sharks waiting in the water.

'In the name of...!' Melcorka said. 'I've never seen anything like that before.'

'We are Chola,' Kulothunga said. 'We are the most powerful empire in the world.'

The other Thiruzha vessels steered away from the horror, so the sea was a mess of retreating Thiruzha ships and triumphant Chola vessels. The thirisdai continued on, slow, ponderous and dangerous, with Thiruzha vessels scattering before it, until one brave Thiruzha scout vessel rowed close, with her archers trying to pick off the engineers that operated the flame machine.

'That's our target,' Jasweer shouted. 'Protect the thirisdai! Come on, lads and lassies – Jasweer's Sharks are needed!'

Jasweer had no need to manoeuvre. Steering straight for the Thiruzha scout, she shouted, 'Up oars' and rammed it in a grinding crash of splintered oars and crackling timber.

'Marines!' Jasweer shouted. The loola's marines poured over the bow, slashing and thrusting at the scout's crew.

'Come on, Kulothunga!' Melcorka leapt across to the scout.

Melcorka only had time to see the thirisdai sail serenely past before three Thiruzha warriors attacked her.

Melcorka ducked the swing of a sword, cut off the swordsman's legs and stepped over the body to deal with the second and third attacker. By the time she had done so, Kulothunga stood grinning over the four men he had killed.

'You are good, Melcorka, but I am better.'

Melcorka did not know what made her turn. One minute she was standing triumphantly on the deck of the scout, and the next, she saw the rakshasa rearing from the water. The creature was exactly as she remembered it from her previous encounter, a great, round head with glaring eyes, a snapping red beak and ten pulsating tentacles that reached from the water onto the thirisdai.

'Kulothunga!' Melcorka yelled and hefted Defender.

A second rakshasa emerged from the sea in a cascade of water and froth. Its tentacles snaked aboard the thirisdai, feeling for purchase along the deck. While some men ran in panic, the marines and engineers struggled to turn the fire-machine to face the monster. Standing square on his quarterdeck, the shipmaster roared orders for the archers to 'shoot those damned monstrosities off my ship!'

'Archers!' Jasweer screamed. 'Fire at these things, aim for the eyes!'

One tentacle lifted a thirisdai oarsman high into the air and tossed him backwards into the sea. Another arm swept along the deck, knocking three marines off their feet as the engineers succeeded in pointing the fire-machine at the monster.

'Come on, Melcorka!' Kulothunga shouted. 'There is more work for our swords!'

The engineers operated their weapon, with a stream of liquid pouring onto the first monster. When it closed its eyes and extended two tentacles towards the flame machine, the engineers promptly ran. Two brave marines stepped in to take their place.

'No!' The shipmaster roared. 'Don't use the flame! You'll burn the ship as well!'

The order was too late, as the marines set flame to the liquid. Within a moment, the creature was enveloped in fire, with its tentacles writhing in the air, and then, still burning, it pulled itself along the deck, lifted the machine from the deck and threw it away. The marines scattered, with the creature curling its tentacles around them. It tore one man in half in a shower of blood and intestines and thrust another into its great beak of a mouth.

'Steer for the monsters, Jasweer!' Kulothunga shouted. 'Let me kill them!'

'I'll not hazard my ship!' Jasweer yelled. It was the first time Melcorka had seen her rattled.

'It's our duty to protect the thirisdai,' Kulothunga reminded her. 'We are expendable. Steer for it!'

'May Shiva protect us all!' Jasweer's voice shook. 'Helmsman, steer for these things.'

All this time, the Chola archers had continued to fire, with their arrows thudding into both rakshasas without effect. The burning rakshasa plunged into the sea, emerging a moment later with the fire doused.

'Arrows cannot hurt them and fire does not kill them,' Kulothunga said in wonder. 'How do we destroy these rakshasas?'

'I do not know.' Melcorka ran her hands along the blade of Defender. 'Let's see if we can do better.'

'Shiva go with you!' Jasweer shouted, as she steered her loola to the stern of the thirisdai. Melcorka and Kulothunga jumped onto the steering oar of the much larger vessel and climbed onto the quarterdeck. The rakshasas were creating havoc, throwing men into the sea, pulling off legs, arms and heads, biting marines with their great beaks and tearing holes in the hull.

'I am Melcorka of Alba!' Melcorka announced her presence. 'Fight me, rakshasa.' Out of the corner of her eye, she saw Kulothunga run to challenge the second rakshasa and then she was too busy to notice anything.

The rakshasa reared up on three of its tentacles until it was three times as tall as Melcorka, and then swept the remaining five arms toward her. Bracing herself, Melcorka sliced the ends of two of the tentacles. 'You can be killed!' She thrust for the great glaring eyes. 'Die, you thing!'

Once again, Defender bounced off the eyeball. The shock jarred Melcorka's arms, forcing her to step back. She tried again, putting all her weight behind the thrust, only for Defender to jar against the eye. The rakshasa lunged at her, ripping its beak down the length of Melcorka's left arm.

Melcorka gasped with the pain. 'Oh, Mother, where are you when I need you most?' She slashed at a tentacle that tried to curl around her ankles, skiffing the wriggling end-piece off the deck.

The rakshasa snapped at her again and lashed out with three tentacles at once as it slithered along the deck, its eyes wide, glaring and undamaged.

'What kind of demon are you?' Melcorka backed away, cutting another tentacle in two, holding Defender in front of her, thinking of a new method of offence. 'I can cut your arms but not damage anything vital.'

'I am the kind of demon that you cannot kill.' The words formed inside Melcorka's brain. 'I am your nemesis, Melcorka of Alba. I am the death you have been seeking.'

'I do not seek death,' Melcorka said. 'I am Melcorka the Swordswoman.'

'All warriors seek death.' The words crept around her head. 'It is the ultimate end for the way of the sword. Either glorious death in climatic battle witnessed by thousands, or a sordid end, dying by inches in a ditch, unknown and uncared for.'

Melcorka had said nearly the same words herself. Trying to shake away the voice, she advanced again, thrusting Defender into the great mass that surrounded the two eyes. The blade sunk deep and stuck there, sucked in by the rakshasa's rubbery body. The rakshasa pulled away, nearly tearing Defender from Melcorka's grip. Melcorka held on, gasping, wrestled the sword free and only just managed to parry a swipe from a tentacle.

'You cannot defeat me, Melcorka. No mortal weapon can kill me. Accept that you will die now.'

'I am not here to die!' Melcorka attacked again, slicing sideways. Defender dislodged a chunk of the rubbery mass. It lay quivering on the deck, obscene, ugly and useless. A squad of marines ran to help, yelling their battle-cry as they thrust long spears into the creature. It retaliated with a swing of a tentacle that swept three men overboard and shattered the legs of a fourth. He lay on deck, refusing to scream.

Panting, Melcorka tried again, slicing another piece from the creature. 'I'll kill you bit by bit,' she said, as the rakshasa slithered toward her with a marine's blood dripping from its beak.

At that point, Melcorka heard Kulothunga roar. He was standing on the head of the other rakshasa, digging into the mass with his sword. The thing coiled its tentacles around him and slid into the sea, to disappear beneath the surface with Kulothunga on top, still thrusting with his sword.

'So dies Kulothunga,' the voice said in Melcorka's head. 'The best warrior that the world has ever seen.'

'You foul vermin.' Melcorka felt her anger rise. 'I don't know what you are or from what filthy place you come, but I will send you back in little pieces.'

Rather than a headlong attack, Melcorka slipped sideways, hacking at one of the remaining tentacles. 'You cannot move without your legs,' she said, 'so I will cut them off one by one and push you overboard for the sharks.'

The thirisdai lurched to the side as water poured in from the massive damage the rakshasa had caused.

'Abandon ship!' the shipmaster shouted. 'May Shiva protect you all!'

Barely glancing at the rakshasa, the crew reacted at once, slipping or jumping into the sea from the rapidly tilting ship.

'It seems that we will both die here,' Melcorka said. 'Come, creature.' Slicing off another of the tentacles, Melcorka again thrust at the rakshasa's eye. Once again, Defender bounced off. The rakshasa lunged with its beak. 'My arms will grow back, Melcorka.'

'Not yet, they won't!' Melcorka said, just as the ship gave a final lurch, tilted heavily forward and sank. Melcorka fell backwards into the water, narrowly avoiding the rakshasa's final swing with its remaining tentacles. When a current dragged them apart, Melcorka found herself swimming in tepid water among the wreckage of battle and the circling fins of sharks.

Failed again! That's twice I've fought that thing, and twice I've failed to kill it.

Treading water, Melcorka searched for the rakshasa. She only slid Defender into her scabbard when she thought it safe. The battle continued to rage all around as Chola and Thiruzha ships clashed, recoiled and manoeuvred across the sea.

'Mel!'

Bradan leaned over the side of a small boat. 'Out you come! I tried to come to help you.' He hauled her into the boat. 'You were too fast.'

'I was fighting that rakshasa for hours,' Melcorka pointed out.

Bradan shook his head. 'No you weren't, Mel. It was barely two minutes.'

'Two minutes? It seemed like ages!' Melcorka dried Defender on Bradan's jacket. 'I couldn't kill it, Bradan. Not even Defender could kill it.'

'You chopped off its legs, though.' Bradan pointed to the tentacles that still writhed on the surface of the water.

'It will grow new ones. I could not kill it.'

'You'll find a way,' Bradan said. 'We'll find a way.'

'Did you see Kulothunga? Did you see what happened to him?'

Bradan shook his head. 'I was watching you, not him.'

'He was fighting the other rakshasa,' Melcorka said. 'They fell into the sea together.'

'He's gone then,' Bradan said. 'I never liked him, but he was a brave man.'

'He was the best warrior I've ever met.' Melcorka looked at the sea with its litter of battle-wreckage. 'God only knows how we can kill these rakshasas.'

'We'll find a way if we can work out the Siddhar's riddle.' Bradan repeated it again. 'Use the steel from the west bathed in the water from the north to defeat the evil from the south when the sun sets in the east.'

Melcorka shook her head. 'I have no idea what that means. Why are these very clever people always so obscure with their sayings?'

'Perhaps they are so clever that they don't know they're obscure.'

With both rakshasas back under the water, Rajaraja regrouped the Chola fleet. He ordered the larger ships to resume their positions and divided the loolas, with some searching the battle site and the remainder returning to their primary tasks of scouting around the fleet.

'Forget the rakshasas.' Rajaraja sounded grim. 'We have the Thiruzha to defeat. Make sure we pick up all our survivors. I'll not leave any of my people for the sharks.'

The fleet sailed on, grimmer now with the loss of a battleship, grieving over the death of Kulothunga. As seamen buried their comrades at sea, marines sharpened their swords and counted their arrows. Melcorka perched on the ship's rail and began to clean Defender.

I'm not dead. Melcorka, we have a bond. I'm not dead.

The deep-voiced words resounded in her head. Melcorka looked up. 'Kulothunga? Was that you?' She scanned the sea; wreckage and the occasional dead body, a twirl of blood around a floating arm, the fin of a shark. 'Look! Over there! What's that in the water? It's Kulothunga! Is he alive?'

'Steer for that man,' Rajaraja ordered.

Kulothunga lay on his back amidst a welter of nautical litter, with his leg bleeding, a fresh scar across his chest and his sword still firm in his hand. Willing hands dragged him onto the flagship as morale soared.

'Kulothunga's alive! The Rakshasa could not kill him!' The news spread round the fleet to loud cheers.

'He's unconscious, though!' Bradan pumped the seawater from his lungs while Melcorka tended to his wounds.

'He has two deep cuts and a few bruises and scratches,' Melcorka said. 'But he's alive.'

'I defeated the rakshasa,' Kulothunga said, as soon as he stopped spewing seawater. 'After I cut off all its arms and legs, it could not swim.' He grinned to them. 'It sunk to the bottom of the sea.' Being Kulothunga, he preened his moustache. 'Am I not the best? I am Kulothunga, the best warrior there has ever been.'

'You fought well.' Melcorka kept her voice solemn. 'It is a pity you ended up floating in the sea so that a foreign woman and a man with a stick had to save you.'

'I killed the rakshasa.' Kulothunga lifted his sword. 'Nobody else can say the same.'

Melcorka nodded. 'I hope you are right, Kulothunga. I only hope that you are right.' She did not doubt Kulothunga's words; she only doubted that the rakshasa would stay dead after he had killed it.

* * *

Thiruzha lay ahead, with the walls of Kollchi waiting behind the island fort of Kalipuram. The defenders were ready, with the sun flashing on helmets through the ominous smoke that clouded the island. 'Now we will see how the Chola can fight,' Melcorka said.

'Bradan.' Rajaraja beckoned Bradan closer. 'Remind me about the defences of this island of Kalipuram.'

Bradan explained about the catapults, the boom and the bolt-firing machine.

'It is a formidable fortress then,' Rajaraja said.

'It is. You lost about a third of your fleet at Kalipuram,' Bradan said. 'By the time the remnants eased past, they were low in spirits and bereft of ideas, I think.'

Rajaraja grunted. 'You confirm what I thought,' he said. 'We will not make the same mistakes again. I will not lead my ships through a narrow channel under fire from hundreds of thousand archers and fire-throwing catapults. We will take Kalipuram Island before we enter the harbour.'

'That would be best.' Bradan noticed Kulothunga watching from amidships. He wondered what that warrior was thinking. 'I am sure Your Majesty remembers that I was only an observer. Any military man knows more than I do.' Bradan saw Kulothunga grunt in disgust, shake his head and walk away.

I never liked that champion, anyway. Bradan joined Melcorka in their cabin.

'Did Rajaraja tell you his plans?' Ever since the curse had been lifted, Melcorka had eaten sufficient for two. Now, she munched on a banana as she lounged on her bunk.

'No.' Bradan slumped to the deck. 'He listened to all I said and told me nothing. Kings don't often share their plans with me.'

'Nor with me.' Finishing her banana, Melcorka started on a handful of nuts. She looked up as the cabin door opened.

Kulothunga stood in the doorway with his sword at his side. Silhouetted against the dying sun, he looked even taller, with the breadth of his chest emphasised. 'It will be a busy day tomorrow, Melcorka. You will need some company.'

'I have Bradan,' Melcorka said.

'You need a man, a warrior, not a man who walks with a stick.' Kulothunga pushed into the cabin. 'You, Bradan, get out.'

'I am going nowhere,' Bradan said.

'Go, or I will throw you out. If you were not Melcorka's friend, I would kill you where you stand.'

'If you put one finger on Bradan, you will no longer be my friend.' Still gripping a handful of nuts, Melcorka stood up from the bunk.

'I thought you were a warrior. We fought side by side together. We have a special bond, you and I.' Kulothunga put a hand on his sword. 'A warrior needs another warrior, not a weakling who avoids battle.' He glanced at Bradan again. 'I could kill him before you drew blade.'

'Your weapon is too long to use in this confined space,' Melcorka said. 'I think you have made a mistake, Kulothunga. For the sake of our friendship, it will be better if you leave.'

Kulothunga stepped inside the cabin. 'I will take you willingly or by force, Melcorka, and I will send out your half-man, or he can stay and watch.' His lips twisted into a smile. 'You know I can best you at archery, wrestling or in swordplay, Melcorka, so why fight it?'

Melcorka swallowed her nuts before she spoke. 'You are a personable and handsome man, Kulothunga. You can get any woman you wish, and they would come willingly. Why do you want me when I already have a man?'

'You are different,' Kulothunga said. 'You are worth fighting for.'

'Goodbye, Kulothunga,' Melcorka said. 'Find another woman.' It was only when she pushed Kulothunga outside that she noticed Bradan had her dirk in his hand. 'You are not a fighting man, Bradan.'

'No,' Bradan agreed, 'but I am still a man.'

'There was never any doubt about that.' Melcorka perused him for a long moment. 'You are more man than any other I have ever met.' Before Bradan could reply, she changed the subject. 'I've never known Kulothunga act like that before. He was always arrogant, but never aggressive. Killing the rakshasa has altered him, somehow.'

'Maybe he's excited at the prospect of tomorrow's battle,' Bradan said.

'It could be that,' Melcorka agreed. She did not share her doubts.

The night before a battle was always tense. The ships' crews checked their weapons, or grabbed what sleep they could. Some sang, or had a last meal. Some prayed to Shiva, Ganesha or Krishna. A few secretly wept, wishing they were safely at home. Others boasted of the deeds they had done in the past and the heroics they would perform in the future. Melcorka slept most of the night, woke up to feast on fruit, fish and nuts and slept again. She woke before dawn and reached for Defender, with her movements awakening Bradan.

'Another battle today,' Bradan said.

Melcorka looked up. 'Another battle,' she agreed.

'What then, Mel? What will we do after that?'

'We will finish this war and move on,' Melcorka said. She looked away. 'Sometimes I think I have had sufficient wandering, Bradan. I want to settle somewhere.'

'I thought you did,' Bradan said. 'Can you defeat these rakshasas?'

Melcorka gave Bradan space to think. 'I don't know, Bradan. I can injure them, I can lop off their tentacles but I cannot kill them. Even Defender did not make any impression on their eyes. Kulothunga says he killed his rakshasa, so perhaps it can be done.'

'Perhaps,' Bradan said. 'You sliced bits off yours.'

'It still lived, and it told me it could grow more arms.' Testing Defender's blade, Melcorka began to sharpen it. 'The marines tried fire, and the archers must have hit it a hundred times, and it did not flinch. I don't know what else we can do. That riddle of the Siddhars means nothing to me.'

'You could ask Kulothunga,' Bradan suggested. 'He may know some new tricks.'

'Maybe so.' Melcorka added candle wax to Defender's scabbard so the sword would slide free more easily from her scabbard. 'Do you remember that woman back in the islands?'

'Hadali. She said she saw a tall man standing over you and one day you would meet a warrior whose sword is superior to yours.'

'That's right,' Melcorka said. 'What if the rakshasa is that warrior? Oh, I know these things don't have swords, but even so, I can't continue to be victorious forever.'

'You have Defender,' Bradan said.

'I know I have.' Melcorka tested her draw, added more wax and hung the sword on the bulkhead.

'Defender is a magic sword.' Bradan tried to cheer her up.

'It won't be the only blessed sword in the world,' Melcorka said. 'Someday, I will meet somebody who has a sword with equal powers and then it will depend only on my skills.' She faced Bradan, her face troubled. 'Bradan, I don't have many skills of my own.'

'Your skills are growing with every fight,' Bradan tried to reassure her. 'You are constantly learning new techniques.'

'When I did not have Defender, Kulothunga defeated me with ease.'

'Kulothunga is a superb warrior. He would defeat anybody with ease,' Bradan said. 'This attitude is not like you, Mel. What's wrong?'

Melcorka forced a smile. 'I'm probably only weary, Bradan. I don't think I have fully recovered from that curse, or my time in the dungeon while you were romping with that rakshasa-woman.'

'Romping is one word for it,' Bradan said. 'Surviving is another.'

'Tell me.' Melcorka crawled toward him with a new light in her eyes. 'What was she like?'

Bradan met her smile with one of his own. 'There are some things a gentleman does not discuss.'

'I might have to make you discuss them.' Melcorka crept closer. 'Kulothunga taught me all about pressure points.' She smiled. 'I also have other methods of persuasion.'

Bradan laughed. 'I know some of your pressure points too, Mel.' He rolled toward her. 'Here, let me demonstrate...'

* * *

Rajaraja stared at the island. 'Well, Bradan, there it is.'

Kalipuram looked no different from Bradan's previous visit, long and lethal, with the fort taking up most of the space. Smoke drifted across the battlements, while the masts of a few ships hugged the rocky coastline.

'I'm going closer,' Rajaraja decided. 'Bradan, come with me. You'd better bring your bodyguard as well.' He raised his voice. 'Signal for Jasweer. She and her sharks are the best in the business for this sort of thing.'

The instant Jasweer brought her loola alongside, Rajaraja stepped on board with his giant bodyguard at his side, followed by Melcorka and Bradan. As soon as their feet touched the deck, Jasweer had the oarsmen take them toward Kalipuram.

'They'll send out their scouts to warn us off,' Jasweer said, 'or maybe lob a few rocks at us.'

'If they knew I was on board, they would send out half their battle fleet,' Rajaraja said.

'Oh, that's no problem.' Jasweer was quite confident speaking to her raja. 'We can outsail and outmanoeuvre anything the Thiruzhas have, and with that ugly foreign woman on board,' she jerked a thumb at Melcorka, 'we can probably outfight them, too. She's nearly as good as Kulothunga.'

'She's better.' Bradan ignored the frosty looks.

Jasweer approached Kalipuram at speed, as she did everything. 'You stay near the stern, Rajaraja. If the Thiruzhas start to fire at us, keep your head down; I don't want to be known as the captain who lost her raja.' She yelled a mouthful of orders that saw the loola veer from left to right. 'And keep out from under my feet, Your Majesty, if you please.'

'I won't get in your way,' Rajaraja promised. Bradan noticed the smile that twitched the corners of his mouth.

Two Thiruzha scout boats sped from the lee of the island, both wearing a giant flag.

'Here they come,' Bradan said.

'Archers! Port bow!' Jasweer shouted orders. 'Helmsman, on my mark, two points to starboard. Trim that foresail, you lubbers! It's flapping like your granny's sari on a windy day.'

The Thiruzha scouts closed rapidly, with their archers opening fire the moment they thought they were in range.

'Amateurs.' Jasweer shook her head as the Thiruzha arrows fell well short. 'Helmsman: now! Archers: fire at their quarterdeck!' The loola eased to starboard, giving the archers a clear view of the closest Thiruzha scout. They fired in a body, with a dozen arrows flying toward the Thiruzha boat. 'Marines, take your shields and cover the raja, but for Shiva's sake don't make it obvious!'

As the first Thiruzha ship veered sharply away, the second joined it, so both were side by side, observing rather than attacking.

'Lookout!' Jasweer shouted. 'Keep your eyes open! The Thiruzha might try to block us from returning. They're up to something.'

The first rock landed fifty yards from the loola, raising a large fountain of water but doing no damage.

'That's what they're up to.' Jasweer had not flinched.

'Take us closer to the fort,' Rajaraja ordered. 'I want to see this place for myself.'

Dodging the occasional rock and keeping a wary eye on the two scout ships, Jasweer steered them to within two hundred yards of the island, where the sea shattered on ragged rocks. Thiruzha archers tried vainly to reach them with the lightest of their arrows.

'There, Your Majesty.' Bradan pointed to a cleft in the rocks. 'The Thiruzha have a chain boom beneath the water at that point. When the previous fleet sailed that way, the Thiruzha allowed some to pass and then hauled the chain up from the seabed to block the remainder.'

Rajaraja nodded. 'All right, Jasweer, I've seen enough. Take us back.'

Melcorka saw the movement on the battlements and looked up. She knew instinctively who the figure was, even at this distance, and nudged Bradan with her elbow. 'Can you see that woman?'

'That's Dhraji,' Bradan said at once. 'She's been watching us ever since we left the main fleet.'

'How could you see her all that time?'

'I couldn't.'

'So how?'

'I don't know how,' Bradan said. 'It feels like she is still inside my head, as if she is watching everything I do.'

Melcorka shivered. 'Maybe she is.' She looked back at the fort. Dhraji was still there, with her glare never straying from the loola. Melcorka wondered if Dhraji was the rakshasa she had fought two days before. Walking slowly to the mast, she climbed until she could balance on the yard and directly face Dhraji.

'Have a good look, Dhraji. Next time we meet, I will kill you.' Melcorka could feel the power of Dhraji's gaze like a physical force.

'Helmsman!' Jasweer yelled. 'Now!'

The loola eased round, followed by two catapult shots that soaked half the crew. The marines adjusted the shields that protected Rajaraja.

'It's all right, men, I've been wet before,' Rajaraja said. 'I'm not completely fragile.' He smiled. 'I've learned a lot this trip, thank you, Jasweer.'

The disturbance in the water erupted two hundred yards in front of them, raising a surge that crashed against the loola's hull.

'Hard a-starboard,' Jasweer ordered. 'Pull, lads! Pull!'

'I don't like the look of that.' Melcorka slid down the backstay to the deck. 'Or that!' She pointed to the tentacles that had just thrust out of the water, waving in the air as if seeking something to hold onto.

'It's a rakshasa.' Jasweer spoke as calmly as if she was talking about a cloud in the sky. 'Marines! Line the bulwarks, cut off these tentacles the second they touch our ship. Spearmen and archers, you can't miss that target!'

'I like this woman.' Stepping to the bulwark, Melcorka drew Defender.

'So do I.' Bradan lifted a spear from the deck.

'Oh, you would,' Melcorka said. 'You would like anything female, even if it has tentacles and a sharp red beak.'

'You've been looking in the mirror again.' Bradan followed Melcorka with his heart hammering inside his chest.

'Rajaraja!' Jasweer shouted. 'Get below deck. It's not much protection, but you'll be a bit safer here. That big lump of a bodyguard can look after you.'

'I'm not hiding when my people are in danger,' Rajaraja said. 'You concentrate on working your ship, Captain.'

The rakshasa shifted through the water with its tentacles spread out like a spider's web.

'We can't get past it,' Jasweer said, 'so let's go through it. Let's see how it likes a fully-laden loola smashing into it at full speed. Put your muscles to work, boys! We'll ram the thing.' She glared at Rajaraja. 'Get below when I order you! On this ship, I am in command!'

Melcorka touched Bradan's arm. 'Stay with the raja, Bradan. Don't let him leave the hold unless the ship goes down.'

'Be careful, Mel!' Bradan shouted, as Melcorka dashed forward.

Melcorka felt the usual surge of power as she held Defender, mixed with a new sensation of trepidation. She did not know how this fight would turn out. She had failed to kill the demon on two previous encounters, so why should this one be any different? Try again! If Kulothunga can kill it, so can I.

'Come on, you foul beast!' Placing herself in the bow with the wind tossing her hair and Defender held two-handed in front of her, Melcorka stared into the shield-sized eyes of the rakshasa.

The worst thing I can do is allow the rakshasa to know I am nervous. Predators can sense fear; it gives them strength and emboldens them. So do the unexpected! Unsettle this monster about which I know so little.

Lifting her head, Melcorka pointed to the rakshasa and forced a laugh. 'Join in, lads! Laugh. Bullies don't like getting mocked!'

Some of the crew joined in, but most were too preoccupied with their own affairs to waste their breath. The rakshasa seemed unmoved.

Melcorka balanced on the prow of the loola, holding Defender above her head. 'I am Melcorka of Alba,' she roared, 'and who dare meddle with me!'

'I dare!' The words formed in her mouth, a deep, clear threat to her very existence.

'Come on then, you demon from hell!' Melcorka challenged. 'Come and face me.'

The rakshasa's laugh was as sinister as anything Melcorka had ever heard.

'Get off the prow, you blasted fool!' Jasweer shouted. 'When we ram, the shock will knock you down!'

That made sense. Melcorka leapt down an instant before the loola crashed into the rakshasa. She had expected an intense jar that would shake the masts and send people to the deck; instead, the loola sank into the dense, rubbery mass that was the creature's body, without any apparent damage to either side.

Jumping back onto the prow, Melcorka slashed with Defender, hoping to cleave slices off the rakshasa to reach something vital. Two tentacles curled around her, one grasping at her legs, the other at her neck. Altering the angle of her attack, Melcorka hacked at the tentacles, slicing them apart before returning her attention to the body of the beast.

In the time it had taken Melcorka to dismember the tentacles, the rakshasa had reared closer to her, with the open beak revealing a deep black chasm that seemed to extend forever. Recoiling in disgust at the rakshasa's stench, Melcorka plunged Defender into the mouth, hoping to strike something vital.

'There, you foul beast!'

There was nothing to strike. The blade of Defender entered a blank space, darkness without end that sucked at Melcorka, so that she teetered on the edge of oblivion. She recovered with difficulty, stared into the black void and slashed sideways. Defender made contact with something that trapped the blade, holding it close. Cursing, Melcorka struggled to pull her sword free.

'What does it feel like to lose a fight, Melcorka?' The words taunted her, eroding her self-confidence, corroding her strength. 'How does defeat sound in your ears?'

'I am not interested in the possibility of defeat!' Melcorka shouted. 'It does not exist!'

The rakshasa's laughter mocked her. 'There is more than one way to lose, Melcorka the Swordswoman, Melcorka of the Cenel Bearnas, Melcorka of Alba, Melcorka, the lover of Bradan.'

The mention of Bradan brought new fear to Melcorka. 'This fight is between you and me, demon!'

The laughter sounded again, tearing at Melcorka's sanity as it wound around her like a living thing, penetrating her mind, until she could think of nothing except the mocking sound and the void that invited her to sink down and down forever into the bottomless chasm that was the interior of the rakshasa.

'Oh naivety, thy name is human, thy errors are in believing you can ever defeat me. Your weakness is my strength, Melcorka.'

Shaking her head to dislodge the words and sounds that confused her brain, Melcorka slashed sideways with Defender. There was no contact and nothing to see except eternal blackness as the rakshasa seemed to envelop her, encompassing her within its beak as its tentacles writhed around, coiling and uncoiling, searching and grasping, taking and tearing. Each tentacle was armed with a dozen circlets of ragged teeth that ripped into Melcorka's skin, worried the flesh and bore deeper into her muscle.

'You can be defeated!' Melcorka yelled. 'I can defeat you!'

With the words, Melcorka heard, faint but distinct, the sharp piping of an oystercatcher, her totem bird. 'Mother?'

The black-and-white bird appeared momentarily, circled sunwise around Melcorka and flew to her right. Unhesitatingly, Melcorka followed, striding into the darkness with Defender held before her like a lance. Two steps and she was back on the solid deck of the loola with the wind in her hair and the writhing monstrosity of the rakshasa before her.

'Now I see you!' Melcorka shouted, slashing with Defender, so two more of the creature's tentacles parted and fell. 'I will kill you piece by piece!'

The jeering laughter was so loud that Melcorka winced. It was a sound like no other as it boomed within her head, dominating all thought. She struck out, circling Defender around her head and then thrusting in front of her.

'Look, Melcorka. Look who I have!'

The rakshasa's voice jerked from her mind. With a sick slide of dismay, Melcorka saw the creature withdrawing into the water, with one derisive tentacle raised in mocking farewell. The tentacle was coiled around Bradan.

Chapter Nineteen

'No! Bradan!' Shouting his name, Melcorka jumped into the water, desperate to recapture her man. She was too late. The rakshasa had already vanished, sliding into the depths from whence it had come.

'Bradan!' Melcorka yelled again, took a lungful of air, thrust Defender before her and dived as deep as she could. She could see nothing of the rakshasa, only the clear water and a few scurrying fish. Melcorka dived until she felt her lungs would explode, frantic in her searching, swimming until faintness forced her to surface.

Gasping, Melcorka glanced frantically from side to side. There was no sign of Bradan, and Jasweer's loola was two hundred yards away, sailing for the fleet. The safety of Rajaraja was more important than that of a stray foreign warrior. Gasping, Melcorka returned to the depths, swimming until she could swim no more and still finding nothing. She surfaced, took a deep breath, dived again, searched and surfaced, dived, searched and surfaced, gagging, with her limbs aching and the breath burning in her chest. She was finished; she could not swim any longer, but she would not give up.

'Is that you, Melcorka?' Kosala leaned over the side of a small boat. 'You can't swim about all day.' He extended a hand. 'In you come.'

Gasping, Melcorka allowed Kosala to help her into the boat. 'The rakshasa grabbed Bradan.' She looked up. Banduka and Chaturi were also in the boat, shaking their heads in sympathy.

'May Shiva help him,' Chaturi said quietly. 'Don't give up hope, Melcorka. The rakshasa might not kill him. Bradan survived Dhraji's captivity before. He can do the same again.'

'I hope so,' Melcorka said. 'I must save him.'

'It might be too late,' Kosala said. 'Don't expect too much, Melcorka.'

'I must save him,' Melcorka repeated. 'Take me to the fleet.'

'We'll come, too.' Kosala touched his sword. 'I want to fight the Thiruzha.'

The demon's laughter rebounded within Melcorka's head, cruel in its mockery.

* * *

Rajaraja's admirals and marine commanders sat around a low table in his state cabin, with large moths fluttering around the lanterns. A sentry propped the door open to allow free passage to a cooling breeze.

'We all saw how strong the defences of Kalipuram Island are. If we pass in daylight, we'll lose ships and men from their catapults and archers, while that chain boom virtually closes one of the two channels. If we go in at night, we will not see the rocks and other hazards, and the Kalipuram archers and catapults will know exactly where we are.'

The assembled men nodded agreement.

'Are there any suggestions?'

Kulothunga stamped both feet on the deck. 'Use a third of the fleet to keep the fort busy while the rest push through.'

'That might be the best way,' Rajaraja said. 'However, I don't like the idea of splitting our fleet to such an extent, or of sacrificing men in what is little more than a diversion.'

Melcorka sat in a corner, sharpening Defender. 'Take the island first,' she said softly. 'Send the marines to assault the place at night and neutralise the defences.' She ran her whetstone up the blade of her sword, the sound strangely sinister in the crowded cabin. 'Kill them. Kill them all.'

'We don't know the make-up of the defences,' a marine commander pointed out. 'The last time we tried to attack Kalipuram, the defenders beat us back. We lost two hundred men. I'm not sending my men to certain death.'

Kosala had slipped in beside Melcorka. 'I know some of the defences.'

'Who are you?' Rajaraja asked.

'Kosala of Ceylon. I was a slave on Kalipuram.'

The marine commanders grunted. 'A Singhalese pearl diver. What would he know of military matters?'

'Kosala is a warrior,' Melcorka said. 'He helped us escape from the Thiruzha.'

Smoothing his fingers over his moustache, Kulothunga eyed Kosala up and down. 'Do the Singhalese have any warriors?'

'He is as good a warrior as any I have ever met.' Melcorka was no longer inclined to humour Kulothunga's ego.

'Let him speak,' Rajaraja said.

When Kosala approached the table, Melcorka was surprised that he did not appear nervous when talking to such a high-profile group.

'I helped build some of the defences.' Kosala gave a wry smile. 'Not by choice.'

'Tell us,' Rajaraja ordered.

Kosala salaamed in Rajaraja's direction. 'There are two concentric walls with archers and spearmen on the front row and catapults and a huge crossbow further back. They also have facilities to launch fire-burning missiles.'

The marine commanders paid close attention as Kosala drew a quick sketch of the walls and the barracks inside the fort.

'Are there any weak spots?' the one-eyed Admiral asked.

'No,' Kosala said. 'The defenders can cover every approach to the walls. Every member of the garrison is covered by at least two others.'

'Is there anywhere in the fort that is not defended?' Melcorka asked. 'A water culvert, perhaps, or even a latrine?'

Kosala shook his head. 'Not that I know of. The walls rise sheer from the cliff. Nobody can climb them.'

Melcorka looked up sharply, tested the blade of Defender and slid it into its scabbard.

'How does the garrison enter the fort?' the one-eyed Admiral asked.

'There is only one gate,' Kosala said. 'The Seagate, at the lee side of the island, the side closest to the land and that is only opened when a Thiruzha vessel approaches.'

'What is the gate made of? How is it opened?' Melcorka asked, as the germ of an idea entered her mind. 'How do the ships enter?'

'The gate is of long iron strips, riveted together,' Kosala said, 'similar to the gate at Rajgana but many times larger. There is a permanent watch from a guardhouse immediately beside the gate.'

'How is the gate opened?' Melcorka repeated.

'There must be a mechanism within the guardhouse.' Kosala said. 'I do not know how to operate it.'

'A pity, but that cannot be helped,' Melcorka said. 'Next, how do the boats enter?'

Rajaraja held up a hand as one of the admirals tried to interrupt. 'Let him talk,' Rajaraja ordered.

Kosala continued. 'There is a gap in the cliff that leads to a small harbour within the fort. The slaves are constantly enlarging and improving the anchorage.'

'How many men are in the guardhouse?' Melcorka shot out her questions.

Kosala screwed up his face. 'I was never in there. Maybe a dozen men.'

'Warriors? Or just garrison troops?' Melcorka's idea grew by the minute.

'I don't know,' Kosala said, honestly.

Melcorka nodded and addressed the gathering. 'Do you gentlemen have any plan to pass this island?'

Rajaraja nodded. 'I can think of only one answer. We launch a full frontal assault just before dawn on the eastern side, so the rising sun is in the defenders' eyes. As the sun rises, it will give us light to see by. We'll need scaling ladders, but our carpenters can knock them up in half an hour.'

'If I can get the Seagate open, can you bring in a couple of loolas in the dark?' Melcorka broke in.

'Your Singhalese friend told us that the gate's well guarded,' Kulothunga said.

'If I can get it open,' Melcorka repeated, too focused on her plan to listen to any negatives, 'could you get a couple of loolas in?'

Rajaraja lifted a hand to stop the immediate outcry from the commanders. 'If you could get the gate open, I would send in a couple of loolas.'

'I need one volunteer warrior,' Melcorka said.

Although Kulothunga looked up, Kosala spoke first.

'That's me,' Kosala said.

'He's Singhalese,' a hard-eyed marine said. 'I'll find you an experienced Tamil you can trust, or you can take Kulothunga.'

'I'll trust Kosala,' Melcorka said. 'I'll trust him to follow my instructions. Kulothunga is too much his own man. Kulothunga would be a rival, doing what he thought best rather than carrying out my plan.' She grinned at the warrior. 'In an open battle, there is nobody I would rather have at my side than Kulothunga. In the expedition I have in mind, I would like Bradan or Kosala.'

Rajaraja had listened intently. Now, he nodded. 'I understand. What do you need?'

Melcorka thought for only a moment. 'I want a long, knotted rope with a grapnel hook at one end, and I want to borrow Jasweer's Sharks for an hour.'

'Why?' Again, Rajaraja raised a hand to stop the babble of sound. 'Silence!'

'I need a loola to take Kosala and me closer to the island,' Melcorka said, 'then we'll swim the final few hundred yards. Jasweer is one of the best mariners I have ever met.'

'Send for Jasweer.' Rajaraja lifted a finger.

Kulothunga leaned against the bulkhead, saying nothing as he stroked the hilt of his sword. When his gaze strayed to Kosala, his eyes were like acid.

* * *

Jasweer was experienced in clandestine operations. First, she unshipped her mast to alter the profile of her loola. 'All you Sharks,' she ordered, 'wear dark clothing. Muffle the oars. Blacken everything metallic. I don't want the gleam of moonshine on steel to give us away.'

The Sharks obeyed with a will, trusting their captain.

'Don't whisper, when we're out there,' Jasweer said. 'Whispering can be a strain. If you must speak, use a low tone. Row gently. If anybody catches a crab, I will personally keelhaul him.'

'Drop us off a hundred yards offshore,' Melcorka said.

'There will be no swimming, Melcorka,' Jasweer said quietly. 'We'll take you right up to the base of the island in this foolish adventure.'

'Thank you,' Melcorka said.

'Don't thank me,' Jasweer said. 'I don't like you. To me, you are a foreign mercenary involving yourself in a war that's none of your damned business.'

'I don't like you, either.' Melcorka adjusted Defender more comfortably across her back. 'To me, you are a big-headed, bad-tempered sea-pirate.'

The two women considered each other in a mutual respect neither would acknowledge.

'So why are you doing this?' Jasweer asked.

'I want to win this war that's none of my damned business.' Melcorka said. 'Not that I give a rat's tail for the glories of your empire, but because our mutual enemy Dhraji has got my man and I want him back.'

'Bradan?' Jasweer grunted. 'He'll be dead by now.'

'That is possible,' Melcorka said. She knew that Defender would not fight for revenge. If Bradan was dead, she could not avenge him; however, she was fighting for the cause of right over wrong, good over evil – or so she hoped.

Was the cause of any expanding empire ever good? Was it ever right for one state or nation or culture to spread their ideas and political domination over other, weaker neighbours?

Melcorka shook her head. She could discuss such philosophies with Bradan. It was to determine such ideas that he walked the dusty roads of the world to seek out learned men and women. She was Melcorka the Swordswoman. She followed the way of the sword, not the insight of the mind.

Is that all I am? A wandering killer?

The black-and-white bird perched on the gunwale of the loola, its long red beak pointing toward her and its eyes far too intelligent for any bird.

'You are thinking deep thoughts, Melcorka.'

'Mother!' Melcorka hissed. 'Not now! I am busy.'

The oystercatcher metamorphosed into Bearnas, Melcorka's mother. 'I know how busy you are, Melcorka.' She smiled at her daughter. 'It's all right, nobody can see or hear me. These good people will think you are praying, which you are, in a way. After all, I am dead.'

'Is Bradan alive, Mother?'

'You know I can't tell you such things, Melcorka. You must forge your own destiny. It is the life you chose when you picked up Defender.' Bearnas extended her hand and ran it through Melcorka's black hair. 'I hear you are growing up now, my daughter.'

'You hear?' Melcorka was puzzled.

'I listen to your thoughts, about life and the meaning of it, and about other things, too.' Bearnas laughed when Melcorka gasped. 'Yes, even these ones! Bradan is an interesting man, isn't he?' Bearnas' eyes drifted to Kosala. 'Oh, I see! That Singhalese does have a fine body. He has similar thoughts for you, my daughter.'

'That is Kosala. He wants to defeat the Thiruzha.'

'He wants more than that, Melcorka,' Bearnas said. 'You seem to be attracting men now. You could have Kosala or Kulothunga, yet still you retain Bradan.'

'Bradan is my man,' Melcorka said. 'Kulothunga loves himself more than any woman. He only wishes a woman to worship him, not as an equal. Kosala, I do not understand.'

'You are still naïve in some ways, Melcorka,' Bearnas said. 'Life has lessons for you yet.' Her tone altered. 'Be careful of Kulothunga; he is not all he appears. I cannot say more than that.'

Melcorka dismissed that delicate subject. 'Mother, can I defeat this rakshasa? Will I defeat this rakshasa?'

'I can tell you that you *can*,' Bearnas said. 'I cannot tell you if you will. You are the mistress of your own destiny. Your life and victory depend on your actions, not on my words. I can only advise.'

'Give me your advice, Mother, *please*!' Melcorka was a small girl again, standing on the shores of her Hebridean island with the salt air of the Western Ocean tangling her hair.

'Do what seems right, Melcorka,' Bearnas said. 'As you always do.' Her eyes hardened. 'Remember what the Siddhars told Bradan. Use the steel from the west washed in the water from the north to defeat the evil from the south when the sun sets in the east.'

'Mother, what does that mean?' Melcorka asked.

'You must work it out,' Bearnas said. 'I cannot tell you more. Except that you are fighting a familiar evil that has taken a new form. That is all.'

'Mother...' Melcorka could only watch as Bearnas transformed into the oystercatcher. The bird's final whistle pierced the velvet Oriental night and then it faded away. Melcorka felt more alone than she had in years.

Oh, dear God. What will I do if Bradan is dead? The sadness of isolation descended like a cloak and Melcorka fell to her knees. She touched the hilt of Defender.

I will find him, Melcorka told herself. *I will fight, and when the sun sets in the east, I will destroy this ancient evil.* Melcorka pushed herself upright and faced the wind.

'I am Melcorka the Swordswoman! I am Melcorka of Alba and who dare meddle with me!'

'I'll dare, if you don't keep your blasted mouth shut!' Jasweer's hiss cut through the dark. 'We're all trying to be as silent as possible to give you a fighting chance, and here you are, yelling and shouting like an idiot!' Jasweer strode up to Melcorka and prodded her with a hard finger. 'Bloody pale-faced foreigners! Keep your teeth together, can't you?'

'Sorry, Captain,' Melcorka said.

'So you should be, jeopardising my crew like that.' Jasweer glowered at her for a moment. 'We're approaching Kalipuram now, so get yourself ready to do whatever it is you want to do before the Thiruzhas kill you.'

'Thank you for your confidence,' Melcorka said.

'I told you to keep quiet,' Jasweer hissed, 'or I'll have you gagged with a tarry rope!'

The island of Kalipuram loomed ahead, with the fort a smudge against the starlit night and a silver smear of surf marking the edge of the sea. Jasweer ordered 'up-oars' as a guard boat rowed noisily past, and then she guided the loola to an outlying shelf of rock.

'Here's where we part company.' Jasweer kept her voice low. 'May Shiva go with you, damn your pale skin.'

'Thank you, Jasweer.' Melcorka salaamed. 'Take care on your voyage back. Come on, Kosala.' Taking her coil of rope, Melcorka stepped from the loola onto the rocky shelf. She felt the sinking depression of evil as soon as her feet touched land. Somewhere in this terrible kingdom, Dhraji held Bradan or had already killed him. Melcorka took a deep breath, watched as a colourful snake slithered past, and contemplated the cliff beneath the fort.

Climbing to gain birds-eggs for food was the way of life on the island she had called home. Now, she had to use these childhood skills to enter this fort.

'Stay here and keep quiet,' Melcorka said. 'When I reach the top, I'll drop the rope down to you.'

Kosala was sensible enough to recognise Melcorka was the better climber. Nodding, he snuggled into a cleft in the rock, where the shadow would hide him from prying eyes from above or from the guard boat out to sea.

The cliff was smooth, with only minuscule cracks for handholds or footholds. Melcorka hoisted herself up a few feet, testing each hold, took a deep breath and began the ascent. Trusting to the instinct gleaned from a thousand climbs in the past, she hauled herself up, foot by foot, hoping the defenders were over-confident within their defences. She cursed when a fickle wind blew clouds from the moon, easing light across the face of the cliff and casting her elongated shadow onto the rocks below.

'Hi!' The call came from above. 'I see you!'

Melcorka froze against the cliff. She moved her eyes a fraction, trying to see if the moonlight emphasised her shape against the cliff face. The shadow of Defender seemed to mock her ascent as it wavered against a patch of vegetation. Melcorka took a deep breath, remaining still as a stone rattled down to bounce from the rocks far below. There was a murmur of voices above her, a high-pitched laugh and the soldier moved on.

'That got you worried,' the same voice said, laughing.

Melcorka breathed out, guessing that the soldier had been teasing his colleagues. She inched upwards again, handhold after handhold, until she came to a fingernail-wide ledge. She rested, looking over her shoulder. Moonlight glossed the sea, showing the masts of the Chola fleet on the horizon and the vast expanse of water beyond. How foolish was Man to try and impose his will and culture on the world, when nature provided sufficient for everybody, if only they learned to share.

Is that Bradan's influence again, forcing me to think beyond the immediate?

There were no more scares as Melcorka reached the base of the fort's defensive wall. Tying the rope around a stone that projected from the nearest buttress, she dropped it into the dark depths below. There were a few seconds of doubt before she felt the slight jerk as Kosala grabbed hold. Now, she had to wait for the Sinhalese to negotiate the cliff, with the Thiruzha defenders only thirty feet above her head and the night slowly passing.

A flight of birds fluttered from a cranny in the cliff, momentarily causing Melcorka to reach for Defender, and then silence returned, broken only by the occasional scrabble from Kosala as he fought his way upward. A sentry passed above, his tread slow and measured.

Kosala dragged himself up the final few feet to Melcorka, his grin evident even in the dark. Melcorka coiled the rope up hand over hand as she balanced on the ledge. She did not speak, for she knew that voices carry far in the night and she did not know how close the guards might be.

Tapping Kosala on the shoulder, Melcorka searched for holds in the wall of the fort. The builders had been immensely skilled, putting the blocks together with hardly a seam between them, so even she had difficulty finding any purchase. Pushing her fingertips into a near-invisible crack, Melcorka hauled herself up, scrambled to find a hold with her toes and pushed on.

The wall had a slight overhang, necessitating Melcorka to hang backwards with her head further out than her body. She remained like that for a moment, then vaulted onto the battlements and rolled through a crenel, swearing inwardly when the hilt of Defender caught the final merlon with an audible click.

'Who's there?' The nearest sentry spun round. 'Who's that?'

Leaping forward, Melcorka clamped a hand over the sentry's mouth. Without drawing Defender, she jabbed her straight fingers into the pressure point nearest his throat. When the man stiffened into paralysed silence, Melcorka pulled the dirk from under her arm and thrust it into his heart. Tossing the body over the wall, she dropped the rope for Kosala and looked around, just as clouds covered the moon, obscuring her view. She barely had time to see starlight glinting on helmets and spear points before Kosala joined her.

'Now what, Melcorka?'

'Now this.' Melcorka unfastened the rope and tossed it over the wall. 'There is no going back, Kosala. Either we succeed, or we die here.'

'That is the warrior's bargain.'

'Take me to the guardhouse above the gate,' Melcorka said.

Nodding, Kosala set off at a trot. Stairs descended from the interior of the outer wall to an internal courtyard, with the squat bulk of the keep rising beyond. Guards patrolled both the wall and the courtyard, some looking efficient, others evidently lulled into slackness by a sense of the fort's impregnability.

Kosala led them around the shadowed rim of the courtyard, dodging into a dark corner as a patrol tramped past. 'That doorway leads to the interior of the fort.' Kosala nodded to an iron-studded door outside which two guards were lounging, one chewing betel nuts and the other crooning a song of love and lust.

'The guards don't look very alert,' Melcorka whispered.

'Why should they be? Nobody has captured this fort in a hundred years.' Kosala shrugged. 'Only a few weeks ago, they swatted aside a Chola assault with the loss of only two men.' He moved on another twenty paces and ducked into a recess. 'If you plan to go inside the fort, we will have to use that door.'

'Where are the slaves held?' Melcorka asked.

'Through that door and down in the dungeons.' Kosala's eyes darkened. 'I'm not going back down there.'

'Bradan might be there,' Melcorka said.

'Are we not here to open the Seagate?' Kosala asked.

'Yes.' Melcorka stiffened against the wall as another patrol shambled past. 'I'm also looking for Bradan. He is more important to me than the fate of the Chola Empire.'

Kosala nodded. 'He is a fortunate man to have a woman such as you.'

'We have had many adventures together,' Melcorka said. 'I hope we shall have many more. Do you have any suggestions for getting through that door? Or is there another way into the keep?'

'No.' Kosala shook his head. 'The fort was designed for defence, not comfort. Everybody uses that gate.'

'How about the catapults? They could not have been carried through that small gate.'

'The boats brought them in pieces from the mainland and engineers assembled them here.'

'Where is the anchorage for the boats?' Melcorka's mind was three steps ahead of Kosala's.

'Over that way.' Kosala pointed left. 'Down those stairs.'

'Is there access from there to the dungeons?'

'Oh yes. The Thiruzhas took us directly from the boats to the dungeons.'

'That's our way then,' Melcorka said.

'I did not think of that,' honest Kosala admitted.

The fort was built around an inlet in the cliffs, which industrious engineers had widened into a harbour at some time in the past. Melcorka stood watching for a moment, but the harbour was quiet, with a single-masted vessel berthed alongside a stone platform. A pile of sacks sat beside the ship, together with a few score leather bottles.

'Which way is it to the dungeons, Kosala?'

'Over there.' Kosala sounded tense.

Set into the wall of the cliff, the door led to a flight of stairs that descended into stygian blackness. 'I'll go first.' Melcorka drew Defender. 'What else is down there?'

'A nightmare,' Kosala whispered, gripping his sword. 'A place that makes you wish to die rather than live.'

'Are there any guards?'

Kosala nodded. 'Sometimes they visit.'

'The security on this island is very lax,' Melcorka said. 'I thought it would be much more stringent.'

The stench hit Melcorka even before she reached the dungeon. The gut-wrenching, stomach-heaving stink of unwashed humans held in close confinement after hours, days and weeks of constant hard labour. The slaves were confined in a single colossal chamber, chained together at the ankles as they lay on bare, weeping stone. A single guard leaned on a short spear, his head nodding in near-slumber. Without a word, Kosala thrust his sword through the man's throat.

Melcorka watched the guard slump to the ground.

'I remember him,' Kosala said, shuddering at a bitter memory. 'He was a brute.'

Fighting her nausea, Melcorka peered into the unlit chamber. The slaves lay side by side, a dark mass of exhausted men and women. 'Is there a torch?'

'No torch. No light,' Kosala said.

'I want to find Bradan,' Melcorka said. 'How can we free them?'

'Simple. The slaves are attached to a mutual chain.' Kosala pointed to a key at the guard's belt. 'That key fits a single lock that releases everybody.'

'Release them,' Melcorka ordered.

'A couple of hundred slaves charging around the place will alert the garrison that we are here,' Kosala warned.

'I can think of no other way of finding Bradan,' Melcorka said. 'Besides, could there be a better diversion to drag the defenders away from the guardhouse?'

'The guards will slaughter them like sheep,' Kosala said.

'Some might survive, and better a quick death by the edge of a sword than a lingering death as a slave.'

The key turned with an audible click. Some of the slaves looked up with dread in their eyes. 'You are free,' Melcorka said. 'Go and attack the guards. Kill your tormentors before they kill you.' She raised her voice above the increasing hubbub. 'Bradan! Is Bradan the Wanderer in here? Has anybody seen a pale-skinned foreigner?'

There was no response as the slaves either cringed in fear, stared at her in astonishment, or ran out of the chamber.

'Hurry!' Kosala shouted at them. 'Get out, find the Thiruzha guards and kill them.' He watched the slaves pass in a stinking rush of bewildered, naked humanity. 'Poor, deluded fools. They won't last a minute.' Lifting the guard's spear, he shoved it into the hands of the nearest man. 'Here, take this.'

Melcorka stood at the entrance, her hope fading as the chamber emptied. She grabbed a few of the slaves, asking them the same question. 'Have you seen a fair-skinned stranger?'

They stared at her in bewilderment, shook their heads and wriggled free.

Melcorka swore softly. 'Bradan, where are you?'

'Dhraji may be holding him in the dungeons of Kollchi,' Kosala said. 'If he's there, we'll only find him if we take the city, which we can't do unless we capture this island.'

'You're right.' Melcorka heard the rising noise as the slaves erupted into the fort. 'Lead me to this guardhouse.' She drew Defender. 'Let us kill.'

They ran from the dungeons, pushing aside any slaves that lingered in their path.

'This way.' Kosala led Melcorka up a narrow flight of stairs. 'The slaves will go up the broad steps and the garrison will meet them there. This is the officers' route.'

Melcorka grunted. 'I thought these stairs were better kept. Even rakshasas have a class system.' She heard footsteps ahead, saw the flicker of torches and motioned Kosala to stop.

The group of officers were half-dressed and only half awake. Melcorka killed the first two before the remainder realised what was happening. She watched Kosala slice the third man's head clean off and finished the fourth with a neat thrust to the chest. Stepping over the jumbled bodies, Melcorka continued upward. 'How far?'

'Three more flights of stairs,' Kosala said.

The noise was increasing as the slaves attacked the now-waking garrison. Another group of officers rushed down the narrow stairs, this time with their swords ready. Melcorka had to fight harder to dispose of them.

'They are learning,' she said.

'This way.' Kosala bounded ahead.

They met more guards now, singly, or in squads rushing to see what all the noise was, and Kosala disposed of them with Melcorka guarding his back. Only one spearman gave serious opposition as he thrust at Kosala from a higher position. Kosala sliced through his spear, grabbed hold of the broken shaft and pulled him down for Melcorka to kill.

'We fight well together.' Kosala scampered light-footed up a final flight of stairs and halted before a closed door. 'It's always barred on the inside.'

'Knock politely and demand access,' Melcorka suggested. 'Pretend you're an officer. Your accent is far better than mine.'

Kosala rapped loudly on the door. 'Open up! It's the commander!'

There was a pause before a voice replied. 'Which commander?'

'Don't be impertinent! Open this door or you'll be kissing the elephant's foot before the day is out.'

Melcorka heard the rumble of wood as the beam was withdrawn. 'The voice of authority,' she said. 'That's the downfall of rigid discipline. People lose the ability to think for themselves.'

The second the door inched open, Melcorka shoved it as hard as she could and ran in, sword swinging. The room was larger than she had expected, with about thirty men in various stages of readiness. The first two stepped back in surprise, so she killed them with a single sweep of her sword and launched herself in an attack on the others, with Kosala following her.

After only a few moments, it became obvious that the guardhouse garrison had no stomach for a fight. Some immediately fled, others begged for quarter and only a few dared to face Melcorka and Kosala sword-to-sword.

'They're running,' Kosala said, as the remnants of the garrison crowded out of the door. He shouted after them. 'Fight me! Fight me so I can kill you!'

'Never mind them,' Melcorka said. 'Let them go and bolt the door. Keep the Thiruzhas out until we can raise the gate.'

While Kosala banged shut the door and slammed the beam into place, Melcorka surveyed the mechanism for raising the Seagate. 'This looks simple enough,' she said. 'We haul on these levers and they wind the chain around that drum and draw the gate back from the opening.'

Kosala grunted. 'There are only two of us and that thing was designed for at least six. We should have kept some of the Thiruzhas to help us. See how they like being slaves for a change'

'Too late now.' Melcorka took hold of the closest lever. 'Come on, Kosala.' She pulled, with no effect. The drum did not shift.

'Jump on it,' Kosala suggested.

That did not work, either. The drum remained static. Melcorka cursed. 'I'll not be beaten now,' she said. 'Try again.'

They pulled, straining with effort but the lever remained stiffly static, the drum immobile. Melcorka swore loudly, in Gaelic, Tamil and Singhalese.

Kosala smiled. 'You do have a temper, don't you, Melcorka? Life with you would be full of interest.'

Before Melcorka could reply, something crashed against the door.

'Kill them!' a score of voices shouted. 'Kill the Thiruzhas!'

'Shiva has sent us help.' Melcorka said. 'Some of the slaves have arrived.'

Kosala grinned. 'I hope we can convince them that we are not Thiruzhan.' He raised his voice to a shout. 'Who's there? We are the people who freed you!'

'Kill the Thiruzhas!' The chant came from outside the door, accompanied by a steady crashing as the slaves tried to break down the door. 'Kill the Thiruzhas!'

'I doubt if they will listen to reason,' Kosala said. 'Join me, Melcorka. Let them know we are on their side.' He shouted again: 'Kill the Thiruzhas!' Removing the beam, Kosala eased the door open a crack. 'Kill the Thiruzhas!'

A horde of slaves poured in, some blood-smeared, some carrying swords or makeshift weapons, and all frantic-eyed with the lust for vengeance.

'Welcome, lads and lassies,' Melcorka greeted them calmly. 'Could you lend a hand here, please?' She indicated the lever for the drum. 'We're trying to open the Seagate to let the Chola fleet in.'

When the first man swung a stick at her, Melcorka dodged the blow and pressed her finger against the pressure point on his solar plexus. The man fell, temporarily paralysed.

'Anybody care to help us?' Melcorka ensured she remained calm. 'The sooner the Seagate is open, the sooner the Chola fleet can come in.'

Staring at their fallen companion, a group of slaves shuffled toward Melcorka.

'Come on then.' Melcorka grabbed the nearest. 'Take hold here and push that lever as hard as you can.'

The man stared at her through vacant, slave-dull eyes.

'Just do as I say,' Melcorka demonstrated. 'We're trying to open the Seagate. Next, please!' She pushed a dozen into place, closed their hands around the levers and shouted: 'Now, on my word, push! Put your weight into it!'

'I'll watch for any stray Thiruzha warriors.' Kosala positioned himself at the door, sword held across his chest.

'Push!' Melcorka ordered again, leading by example. 'Come on, lads and lassies. If we don't open the gate, Rajaraja can't get in and we'll all be slaves forever! Push!'

With the extra weight the slaves provided, the drum creaked an inch and a single link of the chain clicked into place.

'Push!' Melcorka ordered. 'Come on, people!' She lifted herself off the ground, pushing as hard as she could. The chain creaked another link, and then another, until the slaves got the hang of the procedure, worked together and the drum began to roll faster.

'That's it!' Melcorka said. 'We're getting there!'

At that point, the Thiruzhas launched their counter attack.

Chapter Twenty

Melcorka heard the Thiruzha war cry, and the resonant crash of feet, followed by the crisp yell of disciplined orders. Kosala stepped aside as a flight of arrows hissed past him. Some found targets in the slaves that crowded the guardroom. Men screamed in pain or shouted in shock or sheer frustration, and a few hefted their makeshift weapons and rushed past Kosala toward the Thiruzhas.

'Get the Seagate open!' Melcorka pulled a slave back. 'Keep turning the crank! Don't stop. Kosala and I will deal with the Thiruzhas.'

Unsheathing Defender, Melcorka stepped toward the doorway. Kosala was already there, peering past the mob of slaves with his sword held across his chest.

'How many?' Melcorka asked.

'I can't tell.' Kosala flicked an arrow from the air with his sword. 'I can hear more coming up the stairs.'

'Can you hold the door?' Melcorka glanced over her shoulder to where the slaves had stopped hauling on the levers. 'If you keep the guardroom secure, I'll get the Seagate open.'

'I'll hold the door.' Kosala sounded as calm as if he was sitting inside his own house.

'Good man!' Melcorka held his gaze for a second. 'I'm glad you're here, Kosala.' She saw the pleasure her few words gave him, touched his shoulder and returned inside the guardroom. 'Come on, people! Let's get this gate open!'

The second she had left, the slaves had stopped working. Melcorka had to motivate them again, cajoling, encouraging, and leading by example. It was another few moments before the slaves were hauling again.

'Come on!' Melcorka yelled as the drum inched around, chain-link by chain-link. 'Come on!'

'Melcorka!' Kosala roared. 'Over here!'

Melcorka glanced over her shoulder. Kosala was struggling against a press of Thiruzha warriors, fighting desperately. 'I'm coming!'

She dashed across, in time to see Kosala dispose of a young warrior with a deft thrust to the throat. Five more Thiruzhas pressed forward, mouths open in loud yells. For a moment, Melcorka had to fight desperately, slashing, blocking and thrusting, and then there was silence save for the steady clanking of the chain, Kosala's harsh breathing and the moaning of the Thiruzha wounded.

'You are a great warrior, Kosala,' Melcorka said, once she had got her breath back.

'I just follow your example.' Kosala grinned across to her.

'Listen.' Melcorka stood erect. 'Something's happening down there.' She stepped forward.

'More Thiruzhas are coming up the stairs!' Kosala shouted, stepping to her side with his sword held low. 'You and me, Melcorka – it's you and me against all of Thiruzha!'

Melcorka nodded as she heard the thunder of feet on the stairs. 'It sounds as if there are hundreds of them this time.'

The Thiruzhas rampaged up the stairs in chain mail and iron helmets, with spears held horizontally and swords poised to kill. Most had a small, round shield on their left arm, and all looked hideously efficient. Leading them, shaded by the darkness, a tall man mounted the steps three at a time.

'The man in front looks like a giant,' Kosala said.

'Let me take him.' Melcorka tried to push in front, only for Kosala to block her.

'No, Melcorka.' He grinned at her. 'Don't you realise yet that I am trying to impress you?'

'You have no need to do that,' Melcorka said.

'I must. I need to win your favour.' Kosala stood in a half-crouch. 'Come on, you dogs of Thiruzha! Come on, you followers of a rakshasa! Kosala is here!'

Melcorka shook her head as the giant strode forward, laughing. 'Melcorka!' Kulothunga dropped the point of his sword. 'I thought there was still fighting up here?'

'No,' Melcorka said. 'Kosala and I have things well in hand.' She glanced at the Singhalese warrior, who grinned at the praise. 'I presume the Seagate is open and our ships are in?'

'You presume correctly,' Kulothunga said. 'I was first into the fort.'

'I would not have thought anything else.' Melcorka kept her voice solemn. 'How many Chola ships are in?'

'Five. Jasweer's Sharks and four more loolas, all packed with marines.' Kulothunga jerked a thumb to the men behind him. I'll lead them around the defences and get rid of the Thiruzhas.'

'They're not fighting hard, Kulothunga. The defence has been lacklustre at best. I wonder if Bhim is laying another of his traps?'

'Let him.' Kulothunga shrugged. 'I can defeat his army single-handed.'

'There are catapults on the far battlements,' Kosala broke in. 'They can still cause damage to the Chola fleet. Maybe it would be better to get them first.'

'No!' Jasweer pushed through the hard-faced marines. 'I believe there's a boom blocking the North Channel. Our priority must be to destroy that, to clear passage for the rest of the fleet.'

'The catapults and the boom are close together, Jasweer. We can destroy them all together.'

'Show us, Kosala,' Jasweer ordered.

Kosala glanced at Melcorka as if asking her permission. 'Are you coming with us, Melcorka?'

'There is no need for the woman.' Kulothunga struck a dramatic pose. 'I am here.'

'I'll come along anyway,' Melcorka said.

Jasweer grunted. 'Don't get in my way, landswoman.'

With Jasweer in charge and Kulothunga and the marines disposing of any defenders foolish enough to make a stand, Melcorka found she had little to do.

'Burn these,' Jasweer ordered, and the marines set fire to the catapults. Jasweer watched, with her hands on her hips and her head tilted to one side. 'Good. Where is this giant bow I have heard so much about?'

'Over there, Captain.' Kosala pointed.

'Destroy it.' Jasweer watched as her marines dismantled the mechanism and set fire to the timber. She stood erect among the wreaths of smoke, a sea-woman equally at home on land. 'Find me the chain boom.'

'Over here.' Kosala led her to a vast drum, around which was coiled a chain, each link of which could encompass a man's forearm.

'It's completely unguarded.' Melcorka looked around. 'The captain of Kalipuram deserves a good hanging.'

'Marines!' Jasweer shouted. 'Destroy this thing, detach the chain and throw it into the sea.'

Melcorka nodded. 'That is best. It seems as if we have captured this fort.'

'Thanks to you, Melcorka.' Kosala laid a hand on her arm. 'You are not like any woman I have met before.'

Melcorka allowed Kosala's hand to rest where it was. 'I am what I am. It was Jasweer's Sharks who did the important part.' She noticed Kulothunga watching. 'And Kulothunga, I suppose. He has the makings of a reasonable warrior.'

'I led the assault,' Kulothunga reminded her.

Kosala smiled, shaking his head. He spoke only to Melcorka. 'You fascinate me,' Kosala said simply. 'I would do anything for you.'

'No, Kosala,' Melcorka said. 'Thank you for the compliment, but there is no future between us, except in friendship or as fellow warriors.'

'We would be a formidable combination,' Kosala said.

'We are already a formidable combination.' Melcorka removed Kosala's hand. He did not resist.

'If you ever grow tired of Bradan,' Kosala said, 'or if you find the rakshasas have killed him, I will be here for you.'

'Thank you, Kosala.' Melcorka cleaned the blood from her blade. 'I cannot think of a better man.' She ignored Kulothunga's glare.

'We have conquered Kalipuram,' Kosala said. 'Only because of you, Melcorka.'

Melcorka looked around, frowning. The conquest of Kalipuram had been too easy. 'There is something wrong, Kosala. The garrison hardly fought. These were not the men who defended this island last time, or who defended Rajgana Fort. The Thiruzha are up to something.'

'You may well be right.' Shoving Kosala aside, Kulothunga turned over the body of the last man he had killed. 'Look at this fellow. He must be fifty if he is a day, much too old to be a front-line warrior. While this man here...' he lifted the head of the next corpse, 'I doubt if he is twelve years old. He has not even started to grow his moustache yet.'

239

'Why put second-rate soldiers in a frontline fort when you know the enemy is coming?' Melcorka asked.

'You put your less valuable men in forward positions when you are preparing a trap,' Kosala said. 'The Thiruzhas have got something ugly in store for us.'

'I agree,' Kulothunga said.

Jasweer was breathing heavily. 'Our duty was to capture the fort and clear the way for the fleet. We did our duty.'

'I came here to look for Bradan,' Melcorka said.

'You don't need Bradan when I am here.' Kulothunga puffed out his chest. 'You need a warrior, not a man with a stick who is probably already dead.'

'Bradan is a brave man,' Kosala said quietly. 'He does not deserve your insults.' He stepped in front of Melcorka as if to defend her.

'When you children have stopped bickering,' Jasweer said quietly, 'you can perhaps welcome Rajaraja. He is approaching now.'

Melcorka stamped her feet. 'Good,' she said. 'The sooner we get into the city, the better.'

* * *

Leaving a company of marines to garrison Kalipuram, Rajaraja anchored his fleet just out of range of the catapults of Kollchi. Ahead of them, the surviving Thiruzha vessels were pulled up on the horseshoe-shaped beach, while smoke drifted from the battlements as the defenders prepared to resist. A fitful breeze fluttered the blue and yellow flag of Thiruzha above the city.

'I want your ideas and input again, gentlemen.' Rajaraja sat in a carved chair on the quarterdeck of his royal yacht. 'The enemy will expect us to attack. Do we launch our assault now, or starve them out?'

'We should attack,' Kulothunga said. 'The longer we wait, the more warriors the Thiruzhas can gather and the more we will lose from disease and accidents. One swift, glorious assault will gain us the town.' He smiled. 'Think of the booty, gentlemen. Think of the women, think of the stories that will resonate for centuries.'

'They will expect us to attack,' Rajaraja said. 'They do not know of our artillery. We will teach them how powerful we are and hope they surrender before we have the casualties an assault would bring.'

'I need to search for Bradan before Dhraji kills him,' Melcorka said.

Rajaraja shook his head. 'I am sorry, Melcorka. I appreciate your bravery in helping us capture Kalipuram, but I will not alter my strategy for one man.'

Melcorka stiffened. 'I need to search for Bradan,' she repeated, without a change in her tone. 'Your strategy is your affair, Your Majesty. Up until now, our aims have coincided. Now, they diverge. Your priority is to capture the city. My priority is to rescue Bradan.'

'By now,' Kulothunga said, 'Bradan might be dead. There could be nobody to rescue.'

'I'll take that chance.'

Kulothunga gave a mocking bow. 'I rather thought that you would.'

Something in Kulothunga's voice made Melcorka shiver. She stared at him, wondering what he had in mind.

Kulothunga openly gazed over Melcorka's body. 'As I have told you repeatedly, you deserve better than a man with a stick.'

'If Dhraji had intended to kill Bradan, she would have torn him apart in front of me.' Melcorka ignored Kulothunga's advances. 'She is holding him prisoner for some reason of her own.'

Kulothunga stroked his moustache, saying nothing.

Why? Melcorka asked herself. *Why would Dhraji hold Bradan prisoner?* There was only one answer she could think of, and that gave her both hope and despair. Dhraji was genuinely attracted to Bradan. The thought was hideous. Yet that attraction might keep Bradan alive.

'I have to destroy Dhraji,' Melcorka said.

'No mortal weapon can kill a demon.' Kulothunga touched his sword. 'I am the only man who has ever been victorious over a rakshasa.'

Melcorka allowed herself a small smile. 'If a man can do it, I can do it,' she said, although she did not feel the confidence she hoped to portray. On her three previous encounters with the rakshasa, she had failed to kill it. Why should the next attempt be any different?

Bearnas' words came to her again: *'Use the steel from the west bathed in the water from the north to defeat the evil from the south when the sun sets in the east.'*

What had that meant? The sun never set in the east. That was against nature.

Melcorka shook her head. Until she worked out the riddle, she could not defeat the rakshasa. The longer she took to solve the enigma, the more chance there was that Dhraji would kill Bradan in some hideous way, or use him for some other unimaginable purpose.

'Excuse me.' Melcorka left the quarterdeck. She needed space to walk and think. Pacing the deck, back and forward, while the walls of Kollchi wavered under the heat and seabirds screamed around the fleet, Melcorka ran the words through her head a hundred times, always with the same result.

Nothing.

Use the steel from the west bathed in the water from the north to defeat the evil from the south when the sun sets in the east.

The riddle seemed unsolvable. Melcorka teased it apart, seeking possible meanings. Evil from the south may mean the rakshasas. Steel from the west could refer to Defender. The other references made no sense at all. She became aware of Kosala watching over her only when he detached himself from his position beside the mainmast.

'You'll wear yourself out, Melcorka. You've been walking for hours.'

Melcorka saw that the sun was dipping in the west, silhouetting the Chola ships against a glorious purple-orange sky.

'Thank you, Kosala. Maybe I had better get some sleep now. Tomorrow could be a busy day.'

Kosala touched her forearm. 'It will be, Melcorka. Rajaraja plans to soften the city with a bombardment before he attacks.'

'My day will be busy whatever Rajaraja decides to do,' Melcorka said.

'You intend to rescue Bradan,' Kosala said. 'I will come with you.'

'No, Kosala.' Melcorka gave a small smile. 'There is nobody I would rather have at my side, but this I must do alone.'

'Why?' Kosala asked.

'Because I do not expect to survive.'

Chapter Twenty-One

Waiting until the darkest hour of the night, Melcorka slipped over the ship's rail and swam toward Kollchi. From now onwards, she was alone. The fate of the Chola Empire and the war against Thiruzha was no longer her concern. Only one thing mattered: rescuing Bradan.

The battered vessels of the Thiruzha fleet sat beneath the walls of Kollchi with a few nervous seamen left as guards. Melcorka strode from ship to ship, ignoring the shouted challenges, until she found *Catriona*.

'Who are you?' a startled guard asked. Melcorka killed him with a swift thrust to the throat and pushed his body into the sea. She stepped onto the deck of *Catriona*.

'Hello, old friend,' Melcorka looked around, recalling old memories. 'You won't be lying here for much longer. You deserve a better fate than to rot beside a bunch of pirates.'

Dipping into the cabin, Melcorka opened her sea chest. Every object was redolent of her shared history with Bradan. Smiling, she removed her hooded cloak. Her foot skiffed something on the ground; she looked down and lifted up Bradan's rowan-wood stick.

'You've travelled a long way. We'll get you home.' On an impulse, Melcorka tied the staff to Defender's scabbard. It was cumbersome, yet for some reason, she knew she should take it.

Pulling on her cloak, Melcorka adjusted the shoulder to ensure that the thick wool concealed the hilt of Defender. 'That will have to do.' She patted *Catriona*'s gunwale. 'We're not neglecting you,' she said. 'Either we'll come back for you, or you'll find a worthy owner in Jasweer.'

Morning sunlight glared from the east, heating up the long walls of Kollchi and glinting from the helmets and spear-points of the defenders. Every hour, the catapults on the decks of the Chola thirisdais unleashed rocks that either hammered at the city walls, or arced over the battlements to crash on the streets inside. Melcorka waited for the next bombardment to start and then began to scale the walls. It was natural for men to take shelter when great rocks were hurtling through the air at them, so she was not disturbed. The possibility of being struck by a missile on such a long target as the walls of Kollchi was too remote to concern her.

As Melcorka had expected, not a single man looked up to challenge her as she slipped over the battlements and down the inside of the walls. Camouflaged by her cloak and hood, Melcorka ignored both the sheltering warriors and the occasional falling rock as she made her way to the palace.

The Kollchi catapults were also busy, loading and firing as they sought to reduce the Chola fleet, with slaves carrying the rocks to the great machines and the engineers firing them. Melcorka contemplated attacking one or two of the catapults to reduce the effectiveness of the defence, but decided that such an action would compromise her presence without seriously reducing the Kollchi defences. Once she had discovered what had happened to Bradan, she might help the Cholas.

Despite the bombardment, two stalwart guards remained at their posts in front of the palace. One man flinched every time a rock landed close, while the other stared fixedly ahead as if in a trance.

Melcorka ran to them, head down and panting. 'Please help.' She grabbed hold of the staring guard's sleeve. 'It's my mother. A missile hit our house, and she's trapped. Please, you must help me!'

The guard pushed her away. 'I can't leave my post,' he said.

'Please, sahib!' Melcorka approached the second, nervous guard. 'She's trapped and bleeding. I need help!'

'I can't.' The man looked sympathetic, and Melcorka detected a decent human being beneath the Thiruzha uniform. 'I'm not allowed to.'

'I'll get somebody else then.' Melcorka dashed past them into the palace. She knew the guards could not follow her and it was unlikely that they would report their failure to stop her. If they did, Bhim or Dhraji would probably order them to be thrown from the roof or chained to an elephant's foot.

Striding through the corridors, Melcorka headed for the dungeons. The atmosphere of luxurious vice closed in on her, with the decadence of soft carpets and gold-fringed tapestries, peacock feathers and ornate windows only partially concealing the sickness beneath. As she strode, Melcorka thought of the austere winds of Alba and the rough straw beds of the kings and chiefs in Dunedin and the West. She felt a sudden longing for her homeland, with its plain speaking and homely fare, its brisk autumnal winds that lifted the brown leaves and the invigorating snows of winter.

'I'll get you out of here, Bradan,' she promised. 'If you are still alive, I'll get you out.'

With the memories of Alba renewing Melcorka's energy, she lengthened her stride, ignoring the stares of the scurrying servants. As she came close to the even more luxurious sector inhabited by Bhim and Dhraji, Melcorka began to step more warily. In any other building, she would have thought it strange that the rulers lived in such close proximity to the dungeons, but she knew Dhraji's love of others' suffering.

The sound of voices drifted to her. Melcorka stopped. One voice was female – bright, deep and strangely alluring. The other belonged to Bradan, and he was laughing.

Melcorka felt her heartbeat increase. Bradan was still alive, that was the most important thing, but, rather than being chained in some foul dungeon, he was free in the most sumptuous sector of the palace, and seemed to be enjoying himself. Emotions rushed through Melcorka, a mixture of relief and agonising doubt. *Has Bradan willingly chosen to remain with Dhraji?*

Throwing back her cloak to allow herself easier access to Defender, Melcorka approached the door through which the voices came. When Bradan laughed again, Melcorka heard the clink of glass on glass, as if two people were toasting each other.

'When you grabbed me like that,' Bradan said, 'I wondered what was going to happen.' He laughed openly. 'I thought you were going to tear my head off for being back with Melcorka!'

The woman's melodious laugh tore at Melcorka's heart. 'Oh, no, Bradan, I just wanted you back where you belonged, with me.'

'I'm delighted you did.' Bradan laughed again. 'I am no longer Bradan the Wanderer. Now, I am Bradan the Settled.'

Melcorka pushed the door open a fraction and peered in. Bradan lounged full length on a settle, wearing baggy satin trousers and an open yellow top set with pearls. His red turban would have been quite fetching in different circumstances. Beside him sat Dhraji. She was strikingly beautiful, with transparent tight trousers hugging her shapely hips, while three strings of pearls highlighted the splendour of her naked breasts.

Melcorka felt the breath catch in her throat. For a moment, she looked down in dismay at her body, still thin from her time in confinement, slim-hipped, battle-scarred in various places and dressed in old, serviceable clothes that hard wear had faded to an indistinguishable grey colour. Melcorka swallowed hard. What man would ever want her, when such a prize as the voluptuous Dhraji was available?

When Bradan laughed again, lifted his glass and drank, a dribble of the ruby-red contents dripped onto his chin. Dhraji bent closer, wiped Bradan's chin clean with her fingertip and licked it clean.

'You are immensely desirable, Dhraji.' Bradan's eyes were busy on her breasts.

Melcorka opened the door wider. Midday sunlight seeping in from an ornate window caught the pearls that circled Dhraji's forehead and reflected on the strings of pearls around her hips. The leopard lay in the corner of the room, its head resting on its paws and its great yellow eyes watching everything.

'Dance for me.' Bradan leaned back on his couch, smiling. 'Dance for me, Dhraji, as you used to do.'

Placing her glass on an ebony table, Dhraji began to dance, with her hips wriggling suggestively as she rotated her breasts toward Bradan. The strings of pearls rippled and bounced, enhancing the sensuousness of her movements. Even Melcorka could feel the sexual tension in the atmosphere, while Bradan's breathing hardened as he watched her.

'That will do, I think.' Melcorka pushed into the room. 'We have unfinished business, Dhraji.'

Dhraji's laugh was high-pitched. 'You have no business here, Melcorka of Alba.'

'Bradan,' Melcorka spoke quietly. 'You have a choice now. You can bid a fond farewell to Dhraji and walk out the door with me, or you can remain with the rakshasa until I kill her.'

Bradan looked from one woman to the other. Melcorka saw the expression in his eyes as they focussed on Dhraji's curves and then switched to her own stringy flanks. On an impulse, Melcorka threw back her cloak. She heard Dhraji's laugh as Bradan smiled in derision.

'Your man seems hesitant to choose you, Melcorka,' Dhraji sneered. 'He prefers a woman to a…' she hesitated, 'to whatever you are, a creature without either shape, form or grace.'

'Choose, Bradan.' Melcorka blocked out Dhraji's taunts.

Bradan lifted his glass again. 'There is no choice to make,' he said.

'This may help you decide.' Freeing Bradan's staff, Melcorka balanced it in her hand and tossed it across to him. It landed on the carpet with a soft thud.

'A length of stick?' Bradan allowed the staff to lie at his feet.

'That staff supported you from the coast of Alba, to Greenland and down the Mississippi River,' Melcorka reminded him.

'It is only a length of stick to me now,' Bradan said. 'It might be useful as firewood for the cool nights.' Dhraji echoed his loud laugh.

'You will remember the seer who gave it to you,' Melcorka said.

'Of course,' Bradan said.

'And you will remember that it is made from rowan wood, which repels evil.' Melcorka continued. 'It has the cross of St Columba on the tip.'

Melcorka felt a perceptible tautening of the atmosphere as Bradan looked at Dhraji. Picking the staff up, Melcorka thrust the cross towards Bradan, who backed slightly away.

'Take your staff, Bradan,' Melcorka urged. 'Take it if you dare.'

'I don't want it,' Bradan said.

'Why not?' Melcorka took another step forward. 'It's yours.'

Bradan glanced at Dhraji, as if for support.

'You choose her, do you?' Melcorka dropped the staff. 'Well, Hell mend you then!' In a surge of anger, Melcorka threw the staff onto the carpet, drew Defender and, in one quick movement, sliced off Bradan's head.

'Now you!' Melcorka whirled around with Defender held ready.

The room was empty except for the teetering corpse of Bradan. Even the leopard had gone. 'Dhraji! Come and fight!'

There was no response. Still holding Defender at the ready, Melcorka knelt beside Bradan's body. 'You look like Bradan.' Ignoring the still-spouting blood from the headless trunk, she opened his top. 'You feel like Bradan, but you're no more Bradan than I am.'

What had she been told? She could not kill the rakshasas, even when they took human form, but humans had to be alive for the humans to take their shape. Bradan was still alive, somewhere.

Now, where would my Bradan be? Lifting the staff, Melcorka slipped it into Defender's scabbard. *I know that Dhraji is a rakshasa, and as another rakshasa took Bradan's place, there are at least two to worry about. One is bad enough.* Melcorka shook her head and repeated what Bearnas had said. *Use the steel from the west bathed in the water from the north to defeat the evil from the south when the sun sets in the east. What does that mean?*

Holding Defender in front of her, Melcorka pushed out of the room with her mind working overtime. *I came from a long way west of here, and so does Defender, so my sword could be the steel from the west. Yes, that makes sense. That's one part of the riddle.*

Melcorka circled, checking all around. The corridors were eerily empty, not even a servant in sight, with the tapestries moving in a slight breeze. *The evil from the south must mean Dhraji and her cohorts. That is two.* Melcorka crouched at a sudden sound and held Defender ready, only for a cat to scurry from an open door, look at her in evident alarm, turn and run again.

Melcorka shook her head to free it from sweat. *What does the water from the north mean? And the sun setting in the east? The sun never sets in the east.*

Running down the corridor, she checked each doorway in case Dhraji or the other rakshasa was waiting for her. The palace seemed deserted. With no servants and no guards, every sound was magnified. Melcorka's realised that her breathing was ragged and her grip on Defender was slippery with perspiration; her nerves were jangling.

The door was round-headed and studded with iron. About to kick it open, Melcorka instead pushed it with Defender. She gave it only the slightest touch, and it swung violently open.

The warriors rushed from behind the door, yelling. Melcorka took a single step back to gain more space, and met the leading man with a sharp thrust to the throat that stopped him dead. With the space in the corridor limited, the next two warriors could not push past, so Melcorka finished off the first man, ducked down and held Defender like a spear as the second man jumped over the body of his late companion.

Judging her time until the second warrior was at the apex of his leap, Melcorka thrust upward. Defender sliced open both femoral arteries. Leaving the man to bleed to death, Melcorka followed through with a sideways slash that sliced off the sword arm of the third warrior. The remainder fled.

'Fight me!' Melcorka yelled.

The road to the dungeons was clear. Melcorka stepped onto the stairs, gagged at the familiar stench and moved on. 'Bradan! Bradan are you down there?'

Only the echoes of her voice answered, fading into sullen silence.

Melcorka descended into the dark, step after step, wary, alert, knowing every second was vital. The moment she reached the bottom level, a deep voice sounded: 'Here she is!'

A dozen torches flared into life, nearly blinding Melcorka with the sudden glare.

'Good evening, Melcorka nic Bearnas.' Distorted by echoes, the voice came from somewhere beyond the circle of light.

Melcorka turned, holding Defender in front of her, expecting an instant attack. The torches flickered, spiralling smoke into the already foetid air. Still partially blinded by the sudden light, Melcorka circled, waiting. 'Where is Bradan?'

'You have killed him,' the voice echoed from beyond the flames.

'I killed an image that looked like him.' Melcorka narrowed her eyes, waiting. 'Where is Bradan?'

The laughter was not unexpected, coming from two, three, a dozen, a score, a hundred throats.

'Fight me,' Melcorka invited. 'Fight me. I am Melcorka of Alba, fight me or run.'

The laughter continued, louder, filling the space between the flaring torches, filling Melcorka's head, threatening to overwhelm her thoughts. 'Where is Bradan?'

'Where is Bradan? Where is Bradan?' Melcorka's words repeated themselves, echoing round the chamber and around her head, mocking her, taunting her, frustrating her.

'No!' Melcorka shouted. 'You're not playing with my mind!' Rushing forward, she crouched low and swept Defender in a great arc. The blade sliced through the nearest torches, causing them to fall, leaving an angle of darkness into which Melcorka stepped. 'Bradan!' she shouted. 'Bradan, are you there?'

The laughter continued. Melcorka swung again, cutting through the tall stakes on which the torches stood, felling them, so they rolled and spat on the filthy slabs of the floor. Lifting this final remaining torch with her left hand, Melcorka peered into the smoky dark.

'Who is there?'

The echo of her voice slowly faded.

'Bradan!' Melcorka paced through the dungeons, pushing open doors, staring into the stinking cells. Some held chained captives who looked up with terrified eyes; others held decomposing bodies, or peeled skeletons that had once been living human beings. Some cells were empty except for rusted chains and a seething mass of insects.

There was no sign of Bradan.

In the last dungeon, a tall man glared up as Melcorka pushed open the door. 'You may as well kill me, you thing!'

'I know that voice.' Melcorka could not conceal her surprise. 'Kulothunga! How in Shiva's name did they capture you?'

'Melcorka? Have you joined the rakshasa? Or are you a rakshasa that looks like Melcorka?' Kulothunga sat up, grabbed a handful of chain and swung it. 'Come on and try me!'

'No, Kulothunga, I am real. Is there a way out of these chains?'

'There is a catch, out of my reach.' Kulothunga said. 'Over there by the door.'

'I see it.' Melcorka wrestled with the bolt and pushed it open.

Kulothunga's chains fell open. Naked as a baby, he stood up, stretched and groaned. 'How long have I been a prisoner?'

'Not long,' Melcorka said. 'I spoke to you only yesterday.'

'Yesterday?' Kulothunga had lost a great deal of weight, his cheeks were sunken and a weeks-old beard covered his face. 'I've been here for days!'

'In the name!' Melcorka shook her head. 'When did the rakshasas capture you?'

'When I fought the monster in the sea,' Kulothunga said.

'As far back as that?' Melcorka thought of the times she had spoken to Kulothunga since. 'A rakshasa has taken your place. Your amorous advances were not real then.' She grunted. 'I was quite flattered.'

'What?' Kulothunga looked puzzled.

'Never mind.' Melcorka pushed the thought away. 'I am searching for Bradan. The rakshasas took him as well.'

'I have not seen him,' Kulothunga said. 'I've seen nobody except the jailers.'

'Bradan might be dead by now.'

At first, Melcorka did not see the man who spoke. The voice came from beyond the circle of light her torch created. 'Who said that?'

'I did, Melcorka.' Kosala stood four-square and unafraid in the centre of the dungeons.

'How did you get in here?'

'I followed you,' Kosala said. 'I would follow you anywhere and everywhere, Melcorka.'

'So here we are,' Melcorka said. 'Three warriors together within the heart of Dhraji's realm, and neither of us can kill the rakshasa.'

'I tried and failed,' Kulothunga said.

'As did I. Kosala, tell me what you know about Bradan.' Melcorka did not comment on Kosala's bravery or loyalty. She would address both qualities later.

'The rakshasas no longer need him.' Blood dripped from Kosala's sword onto the stone slabs. 'You killed his rakshasa image, so Dhraji can no longer use his body.'

'Where do you think he is?' Melcorka tried to cut through the explanations.

'The rakshasas will have taken him to the great square,' Kosala said. 'Bradan will be kissing the feet of an elephant any time now.'

'Kissing the elephant's feet!' Melcorka was running before Kosala finished speaking. Bounding up the stairs three at a time, she did not respond to the challenge of the single Thiruzha warrior, but pushed past without a word. She heard Kosala dealing with the man as she raced through the corridors of the palace and into the streets outside.

The humid heat of late afternoon greeted her, accompanied by the stinks and noise of the city. Melcorka ignored the occasional rock that crashed down from the bombardment that she had all but forgotten. The squabble between Thiruzha and the Chola Empire was no longer her concern. Only Bradan mattered.

'I am no good to anybody like this.' Kulothunga had followed. He looked down at himself. 'A naked man with no weapon is no threat to the rakshasas.'

'Where will your sword be?' Melcorka asked.

'I will find a sword,' Kulothunga replied at once. 'I'll join you later.' Turning away, he slipped back inside the palace.

'Somebody will kill him, for sure,' Kosala said.

'He's big enough and ugly enough to look after himself,' Melcorka said. 'I must find Bradan.'

Melcorka had left by the nearest door, emerging into an unfamiliar part of the city. People thronged the narrow streets, or peered out from the small, barred windows of the houses. 'You!' She grabbed the nearest man. 'Which way is the great square?'

The man goggled at her through big brown eyes, unable to say anything. Melcorka pushed him away in disgust. 'Anybody!' She raised her voice. 'Which way is it to the great square?'

'Melcorka!' Kosala touched her arm. 'This way!' He led on, turning every few moments to ensure that Melcorka kept up. 'We may be too late.'

The square opened up before them, lined with soldiers, while the citizens watched and waited in near silence. Even as Melcorka approached, a rock smashed down, crushing three people in the crowd. Once the initial yells and screams died down, the remainder shuffled over the smeared copses as if nothing had happened. They stared toward the central space.

'This is surreal,' Melcorka said.

'Welcome to the world of the rakshasa,' Kosala said. 'Welcome to a world of never-ending suffering and pain. Welcome to a land bereft of hope, where life is a torment and death a gateway to darkness.'

'Where is Bradan? Melcorka balanced Defender on her right shoulder. 'Where is my man?'

She did not have to look far. A blare of trumpets battered her ears, and a squad of Thiruzha warriors pushed aside one section of the crowd. Melcorka did not see where the elephants came from. One moment the centre of the square was empty, the next, the animals were there.

Three elephants walked in line abreast, with the sun glinting on the metal spikes that covered their trunks and protruded from their knees. Each elephant had a howdah on its back, with a wiry mahout sitting behind the ears. Bhim occupied the howdah of the elephant on the left, with Dhraji sitting in state on the elephant on the right and a hooded, cloaked figure on the elephant in the centre.

'Who is that?' Melcorka asked.

'That is the mysterious one.' Kosala's voice shook. 'Nobody knows who or what he is, or even if it is a man, demon, woman or god.'

Melcorka ran her hand along the blade of Defender. She felt a thrill of unease. She had never been able to kill even one of these rakshasas, and now it seemed there were three of them to fight at the same time.

Bearnas' words returned: *'Use the steel from the west bathed in water from the north to defeat the evil from the south when the sun sets in the east.'* What could that mean?

Melcorka looked around. The square had an opening on each side, a narrow channel through which the crowds surged when they came to this terrible place. The sun was dipping in the west, highlighting the hills of the Ghats and streaming along the channel between the houses. There would be no sunset in the east this evening. Perhaps this was not the day to defeat the rakshasas. Maybe this was the day to die.

Melcorka took a deep breath. She had always known that death was the ultimate end of any who chose the path of the sword. She would have liked a longer life; she would have liked to see the sun settle behind Schiehallion again... to feel the cool breeze of the Hebrides and smell the perfume of a peat-fire flame. She would have liked to rescue Bradan from his torment. Well, some things were not to be. She must face death as she had met life, with a smile on her face and a jest on her lips.

The high piping cut through the crash of elephants' feet on the ground. The oystercatcher landed on the head of the central elephant, ignored the mahout's efforts to dislodge it and pointed its red bill at Melcorka.

Melcorka frowned. What was the oystercatcher trying to tell her? The message was clear as it exploded within her head.

Why are you giving up? Are you accepting defeat so readily, even before the first clash of steel on steel?

Melcorka shook her head. Bearnas had provided the key to victory. All she needed was to find the lock that it fitted. A surge of hope chased away the gloom.

Melcorka stepped forward. She knew that the rakshasas had been playing with her mind. Depression and hopelessness were their prime weapons. If the rakshasas convinced their enemy that victory was impossible, then their battle was won even before the war began. Wars were won in the mind and the spirit, as much as in contests of steel and muscle.

'Where is Bradan?' Melcorka pushed through the crowd. 'I am here for Bradan!'

The elephants had halted in the centre of the square, with the light of the dipping sun glinting on their armoured shoulders. Dhraji smiled down from her howdah.

'Have you come to die, little girl?' Pearls glinted around her forehead and neck.

'I have come for Bradan.' Melcorka raised her voice. 'I am Melcorka of Alba and who dares meddle with me?'

'Oh, I dare, foolish child,' Dhraji spoke softly. 'Bhim dares, and my friend here also dares.'

Only then did Melcorka see Bradan. He stood at the edge of the square with his hands tied behind his back and a gag in his mouth. Two Thiruzha warriors held him.

'One bound man against three rakshasas with elephants,' Melcorka said. 'That's fair odds.'

Dhraji's smile did not waver. 'Bradan betrayed me,' she said. 'He has to die, but in dying, he has achieved something far more important.'

'What may that be?' Melcorka took a couple of practice swings with Defender. The blade sang as she hissed it through the air.

'He acted as bait to bring you here,' Dhraji said. 'Why do you think there were so few defenders at Kalipuram? I want to kill you myself, Melcorka, slowly and in public.' Dhraji spread her arms wide. 'I don't care about Thiruzha. I can get another kingdom anytime I like. I wanted to get you here.'

'Am I so vital to you?' Melcorka asked. 'I am only a poor girl from the western isles.' Striding across to Bradan, she pushed aside the guards. 'Run,' she said. 'Or die.'

When the first guard drew his sword, Melcorka killed him. The second fled. Melcorka cut Bradan free and removed his gag.

'Melcorka?' Bradan blinked at her. 'Where am I? How did you get here?'

'Dhraji is about to kill us,' Melcorka said. 'Run.' She looked around. Kosala stood at the edge of the crowd with his face set in defiance. 'Kosala, if you want to prove yourself as my friend, I charge you to look after Bradan. Take him to safety.'

'What about you?' Bradan understood the situation at once. He shook his head. 'I'm going nowhere.'

'Nor am I.' Kosala grinned at her.

'You're a pair of fools,' Melcorka said.

At that point, the elephants began their advance with slow, ponderous steps. Melcorka had no more time to argue.

I might not be able to kill a rakshasa, but I can remove its toys.

Running forward, she leapt as high as she could and thrust out, killing Bhim's mahout. The man fell, leaving the beast without any direction. It blundered sideways, barging into the central elephant, which reacted by thrusting sideways with its tusks. As the mahout tried desperately to control it, Melcorka hauled herself up the side of the first beast, slashed casually at Bhim and jumped onto the central elephant. The mahout ducked away, swung his iron goad at her and died as Melcorka decapitated him.

Realising that he was next, the mahout of Dhraji's elephant turned his beast sideways and made it reach for Melcorka with its trunk. Melcorka avoided the curling tip, jumped onto the elephant's back and killed the mahout with as much ease as she had the previous two. Leaping back to the ground, she rolled and regained her feet.

'That was well done,' Kosala said, as the three elephants raised their trunks, trumpeted loudly and barged into each other. Bhim's beast ran through the cordon of soldiers and began to wreak mayhem among the crowd, just as another catapult-fired boulder crashed into the buildings on the north side of the square, bringing down a shower of masonry.

Dhraji slid from her elephant to land on her feet and motioned for the others to follow. They stood side by side, with Bhim still on the left and the mysterious hooded one in the centre.

Melcorka advanced, swinging Defender. 'Fight me,' she said.

The three rakshasas stood side by side. 'Depart!' Dhraji shouted. Her voice resonated above the screams of the crowd and the squealing of the elephants. 'Get back to your posts, soldiers! Go home, the rest.'

The double crash of falling rocks helped speed up the process. The crowd fled, the noise diminished and within minutes, Melcorka, Bradan and Kosala faced the three rakshasas across the empty square, with only the dead mahouts to remind them that the elephants had ever been there.

'This is familiar,' Bradan said, as Melcorka handed him his staff. 'My own staff again.' He ran his thumb over Columba's Cross and tapped the staff on the ground.

'I killed you an hour or two ago,' Melcorka told him.

'Oh? How did you do it?'

'I cut your head off.' Melcorka smiled at him. 'It was a rakshasa that looked exactly like you. Ugly-looking brute it was, too.'

'I didn't feel a thing.' Bradan said. 'Did you know it wasn't me?'

'I was fairly sure.'

'Next time, make wholly sure, please,' Bradan said. 'I would hate you to make a mistake. You'd never forgive yourself.'

'What are you two doing?' Kosala asked. 'We're meant to be fighting the rakshasas!'

'Oh, they can wait,' Bradan said. 'Some things are more important than fighting evil.'

'May I join in?' Kulothunga strolled casually into the square. 'Or is this a private quarrel?' He was dressed in his usual finery, with his face clean and freshly shaved except for his curling moustache.

'You are always welcome,' Melcorka said. 'After all, you are the best warrior there ever has been.'

'You haven't forgotten me, then.' Drawing his sword, Kulothunga kissed the blade in a gesture as melodramatic as anything Melcorka had ever seen.

'How can anybody ever forget you?' Melcorka asked.

'That is true.'

'Are we going to fight?' Kosala asked.

'You are very impatient to die,' Dhraji said. 'For that, I shall kill your friends first and save you to the last.'

The mysterious one stepped back and lifted its hand. Immediately, a circle of mirrors appeared around the square.

'What is that for?' Kosala wondered.

'Don't you wish to watch your friends die from a hundred different angles?' Dhraji asked.

'I wish to kill you,' Melcorka said. 'And I shall kill you.'

Dhraji laughed. 'Vanity, vanity.' She smiled. 'You will fight and die in ignorance.'

Vanity! The weakness of the rakshasa!

Melcorka shook her head. 'Fight me, Dhraji. We have affairs to settle, you and I. Bradan, Kosala and I are ready for you.'

'You have forgotten me,' Kulothunga said. 'Don't you remember who I am?' He stood in front of the mirror with his back to Melcorka, grooming his moustache.

'I know you are not Kulothunga,' Melcorka told him. 'I rescued the real Kulothunga from the dungeons not an hour ago. You are another rakshasa.'

'I have all Kulothunga's skills and memories.' The rakshasa did not seem surprised to be discovered. 'I know he has defeated you already in swordplay, archery and wrestling.' He preened himself. 'I also have Kulothunga's clothes and sword.'

'Try and defeat me again,' Melcorka stepped back. 'Fight me.'

The rakshasa lifted its sword and advanced, with Kulothunga's smile on its face and Kulothunga's sword in its hand. Melcorka parried its swing, felt it twist its sword in an attempt to disarm her and thrust suddenly forward. As the rakshasa pulled back, Melcorka swung Defender, only to find Kulothunga had parried in turn.

'I am the best there has ever been,' the rakshasa that looked like Kulothunga said.

'You are good.' Melcorka advanced again, using her figure-of-eight attack.

When the rakshasa tried to push aside Defender, Melcorka parried, pressing on, knowing that she was stronger and fitter than she had been during their previous bouts. 'Is that your best, Kulothunga? I thought you were good.'

The words stung Kulothunga, as Melcorka had intended. He locked his blade with Defender and held Melcorka, muscle for muscle, with his eyes staring into hers.

'You cannot defeat me, Melcorka.'

Melcorka felt herself pushed backward. Defender slipped in her grasp. 'You are strong,' she said.

'I am,' Kulothunga agreed.

Melcorka tried to twist Defender to disarm Kulothunga. He shifted with her twist, countering her move.

'You are very good,' Melcorka gasped, giving ground. 'I think you are better than me.'

Kulothunga laughed. 'I am the best,' he said.

'You are my master with the sword.' Melcorka slipped and fell to the ground, with Kulothunga standing proud over her. 'I cannot fight any more.' She heard Bradan's shout of despair.

Kulothunga loomed over her, preening his moustache. As he did so, Melcorka rolled to the side and thrust upward into Kulothunga's groin.

Kulothunga stared at her with his face contorted in agony.

'Die, you thing!' Melcorka shoved Defender further up, twisting to enlarge the wound. Kulothunga gasped, dropped his sword and stood rigid above her as his blood flowed up the blade of Melcorka's sword.

Kosala stared, open-mouthed. 'You defeated Kulothunga!'

'The creature was good,' Melcorka said, 'but I knew its weakness. It combined the vanity of Kulothunga with the vanity of the rakshasas.'

'I hope you got the right man,' Bradan said, as Melcorka tore Defender free and the rakshasa crumpled to the ground. 'That looked and sounded very like Kulothunga to me.'

'I hope so, too,' Melcorka said. 'Trust nobody. 'Here they come now.'

Four; there are four rakshasas; the copies of Bhim, Kulothunga and Dhraji as well as the Mysterious One. How can I defeat four of them?

There was no more pretence. The rakshasa that was in the image of Bhim altered into a leopard. It sprang at Bradan, with its claws extended and its jaw wide open.

'I wondered what you were, Bhim,' Melcorka said. 'I never saw Dhraji without her leopard unless Bhim was there. What a strange creature you are.' She swung Defender, swearing when the blade bounced off the body of the leopard. Only the force of the blow pushed the leopard back.

'No mortal blade can kill us!' The words resounded inside Melcorka's head as the other rakshasas altered into their multi-legged shapes and ran forward, tentacles grabbing and beaks snapping. Three of them now, as the creature that had copied Kulothunga assumed its other form.

'Get behind me, Bradan! You're no warrior!' Melcorka stepped forward, Defender held ready. As the first rakshasa curled its tentacles around her, she slashed with Defender, sliced off two tentacles and thrust for the eyes. Once again, Defender bounced off the pupil without inflicting any damage.

'I can't be killed by any mortal weapon.' The words eased into Melcorka's mind again.

'I'll chop you up, piece by piece,' Melcorka said, slashing sideways. 'And this time you have no sea to escape into.'

The three multi-legged rakshasas were attacking her; one had its tentacles wrapped around her legs, holding her while the others slithered up with their beaks poised to strike. Looking in the mirrors, Melcorka could see a hundred rakshasas surrounding her. She slashed at one, to realise that it was only a mirror image as Defender hissed through empty air.

'Is that why you put the mirrors there?' Melcorka asked. 'That's how you work, isn't it? First, you remove hope by spreading depression in people's minds, and then you spread confusion, so they don't know fact from fiction.'

Melcorka saw Kosala fighting the leopard, hacking at its limbs and avoiding the slashing claws. Then the leopard altered, growing more legs as it copied its fellow rakshasas.

'You will die slowly, Melcorka,' the voice sounded in her head, laughing, mocking, seeking to unsettle her. 'Very slowly. You will suffer for weeks while I kill Bradan as you watch.'

'The Chola army will reduce your city,' Melcorka said. 'Rajaraja will break down your walls and scatter your army!'

That laugh sounded again. 'You still don't realise, Melcorka, do you? You are still the naïve little island girl from the far west. I don't care about these little pirates or this city. They are tools.' The voice was deep and cold and utterly uncaring. 'They call me the Mysterious One, for they do not understand anything I do. My fight is far beyond anything you can ever imagine, with your little sliver of steel and your wandering man with his piece of stick.'

'Who are you?' Melcorka freed her legs with a back-handed slash of Defender. 'What are you?'

'For every force, there is a counterforce,' the voice said, 'and this world is a stage for the battle of the two. We are the game masters; kings and rajas and emperors are only pawns in our game.'

'Good and evil.' Melcorka stepped back. She saw Kosala and Bradan standing back to back over the corpse of the false Kulothunga, desperately trying to fend off the Bhim rakshasa. There was a rising din in the background, the clash of steel on steel and the hoarse cries of fighting men. Rajaraja's army must have finally stormed the city and was engaged with the defenders.

Bradan swung his staff, saw it bounce from the rakshasa, and kicked out in frustration. Stumbling over the body of the false Kulothunga, he looked away, temporarily blinded as the dying sun reflected in the mirrors.

Is it that late already? Time goes fast when one is fighting.

Melcorka saw Bradan catch his foot in Kulothunga's jacket. She saw Bradan kicked the jacket free, and a small flask slipped from an inside pocket to roll on the ground.

'Sweet Lord in his heaven,' Melcorka said. 'Thank you, Kulothunga. Thank you, Mother! Thank you, Bradan.'

The water from the Ganges! Kulothunga tested Rajaraja's admirals and generals with water from the Holy River!

Melcorka raised her voice. 'Bradan! Kosala!'

Kosala looked over. 'I can't hurt it.' Frustration edged his voice. 'My sword just bounces off!'

'I know how to destroy them!' Melcorka shouted. 'Do you see that little flask beside Kulothunga?'

Kosala looked down, nodded and sliced off one of the tentacles of a rakshasa. The creature wrapped another around his leg. Kosala did not even flinch. 'I see it!'

'Can you throw it this way?'

The rakshasas made another attack, forcing Melcorka further back as tentacles coiled around her arms. That voice was back inside her head, probing. 'Do you remember meeting me before, Melcorka?'

Melcorka hacked at another tentacle, only to miss as the rakshasa recoiled. 'I have fought you three times.'

'You have fought me more than that,' the voice said. 'Look, Melcorka.'

With her eyes narrowed against the glare of the sun, Melcorka was standing on the golden sands of a beach with the Kalingo warriors before her and the peaceful Taino at her back.

Only a single Kalingo stood. A lone female faced the attackers, pointing two fingers at Melcorka.

'Run, you fool!' *Melcorka yelled.* 'All your friends have gone.'

Kanaima remained standing, pointing, so that Melcorka slowed down, curious to see why her adversary did not run.

Kanaima took a single step forward. 'I curse you. I curse you in your body and in your mind. I curse you in your possessions and your strength. I curse you in your travels and your weather. I curse you until the balance of the world is restored...' *She got no further as Melcorka swung Defender and neatly cut off her head.*

'You!' Melcorka said.

'Me,' the Mysterious One said. 'I am the kanaima you fought.'

'I killed you thousands of miles away.' Melcorka hefted Defender again.

The vision faded until once again Melcorka was in that glare-lit square, with the rakshasas ready to pounce.

'You think of distance and time as though it was fixed,' the voice said. 'Look beyond that, Melcorka. Look beyond time and space. We are everywhere, and we are always. A life, any life, is part of a whole and a speck of goodness or a speck of evil is only a fragment of the spiritual body.'

Melcorka saw Kosala slide under the terrible swing of a tentacle to scoop up Kulothunga's bottle. He lifted it and threw, just as another tentacle grabbed at his arm, knocking the flask upwards, rather than toward Melcorka.

'Bradan! The flask!' Melcorka yelled.

The bottle rose high, spiralling in the air. The rakshasa reached for it with half a dozen tentacles.

'You cannot win, Melcorka. We will fight until I have removed every trace of you from the land. I am of the spirit, but you are corporeal. You cannot kill me.'

Bradan lifted his staff and batted the flask toward Melcorka, who leapt up and grabbed it.

'Do you know what this is?' Melcorka opened the flask and poured the contents onto the blade of Defender. 'It is Holy water from the Ganges. Kulothunga always carries it with him when he goes on campaign.' Melcorka rubbed the water along the full length of Defender's blade. 'It is now on my sword, which is already blessed by the goodness of my own people. You may be of the spirit, but now you face the spiritual good of two ancient cultures, one from the East and one from the West.'

The roar of the fighting intensified. An arrow flew over the most eastward of the mirrors, to skiff along the ground without doing any harm. Another followed and then came a crash as a tall man shoved over the mirrors on the westernmost side of the square. The genuine Kulothunga strode in, with a far-too-tight chain mail coat over his chest and a borrowed sword in his hand. He glanced at the body that looked like him, shrugged and strode on.

Behind Kulothunga, the final rays of the sun streaked along the narrow corridor of buildings, over the mirror he had dislodged, to reflect in the mirrors on the opposite side of the square. Melcorka smiled as the final piece of her mother's jigsaw clicked into place.

'I have steel from the west bathed in water from the Ganges in the north,' she said, 'to fight the evil from the south while the sun is setting in the east.' Melcorka pointed to the mirror that reflected the golden-red sun. 'There is my eastern sunset!'

That's my girl! Bearnas voice was proud in Melcorka's head. Now, fight and win!

You can't kill us, the other voice said.

Melcorka's first swing sliced off two of the rakshasa's tentacles. She laughed, dodged the vicious beak and thrust the point of Defender into the creature's eye. This time, the sword penetrated with ease, as far as the angled quillons of the guard. The voice intruding inside Melcorka's head screamed, as much in disbelief as in pain, until Melcorka twisted Defender left and right, ripped her sideways and dragged it free. She spared a moment to watch the rakshasa crumple to the ground.

The other three rakshasas leapt on her, flailing with their tentacles and thrusting with their beaks. Melcorka had expected nothing else and used Defender with her favourite figure-of-eight movement that was nearly impossible to penetrate. Slices of rakshasa body and legs flew through the air.

'Kosala and Kulothunga,' Melcorka yelled. 'Chop off the tentacles! I will take the eyes!'

One thrust, two thrusts and the nearest rakshasa recoiled. Melcorka finished it off as it writhed on the ground and killed the next with a single swing that sliced through its head. The remaining rakshasa charged at her, squealing inside her head.

'I am Melcorka of Alba,' Melcorka said, thrusting Defender into its eyes. She stood back, panting, as it collapsed.

It's finished. Oh, dear God, it's finished.

Kulothunga grinned at her over the hilt of his sword. 'Melcorka!' He was still unshaven and dirty but carried his borrowed sword as adroitly as ever. 'You've killed all of them. I wanted one for myself.'

'You helped.' Melcorka indicated the flask of Ganges water. 'Without your knowledge, without your foresight, the rakshasas would have won, and if you had not kicked over that mirror, the sun would never have set in the east.'

Rajaraja joined them, sheathing his sword. He looked at the dead creatures on the ground. 'Is that them all?'

'I believe so.' Melcorka began to clean Defender. 'Kulothunga's sacred water and my blessed sword have killed them all.'

'The remainder of the conquest should be easy then,' Rajaraja said. 'My son Rajendra has sent a messenger to tell me he has already captured Rajgana.'

'There will be no need for any conquest.' Melcorka inspected the blade of Defender. 'It was a false Bhim and Dhraji that led the Thiruzhas astray. The genuine Rani and Raja are in the dungeons. When you free them, there will be no cause for war.'

Rajaraja looked around the wreckage of Kollchi. 'That is good news.'

Melcorka slid Defender into her scabbard. 'It is finished,' she said. 'Peace may now come to this land.'

Chapter Twenty-Two

They stood on the deck of *Catriona* with the tide about to turn and all the colour and noise of the sub-continent behind them.

'You don't have to leave,' Jasweer said. 'We always have room for a skilled mariner in the fleet, while Kulothunga needs a rival to keep his ego in check.'

'Melcorka shook her head. 'Thank you for the offer, Jasweer. It is most kind of you, but the world is calling.'

'Where are you headed?'

'Wherever the sea takes us, or to whichever land that calls.' Bradan gave a final check to the stays that held the mast secure. 'I am a wanderer. It seems that I cannot stay long in one place.'

Jasweer nodded. 'You have restless blood in you both. One day, you will find your place.'

'Maybe...' Melcorka looked to the far horizon. 'Wherever we go, we will always carry a little piece of this land with us.'

'Chola is like that,' Jasweer agreed. 'You may be back.'

'We may well be back.' Bradan sniffed at the wind.

Kulothunga waded into the water, preened his moustache and held out a hand. 'You are a fine warrior, Melcorka. You are nearly as good as I am and I am the best there has ever been.'

'I'd be careful of that title,' Melcorka said. 'Kosala saved us all when he held back the rakshasas and threw across the flask of sacred water.'

'Everybody helped,' Bradan said. 'When we face evil, everybody is needed.'

The wind increased slightly, rustling *Catriona*'s sail and skiffing spindrift from the surface of the waves.

Melcorka lifted a hand in farewell as Bradan adjusted the sail.

'To adventures new,' Bradan said.

Tossing back her hair, Melcorka placed Defender in the small cabin. 'To a calm sea and a smooth passage.'

'Melcorka,' Bradan said, 'do you realise that Dhraji was only scared of one warrior, the best there has ever been?'

'I do,' Melcorka said. 'That would be Kulothunga.'

'No,' Bradan shook his head. 'It was not Kulothunga. You defeated his rakshasa. You are that warrior, Melcorka. You are the best there has ever been.'

'Nonsense,' Melcorka said. 'Take us onward, Bradan.'

'Which way?'

'Whichever way the wind takes us,' Melcorka said.

'That suits me.'

They smiled at each other as the wind bellied the sail.

Dear reader,

We hope you enjoyed reading *Melcorka of Alba*. If you have a moment, please leave us a review – even if it's a short one. We want to hear from you.

Want to get notified when one of Creativia's books is free to download? Join our spam-free newsletter at www.creativia.org.

Best regards,
Malcolm Archibald and the Creativia Team

Historical Note

Although this story is entirely fiction, the Taino and Kalingo people of the Caribbean were contemporary with Melcorka and Bradan. The Kalingo were fierce warriors and the Taino were a peaceful people, as Columbus discovered when he came across them, four centuries later.

The Chola Empire also existed. It was one of the more successful empires of the Middle Ages and at its peak, extended from the southern tip of India to the Ganges and included Sri Lanka, the Andaman Islands and parts of what is now Malaysia and beyond. Rajaraja was a real Emperor, but he did not have to contend with Melcorka or rakshasas. He did have a fleet and a powerful army to help spread his power, while his son and heir, Rajendra, led a Chola army to water its elephants in the Ganges.

Malcolm Archibald
Moray, Scotland, October 2018

About the Author

Born and raised in Edinburgh, the sternly-romantic capital of Scotland, I grew up with a father and other male relatives imbued with the military, a Jacobite grandmother who collected books and ran her own business and a grandfather from the legend-crammed island of Arran. With such varied geographical and emotional influences, it was natural that I should write.

Malcolm Archibald

Books by the Author

The Swordswoman
The Shining One (The Swordswoman Book 2)
Falcon Warrior (The Swordswoman Book 3)
Malcorka of Alba (The Swordswoman Book 4)
Jack Windrush -Series
Windrush
Windrush: Crimea
Windrush: Blood Price
Windrush: Cry Havelock
Windrush: Jayanti's Pawns
A Wild Rough Lot
Dance If Ye Can: A Dictionary of Scottish Battles
Like The Thistle Seed: The Scots Abroad
Our Land of Palestine
Shadow of the Wolf

Lightning Source UK Ltd.
Milton Keynes UK
UKHW010936111121
393791UK00001B/29

9 781715 492014